FENWICK

FENWICK

EDWARD WILDING

Troubador Publishing Ltd
Unit E2 Airfield Business Park,
Harrison Road, Market Harborough,
Leicestershire LE16 7UL
Tel: 0116 279 2299
Email: books@troubador.co.uk
Web: www.troubador.co.uk

ISBN 978 1836283 577

British Library Cataloguing in Publication Data.
A catalogue record for this book is available from the British Library.

The manufacturer's authorised representative in the EU for product
safety is Authorised Rep Compliance Ltd, 71 Lower Baggot Street,
Dublin D02 P593 Ireland (www.arccompliance.com).

Printed and bound by CPI Group (UK) Ltd, Croydon, CR0 4YY
Typeset in 11pt Minion Pro by Troubador Publishing Ltd, Leicester, UK

The belief in a supernatural source of evil is not necessary; men alone are quite capable of every wickedness.
Joseph Conrad, 'Under Western Eyes.'

Hell is empty and all the devils are here.
Shakespeare, 'The Tempest.'

Governments do not govern, but merely control the machinery of government, being themselves controlled by the hidden hand.
Benjamin Disraeli.

ONE

THE OWL WOMAN

Whenever anyone asked Michael Tyler about the missing index finger on his left hand, he'd spin a yarn that was as enthralling as it was misleading. Not always the same yarn — he loved spinning new ones — but his favourite version of events was that he'd lost the finger at a shooting range some years previously, a mishap with a Luger 9mm Parabellum. According to his account, the antique handgun had jammed, and when he tried to clear it, the breech exploded in his grip, mangling the digit so severely that the doctors at his local hospital had no choice but to amputate.

The truth was far more prosaic. Michael Tyler was not left-handed; he'd never held a pen with that hand, let alone a gun. The real story of his missing finger took place twenty-two years earlier, in the quiet town of Berkhamsted. On that fateful day, Tyler was trimming the hedge in his garden, wielding a Black and Decker power-strimmer with more confidence than skill. It was entirely his fault when the strimmer slipped from his grasp and severed his finger clean off. The unfortunate appendage sailed into the thick undergrowth, lost forever to the bushes.

Tyler had been alone that day, and in the immediate aftermath, his mind raced with the horrifying possibility he might bleed to death before he could reach help. But somehow, amidst the panic and pain, he managed to fashion a makeshift tourniquet. He wrapped his shirt sleeve around the wound, tightening it with a stick until the bleeding slowed. Only then, with trembling hands, did he fumble for the phone to call an ambulance.

Tyler didn't like people knowing too much of the truth about himself. He habitually told such lies — or, more precisely, small but memorable insinuations, hinting at secretive affiliations and acts of derring-do. In weaving this deception as a man of mystery, Tyler was wise enough rarely, if ever, to volunteer information or specifics that might be independently checked or verified. With Tyler, people had to keep guessing — assuming that is, they cared enough to guess.

Nowadays, with his career in gradual descent, not many people did. As a forensic accountant — or 'financial crime investigator', as he haughtily described himself — there was little to excite or whet the appetite. Despite appearances otherwise, Tyler's world was predominantly of ledgers and spreadsheets, and whichever way it was cut there was nothing sexy, seductive or alluring about 'data mining' or 'breakpoint clustering'.

Nevertheless, Tyler had worked hard to preserve and build a reputation as a tenacious and skilled investigator, with a track record of exposing corruption in public office and high places. Rightly or wrongly, he'd forged the image of a man who spoke truth to power. To the public, he was a defender of the downtrodden, the forgotten, and the marginalised. But behind closed doors, in the privacy of his inner sanctum, Tyler's sharp tongue betrayed the cynicism that lurked beneath his carefully constructed facade. With a smirk, he referred to those he supposedly defended as 'plebs', or worse, with a biting disdain, 'retards'. It was a cruel joke, one he shared only with those few who truly knew him, a glimpse into the darker corners of a man who had learned to wear masks as cynically as he uncovered them.

Calculatedly honing this profile of a latter-day Robin Hood, Tyler had assiduously courted publicity, carving a niche for himself in news media circles and on the conference circuit. He was never averse to reminding his various audiences of his high-profile cases. The colourful, animated PowerPoint slides that accompanied his lectures were crammed with BBC news reports and lurid tabloid headlines of his past glories. Much like an ageing film star, Tyler still had his 'groupies', and for a fair few he remained an ideal 'soundbite man' or 'go-to guy' whenever the issues of fraud, corporate malfeasance and corruption reared their ugly heads.

Thus, on a cold, damp November afternoon in London, Tyler found himself on stage yet again, wheeled out perhaps for the last time, expounding his tradecraft and peddling his theories at an unspeakably dreary symposium on the subject of corporate governance. The event, EXPO CG23, was hosted at the prestigious Queen Elizabeth II Centre near

3

Parliament Square. The anointed speakers for the two days comprised an ill-assorted mix of academics, statisticians, regulators, lawyers, judges and second-tier politicians. Tyler was the only 'practitioner' present, lauded as an investigator of real fraud and corruption at the coalface — 'up close with the Devil', so to speak.

His session for the event was billed as a hair-raising 'whites of the eyes' exposé. A puff piece in the event's brochure, penned by Tyler himself, hinted at 'shock and awe' revelations to come. Tyler knew well the power and value of 'war stories', those slightly contrived and exaggerated reminiscences that were necessary in holding any audience captive.

During his presentation, Tyler also injected some much-needed humour. When the electronically controlled blinds in the conference room started ascending and descending with a mind seemingly of their own, he spontaneously quipped: 'Just like the FTSE.' It was a good pun at a time of extreme market volatility — and, judging by the laughter, the audience agreed.

With his hour-long slot completed to resounding and appreciative applause, Tyler headed off for a cup of tea. He thought he might exchange a business card or two, and there was always the possibility of a chance encounter. Despite a long and surprisingly trouble-free marriage, Tyler had a roving eye, and the conference circuit was an ideal hunting ground — the audit, regulatory and compliance professions were increasingly staffed by young women, many of whom Tyler considered attractive, some of whom had proved compliant also.

Imagine his disappointment, therefore, when he now found himself pinned to the wall by a woman whom he found singularly *unattractive*. This particular lady had sallow, ageing skin, pockmarked cheeks and thick-rimmed tortoise-shell spectacles with lenses like pint mugs, which magnified her eyes grotesquely within the narrow confines of her skull. She also had a hooked nose — not unattractive in itself, but it only added to Tyler's impression that he was being accosted by an overgrown barn owl. To add insult to injury, the poor woman had arguably the worst haircut imaginable, and when she spoke there was just the hint of spittle and halitosis.

This was an unmitigated disaster, the diametric opposite of everything Tyler had planned. Flapping and gasping for relief like a floundering fish, Tyler desperately sought to catch the eye of the notably desirable Georgina, the international events coordinator, whom he espied across the floor. Alert to Tyler's evident discomfort and playfully amused by the vignette, Georgina — herself besieged by admirers, all male — studiously feigned short-sightedness throughout his ordeal.

On and on the wretched owl woman went, prattling away in a deep, low, guttural baritone, like Henry Kissinger on his deathbed: 'Mr Tyler, Mr Tyler, what would you do in my position? The entire human race! What, what would you do? If you know something so dangerous, so damaging... and you, alone, have the evidence... what would you do? And then the very people who send you for this evidence... they ignore you! They turn their backs on you! They do nothing, Mr Tyler, they do nothing!'

Tyler, sixty-three, a little over five foot nine and progressively hard of hearing, had to stoop low to hear the owl woman, as she was significantly short of stature and her granular, heavily accented voice did not carry well. Her remonstration continued relentlessly: 'This is so serious, so frightening! What would you advise? Snake venom, it turns the blood to glue. To kill billions! It must be exposed; the world must know. Now! A catastrophe! A scandal! You must help me! You have the connections, the contacts, the reputation, the influence. Could you help me, Mr Tyler? Will you help me?'

For God's sake, woman, get to the point! thought Tyler.

His lower back was playing up — muscular pain and sciatica. He was itching to get away. Nor was there any abatement to the deafening noise in the room, full to the rafters as it was with chitchat and laughter, greatly amplified by poor acoustics. He struggled with his teacup and saucer, for there was no level surface to hand where he could leave them. He felt a wave of tiredness crash over him. He was bored senseless and was neither listening to nor comprehending a single word that was uttered by this ghastly woman.

He thought briefly of Sartre: Hell was, indeed, other people.

As the minutes ticked by, Tyler's despair intensified, but the owl woman only became more energised and insistent: 'What would you do? What would you do? They will kill us all. Do you understand? They will kill us all!'

How much longer must he suffer this babbling crone and her interminable nonsense?

Then, as though anointed by God himself, a real hand tugged hard on Tyler's jacket elbow. It was Georgina. A heavenly apparition! A saviour! An angel! Tyler couldn't believe his luck.

'Come on, old man,' she said, taking his arm: 'it's time you were home.'

The relief, thought Tyler, was akin to the most explosive bowel movement. Finally, at last, he was unburdened of this freak!

He bid the owl woman farewell. His firm, determined handshake and imposing, meaningful stare conveyed a clear message: 'Never cross my path again!' There was a ritualistic exchange of business cards, as polite and restrained as a Japanese tea ceremony. In Tyler's case this was entirely a formality: he had absolutely no intention of ever re-encountering this succubus. With the briefest glance at her card, he noticed her surname — eastern European, he presumed — it began with a Z.

On approaching the exit door, Tyler was thrilled beyond delight when Georgina took his arm with teasing flirtation and snuggled generously close to him. But subjected to an insistent tapping upon his left shoulder, his joy instantly evaporated.

Not the bloody owl woman again, surely? Was he going to need a restraining order?

Feeling a twinge of anxiety, even fear, Tyler turned around. A severe reprimand was more than justified. But the owl woman, sensing Tyler's ire, now shrank really rather sweetly, and then retrieved from her shoulder bag a thick bible, garish in red, with Christ on its cover.

'It's all right, really, keep it,' hissed Tyler, making no effort to hide his impatience — a bible was the last thing he needed.

'No, you will need it, you must take the book. You must!'

Sensing Georgina's disapproval of his harsh tone, Tyler shrugged resignedly and took the wretched bible, stuffing it into his laptop case, causing its leather to strain with the bulk. Turning on his heel, he departed, with Georgina in somewhat bemused pursuit.

In the cool, damp, autumnal air outside the conference centre, Tyler drew breath dramatically, signalling his exasperation and sense of relief. Georgina, amused and with some empathy, hugged him. Rather too briefly and guardedly, thought Tyler. Then, with a quick peck on his cheek, she was gone.

He watched ruefully as his beautiful saviour slunk away like a panther into the night, trailed by a flotilla of much younger men, her entourage during the tea break. Tyler instinctively knew that none of them stood a chance, but he felt dispirited nonetheless.

Along the damp, cloying and faintly sticky walk to the tube station, Tyler deliberated. He thought momentarily of binning the owl woman's stupid bible in a rubbish skip along the way, but an inner voice cautioned him not to. She'd focused so intently and insistently on him, and him exclusively. It was as though he, Michael John Tyler, had been targeted for some specific reason. Oddly, despite her vocal and emphatic protestations, everyone else present at the gathering had been oblivious to her ranting. As with Cassandra, her prophecies of doom had evidently fallen on deaf ears.

Tyler was struck by the absurdity of the episode. Perhaps he had imagined the incident, or had someone perchance 'spiked' his tea?

With the prospect of a long and tedious journey home, Tyler persuaded himself with effortless ease into *Cahoots*, a welcoming bar with high stools and youthful staff.

He ordered a rum and coke. 'Single or double?' enquired the barmaid, a coquettish tousle-haired sprite, with many body piercings in interesting places.

'A treble' said Tyler with a salacious grin. The owlish ghoul, and even the beguiling Georgina, were fading memories. The evening was fast improving, with the tantalising prospect of pierced flirtation.

TWO
THE CIPHER

Arriving home in the early hours, Tyler went straight to his office and consigned the demented owl woman's bible to a shelf, unthumbed, unloved and unopened.

For several weeks, he focused all his attention on the management and upkeep of the house and estate he'd recently acquired in upmarket Forest Row in East Sussex. It was a merry-go-round of wheelbarrows, ladders and cement mixers, of 'pointing', roofing, plastering and crazy paving. Susan, Tyler's wife of thirteen years, seemed happy and relaxed, gardening in the sizeable grounds of their new home, walking their energetic and handsome Irish setter Basil, and continuing her stunningly successful career in retail fashion.

All appeared well… until, out of the blue, Tyler's phone pinged, shattering the stillness of his office.

The screen illuminated with a new WhatsApp message, its notification icon glowing ominously. He glanced at the sender's name and felt a jolt of recognition. There she was:

the owl woman. Her stern visage, peering out from behind thick lenses, mocked him from the tiny icon.

The message itself was stark:

URGENT: EXTINCTION EVENT — IMMINENT!

Tyler blinked, bewildered. How the hell had she obtained his number? He racked his brain, struggling to remember if he'd ever given her his card, but his memory came up blank.

The body of the text was just as perplexing:

Mr. Tyler, we talked in London last November.
Urgent! Use the book.
Danusia Ziętek

Beneath her terse words was a long, disjointed string of numbers, ordered in ones, pairs, triplets, and quadruplets. The sequence was as indecipherable as it was bizarre.

Tyler leaned back in his chair, the faux leather creaking under his weight. This was clearly nonsense, a prank designed to rattle him. Ziętek, the owl woman, had likely been persuaded on this course by others. He briefly considered reporting the message to the police as an attempted extortion or threat, but he quickly dismissed the notion.

Instead, he read the message again, more slowly this time. He now recalled the conference at the QEII back in November. The details had blurred with time, but one phrase stood out, echoing in his mind like a haunting refrain: 'Snake venom, it turns the blood to glue.' The words had resonated even at the time, but he'd later dismissed the notion as delusional rambling.

Now, in the cold light of this strange message, the phrase took on a new, more sinister significance.

Where would he find the matrix, the essential table to crack this bizarre code? *Use the book*, Ziętek had instructed. The Good Book? The bible? Tyler sneered at the thought, but he found himself unable to resist the lure of the puzzle.

He walked over to the bookshelf, his fingers tracing the spines of the neatly ordered volumes until they landed on the bible — *her* bible. He eased it out from among its brethren and opened it for the first time. There, inscribed on the inner jacket, was a set of handwritten instructions. The neat, precise handwriting was Ziętek's, presumably. The instructions were a formula: references to page numbers, paragraphs, lines and character counts.

Tyler's pulse quickened. He was holding the key to a code, a cipher that would unlock a secret message meant for him and him alone.

He leaned back in his chair and let his mind drift. Memories surfaced of books long discarded — particularly *Crypto* by Steven Levy, with its deep dive into the world of codes and ciphers. He'd forgotten much of what he'd learned from this and other books on codebreaking, which had rarely, if ever, been relevant to his day-to-day work. Yet he still remembered enough to recognise the method Ziętek had employed: a book cipher, unbreakable as long as the specific book used remained a secret between them.

It was a simple yet elegant solution, one that hinted at a deeper knowledge of cryptography than he'd given her credit for.

Had Ziętek been trained in this? If so, then by whom, and for what purpose? Tyler's mind whirred with questions as he prepared to dive into the decryption process, a strange mixture of dread and anticipation tightening his chest.

He hunched over the desk, an angle-poise light illuminating the pages of the bible. His fingers traced the numbers, guiding him through the cipher one painstaking step at a time.

The first sequence, 1382:16:0:4, led him to page 1,382 – a passage from Jeremiah, chronicling idolatry and the moral corruption of Judah. He dropped to paragraph sixteen, line zero, and then counted to the fourth character of the line. It was a capital 'P'. He scribbled the letter on a piece of paper, his pulse quickening. The next group, 1018:19:0:1, chronicled Psalm 117, a solemn call to all nations, which led him to a capital 'O'. Then came 'R' and 'T'. He could see the word forming, tantalisingly close yet still incomplete.

He glanced at his Rolex — a silent stylish reminder of his success, bought on a whim in Dubai, tax free and undeclared. It was mid-afternoon. He had to remember to take his medication; he couldn't afford to let this distraction derail his routine.

Yet the allure of the puzzle was too strong to resist. Hours slipped by unnoticed as Tyler decoded the message, each new letter adding to the growing sense of urgency.

The process was slow, laborious and exacting, but Tyler persevered, driven by an overriding compulsion to see it through.

Finally, after what felt like an eternity, he leaned back and surveyed his handiwork. The words on the jotter formed a coherent, if disturbing, message:

```
PORTO SANTO, TEL 351 964 875 228 /
Mr Tyler,
I reach out to you most urgently. There is a
plan for mass murder, genocide. A pathogen to
annihilate humanity. It turns the blood to glue,
like snake venom. Death is certain, it comes in
seconds. They plan to release it within months.
I have the molecular specification but must be
careful. Other information also. I will send
production schedules, manufacturing agents,
methods to disperse.
C12b3BO091944Cd88L29
```

'Alakazam,' muttered Tyler, a grin spreading across his face. But his smugness was quickly tempered by the gravity of the message. A pathogen that turns blood to glue? The idea seemed absurd, yet the eerie repetition of the snake venom motif struck a chord deep within him. Was this just an elaborate hoax, or was there something infinitely more sinister at play?

Tyler looked intently at the jotter on his desk, with his handwritten decoded message. He could pick up the phone now, right this minute, and make the call. He might speak directly to the owl woman, who would immediately confess the hoax. But if this was an elaborate practical joke, it was a pathetically insipid one, feeble and banal, without a dénouement. Why go to all that effort? Where was the punchline?

Tyler flicked through his mental rolodex, seeking out and profiling his personal and professional enemies. There were quite a few, but would any of them be so motivated as to engineer such an elaborate but ultimately sterile prank?

Susan was at the AGA, cooking one of her incomparable Sunday roast dinners, with all the trimmings, including the most scrumptious and irresistible roast potatoes. A mouth-watering aroma wafted from the kitchen and permeated through the frame of the closed office door.

With a feast in the offing, and a bottle of something special to celebrate his cryptographic mastery, Tyler decided to call it a day.

Tyler lay beside Susan. The piercing rays of first light penetrated their bedroom window. Her naked back radiated an immensely powerful heat — a phenomenon consistent with every other woman with whom he'd ever shared a bed. In the half-light, Susan looked peaceful, sweet and serene.

Tyler inwardly cursed himself for his serial infidelity. He knew he was a lying, degenerate, faithless bastard.

His mind started racing. Shelving his conscience, he focused instead on the strangeness of the previous day. Should he dial the number in Porto Santo?

It had already occurred to him that Ziętek's bible

provided the matrix with which to encrypt a response to her using precisely the same formula: her formula, known only to them, as in a mutual and exclusive covenant.

It was a perfectly secure, impenetrable communication link.

With a smirk, Michael Tyler buried his head in a sweet-scented yielding pillow.

He might be a faithless bastard, but he was a bloody smart one, too.

After breakfast, Susan departed for London, driving her prized black Audi RS4, which Tyler had given her for her fiftieth birthday. She had engagements and business meetings in preparation of spring collections for various boutique and high-street retail clients. She'd be away for three days, staying in a hotel in Bayswater.

Tyler watched as Susan's car turned right at the driveway and disappeared from view. 'While the cat's away...' he mused.

Porto Santo... he vaguely recalled the name — an island, he thought — but couldn't place it in his mindscape. He could google it, of course, but he was hesitant to do so; a sixth sense within him urged caution.

There was an aged world atlas gathering dust and cobwebs in the garage, destined at some point for a jumble sale. He'd refer to that instead.

With its index consulted, Tyler thumbed impatiently through the book's faded, brittle, water-stained and yellowing contents, until he landed determinedly on the twenty-sixth page.

Sure enough, there was Porto Santo, a diminutive island in the Atlantic, fifty or so nautical miles to the north-east of the larger and better-known island of Madeira, an enduring favourite of Tyler's aunt. She and her late husband had both waxed lyrical about the capital Funchal, to the extent that they'd even contemplated investing in a timeshare there.

Tyler smiled; he felt a sudden hankering for warm and sunny Madeira. He relished the prospect of a week in the sun and, frankly, he deserved a holiday.

He wouldn't take Susan, nor would he tell her the destination or even the purpose of his trip. If she enquired, he'd only tell her he was meeting an informant, which wasn't strictly untrue.

As was usual with Tyler, he had hidden agendas. He decided to cross-charge the exercise to his most gullible client, and he'd claim tax relief on the entire trip. He started planning several days of self-indulgence and hedonism, assessing locations and opportunities, particularly with the intent to 'play away'. Although, demographically, Madeira was a draw for the retired and the elderly, Tyler felt confident there would also be sizzling young flesh to be had.

Wary of googling on his own computer, Tyler resolved on two courses of action. Firstly, he'd research flights and hotels anonymously on a computer that couldn't be traced — from an internet café, he thought.

Secondly, he'd book his flights and hotel with his preferred travel agent by phone.

There were some limited direct flights from the UK

to Porto Santo, but he balked at the idea of being stuck on such a small island with Ziętek, whom he knew at first hand to be cloying, intrusive and, frankly, repellent. Instead, he'd fly directly to Madeira and stay in the island's capital Funchal.

Regarding hotels, he soon settled on Reid's Palace — a stunning pink monolith set amongst beautiful gardens, presiding high on sea-cliffs overlooking the sparkling Atlantic. Reid's had a reputation for service and pampering second to none. It all looked exquisite — just the sort of place that might attract an aspirant Hollywood starlet or two.

As to Ziętek, Tyler would keep their meeting brutally short: either a quick hop over by turboprop, or perhaps across the sea by ferry — which, he'd noted, sailed twice daily. Ziętek was the cover for his visit and could prove troublesome if he didn't meet her at least once during the trip. He dreaded the prospect, but, as he quipped to himself, all silver linings must have a cloud.

The more Tyler thought about it, the more preposterous Ziętek's story seemed — most likely nothing more than harmless, delusional nonsense, a convenient excuse for a well-earned 'jolly'. Yet there were also clear risks. Was Ziętek insane, or at least in need of psychiatric help? Was he himself the subject of a dangerous fixation, as in *Fatal Attraction*?

Another terrifying possibility, albeit an extremely remote one, still lingered in Tyler's mind: what if Ziętek was telling the truth? That would place him at the centre of a maelstrom. He'd be riding a tiger.

And yet, what an opportunity! What if he heroically exposed the dastardly masterminds behind an horrific doomsday plot, dragging the fiends from the shadows, kicking and screaming, into the purifying, searing light of justice? He, Michael John Tyler, would be the Saviour of the World!

His imagination went into overdrive: television interviews, talk shows, book deals, screenplays, even Hollywood... and infatuated girls, hysterical in adoration.

The next morning, Tyler set about composing his encrypted response to Ziętek. With meticulous care, he entered the correct coded groups into his phone that corresponded to his simple, handwritten plaintext message. Transposition by reference to Ziętek's bible was childishly simple but very time-consuming: the ciphertext completed on screen had taken nearly an hour. His cleartext message read:

LET'S TALK. ON THIS CHANNEL. MT.

Satisfied with his transposition and the corresponding code groups, he tapped the send button. With a 'handshake' and the most fleeting hesitation, his message was delivered and marked as read with two blue ticks.

Near instantaneously, Tyler was surprised to see an incoming transmission appear in the chat thread. Attached was a compressed ZIP file. The accompanying message read:

USE PASSWORD.

Password? What bloody password?

Tyler was tired and hungry — with Susan away, he had not had breakfast and his stomach and bowels gurgled and grumbled insistently. He sighed now, annoyed, frustrated and resentful at this game-playing.

He eyed the desk jotter and his handwritten notation from the previous day, noting the last line:

```
C12b3BO091944Cd88L29
```

Of course!

With no means to open the ZIP file on his phone, he launched the WhatsApp web application on his PC and downloaded the transmitted file to the computer's desktop. Deactivating the wireless connection, he clicked on the transferred ZIP file.

As expected, there was the password prompt. With reference to the jotter, Tyler proceeded to type carefully and methodically — as he'd noted, the sequence was case-sensitive: capital C... 12b3... capital B... 009... 1944... capital C... d88... capital L... 29.

Expectantly, Tyler pressed return, only to be confronted with the message:

```
Password incorrect, please try again.
```

In anger and frustration, Tyler threw his pen forcefully at the computer, it bouncing off the screen with a glassy high-pitched 'ping'.

'Bollocks!' he shouted. 'Bitch!'

Tyler thought and thought. He looked again at Ziętek's password. After five minutes of fruitless reading and rereading, his error suddenly became clear: it was not 009, but O09. A capital 'O', not a zero.

Idiot!

The ZIP file now unfurled, instantly revealing two PDF graphics files and an Excel spreadsheet — all standard format but each capable of inflicting mayhem if boobytrapped with malware.

Oh well, he thought, in for a penny, in for a pound. If he trashed the hard disk and even the machine itself, so what?

He selected the first file, clicked the mouse with almost casual abandon and was surprised and reassured to observe the file open gracefully. Before him was a single page, photographed.

Tyler viewed the document's lateral dimensions: this was American Quarto paper — a stock rarely, if ever, seen in the UK, but more so in Europe. Jet-black punch holes to the left of the page indicated this originally was a photocopy, possibly an extract from a much larger sheaf held in a lever-arch file or a ring binder. Tyler got the impression this page was a mere taster, an apéritif, which Ziętek had submitted to whet his appetite. He wondered if she'd had only a very limited opportunity to snatch this evidence.

No, don't be a fool, thought Tyler. She's a crank — her charade an elaborate but crude hoax.

As for the first PDF's content, it was all Greek to Tyler. Molecular stuff, with symbols and complex formulations.

Words and expressions alien to him filled the screen: nucleosides, peptides, amino acids, amines, lipids and amyloid proteins. Other compounds included widely known elements: sodium, calcium, potassium and magnesium. This could all be ascertained in seconds from the internet… and yet there was something about the document. It looked and felt 'right'; it had that intangible quality which, in Tyler's mind at least, attested to its authenticity.

In the lower right quadrant was an originator's watermark, a stamp which read 'Endpoint Pharmaceuticals'.

Really! Tyler sneered. If this truly was a blueprint for mass murder, would the evil geniuses behind such wickedness imprint themselves so blatantly?

The second PDF proved even more problematic. It was a digital copy of a memorandum on plain paper with no accreditation or affiliation shown, nor any clue to its provenance. It was densely written in Polish, with a character set full of diacritical signs, digraphs and trigraphs. Viewing it on screen, Tyler regarded the document as impenetrable. Normally, he'd have cut and pasted the entirety of the Polish text into Google Translate, but given the potentially sensitive subject matter, such an option struck him as unwise.

He definitely wasn't going to pipe the material through any platform hosting CHATGPT. Like millions of other people, he was instinctively cautious of the Artificial Intelligence model, believing it to be a CIA information harvester or some such.

Instead, Tyler downloaded a Polish-English translation application and copied and pasted the Polish text into it.

The text was technical in nature, with clinical data supplied from an unnamed laboratory in Katowice. He found it utterly unfathomable, with one notable exception: an experiment described as a 'lethality trial' with a '100 percent fatal reaction'. 100 percent of what? Lab rats? Macaques?

Tyler turned his attention to the remaining file, noting the filename: UKRAINE_BSL4_ROLLOUT. It was an Excel spreadsheet, an indecipherable and boring one at that. He recognised it as a manufacturing ledger, scheduled with production dates, manufacturing locations, volumes and product types, coded numerically. Although underwhelmed by the document as a whole, he was impressed by the production volumes shown. By rudimentary mental arithmetic, he calculated that the tally ran to several billion 'lots' — quite the most voluminous he'd ever encountered.

But billions of what? Widgets?

The manufacturing plants shown, unidentified but indicated by location, were many, various and international — located mostly in industrialised nations in the northern hemisphere.

It was all a bit of a disappointment.

As was his habit, but with little enthusiasm, Tyler commenced a case file. He ran a clean uncut fingernail along the cellophane shrink-wrapped package of Ryman A4 office files. He extracted a pale blue folder with a treasury tag, marking the file in neat capitals, top right, with a black felt-tip pen: 'UKRAINE'

In Cheltenham, 120 miles north-west of Tyler's home, Martyn Stowell was busy loading a black plastic processing cartridge, or 'mission package' as it was known, into an HPE Cray EX supercomputer, affectionately nicknamed 'the Beast'. Stowell, a computer analyst assigned in support of the secretive Scavenger team, knew nothing of the preparatory cryptanalysis, but he would now press the buttons to initiate the full cracking of the code. The first to show on the morning shift, Stowell saw that the cartridge was a targeting priority, and following a hastily brewed mug of Nescafé, he wasted no time in loading it.

With the cartridge's checksum authenticated, Stowell entered his authorisation PIN and the decrypt commenced. He knew this processing 'run' was the product of a direct pipeline tunnelled into the backbone of a Virtual Private Network (VPN) hosted in Germany. Despite the defection of Edward Snowden years previously and his revelations that the prominent internet service providers were almost universally in league with Western intelligence agencies, the hapless public still trusted VPN providers to protect their privacy.

Stowell chuckled at the thought. His team had been downloading emails and other traffic from hundreds of VPN providers for years, following highly secretive agency-platform agreements, or 'accommodations' as they were termed. You couldn't trust anything these days, he chortled.

But this mission package must contain a singularly intractable conundrum, thought Stowell. The HPE Cray EX supercomputer was the most powerful available; its phenomenal processing power judiciously deployed as a much-prized commodity. The targeting team must be trying to break something 'uncrackable'. A 'one-time pad' perhaps?

The telephone box in the village was the last vestige of a bygone era, an ugly anachronism soon destined for the scrapheap. Its once proud Post Office red gloss paint had long since faded to a lacklustre faded grey-purple. The veneer was peeled and rotting, and moss and lichen encroached. Glass panes were shattered and smashed out, with graffiti scrawled on every surface.

Tyler palmed a fresh sheet of Kleenex, pulled the heavy metal door open and squeezed himself inside, where he was met by a reek of urine and rotting takeaway. There was a slot for a card — credit or debit — but he opted for a cash call. He lifted the greasy receiver with the Kleenex hanky and pushed in five one-pound coins, one after the other, each one making a loud clunk after insertion.

Astonished to hear an active dial-tone, Tyler keyed in the number: 00 351 964 875 228. The ringtone sounded interminably.

At last, a female voice answered: 'Good morning, Excelsior Apartments, Porto Santo. How may I help?'

Tyler, genuinely surprised, stammered: 'May I speak to Miss Ziętek… Danusia Ziętek?'

After a few moments, the female voice replied: 'I'll transfer you. Please hold.'

The rasping, guttural, accented voice that answered a few seconds later was unmistakable: assuredly, it was Ziętek, the owl woman, the harpy from hell. Tyler shuddered at the prospect of having to face this fetid creature yet again.

The Professor was adamant. The cryptographic patterns were indisputable: either a 'one-time pad' or a book cipher, and if the latter, the high page numbers pointed to a substantial, weighty tome. The advice to the Scavenger team had been precise: let the supercomputer keep crunching, but in the meantime, the simplest path to crack the code lay in identifying the exact book referenced by both targets. It had to be the precise edition, down to the International Standard Book Number.

Ziętek's work computer and laptop had been placed under relentless surveillance ever since the security breach. Her email traffic had been intercepted and scrutinised, but so far, those to and from Tyler had all remained obstinately encrypted.

It was Ziętek's internet activity that finally exposed the crucial clue. An Amazon Prime purchase, made with her bank card, stood out like a flare in the night: two copies of the CTS New Catholic Bible, 2007 edition. This had to be the book they were using.

The order was placed immediately. Amazon's vast automated warehouse whirred into action, and by first light the next morning, two copies of the bible arrived at Scavenger's secure facility. The unit's top cryptographers set to work without delay, aware that the clock was ticking and every second counted

THREE
PORTO SANTO

Tyler had booked his flight to Madeira three full days ahead of his appointment with Ziętek — an intentional ploy, giving him time to survey the lie of the land and to luxuriate.

He'd immediately warmed to Reid's, with its beautiful reception and terrace. Everything about the hotel was exquisite, oozing old-school style and quality. The staff were respectful and attentive but never obsequious; they were there when needed and discreetly absent when not, which was just as it should be.

Tyler's room, 518 in the garden wing, was perfect, too, with a balcony that provided an unhindered view over the hotel's sun platform and well-proportioned swimming pool. Strategically placed palms and trees on the periphery provided shaded relief. Sprinklers spun quietly and rhythmically, refreshing the immaculately tended arboretum and ornamental gardens beyond. In the distance was a sweeping panoramic view of the city of Funchal, with row after row of glistening white stucco villas and smaller family dwellings topped with distinctive blood-orange terracotta roofs. At night, as Tyler had witnessed the previous evening, the city's lights twinkled and sparkled majestically like a richly jewelled necklace.

The Atlantic glistened in the rays of the evening sun. Motorboats, yachts, skiffs and small fishing vessels weaved expertly, dancing around each other in mutual and respectful recognition, while the occasional jet-ski throttled and bounded at speed. Huge cruise ships — floating citadels — were docked, tethered precisely alongside the lengthy and accommodating wharf of the port.

The sunset was breathtaking: a gorgeous, seamless, radiating palette of gold, crimson, copper and violet. Tyler, reflecting briefly on the miserable winter evenings behind him, pinched himself.

As the warmth of the day dissipated, the shadows extended. Surveying the pool below, he watched intently as a svelte and tanned brunette, early thirties, shapely and tantalising in a red bikini, arose from her sun lounger to depart for the evening. Tyler had kept a keen watch and was now despondent as she disappeared from view. He made a mental note of her chosen sun lounger.

From the sublime to the ridiculous, alas. Tyler's thoughts turned with little enthusiasm to Ziętek. Their correspondence by encrypted texts and emails had culminated in a place, date and time to meet. Tomorrow at 2 pm, he'd meet Ziętek at a location chosen by her: *Moinho das Lombas*, a well-appointed beachside bar-restaurant with a sizeable terrace, situated along the eastern coastal road of Porto Santo Island.

Ziętek, brusque to the point of rudeness, or perhaps just overwhelmed by the tedium and sheer laboriousness of scrambling her messages, had volunteered little detail, other than that she had 'much information' to impart 'in many forms' and he should come 'prepared'.

Tyler cast his mind back to litigation cases at the Royal Courts of Justice, at the Inner Temple and the Inns of Court, as well as criminal prosecutions. Prior to courtroom automation, legal cases had invariably entailed voluminous boxloads of documentation, folders and printed exhibits stacked high, all wheeled into proceedings on hand-trolleys by paralegals and junior solicitors.

Boxloads of printout… surely not? But if so, he'd need a car.

Hiring a car made sense in any event, crossing over by ferry, which sailed back and forth daily, departing in the early morning and returning in the late afternoon. He would therefore be in Porto Santo for several hours. Tyler had mentally scheduled a mere forty-five minutes with Ziętek, hopefully rather less.

With a car, he could drive around the island at will, sightseeing. Then, with Ziętek, when the whistle blew, he could escape her clutches, swiftly and efficiently beating a retreat with an easy grin and a plausible excuse.

He didn't want to be dependent on buses or taxis at any point.

Very early the next morning, Tyler visited a Hertz car rental office. His driving licence was duly photocopied and there were the usual forms to be filled out. He then took charge of a charcoal grey Fiat Punto. After a cursory familiarisation with the controls, he hit the road, driving swiftly down steep narrow alleyways to the port and the ferry embarkation point.

Foot passengers, cars, some vans and even a few trucks converged at the dock, with new arrivals by the minute. Amongst them, unnoticed by Tyler, was a Suzuki motorbike, the rider of which had dismounted before striding purposefully to the ferry's booking office.

The Porto Santo Line's ferry *Lobo Marinho*, the 'Sea Lion', was docked, reversed with its gaping and expansive car deck marshalled and cordoned off. With a sailing time of two-and-a-half hours, the ferry was the right decision; a plane, with a flight time of just twenty minutes, would have been frustrating, what with security checks and the interminable waiting around inherent to air travel. The fresh sea air would do him the power of good. Having skipped the hotel's breakfast, he also savoured the prospect of a snack in the ship's lounge.

Disembarking at Porto Santo, he drove off the ramp and followed the designated lane along a steeply left-veering quay which ended at a sharp road junction. The traffic flow was surprisingly dense, and Tyler stalled, awaiting an opportunity to pull out. He sensed the impatience of the drivers behind. He was oblivious, however, to the Suzuki motorbike, three rows back, which throttled and gunned its engine, or to its rider: male, mid-thirties, athletic, helmeted with darkened visor.

With the most momentary lull in the traffic, Tyler

seized his chance and accelerated violently. The Fiat lurched sharply, tyres squealing and smoking, on to the highway. As he sped away, he wore a smug grin, seeing in his rearview mirror the various tailgaters at the junction, stalled and immobile, now vanishing from view. Gunning the Fiat for three hundred metres, Tyler, without signalling, swung a sharp right turn, then deftly and speedily weaved through the backstreets, intent on joining the coastal road.

Nathan — the alias printed in his Serbian passport — had wasted no time. On arrival at the airport, he'd hired a powerful Renault estate, dumped an overnight bag at his hotel and then had driven immediately to the Excelsior Apartments, a block of serviced flats. All he'd been told was that an ELINT intercept indicated that a high-priority target was at large in this building. He'd considered a stakeout, but the road outside was too busy, with pedestrians — tourists mostly — and traffic. He thought of hiring an apartment himself but considered it pointless: too uncertain, with no guarantee of a result.

At the wheel of the Renault, parked discreetly along the road, Nathan took a long look at the photograph of the target on his smartphone: an unprepossessing woman in her sixties? He checked the date of birth: she was actually forty-eight but looked much older. A lengthy static surveillance of the building would be risky. Given the urgency of the task, and the paucity of resources to hand, he decided on a 'walk in'. He grabbed the sealed DHL package he habitually took on missions, then strode towards the entrance.

At the reception desk was a young woman, a girl really, straight out of school or college.

A package for Danusia Ziętek?

No, said the girl apologetically. Ms Ziętek had vacated the apartment the previous day. There was no forwarding address.

Porto Santo is a small island with a peripheral main road, bled into by only a few tributaries. With uninterrupted travel, it may be toured by car in less than an hour.

Tyler sped along the coastal road, glancing intermittently at the Fiat's integrated screen satnav. The rendezvous point, the bar-restaurant *Moinho das Lombas*, was prominent and listed, quaintly juxtaposed with a windmill, indicated on the screen by a small flashing symbol. Mile upon mile of beach stretched to his right, of pure, rich, golden sand. Along the road in the distance, he spotted the blades of the windmill — outstretched tendrils of wood and bolted metal, long stripped of their canvas sails.

Tyler parked in the ancient mill's shadow, alighted and ambled downward, past the stylish stone restaurant to his left and down shallow steps, shaded by magnificent tall palms with abundant verdant fronds. Reaching the lower terraces, Tyler approved of Ziętek's choice of venue — it was hidden from the road or any observation, buttressed with stone alcoves and recessed nooks, further concealed by groves of fulsome ferns and prickly cactus plants.

His Rolex showed twelve noon. He'd return in two hours, at the appointed time.

Danusia Ziętek was seated bolt upright on an aluminium tubular framed chair that had thoughtfully been brought down the stone steps by a sympathetic, good-humoured waiter with kind eyes. He'd also conveyed her two large suitcases and had even returned, minutes later, with a scattering of cushions, which had marginally eased the pains in her hips and abdomen — the symptoms of osteoporosis and aggressive and pervasive cancer.

Despite the electric-blue sky and the blissful balm of a generous, warming onshore breeze, Danusia shivered. She checked the buttons of her cardigan and, hunching forward, pulled her thick woollen winter overcoat tightly around her. Then she re-knotted her headscarf, readjusting her heavily framed sunglasses with their outsized brown prescription lenses.

Danusia's pocket watch showed five minutes past two. She feared Tyler had got 'cold feet', as the English said. She'd warned Tyler under no circumstances to contact her by mobile telephone, having long since dispensed with the handset shown on her business card. She hadn't even advised Tyler of her current number. The book code was the only channel for communication. With her laptop secured in a suitcase and with no wireless signal, she and Tyler were incommunicado, at least for the time being.

Danusia tried to conjure Tyler's face in her mind, but the image eluded her, dissolving like mist on a cold morning. Had she been wrong to trust him? Had she, in her desperation, been carried away by his overwhelming confidence and breezy charm? Was he just another charlatan?

She'd first stumbled upon Tyler on YouTube, enthralled by a captivating lecture he'd given on corporate fraud. His case studies, with numerous examples of handling informants and whistleblowers, had resonated with her own struggles. In him, she'd seen the solution to her problem, the lifeline she so desperately needed. With that belief, she'd tracked him down, securing her place at the conference, eager for the opportunity to meet him in person.

But doubt now gnawed at her, and her confidence withered. She questioned not only the man's grasp of the intricate scientific details submitted, but also his comprehension of the implications and gravity of what this data actually meant.

And then, as if summoned by her burgeoning doubts, the very man appeared before her. Bounding down the terrace steps like an exuberant puppy was Tyler, ebullient with greetings, glad tidings and transparent bonhomie. Danusia now recalled Tyler's boyish good looks. His face, which had been pale in November, was impressively tanned. But in the harsh glare of daylight, she detected something false, even shabby, about him. His crumpled linen suit, silly cheap necklace worn without conviction in support of some 'worthy' yet baseless cause, the silver rings on his fingers, and the over-cultivated sideburns trimmed to geometric points with such 'careless' precision — it was all just so vulgar.

But to Danusia, Tyler's most unattractive quality was his utter inattention. Nothing she'd tried to impart had made the slightest impression on him. Nothing!

She recoiled at the prospect of this man's company. But her alternatives were not merely limited: they were non-existent. Tyler had been her last hope and refuge; instead, she'd have to put her faith in God alone, in the hope He would enlighten and guide this creep in a creased suit who was uttering such banalities. She cursed herself for her credulity.

She would leave quickly, perhaps aided by the kindly waiter. With a flight reserved from Porto Santo to Lisbon, she'd offer her excuses and make a swift exit.

As Tyler blustered on, full of breezy assurances and unfounded certainties, Danusia inwardly crumpled. She looked over the man's shoulder to the vast Atlantic Ocean, azure and sparkling under the high sun, with undulating waves and galloping white horses. Gulls soared overhead, gliding high on the thermals. The beach and its golden stretch of sand held such promise, at least for those who were young and lucky in love. But life's long trail was now behind her, a distant memory, and an all too narrow and alarmingly darkened path beckoned.

Beyond consolation, Danusia beheld Tyler, her final representative on earth. Her heart sank; she'd chosen unwisely. For she realised that this man, in whom she'd placed such faith, trust and belief, was nothing more than an unbridled idiot.

Nathan fumed. His colleague Xavier — an alias — had lost Tyler upon disembarkation. The target vehicle, a dark grey Fiat, had sped from the ferry, leaving Xavier astride his Suzuki motorbike, high and dry.

Yet Nathan didn't chastise Xavier, for vehicular surveillance was always challenging in the extreme, and this hasty and ill-considered operation was grossly under-resourced. Nathan's team had hit the ground within seventeen hours of the tasking order — their quickest deployment ever. But they were lacking equipment and, crucially, personnel. A task of this complexity would normally have entailed at least ten troops. He had just three.

ELINT had indicated an imminent meeting between Ziętek and Tyler — precise location unknown but on the island somewhere. An exchange of classified information was suspected, the wider dissemination or exposure of which was to be prevented by any means necessary.

Crucially, both targets had been traced: Ziętek to the Excelsior Apartments, Tyler to Reid's hotel in Funchal. They even had his room number: 518. Locating the targets so precisely had been a coup, doubling the opportunity to cover the meeting, and optimal for further surveillance and intervention.

Now, maddeningly, they had dropped both ends of the rope. Nathan suspected that Ziętek, and possibly Tyler also, had been tipped off. If so, the leak was most certainly not from his small, tight-knit team.

Nathan reappraised the territory. The island was forty-two square kilometres — tiny, really. But the task of tracing the targets, whether they were on foot or in the Fiat, was immense and daunting.

The jaundice shocked Tyler. Ziętek's skin was a pronounced deep ochre, and the whites of her eyes were runny yellow, veined and bloodshot, like putrid eggs. On seeing her, he shuddered. His skin crawled at the sight. His mental stopwatch was counting down precisely to the preset moment of his departure. Ziętek's monologue, her monotonous tedious drawl, droned on and on. She never completed her sentences, or parcelled the narrative — to Tyler, it just sounded like a garbled stream of consciousness.

Why, oh why, could she not just write a report, or even a memo, sticking to the facts, clinically and concisely?

At thirty minutes in, the prize Tyler coveted was tantalisingly within his grasp. From a cracked black leather shoulder bag, stuffed to the gunnels with the old woman's flotsam and jetsam, Ziętek dug deep. Gasping in recognition, she hauled from its inner recesses a crumpled, brown, letter-sized envelope.

Heart pounding, but with feigned indifference, Tyler resisted snatching the offering from her yellowing parchment-like claws. It would soon be time to end this charade.

Danusia, sensing and deeply resenting Tyler's restlessness and his eagerness to depart, turned to him balefully. Resigned and defeated, with bitter regret, she surrendered her spoils.

She gestured to the envelope. Two drives, high capacity, a primary and a backup.

Tyler, reaching for the slender package, noted the woman's paper-thin, translucent fingers and her long, brittle, greying fingernails.

Like a hawk's talons, he thought.

He nodded slightly, as respectfully as he could, and then with his thumb he punched a discreet hole in the envelope. Inside, nested together, were two razor-thin flash drives, both silver-plated. With a beady eye, seeing that each drive had a capacity of sixty-four gigabytes, Tyler assessed this haul to be a potential treasure trove.

Tyler's 'bubble' was short-lived, burst almost straight away by Ziętek, who suddenly thumped his collarbone with surprising force. What now? Looking down, he saw a dayglo pink Post-it note, freshly stuck to his jacket lapel. Inspecting the note more closely, he could see a handwritten sequence.

'The access code,' said Ziętek.

Another ludicrously convoluted one, thought Tyler.

This intimate, abrupt and irreverent act by the owl woman was strangely endearing, in stark contrast to all else about her. But in an instant, her mood changed.

In pain, bone-tired and feeling ineffably sad, Danusia could take no more. She let her head droop and closed her eyes.

With his bounty secured, Tyler turned sharply and headed determinedly up the shallow steps, towards the sanctuary of his car.

Referring to the flash drives, Danusia muttered, only half-jokingly and very intentionally within Tyler's earshot: 'I hope you choke on them.'

The manhunt that afternoon was frenetic. Xavier, on his powerful Suzuki motorbike, had been tasked to cover every single road, street, track and trail on the island, however minor, working from north to south on a repeat circuit. Meanwhile, Nathan and the third member of the team were in the hired Renault estate, working in the opposite direction.

The priority was to locate the grey Fiat, registration FE-37-BD. Xavier, in hot pursuit, had earlier taken a clear phone-camera photo of the Fiat, which he'd circulated to the team. If they could find the car, they could wait on its occupant: Tyler. A GPS tracker could be installed also. The team had a recent passport photograph of Ziętek, and a grainy shot of Tyler from an old conference brochure downloaded from a website. Nathan was assured that Tyler's passport photo, much clearer, would be transmitted imminently.

From long experience, Nathan knew that if the Fiat was hidden, perhaps in a garage or secreted in a remote sideroad or otherwise, the chances of finding it in the few hours available to them were pitifully small. Moreover, if Ziętek and Tyler were indoors or otherwise shielded from view, perhaps in any of the thousands of dwellings, cafeterias, restaurants or commercial buildings in the island's capital Vila Baleira or in its conurbations, the chances of locating them were next to nil. The same odds applied to the surrounding towns: Camacha, Campo de Cima, Dragoal and Cabeco da Ponta.

All afternoon, there had been urgent 'flash' transmissions back and forth with Control. There had been some talk of deploying a high-altitude surveillance drone, but even if flown in immediately by a transport plane, this notion, without any local support, command infrastructure or operating permission, had been quickly dismissed as wholly impracticable. Satellite surveillance, bypassing official channels, was also ruled out, with all strategic 'Keyhole' assets fully committed to the war in Ukraine or the Gaza assault, or stationed over Taiwan and the South China Sea.

Nathan had suggested a much more realistic option: an 'all ports bulletin' to intercept the targets at Porto Santo airport, or at the ferry port where the *Lobo Marinho* docked. But his request had been emphatically denied. There was to be absolutely no referral to the Portuguese authorities, nor any consultation with them.

This response had confirmed beyond doubt to Nathan that he and his small team were engaged in a 'black op': deniable, unattributable and illegal. But legal, moral or ethical considerations didn't apply.

They never did.

Nathan had been assigned a task; a mission. He was to locate Tyler, locate Ziętek and, by any measures necessary, stem the information leak.

With the targets both lost, a radical change of plan was called for.

Tyler hit the coastal road again with renewed vigour. He headed south, with the stunning stretch of beach now to his left, its sand seared white under the hot mid-afternoon sun. Everything had gone precisely to plan: Ziętek had relinquished the data with no quibbling and no need for any blandishments. He also congratulated himself on the speed of his escape, effected in far less than the assigned forty-five minutes, leaving the haggard crab to stew in her own juices.

Without any planning or forethought, he happened upon the southernmost point of the island, stopping at the tiny commune of Ponta da Calheta. He parked the Fiat in the shade, off the road, behind a windbreak of maturing laurel saplings. He then nestled himself at a beach bar, sitting at a circular steel table shaded beneath a large, multicoloured parasol. The bartender, a young man in shorts and a T-shirt, approached Tyler who ordered a *Sagres* — a light beer, ice cold, and a snack also, a tapas dish of squid, shrimp and mussels.

Tyler looked out to sea. The water was aquamarine, with striking greens and blues of picture-postcard beauty. There was an imposing outcrop — rocky, jagged, prehistoric. Two girls in string bikinis strutted past, squealing with laughter and disdain as they caught his errant eye. He smirked; they were too young, even for him.

Tyler eased back, reflecting on his luck. He could forget the owl woman, and her memory sticks would wait. The afternoon was still young, and Madeira beckoned once more. He still had three more days at Reid's.

Life was good.

High above him, Tyler glimpsed an airliner, glistening red and white, arcing tightly on a north-east bearing. It was an Air Portugal A320, bound for Lisbon. Unbeknown to him, attended to in its business-class cabin was Danusia Ziętek.

An 'owl' in flight.

Nathan and the third teammate, who was with him in the Renault, had missed Tyler's progress south; they'd been busy scouring the town square and a web of backstreets in Vila Baleira. Meanwhile, Xavier, on the Suzuki, was still far to the north.

Tyler had arrived on the island by ferry. Therefore, Nathan thought it safe to assume he'd most likely leave by ferry, too. With this in mind, Nathan instructed Xavier to meet him and the third team member at the ferry terminal, one hour prior to the *Lobo Marinho's* departure, where they would lay in wait.

With luck — a slim chance, admittedly — if Tyler's Fiat showed up, Ziętek might be with him.

FOUR
LOBO MARINHO

The *Lobo Marinho* was scheduled to sail for Funchal at six.

Tyler drove up the ship's vehicle ramp and on to the lower car deck some twenty minutes earlier. Executing a precise three-point turn, he positioned the Fiat neatly in a designated bay of the lower car deck, poised for a quick, hassle-free exit.

The stencilled notification read: '*Estritamente não fumar, aplicar freio de mão*' — 'Strictly no smoking, apply handbrake'. In the enclosed space, the stench of petrol and exhaust fumes was overpowering.

From the pocket of his linen jacket, he retrieved the brown envelope. He inspected the two identical memory sticks. They were Integral Arc USB flash drives. Ziętek had thoughtfully applied adhesive stickers to them — one red, the other yellow — marked in biro: 'MT'. He'd take the yellow one with him, secure in his jacket pocket, but would leave the red one in the car.

But where? The glovebox? Tyler thought it too

obvious. Instead, he pushed the device deeply into a small, tight pouch in the car's red plastic service wallet, which he then wedged into the pannier of the driver's door. Satisfied with this concealment, Tyler locked the car and headed for the exit, climbing its steep steel ladder to the comfort of the lounge above. He would enjoy a drink at the bar, and perhaps partake of a cigarillo on the promenade deck.

Relaxed and at ease, Tyler ordered a glass of chilled Sauvignon. What with the car, he'd kept an eye on the day's alcohol consumption. He congratulated himself on his self-discipline and restraint. He'd recently been diagnosed as prediabetic, and excessive booze also had a bad effect on his heart, causing chest pain. But a couple of glasses in celebration of the day's successes, both great and small, wouldn't hurt.

He checked his jacket pocket again, reassuring himself the memory stick was safe. Opening the notes folder on his smartphone, he discreetly and very carefully transcribed the access code Ziętek had scrawled on her pink Post-it note. He photographed the Post-it also and would keep it, just in case.

Savouring the wine — a light, crisp New Zealand label — Tyler noticed a woman, whom he judged to be in her early thirties, at the far end of the bar. Not just any woman, either — he found her so spellbindingly beautiful that he struggled not to gawp. She had something of the French Riviera about her, Nice or Cannes perhaps? She had classical features: an almond-shaped face, perfectly proportioned with high cheekbones, expressive brown eyes, sensual lips and a cute, slightly upturned ski-slope nose. Her flawless skin was the colour of honey and her hair, auburn with subtle highlights, was immaculately coiffured in a symmetrical bob that fell just below the jawline. Her makeup was artful and elegant, professional even, indicative of a model or an actress.

Tyler, a connoisseur of the female form, admired the woman's proportions, or what he could survey of them. She looked taller than average, possibly five foot eight, and she had a fine neckline, long and slender limbs, a trim waist, and pert upturned breasts.

Tyler felt certain he'd never seen a more beautiful woman in his life — at least, not in the flesh.

Giselle — her cover name — had sensed Tyler's eyes upon her immediately, fleeting but intense and focused, like laser beams. She detected also his feigned indifference, his lack of subtlety almost comical. She would reciprocate, returning the unspoken compliment... but not immediately.

Timing was everything.

Nathan was seated in a far corner of the lounge bar, beyond Tyler's line of sight. He'd chosen his perch carefully, his sight aligned with a wall-mounted mirror to keep tabs on the target. The mirror reflected a clear view of Tyler's shoulders and the back of his head.

Nathan now cursed as he read the incoming message:

```
'Target RV: Moinho das Lombas / beach bar
restaurant. 1400 local, 1500z.'
```

Damn it! The crucial meeting had long since timed out. The mission was surely being sabotaged? But if so, by whom?

An urgent instruction from Control followed in quick succession. The codeword 'ENDGAME' was unequivocal. Nathan had half expected it all afternoon. The target's elimination was now the sole directive and the only acceptable outcome. No easy task in the lounge bar of this ferry, with its staff and disparate patrons as witnesses to their every move. The team faced a dilemma: kill Tyler at sea, or wait for the ferry to disembark and then stalk and dispose of him onshore?

Nathan recalled his training; it had been a gruelling induction into the dealing of death and destruction, bleak in its basic tenets: increase the bleeding, impede the breathing, promote established shock. But what about drowning? Throwing Tyler overboard?

For a drowning to be foolproof, a complicit 'rescuer' would be required to finish the job. If so, either Nathan or Xavier would need to dive in after Tyler with the pretence of rescue, while actually ensuring his demise by pushing his head underwater and drowning him.

The prospect of jumping into the open sea did not appeal at all. In fact, it seemed suicidal.

Men were such ridiculous, instinctual, priapic creatures.

Giselle remembered her field evaluation, years before: 'Of the ten heterosexual men targeted, all engaged, without exception.' Tyler, the proverbial fly in the web, was following her lead to perfection. It was Tyler's third eye contact, marginally more prolonged than was excusable, that assured her.

She didn't avert her eyes, but glanced back at him and even flashed a coy smile. For Tyler, that smile — warm, welcoming and radiant — was a lightning bolt. He shivered with a frisson of unbridled energy, his senses prickling and sizzling. The thrill of the chase — and this was no ordinary quarry. This woman was exquisite, immaculate. If he played his cards right...

Yet a small doubt gnawed at him, his inner voice cautioning him to beware. The woman was too obvious; she was clearly a set-up. A honeytrap then — delectable, irresistible, but a trap nonetheless.

Tyler considered the odds, but it didn't take him long to make up his mind: he would play! He'd turn the tables on her! His imagination ran wild: she and he, post-coital at Reid's, this stunning woman beside him, sharing the room's enormous 'Emperor' bed. The pillow-talk would be scintillating, as he gently, subtly coaxed her into revealing the entire plot to him. It was perfect: he would turn her, and she would become his double agent.

With women, as Tyler knew, it always paid to be in control.

There was the faintest tap on the ferry's window, a single raindrop. And then a second drop, and a third. Only they weren't raindrops: they were tiny hailstones.

Nathan checked the weather app on his smartphone. A storm was fast approaching, a seasonal squall which, according to the forecast, would last for an hour or so.

He sent Xavier a text message: Passenger decks. CCTV. Blind spots.

As soon as he'd read Nathan's message, Xavier knew precisely what his mission entailed. He prowled the deck in the incipient hailstorm, hunting for cameras, assessing fields of vision.

Peripherally, Nathan noticed Giselle. Tyler, as viewed in the mirror, was now clearly on the hook, following the script to perfection.

A command decision was required. Nathan calculated speedily: a freezing sea, a low cloud base which impaired aerial observation or a helicopter rescue, very limited lateral visibility, compounded by an enveloping, dense sea mist, and a target — by the look of him — presenting little or no resistance. Tyler was highly unlikely to survive the sudden immersion in freezing water. So, there would be no need for a false 'rescuer' to finish the job, after all.

Nathan's texted instruction was blunt: Blind spot, Starboard passenger deck, X marks the spot. GO!

Giselle flashed an enticing smile at Tyler, then stood and sashayed calculatedly towards the starboard exit.

Nathan watched the mirror's reflection intently as Tyler drained his glass and headed determinedly after her.

Giselle sensed Tyler on her tail, so eager that his breath almost seared her neck.

Pausing briefly, Nathan now moved also, stealthily in pursuit.

Adrenaline is intrinsic to physical assault, even where minimal contact or resistance is anticipated. Accordingly,

Nathan and Xavier, the heavy lifters of the mission, steeled themselves for action, with pulse rates surging and blood pounding through their arteries.

Giselle, well accustomed to these assignments, enjoyed the tempo and macabre choreography of the occasion.

'X' did indeed mark the spot: having reconnoitred the 'kill box', Xavier vanished dutifully into the recesses as soon as he saw Giselle and Tyler approach.

Time to lower the tempo briefly, thought Giselle. She laughed inwardly at the absurdity of a contrived dalliance on the forsaken deck of a ferry with a man twice her age, all amidst a blizzard of freezing hail. But the old fool had fallen for it, as she'd known he would.

Leaning on the safety rail, she casually surveyed the veiled horizon. Tyler had stationed himself respectfully a few metres away, also leaning on the rail. He'd placed himself, unwittingly, out of shot of the solitary CCTV camera mounted midships.

Giselle watched Tyler struggling with his Zippo lighter. In the powerful breeze, it took cupped hands and several flips of the wheel for him to light the cigarillo. Further flirtation now, nothing too theatrical. She turned to Tyler, invitingly, as they both shrugged and commiserated in mutual dismay at the cold and drizzle.

Nathan and Xavier approached Tyler from opposite ends of the deck, calmly at first but accelerating exponentially on closure.

The hit was executed at lightning speed with a practiced commando efficiency; a deadly ambush against which Tyler stood no chance, afforded no warning and no defence.

Tyler's hair was seized violently and his head hauled backwards, with his ankles grabbed and whipped away from the deck. His body was elevated high above the safety rail and with kinetic inevitability he was hurled mercilessly, head first, down to the roiling sea, some forty feet below.

It was a sheer, uninterrupted plunge into the seething Atlantic, a manoeuvre completed in less than three seconds — so stealthy and stunningly swift that Tyler didn't even cry out, let alone resist. Into the heaving grey sea he went, along with his cigarillo and other remnants also.

Tyler's mobile phone clattered to the deck. Its screen shattered and the battery cover detached, bouncing metallically along the walkway. Xavier, seeing the phone and its components, retrieved them immediately, zipping them in the pocket of his windcheater.

Tossed around like a cork in the violent and powerful wake of the *Lobo Marinho*, Tyler watched helplessly as the ferry powered away, disappearing into the dense mist, out of sight and over the horizon. He had swallowed a significant volume of the ferry's churn, but it was the inhalation of a quarter of a litre of seawater into his lungs that now caused him severe difficulties. That and the cold of the sea, which would soon be bone numbing.

He choked desperately as he fought for oxygen, but his larynx and nostrils were powerless to resist as he gulped and inhaled yet more foul, concentrated brine. His airway was overwhelmed by reflexive spasms — powerful, uncontrollable and terrifying.

Storm clouds enveloped the scene with flashes of lightning. Stair rods of rain and hail sliced the ocean swell. There was not a single vessel or any landmark in sight.

Shocked, traumatised, shivering, abandoned and alone, Tyler would survive in the glacial sea for just another ten minutes.

FIVE
FELLOW TRAVELLERS

Charles Fenwick walked at pace across St James's Park in the direction of Horse Guards, intent on crossing the Mall and up the steps, past the Duke of York Monument. It was a cold afternoon and layers of frost carpeted the ground, still frozen and unperturbed by a watery and anaemic midday sun. It was mid-January, and the few ducks and wildfowl still resident in the park were huddled and mute.

Upbeat, with a spring in his step and freshly returned from West Africa, Fenwick had completed a smooth and efficient 'in-country review', which had culminated with startling revelations. He was on his way to report his findings to Sir Frederick Springer, the seventy-two-year-old chairman and chief executive officer of the Winchcombe Group.

Winchcombe was a FTSE 100 thoroughbred, an international conglomerate on a stratospheric ascent. It was held in awe by even *The Financial Times's* most cynical hacks, not only for its market performance, but also for its social inclusion, ethical practices and environmental awareness. Winchcombe had just come highly placed in a 'diversity, inclusion and equity' index and was fast gaining a reputation as the 'poster child' of caring, responsible capitalism. Winchcombe always invested heavily in public relations and reaped the rewards accordingly.

Springer, at the apex of this megalith, had invited Fenwick to partake of 'coffee' at his club, which Fenwick knew would be generously augmented by a few far more interesting supplements. Wrapping his overcoat tighter against the chill, Fenwick savoured the prospect of a warming cognac or two.

The Travellers Club, 106 Pall Mall, was one of the finest and longest-established London clubs. Founded by Viscount Castlereagh and others at the conclusion of the Napoleonic Wars, it was a favoured retreat of ambassadors, diplomats, adventurers and intelligence officers — the latter contingent quaintly incognito.

As with other London gentlemen's clubs, *The Travellers* had its observances. Fenwick's favourite 'house' rule was that mobile telephone calls within the building were expressly forbidden. Even texting was frowned upon. For Fenwick, a visit to *The Travellers* was a welcome reprieve, extending the opportunity for a brief but necessary electronic 'detox'. At the cloakroom, immediately upon entering, he dutifully switched off his iPhone.

The dress code was formal, jacket and tie, at all times. Shirtsleeves, with trousers suspended by near-obligatory braces, were therefore rarely, if ever, seen. There had, reportedly, been occasional dispensations to the jacket rule — on the hottest summer days — but if so, Fenwick had never witnessed them. He wore his black suit, with a white shirt and a dark tie. Fenwick had never grasped the concept of 'smart casual' or any other fashion diktat. A suit kept things simple — although, catching a glimpse of himself in a glass pane, he did think his appearance a little funereal.

Another convention, not strictly a rule, was that when on club premises, engagement in business matters or deal-making, or even the discussion of work-related issues, should be politely avoided. This had in the past posed some minor difficulties for Fenwick, whose appearance at the club's doorstep often presaged the revelation of a matter of concern, if not impending disaster, for one or other of its patrons. Discreetly, and without anything so crude as a memorandum or any commitment to paper, the club's secretary had decreed, selectively, that Fenwick should have a 'free pass' on this issue.

Accordingly, the doorman and fellow cloakroom attendant who presided over the members' overcoats, hats, gloves and assorted bric-a-brac now turned a blind eye to Fenwick's slim black briefcase, which he clutched protectively.

Sir Frederick, the doorman informed him, was at lunch in the Coffee Room, as the club's restaurant was called.

Fenwick, forty-two, was the confidante of many eminent and powerful people, mostly industrialists and corporate CEOs, entrepreneurs and those in high finance. Nevertheless, his clients also included 'high achievers' and virtuosos in other fields, including actors, artists, sports 'personalities', writers, 'influencers' and even some minor royals.

Accomplished in several fields, Fenwick's most notable attribute was his tenacity. He got things done in great style, without fuss or kerfuffle, and usually in a charming way. His methods, too, were often ingenious. It was no surprise, therefore, that Fenwick's name and details were secreted in the contact lists the of the rich and famous, squirreled away but instantly retrievable at times of sudden alarm or dire need.

Fenwick had another outstanding quality: he kept his mouth shut. However embarrassing or sensational was the issue to be resolved, Fenwick could be relied upon, not only as capable, but also as resolutely discreet.

Over the years, Fenwick had saved many a marriage, shielded countless reputations, and protected from themselves numerous people who really should have known better.

Those whom Fenwick had helped genuinely liked him and usually thanked him, a little undemonstratively at times, but in their own way. He, in turn, was truly fond of those who contracted his services. He wasn't judgmental but had been baffled at times by the antics of his clients, which were often bizarre, sometimes obscene and occasionally borderline illegal. Fenwick had laughed at these instances, regarding them as part and parcel of life's rich tapestry.

His reputation within the inner circles of the *cognoscenti*, those guardians who protected and preserved society's anointed elite, was as an enlightened man who poured oil on troubled waters. Consequently, he was approved not only amongst those in the spotlight, with their tawdry baggage so painstakingly concealed, but also by the hidden forces — unseen, all-seeing, unknown and omniscient.

Fenwick headed for the Coffee Room. Familiar with the topography of the club, he headed up the grand winding oak staircase that led to the restaurant — a large, light and airy room which overlooked Pall Mall. The decor was splendid: heavy polished furniture and crystal chandeliers, with portraits of illustrious club members on the walls. The tables were set immaculately with dazzling white tablecloths, burnished silverware and sharply pressed and folded napkins.

Impressed by the Coffee Room, Fenwick curbed his enthusiasm. With Springer, a low-key appreciation was best — no 'red-carpet fever'. Springer inhabited a rarefied world, whether at his various London clubs, his office in Knightsbridge, his box at Royal Ascot or his private marquee at the Henley Regatta. Fenwick knew he'd been granted only a restricted, albeit privileged, glimpse of Springer's empire. He knew also of yachts, apartments in New York, Monte Carlo and Lausanne, a chateau in the Loire Valley, a villa and a hotel in Tuscany, a Gulfstream G800 and a Lear Jet. There was also a stud farm in Greeneville, Tennessee.

Springer walked the corridors of influence and power at ease and with confidence. He was to the manor born, imbued with privilege which he wore graciously. In the trail of Springer's coattails, Fenwick knew to follow suit as best he could.

Maurice, the maître d'hôtel, instantly recognised Fenwick and greeted him warmly. Maurice and Fenwick were on the same wavelength, having exchanged wry smiles and a few raised eyebrows over many years, at mutually observed mishaps, minor misfortunes and the occasional member's *faux pas*.

Scanning the room Fenwick noticed Springer seated alone in its distant reaches. Amongst the diners, he was pleased to see a sprinkling of women at the tables. Ladies were accepted now, not as members but as guests — a concession approved by a membership ballot that had been heatedly contested at the time. Fenwick, never a clubbable man, had always been cautious of male-only associations and he thoroughly approved of this progress.

As maître d', Maurice breezily took the lead. 'Sir Frederick is by the window, a little way down.'

Closing on Springer's table, Maurice signalled a halt at a respectful distance. With a circumspect bow, he promptly left.

Springer looked out of the window, lost in thought, it seemed. Fenwick resolved not to interrupt: Springer would turn and see him in his own time. He was impressed that Springer dined alone. To Fenwick, it was a sign of a man at ease with himself. He noted Springer's noble profile, with its strong patrician features. He was reminded somewhat of Landseer's lions in nearby Trafalgar Square.

Winchcombe Group was a sprawling leviathan, with hundreds of operations in more than forty countries. As such, the group was subject to the usual commercial stresses and strains, as well as the many run-of-the-mill frauds and acts of petty larceny that afflicted all large commercial enterprises.

Fenwick had declined Springer's offer to be the group's head of corporate security, but he was pleased to serve as a consultant on a contingency basis, not only as a roving troubleshooter but also as a preventative strategist. His skills were engaged only where catastrophic risk was suspected, those contingencies that threatened life or limb, or which were existential threats to the survival or viability of the business.

Fenwick liked working with Springer, and he toiled diligently and vigilantly in protecting his interests. The two men's relationship bordered on friendship, or as near to it as either man would permit.

In recognition of Fenwick's loyalty, there had been many acts of generosity and kindness. Following an unexpected and shocking death in Fenwick's family, Springer had ordered one of his private jets to return him from an assignment overseas, and he had even provided a car with driver for that week also.

Later, Fenwick felt genuinely honoured and privileged to have been invited to the marriage of Springer's youngest daughter Emily, who had wed an officer of the Household Cavalry at the Guards Chapel, Wellington Barracks. Fenwick had even been invited to the reception at Claridge's afterwards, welcomed and embraced as he was within the family's bosom.

Although Fenwick would vigorously deny it, there was a father-and-son dynamic between them.

Springer now turned. With a weather-beaten, tanned face and a shock of snowy white hair cropped close to his skull, he had something of the ancient mariner about him. Not evident while he was seated, Springer was tall — six foot two, by Fenwick's estimate — and unusually lithe and wiry for his seventy-two years.

Springer also had piercing, ice blue, unwavering eyes.

The sort of eyes that melt women's hearts and reduce men to nervous wrecks, thought Fenwick.

On seeing Fenwick, Springer showed no surprise at all; perhaps he was aware of having been watched. With an affable smile, he beckoned, 'Fenwick, please sit. I'm most grateful for your time this afternoon. It's awfully decent of you.'

At a fee of fifty thousand pounds, it was not particularly decent of him, thought Fenwick, as he sat down opposite Springer.

A waiter appeared as if from nowhere. Deftly and without display, he poured Fenwick a glass of red wine.

'*Monte Alpha* 2021, Chilean,' said Springer, gesturing to the bottle. 'Nice and gentle, eminently quaffable.'

Taking a sip, Fenwick swilled appreciatively and unbuckled his briefcase: a thin black leather effort, veined with craquelure, that had seen much better days. It had just a couple of simple straps and buckles to secure the contents. No locks.

He had long since dispensed with bulky combination-lock briefcases, mostly because he'd successfully broken into several of them on various assignments, by systematically rolling through every combination. In his experience, their locks provided no protection — 007, 666 and 999 often granting instant access.

There were, admittedly, far more secure containers to protect documents and reports — aluminium and steel cases, for instance, with fancy biometric access controls. But such cases screamed 'TOP SECRET', much like the Presidential 'football' crammed with nuclear missile launch codes.

Far wiser to convey one's secrets humbly and discreetly, without fanfare.

Rummaging inside the battered briefcase, Fenwick thought momentarily of the other assorted contents held therein, from past cases. His report ten years before, for instance, for the Ministry of Defence, which had detailed the Pentagon's 'backdoor' compromise of the UK's Trident missile launch codes. Or, more recently, the audacious blackmail operation against cabinet ministers, MPs and Whitehall mandarins to leverage the UK's return to the European Union.

So many secrets, all conveyed across town, and further afield, in Fenwick's battered black leather briefcase.

He now removed a brown A4 envelope and handed it to Springer.

'Ghana?' asked Springer in a neutral tone.

'Your bauxite mines. You were right to be suspicious.'

Springer took the envelope and calmly removed a stapled report of ten pages or so. He opened a spectacle case on the table and took out his half-moon reading glasses. He studied the first few pages of the report, skim-reading, while Fenwick stayed silent.

Finally, Springer murmured, with barely suppressed rage: 'Devious bastards!'

Fenwick nodded. 'Devious but stupid. Feeding false data to London, suppressing output by ten percent.'

'Who's getting the undeclared surplus?' asked Springer.

'They're offloading to a competitor: a Chinese Communist Party operation. It would have unravelled eventually, but now we have the jump on them.'

'You name names?'

'Yes, the rogues' gallery is on page ten.'

Springer flicked forward. Fenwick could see, even upside down, the page Springer was on by the photographs that appeared there — the 'mug shots', as he called them.

Springer looked up from the report. 'What do you advise?'

'To stop the rot, you'll need to fire and replace the entire management team. Succession planning will be key.'

'Should I notify Group Legal?'

Fenwick shook his head. 'If you sue, it'll spiral out of control and impact all your African holdings. The last thing you need is a diplomatic spat with the Chinese. If the Foreign Office caves, you'll lose every which way.'

'Hmmm,' Springer contemplated. 'The "Belt and Road Initiative". They're like sharks: they'd eat their own entrails.'

Promulgated by the Chinese leader Xi Jin Ping, the 'Belt and Road Initiative' decreed heavy investment in more than 150 countries, focusing on Africa most aggressively. The Chinese were vigorously flexing their muscles, exploiting all opportunities ruthlessly, which had impacted heavily on Winchcombe's operations in that continent for more than a decade: Winchcombe had lost out to the Chinese on prospecting rights in both Mali and Namibia, and had most recently forfeited its mining certification in the Congo.

Now, clearly, Beijing was at it again.

There was a brief pause, as Springer assembled his thoughts. 'My granddaughter Victoria plays merry hell over my African concerns,' he said reflectively. 'She accuses me of exploiting the natives, stealing their resources and trashing the environment.'

Fenwick smiled inwardly. Springer was guilty on all three counts, not through any malice or wickedness on his part, but because the world of business was always about compromises, some of which were necessarily unsavoury. Fenwick thought also of Victoria's fervour, and then of his own younger self. He'd never been passionate about anything or any cause; nor had he become any more ardent with age.

'Don't be too hard on her,' he said. 'Youthful idealism is in the natural order.'

'Don't get me wrong, Fenwick. I respect her idealism. I just wish she were less preachy and narrow-minded. Victoria is a child of privilege, shielded from life's harsh realities, unaware of how hard it is for most people to scratch a living.'

Fenwick thought briefly of children in Africa, paid a subsistence wage to claw lithium from the dust of crushed rocks under the scorching sun. There was no escaping it:

Victoria was right. Both he and Springer were guilty as charged.

'But enough of my familial bickering,' said Springer, changing subject. 'I thought we might take coffee in the grounds. A matter to discuss.' Lowering his voice and gesturing to the immediate surrounds, he winked at Fenwick conspiratorially: 'And, as we know, walls have ears.'

Moments later, Springer and Fenwick were seated in Carlton Gardens, a well-tended preserve which was shared as a communal retreat by the members of *The Travellers Club* and the residents of its adjacent neighbours. The cold had eased somewhat, and out of the shade there was now a discernible warmth from the sun.

Fenwick was amused to see two squirrels chasing, playing high in the trees, bounding acrobatically between branches. Squirrels didn't hibernate, Fenwick had read.

The two men sat on iron lattice chairs, with coffee and brandy placed on a matching table. Springer was shrouded by a red rug and wore a woollen scarf. 'So,' he said, 'to business.'

He took a single photocopied page of *The Daily Telegraph* from a leather document wallet, and handed the sheet to Fenwick. He pointed to a 'news in brief', which Fenwick scanned: '*British man falls from ferry: drowns in Atlantic*'.

As Fenwick read, Springer murmured: 'The deceased is one Michael Tyler.' With a faint smile, he added: 'He was "off the books", a status you will appreciate.'

Fenwick nodded, for he himself was often 'off the books' when it was convenient or necessary to be so. Moving in the shadows, unacknowledged and, for all intents and purposes, non-existent.

Michael Tyler? Fenwick vaguely recalled the name — something to do with price-fixing or cartels, he thought.

Springer continued: 'Tyler was a fine operator. We parted company a few years ago — a silly, trivial falling-out over fees or expenses. I can't remember the details.'

Springer was far too canny to have forgotten something so significant. Fenwick surmised that Springer knew he'd been in the wrong but couldn't concede the point.

'We then rather lost touch,' said Springer. 'Just the occasional Christmas card. Yet Tyler's death has hit me hard. The police say his drowning is a suicide, but I can't envisage it. He was happily married and successful.'

'Suicides aren't predictable. Depressives may hide their condition, and impulse often applies. Also, you lost touch with him... more recent issues, perhaps?'

Springer shrugged, confused and a little bewildered.

Fenwick continued:

'His sudden departure from Winchcombe Group would have been quite a comedown, what with the excitement and the challenge of it all. Then, suddenly overnight, nothing. For someone like that, his professional status must have been the most important thing in his life.'

'Possibly,' conceded Springer.

Fenwick had rarely, if ever, seen Springer downcast, let alone mournful. The man was normally so full of life, energy and enthusiasm. And yet, sitting before him, huddled in this secluded garden, shrouded in his rug and scarf, Springer looked genuinely bereft.

With age came the inexorable passing of friends and colleagues, and estrangements beyond atonement. The grave extinguished any hope of making amends. There was a poignancy to this unravelling story, and Fenwick felt a genuine surge of compassion. Springer was displaying here his vulnerability, which to Fenwick was a little unnerving, having never before been privy to this aspect of the man.

Springer, after an uncomfortable pause, composed himself.

'Well, if he did throw himself overboard, it's extremely bad news for his wife, and not just for the obvious trauma of it all. She stands to inherit over two million pounds from his life insurance, but if his death is declared a suicide, she won't receive a penny. Mrs Tyler's financial welfare is of paramount importance to me. I feel a duty of care towards her.'

Fenwick had assisted several insurance companies over the years, and in that time, powerful societal shifts and evolving public attitudes had forced some radical rethinking upon the industry.

'Policies are rarely annulled by suicide these days,' he now said.

Springer, clearly advised and better informed, retorted, 'So I understand. But I've made enquiries. The insurers will contest, *vigorously*, if the death is self-inflicted.'

Fenwick knew that Springer could speed-dial the directors and chief executives of almost every high performer on the global indices. He sensed that Springer had already conducted enquiries, cozily by the fireside over a fine claret, cajoling some industry supremo, or other. Springer almost certainly had the insurer's file on Tyler, quite possibly handed to him directly by the CEO of the insurance company itself.

Surveying Springer obliquely, Fenwick sensed the veneer cracking and peeling. The pretence was unsustainable.

'There's more to it, isn't there?'

Springer exhaled, with evident relief. 'Yes. My intuition gnaws at me. Is the death suspicious?'

Fenwick tilted his head inquisitively.

Springer explained: 'Tyler exposed many villains over the years; he ruined several careers and even had a few of them banged up. Might they avenge themselves this way?'

From his own experiences with the Winchcombe Group, Fenwick knew the job was not without personal risk; he himself had been threatened on occasions. Tyler would certainly have faced similar aggression and hostility.

After a long and awkward interval, he broke the silence. 'Am I assigned?'

Springer's striking blue eyes drilled into Fenwick — intense, focused, earnest. 'If you consent, yes. A discreet enquiry, under the radar. Just the facts. What was Tyler doing in Madeira?

'And why did he end up dead?'

SIX

THE GRENADIER

F enwick arrived at *The Grenadier* some twenty minutes before his appointed meeting. He was damp and bedraggled, having been subjected to yet another January squall. The rainfall, slanted at a severe angle by a powerful wind, had confounded his trusty umbrella.

The pub was tucked away, out of sight, on the discreet mews and cul-de-sac of Wilton Row in the district of Belgravia, home to many of London's rich and famous. Projecting the establishment's martial theme, a bright red sentry box, sufficient for a guardsman with ceremonial bearskin, greeted visitors. Entry was by a short series of stone steps to a podium from which cavalry officers of yore, unsteady in drink, had mounted their steeds.

In summer, hanging baskets were bright with geraniums, begonias, fuchsias and petunias. But it was bleak midwinter and, on this day, it was the enticing warmth of the pub's inner sanctum that beckoned seductively.

The Grenadier was one of Fenwick's favourite pubs. He particularly appreciated the absence of a jukebox; he deeply resented paying for a drink or a meal when forced to listen to other people's music.

He sat on a wheelback chair beside the open fire, drawn, moth-like, to its glorious radiating heat and light. The rain had abated, but the exposed areas of his suit and shirt were suffused with damp. Flames flickered and danced — orange, red, pale yellow and blue. The fire spattered with a crackle and a pop. A charred log — the palest ash grey, incinerated to the core — collapsed and disintegrated into flakes within the hearth.

Ensconced, warmed and revitalised, Fenwick dwelt on the matter at hand. A key question was whether Tyler had hit the ocean dead or alive. In his head, Fenwick rummaged through postmortem reports of old. He recalled the pathology textbooks indexed in his 'Black Museum', as his housekeeper Evelyn jokingly called Fenwick's library. If strangulation, it should be evident. Petechiae might show in the eyes — tiny blood spots from burst capillaries. A broken neck should also be obvious, as should any other indication of violence.

But drowning? That was more problematic.

Fenwick thought briefly of the death at sea of the media tycoon and arch-crook Robert Maxwell off the Canary Islands in 1991. The pathologists at the time had considered a test of the body tissues for 'diatoms': microscopic algae in seawater. Their presence possibly indicated the inhalation of water — Fenwick couldn't remember the specifics. If these diatoms were inhaled, the deceased had presumably drowned; if not, the death was possibly from another cause. But as Fenwick recalled, the diatom test was contentious and not universally approved.

A body *in* water… then… *in* a body *of* water.

Fenwick thought of the Atlantic Ocean, impossibly vast and totally beyond forensic enquiry. Immersion in water, even if only temporary, destroyed so much evidence. Fenwick remembered an insurance dispute from years earlier: a shipwreck off the Cape of Good Hope, caused by the vessel's deficient overhaul, with its hull fracturing and buckling on account of grossly substandard steel plates, sheared bolts and inexpert welding. The bodies of the dead, he remembered, had mostly been recovered naked, the tides and elements having stripped them not only of their dignity, but even of their clothing.

A joyful, exclamatory voice interrupted these grim thoughts: 'Charles! Found you! Great fire!'

Startled, Fenwick looked up. Before him was his cousin Lucia, the eldest daughter of his father's brother Richard. Lucia was one of a select few, numbering perhaps just four or five, within Fenwick's inner circle who called him by his first name. Her timing was perfect, as always — she was a professional cellist, for whom good timekeeping and precision were occupational prerequisites. Fenwick, not himself musically talented, had always admired instrumentalists, and he was proud and a little in awe of Lucia's celebrity and accomplishments, which were considerable.

It was the middle of the afternoon on a Wednesday, and *The Grenadier* was quiet, with just a few patrons. Fenwick swiftly secured a chair for Lucia and headed to the bar. He returned minutes later with white wine for his cousin and a Balvenie malt for himself.

Lucia stared appreciatively into the flames. She was slim but not slight, with straight, greying hair, cut relatively short, and a kindly, expressive face with wise grey eyes. No hair dye or makeup. She was a year older than Fenwick, and he regarded her as an elder sister.

'Lovely pub,' she remarked.

Fenwick took a sip of his whisky. 'It's haunted,' he said casually. 'I've never seen a ghost here. Spirits, yes, but no ghosts.'

Lucia chuckled, then leaned in. 'Do tell.'

'1818, a young guardsman, a subaltern, called Cedric. The pub in those days served as an NCO's mess. Cedric had absconded from barracks and was playing an illicit game of cards with the sergeants and corporals of the regiment. He was caught cheating.'

'Go on', said Lucia, genuinely intrigued.

'They beat him to death in the lane outside,' said Fenwick, gesturing to the doorway.

'God almighty! Over a game of cards?'

'I suspect the stakes were quite high,' replied Fenwick. 'I presume he was also playing "poker" with their wives and girlfriends.'

Lucia giggled.

Fenwick regaled Lucia with his story of Cedric, the pub's ghost. He wove a tall tale of glasses that shattered, of tables and chairs that rattled, of moans and groans from the cellar, of lurking, menacing apparitions, and even an instance of spontaneous human combustion.

These terrifying events only ever happened in the month of September; Fenwick assured Lucia earnestly. To keep Cedric under control, happy and, above all, *quiescent*, patrons of the pub had ever since paid him off. 'Hush money,' Fenwick called it.

'How? He's a ghost!' Lucia shrieked with laughter.

Fenwick said simply, 'Look up.'

Lucia raised her head, and gawped in astonishment. Glued and pinned to every square inch were thousands upon thousands of bank notes, from all the nations of the earth, in every denomination issued, since the very first printing of money.

Fenwick caught her eye. 'Money,' he whispered, with a wink: 'the root of all evil.'

Fenwick and Lucia met this way for a drink or a meal, typically twice or thrice a year, to catch up on family gossip and general goings-on. Fenwick now responded to the obligatory inquisition:

'I'm fine, thanks. Better than fine. I'm off to sunny Madeira next week.'

'You lucky bugger! Escaping this horrible winter. A couple of weeks?'

'Not sure. It's a bit left-field,' replied Fenwick, pensively. He would not discuss Tyler or Springer with Lucia. If pushed, he would state the matter an insurance issue and venture no further.

'Well, I hope you like Madeira wine, and Madeira cake,' she said.

'Neither,' replied Fenwick with a smile. 'Sickly sweet.

A single malt and no cake for me. And you? How's the cello?'

Lucia groaned. 'Don't ask. My next concert… it's an impossible piece by Prokofiev at Wigmore Hall next month. It's being filmed for broadcast. I mustn't mess it up.'

No chance of that, thought Fenwick, who knew his cousin to be a consummate professional. The footage would be in the can with just one take.

Lucia cringed inwardly. Fenwick knew nothing about the *Sinfonia Concertante*, a diabolically difficult piece, which had proven the undoing of many a soloist. Fenwick, on occasions glib and nonchalant, knew nothing of the technicalities, or of the demands of the piece.

'I appreciate your confidence,' she replied flatly. 'Misplaced, perhaps?' It was time to reset the conversation. 'A rare night out without Beatrice!' she said gleefully, referring to her daughter. 'She's eight on Monday, by the way.'

'Eight!' exclaimed Fenwick, amazed at the passage of time.

Fenwick liked Beatrice. She was headstrong, spirited, and talked and chattered incessantly, teasing him with embarrassing questions about adult life, which neither Fenwick nor her mother Lucia ever deigned to answer.

With a hastily sought birthday present now in mind, he asked: 'What's her latest "thing"?'

'Minecraft, which I don't understand at all, and Lego, which I do understand, as I keep stepping on her bloody bricks in my stockinged feet.'

Involuntarily, Fenwick blurted out: 'Lego manufactures more tyres each year than Pirelli, Firestone and Dunlop combined.' He winced instantly, sounding like the pub bore he was normally at such pains to avoid.

Lucia raised an eyebrow. Her cousin really was a mine of useless information. 'Forget Beatrice for now,' she said. 'Let's enjoy this liquid therapy.'

For a while, they drank together in companiable silence. Then Lucia's intense grey eyes focused resolutely on Fenwick. 'Now, Charles. To business. Any romantic developments?'

She invariably asked this question with a twinkle in her eye, never expecting an answer in the affirmative.

Fenwick smiled in amused admiration of his cousin's impudence and persistence. Over the years, this little game had become a ritual.

With a sardonic grin, he answered: 'Developments, yes, but not romantic ones.'

Realising, yet again, the futility of this line of enquiry, Lucia changed direction. 'Another whisky?' she asked resignedly.

Fenwick watched as Lucia headed, a little unsteadily, to the ladies. He surveyed the surrounds. The walls of the pub were festooned with military prints, of soldiers, battles and campaigns. Wellington and Waterloo predominated, but earlier and later conflicts were also depicted. Recent operations in Bosnia, Afghanistan and Iraq featured, with framed photographs of the units and soldiers deployed. Uniforms, medals, regimental colours and other militaria were displayed in cabinets.

Fenwick noticed an elderly man seated in a winged

red leather armchair. The man, gaunt with grey, lifeless skin, hollow cheeks and limpid eyes, stared fixedly at him. Sensing the man's hostility, Fenwick averted his view and pretended to look at his iPhone, but he could still sense the old man's eyes boring into his skull, fierce with rage, as though seeking to avenge some heinous injury or injustice.

With a shiver of visceral fear, Fenwick racked his mind: was this demon from his past, someone he knew, or some soul he'd grievously offended? Then his fear gave way to anger — he'd return fire and stare the man down. With adrenaline surging, he snapped his head up aggressively in the man's direction — but to his astonishment, the red leather chair was vacant. The old man had simply vanished into thin air, disappearing so swiftly as to defy the laws of physics.

Was there a hidden portal, perhaps disguised by a *trompe l'oeil*, or a trapdoor to facilitate this disappearing act? Fenwick speedily scrutinised the walls and floors, to no avail. He shot to his feet and walked with urgency to the bar, intent on catching the old man at the exit door, but he wasn't there, nor could he be seen elsewhere.

It was dark outside. Without his overcoat, Fenwick shivered as he stepped on to the stone podium and scoured the forecourt and the extent of the mews.

Nothing.

Utterly baffled but intent on a logical explanation, Fenwick was half-minded to ask the landlord to check the pub's CCTV — a relatively simple investigation, what with the time and location of the man's disappearance being known to him.

But now that he felt calmer and was once again in his right mind, perhaps not. Leave it. Whilst eerie and unnerving, it was a trivial incident, which didn't merit further enquiry.

Upon returning to the fireside, Fenwick saw Lucia seated beside it, huddled and a little hunched. Their table was now cleared, with no sign of a 'round' or refreshed glasses. This minor detail irked him, but as he took a closer look at Lucia, he was more concerned than irritated. Her cheerful, playful demeanour had evaporated.

'Cheer up,' said Fenwick. 'Worse things happen at sea.'

It was an unintentional quip, but the irony was not lost on him.

Lucia looked up. She was strained and fretful and surveyed the surrounds with jerky movements of her head. Her eyes darted to and fro — alerted to something monstrous hidden in the recesses.

In the pub's subdued lighting, Fenwick detected that Lucia was close to tears. She was also trembling, with her hands visibly shaking. Not from cold — the fire now roared — but in fear. Of what or of whom exactly, Fenwick could only guess. He'd never seen his cousin in such a state. She looked exposed and vulnerable and his instincts were now entirely protective. He suspected some affliction, perhaps food poisoning or an infection.

'A doctor? One-One-One?' he asked, reaching for his mobile phone to summon help.

'No. It's not physical. It's an aura… a mental thing… it's difficult to explain. I must go. Something's very wrong. I need to go home. Now.'

It was a short walk to the heaving thoroughfare at Grosvenor Place, which Fenwick knew would be abundant with passing taxis, their electric 'for hire' signs glowing orange and fluorescent in the darkness. He held his umbrella aloft above Lucia, attempting to protect her from the persistent drizzle, which in the luminescence of the streetlamps appeared rather heavier than it actually was.

There was an urgency in Fenwick now, and relief upon his successful hailing of a black cab for his cousin. He wanted her safe, warm and at home without delay. She climbed into the passenger compartment and settled. Fenwick stated Lucia's postcode to the driver, paying with crisp notes and tipping him generously.

Fenwick was about to close the heavy black door, when Lucia stopped him.

'Be careful out there,' she said solemnly.

'Madeira?' said Fenwick, bemused. 'It's just a routine job. There's nothing dangerous...'

Lucia interrupted him. 'I have a bad feeling about it... a gut instinct.' Her wise grey eyes, even in the half-light, radiated urgency and conviction. Fenwick felt as though they were scrutinising his very soul.

'Be careful out there,' she repeated, even more gravely than before. 'I mean it.'

'I'll be fine. I promise,' replied Fenwick somewhat effetely, projecting more confidence than he felt.

He watched the taxi set off towards Hyde Park. It had been a very strange evening, worrisome and foreboding. There was much to reflect on, and despite the miserable damp and drizzle, he needed a walk to clear his head.

SEVEN
FUNCHAL

Sir Frederick Springer, or 'SFS' as he was known to his employees, sat at his desk at the headquarters of The Winchcombe Group in Knightsbridge. His was a spacious office, with nothing on the table whatsoever, apart from a landline with intercom and a charging socket for his mobile phone. Springer believed that clutter signalled inefficiency. 'Tidy desk, tidy mind,' he would say.

He pressed the intercom button and spoke to his PA, located in the vestibule directly outside: 'Montserrat, I've assigned Charles Fenwick to the Tyler case. Funchal next week, business class, and a good hotel.' Springer never used Montserrat's surname.

'Any particular day?' she asked.

'Any, but soonest please,' he replied, ending the exchange abruptly.

Thirty-two years old, preternaturally beautiful, with supermodel features, platinum blonde hair, and placid yet intense blue eyes, Montserrat was admired for her intelligence, her calm efficiency and her exquisite dress sense, favouring as she did the haute couturiers of New York, Paris and Milan. There was something a little other-worldly about Montserrat, who struck many as distant and inscrutable. Intentionally or otherwise, she gave off an air of detachment, which some interpreted as disdain. Her detractors — and there were many — regarded her as robotic, dull and lacking in passion, albeit exceptionally clever. The other women at The Winchcombe Group, perhaps a little jealous or in awe of her, didn't like Montserrat, perceiving her as an aloof 'ice maiden'. Male employees — the straight ones — were agog, but a little intimidated by her also.

There was much gossip, fevered speculation and prurient tittle-tattle about Sir Frederick's PA, whose private life and domestic arrangements were a complete mystery. Reflecting her cold logic and glacial demeanour, her nickname, cautiously whispered and never uttered within earshot, was 'The Vulcan'.

Montserrat had worked as Springer's PA for five years. She initially feared there might be some awkwardness, with clumsy sexual passes or furtive coercion, but her concerns proved groundless. Springer treated her decently and with respect, which she appreciated. He barely suppressed his pride and pleasure in his appointment of such a glamorous, head-turning young woman, now lashed to the wheel, aside him at the helm. He quietly revelled in showcasing her at meetings and events, but it was her skills, judgment and discretion that he truly valued.

Montserrat had met Fenwick a few times. He'd made no impression on her; men rarely did. She'd use British Airways for his flight, and research the hotels available.

Montserrat also had another agenda — undisclosed.

Noticing her office door ajar, she closed it, locking it quietly. At her desk, she opened the computerised passport registry held on the Winchcombe server. Her demeanour — characteristically — was detached, efficient and extremely focused.

The passport registry file had a discrete sub-folder accessible only by herself and Springer. These were Winchcombe's specialist contractors, hired for the most sensitive tasks. Fenwick's passport page appeared on the screen, with his photo ID. The photo showed a man of youthful middle-age with short, dark-brown hair, greying at the temples. The features were regular and quite refined. It was a sensitive and intelligent face, with a learned and professorial bearing — almost ascetic. Quite handsome, Montserrat thought, even attractive... for a man.

Scanning her surrounds, she took her mobile phone from her tote bag and photographed the passport ID page, ensuring that the passport number and the photo of Fenwick himself were in sharp focus.

Montserrat then opened the list of confidential contractors, also on the server and equally restricted. She scrolled to 'FENWICK, CHARLES', which showed no address — only his mobile telephone number. She photographed this entry likewise. With her clandestine mission accomplished, she calmly returned her mobile phone to the tote bag.

As SFS had decreed, it was now time to get Mr Charles Fenwick on his way, first thing on Monday morning.

Montserrat had booked Fenwick on the 'red eye' from Gatwick to Madeira, leaving at 7.10 am.

He'd slept fitfully, waking in the small hours, perturbed by events at *The Grenadier*. Lucia's strange affliction on the night might have been due to carbon monoxide poisoning, the symptoms of which included claustrophobia, extreme cold and a sense of impending doom. Had he been hallucinating that evening, too? He'd report his suspicion to the pub's manager — there might be a dangerous fault or a leak.

Fenwick now sat in business class on a British Airways A320 Airbus. He'd enjoyed a 'full English' breakfast brought to him on a tray, and a couple of Glenlivet miniatures, as sharpeners. Fenwick considered alcohol consumption in airports and on aeroplanes to be beyond censure at any hour — cocooned as he was, lost in time and space.

For most of the three-hour flight, Fenwick studied his old and battered copy of *Dr Iain West's Casebook*, particularly the renowned pathologist's recollection of the death at sea of Robert Maxwell. He read West's chapter slowly and carefully, making notes as he went.

As the plane started its descent to the airport, an elderly lady in the seat next to him piped up, intent on conversation. Fenwick engaged with her, politely but with little enthusiasm. The approach to the runway, she assured him, was amongst the seven most challenging in the world. Fearful cross-winds, swirling and instantly changeable, could tip jetliners dangerously off course, rocking them hazardously and forcing pilots to throttle affirmatively, surging their aircraft skywards, up and away into a holding pattern far off the island, circling over the Atlantic, awaiting clearance.

Fenwick looked out of a starboard window. The runway, carved into the rock face as a plateau, indeed looked perilously close to steep cliffs, both below and behind. The approach, too, appeared hazardous, uncomfortably near to the island's steeply ascending foothills. The runway had recently been extended by a thousand feet or so, jutting outwards, the structure supported by hundreds of concrete reinforced pylons. It was a distinctive triumph of engineering which even featured on the island's postcards and souvenirs.

On this day, fortunately, the gods looked kindly on Fenwick, whose plane touched down smoothly and without incident at 11.20 am local time. The A320 taxied to the terminal and its arrivals hall at Madeira's Cristiano Ronaldo International Airport.

Passport clearance, the baggage carousel and the customs post were each negotiated with speed and efficiency; within twenty minutes, Fenwick was outside the airport at a taxi rank. The thermometer on his mobile phone showed a balmy twenty-three degrees. A gentle sea breeze cooled his skin agreeably.

Fenwick had never been to Madeira before and knew not what to expect. 'Reid's Belmond' he said to the driver, who nodded in immediate recognition. Seconds later, the taxi — a canary yellow Mercedes-Benz E-Class with a pale blue speed stripe — screeched from the kerb. Fenwick, sensing an imminent rollercoaster ride, fastened his seatbelt.

Slipping beyond the airport's periphery, the taxi was soon rocketing along the expressway, powering muscularly through a series of precisely hewn and lengthy road tunnels, then across an ascension bridge before barrelling downwards towards the city. In the fast lane, the driver aggressively tailgated any slowcoach who dared to impede his progress, flashing his headlights and bulldozing these retards out of his way and into the slow lane, where they belonged.

Fenwick, apprehensive yet exhilarated, rechecked his seatbelt.

As they shot along the expressway, the driver caught Fenwick's eye in his rear-view mirror. 'On holiday?' he asked. Fenwick found the driver's question intrusive. 'No. Work. I'm an accountant.' It was a stock answer, guaranteed to kill anyone's 'what do you do?' line of enquiry stone dead.

'Fantastic hotel, Reid's,' said the driver.

'Why?'

'It's beautiful and very glamorous. Many famous people stayed there — your Winston Churchill. He also painted on the island, at Câmara de Lobos. It's a fishing village — you must visit it.'

The driver deftly weaved around a slow lorry that was belching exhaust fumes. Having undertaken the lorry, the driver surged ahead again, his foot hard to the floor. Fenwick maintained a watchful eye on the speedometer; the driver was vastly exceeding the speed limit.

The Mercedes powered out of a chicane and Fenwick caught sight of the city, far below in the distance. He saw a sprawl of gleaming villas and houses — white, yellow and occasionally pink with terracotta tiles — stacked row upon row upon the steep gradient stretching upward to the hinterland. Further down, a few high-rise hotels and apartments jutted into the sky discordantly. The azure sea beyond sparkled majestically in the midday sun. The harbour's jetty stretched out protectively, sheltering three great cruise liners which towered above the bay. Cable cars progressed in a loop, running high above the roadway.

Sensing Fenwick's wonderment, the driver grinned. 'Reid's does a famous afternoon tea, with sandwiches, and cakes. You will love it.'

The driver was on autopilot. Insouciant and oblivious to his passenger's discomfort, he accelerated even faster.

'Afternoon tea?' said Fenwick nervously. 'I'll check it out.' He deemed the prospect most unlikely but made a mental note of it anyway.

'You'll enjoy the view, too. Reid's overlooks the sea and has grand gardens.'

If we get there alive, thought Fenwick, as the scenery tore past the passenger window in a blur.

Fenwick had done no research at all about Reid's. All he knew was that the British Consulate had advised Springer's office that Tyler had stayed at the hotel. Fenwick had asked Montserrat to book a room there also, to familiarise himself with Tyler's environment and circumstances. He'd even asked for Tyler's exact room, number 518, but Montserrat advised him it was unavailable. Fenwick knew he needed to search that room and assess it for access and vantage points that might have facilitated hostile surveillance efforts against Tyler.

The yellow Mercedes swept gracefully into the forecourt at Reid's. The taxi ride of six and a half miles, driven at such breakneck speed, had taken just twelve minutes — an astonishing progress, given the traffic lights and speed restrictions of downtown Funchal.

Fenwick stepped out, uncoiled, and exhaled with relief.

A concierge, smart in a grey suit and tie, stepped forward to help with Fenwick's suitcase. From their evident familiarity, the driver and the concierge clearly knew each other. Small island, mused Fenwick, who paid the driver in cash — he intended to keep card payments to a minimum, restricting his electronic 'footprint' on the island as best he could.

'Say hello to Sir Winston,' said the driver, with a good-humoured wave.

'I will,' replied Fenwick.

Approaching the reception desk, carrying his black laptop in its travel case in one hand and his trusty briefcase in the other, Fenwick thought of Churchill's wartime sign-off: 'KBO'. German Intelligence, the *Abwehr*, had invested incalculable time and resources in breaking Winston's three-letter acronym.

'Keep Buggering On,' said Fenwick to himself with a smile.

The check-in process was effortless, and Fenwick was soon guided to room 509 by one of the hotel's three super-efficient duty receptionists. Reid's was a charming rabbit warren of staircases, floors, mezzanines, and corridors. Fenwick made a careful mental note of the route, which progressed from the lift past the hotel's business centre, an Italian boutique, a billiards room and a bridge room. The venerable polished floorboards squeaked and creaked underfoot in a way Fenwick found reassuring. Photographs, mostly sepia or monochrome, and mementos of notable guests and events were displayed in wall-lined cabinets.

Fenwick's suitcase had already been delivered. The room had everything he could wish for, including a writing desk. The balcony overlooked the pool, the harbour with its grand ocean liners, and the sweep of the sea front and the city. He noted a complimentary offering of both Madeira wine and *bolo de mel*, a traditional Madeiran honey cake. Despite his declared resistance, he would sample both in keeping with the setting and the occasion.

The bathroom gleamed spotlessly with lotions, potions and styling accoutrements which were of no interest or relevance to Fenwick. It also had quite the biggest bathtub he'd ever seen. He opted to take a shower instead — soulless but quick and efficient — with instant, piping-hot water. Revitalised under its powerful jet, Fenwick thought of the taxi driver's exuberance and of his quaint recommendations.

Minutes later, wrapped in one of Reid's sumptuous white bathrobes, Fenwick picked up the room telephone and dialled zero.

'Mr Fenwick, good afternoon,' said the receptionist. 'How may I help?'

'I'm expecting a guest at three o'clock,' he replied. 'Might I book afternoon tea on the terrace for two?'

EIGHT

SOFIA

Sofia Ferreira had taken the call on Sunday afternoon. It was Cathy from the British Consulate, who was speaking from her home in São Martinho. Might Sofia be available to attend an impromptu meeting the next day?

Sofia, forty-one, had undertaken translation and hosting duties for the British Consulate in Madeira for ten years. She liked the consular staff and had enjoyed various assignments, assisting variously with cultural and trade delegations, VIP visitors to the island, and liaising for the British with the Madeiran authorities. She occasionally helped with less portentous issues: hapless tourists with lost passports, medical insurance cover for the suddenly afflicted, and emergency travel arrangements that required expedition.

Cathy apologised for contacting Sofia at such short notice and on a Sunday too, and for the dearth of background information — for as she explained, she was also in the dark. The man she would meet was called F-E-N-W-I-C-K, pronounced 'Fennick', and he'd be making enquiries regarding an insurance issue in connection with an Englishman who had drowned off the island two weeks previously. The death had been in the newspapers and on local TV. Cathy would send some links, if and when she found them.

The following afternoon, Sofia duly reported to Reid's, arriving a little earlier than scheduled. She knew the staff, having assisted the hotel with receptions and events over many years. She was escorted to the hotel's principal terrace, a charming veranda that overlooked the gardens and arboretum below, with trees, plants and herbaceous borders, verdant and glorious under the mid-afternoon sun. Most unexpectedly, a flute of champagne was proffered. Sofia, uncertain of the protocol, declined.

She'd studied the circumstances of the drowning from local news reports and had prepared for this meeting as best she could.

Footsteps approached, resonant on the chequered marble floor behind her.

'Senhora Ferreira?' came an English-accented male voice.

She looked up at the man. 'Yes.'

He extended his hand. 'I'm Charles Fenwick.'

He had a firm but not overly demonstrative handshake and, much to Sofia's relief, a cool, reassuringly dry palm. He sat down beside her and gave her an engaging smile. His card showed simply his name, a telephone number and an email address, but no affiliation. Sofia wondered if she should enquire on the point. Best not, she concluded — at least, not until later.

At that moment, a waiter in a pristine white jacket appeared with a silver cake stand of three tiers. Upon each tier was a cornucopia of exquisitely crafted finger sandwiches, vol-au-vents, scones, cakes and pastries.

Far too much for the two of them, thought Sofia in astonishment.

A waitress followed, gently placing a large fine China teapot on the table with a silver canteen of hot water and a selection of fine teas in a wooden decorative box. A porcelain coffee pot followed with a jug of hot milk. The waitress officiated, filling their cups as indicated, with a steady hand.

Sofia, feeling a little awkward, broke the momentary silence: 'Well, Mr Fenwick, you've certainly started in grand style. This is my first ever tea at Reid's. It's quite an indulgence, for sure. It's very generous of you.'

'It's generous of my client,' said Fenwick. 'All expenses are covered.'

He and Sofia surveyed the feast before them.

'Please tuck in,' he said, gesturing to the food, then easing forward and taking a miniature brie and prosciutto sandwich. Before taking a bite, he continued: 'Thank you for agreeing to translate and interpret; I'll need your help.'

Sofia doubted there would be much interpreting. Most government employees spoke English, particularly the island's senior police officers, doctors and civil servants. 'I have medical and legal phrasebooks to hand,' she murmured, almost apologetically.

'Which will be indispensable, as will your local knowledge. I wouldn't rate my chances here alone.'

Sofia doubted that. This man looked capable enough: shrewd, resourceful and probably ruthless, too. The insurance story didn't ring true at all. She'd have to be on her guard.

There followed some chitchat of little consequence to Fenwick, about the island, its history and culture. Sofia became animated only when discussing her hosting and reception duties: a veritable carousel of corporate functions, anniversary parties, concerts, weddings and celebrations. To Fenwick, it sounded like a charmed existence.

After ten minutes or so, he cut to the chase. 'Senhora Ferreira, tell me: what do you know about Michael Tyler's death?'

'Sofia, please,' she responded, breaking the formality. 'Only what I've read in the local newspaper, which isn't much at all.'

'Then, Sofia — and I'm Charles — you know almost as much as I do.'

Sofia cared little for the man's breezy manner, or for his pretence of ignorance. He hadn't flown from London on a whim.

'Mr Tyler's death is a sensitive issue here,' she said. 'The people of the island value peace and tranquillity. Disturbances of any kind are unwelcome. You won't encounter any hostility, but you may meet some resistance.'

Fenwick looked at her solemnly, eyes narrowing. 'I anticipated as much. It's another reason why I need your help.'

'Not as much as you need Marcos Teixeira's help,' said Sofia. 'Teixeira is the chief of police. We meet him tomorrow at ten. He's highly competent, greatly respected and popular. He was a career detective on the mainland, but he's been with us now for three years. He's become one of us: an islander.'

Fenwick gave Sofia another smile, which she found friendly and disarming, but did little to allay her doubts. 'Marcos Teixeira, you say. Let's hope we don't encounter any resistance from him.'

He watched as two tiny wall lizards scuttled jerkily across the terrace, playful in the heat. The waiter then reappeared, as if on cue. The three-tiered stand still heaved with untouched delicacies.

Fenwick turned to Sofia. 'You have a son, I think?'

Sofia looked perplexed. What had the consulate told him? 'Yes, he's fourteen,' she answered defensively. 'A husband, too.'

Fenwick turned to the waiter and gestured to the tiers of uneaten treats. 'Might we have these boxed? For the lady... well, in truth, for her husband and son.'

Sofia laughed and nodded good-naturedly, in awkward recognition of her barely concealed distrust.

A few moments passed in contemplative silence. Then Fenwick said gravely: 'There's a final question I must ask.'

What now? she thought anxiously.

Fenwick studied the menu, then stared at her intensely.

'Moët et Chandon or Dom Perignon?' he enquired, raising a fluted glass.

NINE
TEIXEIRA

Fenwick was seated on the balcony of his room with a gin and tonic with ice. It was early evening and the sun was setting but the air was still warm. Two massive cruise ships were berthed in the harbour: the *AIDAcosma*, its livery vulgar and cartoonish with a face of lips thick with rouge and a female eye painted on each side of its white bow; and the *Marella Explorer*, refined and dignified, with a stylish blue wave that ran the length of its hull.

At six precisely, a ship's horn sounded, a deep vibrato that boomed across the entire city: three blasts, each of six seconds. Fenwick watched as the *AIDAcosma* slipped its moorings and gently eased its way majestically from the port and out, towards the open sea. Hundreds — maybe even thousands — of passengers, ant-like, lined the railings and the massive hospitality deck at the stern. Many of them were waving.

Not waving, but drowning, thought Fenwick abstractly.

His attention now returned to Tyler and the island's

chief of police Marcos Teixeira. As a senior Portuguese detective, had Teixeira perhaps been involved with the investigation into the disappearance of Madeleine McCann? Google revealed nothing to that effect, but it did list a number of citations and commendations in Lisbon for Teixeira's successful prosecution of various crimes: murders, narcotics, robberies and people trafficking.

Teixeira's career in Madeira also featured, more sedately, with appearances at fêtes, carnivals, pageants and council meetings. Tyler's death at sea and Teixera's detectives were mentioned briefly in a few media reports.

There also were some images of Teixeira — the clearest of which was a portrait of him on the Madeiran police website, which surprisingly was narrated throughout in English. Fenwick took some time to study the command structure. There were three police Command groups: Tactical, Regional and Judicial. The last thing Fenwick needed was to become embroiled in a turf war. Tyler's death, Fenwick assessed, fell exclusively within Teixeira's jurisdiction.

He now studied the photograph of Superintendent Marcos Teixeira. The police chief had thick, jet-black hair, cut shortish, and brown eyes, with a leathery olive skin and pockmarked cheeks, the residual scars of teenage acne. The face was square with a prominent jaw and a low brow. A five-o-clock shadow suggested the portrait had been taken late in the day.

The man's expression exuded confidence, as well as a sly intelligence. He bore a slightly contemptuous air, suppressed in the photograph but detectable. Streetwise, tough, no-nonsense. An alpha male.

Cynical, too, thought Fenwick, and probably arrogant. He sure looked a mean son of a bitch.

Sofia picked Fenwick up from Reid's shortly after 9.15 am and they drove to the headquarters of the Polícia Judiciária, or 'PJ' as it was known, based in an ugly and unimaginative administrative block which appeared to have been built entirely of white Lego bricks. Sofia parked her Renault Megane expertly in a tight space on the *Rua Tenente Coronel Sarmento*, a quiet side-street. It had been a very short drive, but Fenwick, uncertain as to how the day might unfold, had suggested they take the car as a contingency.

They were quickly signed in and handed ID lanyards to be worn at all times. Fenwick and Sofia sat together, huddled on a cramped bench in the foyer, surrounded by walls bearing public information notices and alarmist security advisories. Police officers came and went in ones and twos, dressed in the aggressive paramilitary style now prevalent, with high ankle boots, combat trousers, belts with loops and pouches bearing Taser stun guns, pepper sprays, handcuffs, telescopic batons and the other paraphernalia of incapacitation and physical restraint. They also wore ugly forage caps. And holstered sidearms: Glock 9mm automatics.

Fenwick smirked. It was all so incongruous and over the top. This was Funchal, for God's sake! There could not be a quieter, more peaceable and law-abiding place on earth!

The receptionist, an efficient looking woman in

spectacles with her raven hair tied severely in a bun, at last spoke: 'The superintendent will see you now.'

Fenwick and Sofia followed her along a corridor. She stopped before a door, with an enamel nameplate:

'*Superintendente Marcos Adalberto Teixeira,*
Departamento de Investigação Criminal da Madeira'.

The receptionist knocked firmly but respectfully.

'Enter!' boomed a commanding male voice from within.

Teixeira surveyed Fenwick and Sofia as they sat across the desk from him. Teixeira knew and liked Sofia, who had assisted the Polícia Judiciária on various occasions, mostly with social events and charity fund-raising.

He now studied Fenwick. Teixeira had instructed that the man's passport with ID be transmitted to him immediately on landing. The immigration team at Cristiano Ronaldo had also been ordered to ease Fenwick's transit without obstruction or incident. On seeing the passport photo, Teixeira presumed him to be a bean counter or administrative desk jockey — an unremarkable man. Fenwick looked just as forgettable in the flesh as he did in his photo.

With a round of golf in prospect, Teixeira intended to keep the meeting short, offering his visitors the barest minimum before sending them on their way.

'I've never had a request of this kind from a consulate before,' he opened. 'Your arrival here to investigate

Mr Tyler's death is most unorthodox. The timing is unfortunate, too: we're in the run up to the Mardi Gras and I need to conserve my manpower.'

'It needn't trouble you, superintendent,' replied Fenwick. 'I have no intention of taxing your resources.'

'Nevertheless, you will need my help,' insisted Teixeira, with a hint of menace. He slid a document across the desk. It was a single printed page, bearing his signature, stamped with his official seal of office. 'This is my letter of authority with my contact details, day or night. If you encounter any difficulties, you will advise me.'

Fenwick, in submissive mode, nodded accordingly.

Teixeira continued: 'My help is not unconditional. My main concern is the safety of the island's ferry. Be sure to include this in your investigation.'

Teixeira's request was eminently deliverable and public-spirited also. Fenwick had feared more onerous conditions, and worse: demands for 'favours', or even a payment 'to oil the wheels.'

'The ferry is my priority, too,' he said; 'an inspection is scheduled tomorrow morning.' He turned to Sofia for affirmation.

She nodded.

With the diplomatic niceties now completed, and with his pencil poised above his pocket notebook, Fenwick cut to the chase: 'So, what can you tell me about Michael Tyler?'

Teixeira shrugged. 'He went overboard during a storm. The alarm was raised when the ferry docked — his abandoned car alerted the crew. A fishing vessel spotted the body before nightfall. The island's search and rescue helicopter recovered it.'

Fenwick imagined the pilot wrestling with the helicopter's controls, struggling for stability at low altitude in buffeting winds, in the fading light and with minimal visibility. The lone pararescue winchman, spinning precariously at the end of a steel cable, must have fought strenuously to strap and secure the corpse amidst the heaving waves, before being hoisted aloft. Quite a feat by all the crew — and brave, too.

Fenwick wondered whether he should speak to the SAR team.

'Where's Tyler's body now?' he asked.

'It was flown to Lisbon for the postmortem,' said Teixeira with a carefree wave of his hand. 'We have limited facilities here on the island. It will be repatriated to London in a matter of days.'

'Identity confirmed?'

'Informally, from his passport.'

'And Tyler's car?'

'A Hertz rental. The port authorities inspected it. My officers also had a cursory look.'

'Anything?'

'Nothing, but we didn't carry out a detailed examination. There was no indication of assault, or of any other crime.'

It was clear by now that Teixeira and his officers had closed the file on Tyler. It was an 'NFA': no further action.

'A textbook suicide, then?' asked Fenwick.

'We're treating it as such.' Teixeira stood up and walked

to a steel filing cabinet. He opened a drawer and retrieved a file from a rack of suspended dividers. He pitched the file on to the desk before Fenwick with a casualness that bordered on contempt. 'Photocopies of Tyler's passport, the car rental agreement, his driving licence, the reservation confirmation and itemised billing details from the hotel, and his online ferry tickets.' Teixeira produced a supplementary sheet. 'There's also a list of his personal effects.'

Fenwick removed the photocopies of the passport from the folder. Issued post-Brexit in July 2021, the hotel had copies independently, and had retrieved the passport itself from Tyler's room safe. The regulation photograph, copied from the colour original in monochrome, was overexposed, the features flattened, washed out and indistinct, rendering the subject's face devoid of warmth or personality. Fenwick noticed what appeared to be melasma: darker spots of skin around the crevices at the corners of both eyes. A mole was also discernible on the side of the forehead.

'May I see the pathologist's report?' he asked.

'It's in Portuguese,' said Teixeira, taking two ring binders from his desk drawer. 'You may take notes only. Copying or imaging is strictly forbidden.'

Fenwick bridled at this stipulation, but he understood its necessity. Gruesome postmortem reports and explicit photographs always merited the highest protection, for fear of press leaks or unauthorised disclosure.

Teixera passed the binders to Sofia, who winced slightly on seeing the bound collection of autopsy photographs, explicit in full colour. She passed that file to Fenwick and busied herself with the written report, mentally translating its findings and conclusion. Intermittently, she referred to her *Oxford Concise Medical Dictionary*.

Teixeira remained silent as Fenwick studied the photographs, eighteen in all, each date and time-stamped. The body hadn't been in the water for long enough for any significant decomposition to occur. The skin hadn't sloughed or rotted, the eyes were intact and there was no indication of predatory nibbling, pecking or feasting. The skin on the face was fresh and unbroken. Fenwick noted the melasma and the mole on the forehead, which were present and correct, matching Tyler's passport.

The body, lean but not toned, was stripped, apart from a loincloth for decency. There was no sign of gaseous bloating, but venous marbling was evident on the upper limbs and the torso. No bruises showed, nor any sign of hypostasis, the gravitational pooling of blood to lower dependent areas that resulted in purple or brown discoloration.

Fenwick looked intensely at the neck for signs of choking or strangulation, but saw nothing unusual. Was the hyoid bone intact? he wondered. The upper arms also showed no visible contusions from gripping or restraint.

He next checked the photographs of the wrists for signs of chafing consistent with tethering by cord, wire, rope or handcuffs. Again, nothing. The mortuary, he noted, had attached the ID label twice, tied around the right ankle and the right wrist, both showing '1-090124'.

Fenwick now studied the left hand and noticed a detail

of which Teixeira was possibly unaware. Choosing his words carefully, he asked, 'What did you and your officers deduce from the missing finger?'

Teixeira looked up, suddenly alert. 'The missing finger?'

'Yes, the left index finger,' said Fenwick, showing him the photograph of the corpse's hand.

'Ah, yes, yes… the finger. It was of no consequence,' he blustered.

It was a lie, of course. Fenwick had watched Teixeira closely as he'd uttered it, gauging the man under pressure and studying his 'tell'.

Fenwick looked to Sofia, who now scanned the pathology report. She identified the relevant entry.

'"*A proximal ablation of the left index finger*",' she read. She then consulted her medical dictionary and explained: 'It means a total amputation of the finger at the primary joint — the knuckle.'

Fenwick gave her an appreciative nod. Teixeira's unease was palpable.

Breaking the awkward silence, Fenwick said, in a conciliatory tone: 'I agree with you, superintendent. As you say, inconsequential, of no relevance to the cause of death. Speaking of which…'

Sofia interjected on cue. She read and translated hesitantly, careful not to make any error. '"*No evidence of strangulation, bruising, cuts, lacerations or defensive wounds*."'

Teixeira eased back in his office chair. He wore a smug, 'told you so' expression.

Sofia continued to translate: "*Death due to shock from the cold, inhalation of water, hypothermia and cardiac arrest.*"

Teixeira bore an inscrutable Cheshire-cat grin. 'Arterial sclerosis,' he said, motioning to the pathology report, 'and hypothermia. The warm sunshine here on the island is deceptive. At this time of year, the ocean can be lethally cold. Mr Tyler would have perished within an hour at most.'

Game, set and match! Teixeira, in his head, was already teeing off down the fairway.

'There's an adjunct,' said Sofia, scrutinising an appended toxicology report tucked deep in the binder's nether regions. "*Alcohol present at three times the legal driving limit,*" she read.

This detail unsettled Fenwick, who raised a quizzical eyebrow. 'Three times over the limit? And driving?' There was no mention of alcohol or drink driving by the police, the Attorney General or the public prosecutor's office.

With the air of a weary teacher at an infant school, Teixeira responded, 'People do drink and drive, Mr Fenwick, and it's not uncommon for people to drink heavily before taking their own lives.'

For Fenwick, this finding was a bombshell, indicating Tyler's recklessness and further supporting the hypothesis of suicide resulting from a precariously unsound mind.

Sofia continued her translation: "A medicinal… therapeutic… level of an anti-anxiety drug is detected. Xanax, Alprazolam."

In his notebook Fenwick now wrote: 'DRUGS ALSO!' Drink and drugs, tucked away in the endnotes, to reappear when needed, like a rabbit from a hat. An undisclosed ambush, set in advance like a landmine. Fenwick had seen this 'small-print' ruse many times.

Sofia had made copious notes, running to several pages in a lined writing pad. She now returned the pathologist's report to Teixeira. Fenwick, likewise but somewhat reluctantly, relinquished the binder of autopsy photographs.

He thought now of puncture wounds, injections by syringe, knife blows and scuffs and tears, violently wrought. 'Are the clothes Tyler was wearing available for inspection?'

'I'm afraid not,' replied Teixeira.

Fenwick awaited an explanation, but the police chief stayed silent. He dropped the issue, suspecting the garments had long since been dispensed with as rubbish or incinerated. His attention now turned to Tyler's property, retrieved from room 518 at Reid's and neatly itemised by bullet points in Teixeira's inventory. Had the police searched Tyler's personal effects?

'Yes, nothing of interest, so nothing was impounded,' replied Teixeira. 'The hotel's concierge has Tyler's belongings and baggage. You can inspect anything you wish, provided you don't damage anything or unduly delay their return to London.'

Sofia looked exhausted, utterly drained by the immense mental effort of translation. She wore a sombre expression, wrought by the gravity of the task. It was a far remove from her usual social whirl — the convivial celebrations, events, concerts and conventions that she normally assisted.

Fenwick felt equally bloodied and bruised, as though he too had done ten rounds in a prize fight. He placed in his briefcase the letter of authority and the file of Tyler's paperwork that Teixeira had given him.

Without the need for any prompt, as if by telepathy, both he and Sofia stood. 'Superintendent, thank you for your assistance,' said Fenwick. 'It's much appreciated.'

'You're welcome,' replied Teixeira, devoid of sincerity. 'But I stress: investigate diligently but speedily. Within reason, you may call upon police resources and you'll receive prompt and courteous assistance. But it would be best for all concerned to close this file quickly.'

This was the gypsy's warning — a formal 'get lost', in truth. 'Provided the file isn't closed prematurely,' Fenwick growled with cold intent.

The intimation was not lost on Teixeira. 'Goodbye, Mr Fenwick, Senhora Ferreira,' he said with barely concealed enmity.

Sofia, embarrassed, extended her hand, which Teixeira shook perfunctorily. 'Goodbye, sir,' she said amiably.

Fenwick just walked away. At the door, he turned abruptly and glared at Teixeira. 'Did you recover Tyler's mobile phone?'

'No, there was no mobile phone, nor any car keys,' replied Teixeira. 'I presume they were both dislodged from Tyler's pockets into the sea and sank.'

'That's the simple explanation,' replied Fenwick coolly.

'In my experience, Mr Fenwick, simple explanations are usually correct.'

Fenwick could list at least a dozen cases from his own

experience in which simple explanations had proven *incorrect*.

But he was tired now, of this meeting and of Teixeira.

'Right,' he said wearily, ending proceedings.

On returning to her car, Sofia groaned — a parking ticket was stuck to its windscreen. She checked for a wheel-clamp and was relieved to see nothing attached.

The coincidence was not lost on Fenwick. A shitty memento from Teixeira. A petty and spiteful act of harassment.

The car had roasted under the midday sun, and now, inside, it was like an oven. Sofia pressed the ignition and activated the air conditioning at full blast.

They sat together in silence. The intense heat gradually dissipated, replaced by a salving cool.

Fenwick felt guilty. With no forewarning, Sofia had endured the autopsy photos and the burden of so much grim and depressing translation, which she'd completed in exemplary fashion. Most of all, he regretted the compression and unpleasantness of the meeting itself.

Forget it. Move on. Sofia had volunteered; she was a professional.

He handed her Teixeira's folder, containing Tyler's details.

'Tyler's number,' he said. 'It's in the Reid's registration form and the Hertz rental agreement.' He grabbed his iPhone. 'Read it to me, please.'

Sofia, having weighed her allegiances, fell in line. Unnerved by the morning's proceedings and by Teixeira's obduracy in particular, she would — for now — give this strange Englishman some leeway. She dictated the number, which Fenwick dialled.

To both Fenwick's and Sofia's surprise, the phone number worked — there was a sonorous ringtone — and after about five seconds, to their amazement, the call was answered.

'Yes?' It was a male voice. Fenwick was sure the accent wasn't British.

'Mr Tyler?' he asked uncertainly.

The phone immediately disconnected, the signal flatlining, unresponsive as a dull monotone.

Fenwick glanced at Sofia, who was staring incredulously at his phone. Astonished and alarmed to see tears forming in her eyes, he felt wretched. She'd endured a baptism by fire, and he'd done nothing to protect her.

There was a pause, infinite it seemed. Eventually, he turned to her.

'Are you still with me?' he asked quietly.

Sofia looked away. After a further pause, even longer, she turned to him, dabbed her eyes and forced a smile. 'Yes,' she choked.

Silence again…

'Where next?' she said at last.

TEN

REID'S PALACE

The guests in Reid's room number 518 had vacated and flown home.

With the room now unoccupied, Fenwick was permitted entry for a cursory inspection. He found nothing. The view from the balcony showed no vantage points, or means of access, to effect entry or surveillance. It was an unproductive line of enquiry, but a necessary one, completed.

Fenwick now turned his attention to the police's inventory of Tyler's effects, held out of sight in the hotel's luggage store. The bullet points itemised the contents found in room 518, from Tyler's Samsonite Spectrolite travel case, and from his black Alassio Ponte attaché case, which, Fenwick noted, was unlocked.

Had the police broken the triple locks of the attaché case? Or someone else? If it held secrets, surely Tyler would have rolled the six cylinders to secure them? Alarmingly, where were the contents?

Tyler's clothing was listed — over-prescriptively —

with flat-packed shirts, Y-fronts, trousers, socks, pyjamas and swimming shorts, each meticulously recorded by manufacturer, size and colour. 'Waist thirty-eight,' noted Fenwick — marginally more expansive than his own.

A pair of Loake's brown brogues and some Peter Christian oxblood loafers looked stylish and distinctive. There were also two sports jackets — not to Fenwick's taste, but smart and carefully preserved in Moss Saffiano premium suit carriers. Fenwick's impression of Tyler was of an affluent man on a mission, image conscious and intent on making a statement. A ladies' man, he suspected.

The toiletries were unremarkable: Wisdom toothbrushes (three), Gillette antiperspirant, a Braun electric shaver and two bottles of eau de Cologne, duty free presumably — Fenwick never used the stuff. Tellingly, Durex condoms — 'Extended Pleasure' — were secreted also.

The medications were sparse but interesting: antihistamines, aspirin, statins at forty milligrams, and a blood pressure tablet called Hygroton at fifty milligrams. Arterial sclerosis, thought Fenwick, recalling the pathologist's report. The antihistamine was for hay fever, presumably, but it could also induce drowsiness and was even an ingredient in several over-the-counter sleeping pills. Fenwick smiled faintly on discovering Sildenafil, better known as Viagra at 100 mg. There had been no mention of any of these drugs in the toxicology report.

He now searched every pocket, niche, recess and crevice. He retrieved a few fragments: some crumpled and long-forgotten till receipts, a torn rail ticket from three years previously and a couple of throat lozenges still in a blister pack of eight.

Where, then, was the Xanax?

There was no trace of it, or of any drug at all of the Alprazolam family. No tranquilisers or antidepressants anywhere — no tablets, leaflets, packaging, pharmacy receipts or prescription. Nothing.

A working hypothesis was that Tyler was involved in illegal narcotics and might even be a 'mule'. Alternatively, was he a courier for secret information or assets of some sort? If so, Tyler would have needed a covert means to transport such contraband.

The fingertip search proved fruitless, and Fenwick now considered a forensic inspection. Stripping linings with his Swiss army penknife, or breaking plastic and metal fittings in search of concealed compartments would be unseemly at best and criminal at worst. Better to ask the police to X-ray Tyler's luggage and clothing, perhaps using the security machines at the airport. Sofia could oversee the exercise, swabbing the luggage and clothing for drugs also.

Having retired quietly to the terrace with a cup of coffee, Sofia now joined Fenwick as he approached the reception desk. He was relieved to see her restored: happier, much brighter and refreshed. Sofia had signed neither a non-disclosure agreement nor a liability waiver. This constituted an egregious breach of Springer's rules, but these forms could wait, as Fenwick was determined to earn Sofia's trust.

By far the most important bullet point in the police's inventory was Tyler's computer: a Dell XPS-15 laptop with a Seagate two-terabyte USB external drive. The equipment was held by the hotel's reception, presumably in a safe. Fenwick was intent on securing the equipment for examination. He was still formulating a strategy: fly in a computer forensic expert to copy the data for subsequent analysis in the UK; use Teixeira's technicians; or take custody of the devices and courier them to London.

Best to keep the Polícia Judiciária away from the process in any event, he thought.

Fenwick was well aware of the first rule of digital evidence: '*If it's switched on, do not switch it off; if it's switched off, do not switch it on; seek expert help!*' Computer evidence was notoriously volatile, and information could be lost irrevocably through mismanagement.

The second rule was: '*Never guess passwords!*' Fenwick had no intention of inspecting the data — he would photograph any ID tags, serial numbers or manufacturers' specification labels, and then seal the equipment in evidence bags.

Sofia and Fenwick arrived at the reception desk. The receptionist, a genial woman in her fifties whose name badge read 'Águeda Cadete', was reassuringly attentive and eager to assist. She'd been designated by the police as Fenwick's single point of contact at Reid's.

Might he see Tyler's computer equipment?

Senhora Cadete looked at Fenwick, clearly puzzled. 'It isn't here,' she said. 'The police have it.'

'The police? But we've just come straight from

headquarters. Chief Teixeira gave me a list of Tyler's effects, including the laptop and USB drive.'

'The equipment *was* here,' she explained, 'but an officer came to the hotel two days ago and took it.'

Suspecting crossed wires, Fenwick rifled through the documentation and the inventory. He found no indication anywhere that the equipment would be seized and impounded.

'Did the officer give you a name?'

'No, I'd finished for the day. The night manager, Benedita, dealt with him. Let me check our records. There'll be a scan of the receipt.'

A quick and efficient search yielded rapid results, and a colour printer whirred smoothly into action. Senhora Cadete handed Fenwick two printouts: an itemised receipt with an officer's signature, and a warrant card with an ID photograph.

Fenwick stared intensely at the officer.

The officer stared with equal intensity back at Fenwick:

'Sargento Jorge Leandro. 7659, Departamento de Investigação Criminal Funchal'

The call needed to be discreet and low-key. Sofia could dial police HQ and ask to speak to Sergeant Leandro, who would immediately explain the situation, dispelling any confusion so that all should be crystal clear. On second thoughts, however, Fenwick decided it made more sense to speak to Teixeira directly. He didn't relish the prospect of locking horns with the police chief again, but the computer equipment was by far the most promising line of enquiry available to him.

Sofia sat on a bench in a secluded and dappled spot of Reid's arboretum, surrounded by brightly coloured poinsettia, winter jasmine and cyclamen. Fenwick stood nearby as he spoke, pacing slowly up and down:

'Yes, Tyler's laptop. Taken two days ago by a Sergeant Jorge Leandro. I have his service number and department: 7659 Funchal CID.'

There was a pause while Teixera responded. Sofia strained to hear.

'There's no such officer,' said Fenwick. 'Might he be from Lisbon or the mainland police?'

Sofia couldn't hear Teixeira's reply, but his response was readily interpretable — a plane's wheels couldn't touch down on the runway without his knowing of the arrival and its passengers.

'No, you would know,' said Fenwick. 'Thank you again, superintendent.' The police chief's tone was courteous, without any of the tension so prevalent during their previous encounter.

Fenwick listened thoughtfully to Teixeira's sign-off.

'Yes, it is an interesting development,' he said, nodding. 'As you say, sinister.'

ELEVEN
ON THE DECK

It was half past six the next morning and José Gomes, captain of the *Lobo Marinho*, greeted Sofia and Fenwick at the administrative office of the Porto Santo Line in Funchal.

It was a short walk to the terminal and to the ferry itself: an imposing, sleek vessel which had a sharp bow and was deceptively capacious, with two car decks for 120 vehicles. The stern of the ship was open and the vehicle ramp deployed, with the car deck cordoned off by brightly coloured red-and-white cones.

The darkness of the hour was gradually lifting, and even though a fine day beckoned with no clouds to be seen, the morning chill still gnawed.

Gomes was immaculate in white flannels, the brass buttons on his jacket were brightly polished, and the gold braid on his epaulettes and his peak cap glistened. An officer and a gentleman, thought Fenwick. Sofia clearly approved. Fenwick was quietly amused at her less-than-subtle flirtation with the dashing officer, who had an easy roguish charm and a twinkle in his eye.

With a few formalities completed, Gomes led the way to his ship, speaking and gesturing as they walked. 'The ship complies with all statutory safety standards,' he said, 'but so did the Titanic.' He grinned broadly at Sofia, who sniggered, a little too effusively.

A deckhand moved the cordon and they crossed the gantry on to the primary car deck, which was empty of vehicles other than a red forklift truck surrounded by many palettes, stacked high.

Fenwick used his iPhone to take a gallery of photos. Of what, precisely? Sofia could only guess. Fenwick, now satisfied, followed as the trio climbed the steep metal ladders to the upper decks. Sofia, thinking ahead, had worn jeans, not a skirt.

After a tour of the lounge and the ship's inner accommodation, again with Fenwick taking photographs, they stepped out on to the passenger decks, inspecting both port and starboard flanks. Fenwick caught his breath, looking out over the harbour.

The giant ocean liners had departed the previous evening and the harbour now hosted two much smaller naval craft: Madeira's principal patrol vessel and a French corvette, both battle-ship grey. Nice shore-leave for the French sailors, thought Fenwick ruefully. Further along the quay was a sizeable fisheries protection vessel, the *Ocean Sentinel*, resplendent in blood-orange and white livery.

Never good with heights, Fenwick leaned over the safety railing and looked straight down to the waterline. He felt instantly queasy, reeling, with a weird sensation in his core — or in his balls, to be precise. It was a long drop to the sea, forty feet or so. Captain Gomes had supplied the blueprints of the *Lobo Marinho*, necessary to determine the precise height of the fall. Fenwick concluded that Tyler could not have propelled himself far from the deck, or — if assaulted — he could hardly have been thrown outwards to any significant distance.

Assessing the scene, Fenwick was astonished the body hadn't been hauled under the keel and cut to ribbons by the ship's propellers.

He turned to Gomes. 'The decking — it's non-slip?'

'Yes. Composite, embossed plate. All external decks.'

Fenwick took a couple of photographs of the decking and its tessellated patterning, which were painted a deep blue-green gloss with a water-resistant Hammerite coating.

Fenwick had photographed several CCTV camera vantage points during the inspection. 'Are the CCTV recordings available?' he asked.

Gomes, unsure, thought them to be backed up on DVDs under police seal. He didn't know the protocol to retrieve them for review.

The ferry's CCTV footage was presumably under Teixeira's control. The matter hadn't been broached; it was now a priority.

'Has any structural damage been reported?' asked Fenwick. 'Scuffs, scrapes, dents or bloodstains?'

'No, nothing at all,' replied Gomes. 'But a fall from the passenger deck would be a sheer, uninterrupted drop into the sea.' Fenwick could see that Gomes was right; a body would not have bounced off any abutment or hit anything at all during its descent.

He took out his reeled steel tape measure, an essential part of his toolkit. With long experience, he'd learned the value of measuring things.

Teixeira's ego, he thought with a smirk.

The safety railing measured 122 centimetres — four feet exactly, which was rather higher than was required by regulation. Fenwick wrote the figure in his notebook.

Tyler's height from the autopsy report was 176 centimetres — a little over five foot nine. His weight was 82.5 kilograms — about thirteen stone. The post-mortem photographs had not shown an overweight or top-heavy man. Fenwick, five foot ten, now assessed the safety rail. Sofia took a couple of pictures of him standing upright beside it.

He again surveyed the harbour. Gulls wheeled and soared, with a discordant screeching, scavenging discarded pickings. A work crew in hi-vis toiled and powered on some construction. Fenwick watched the hammer blows from afar; hearing each blow momentarily after seeing it.

The *Lobo Marinho* would set sail for Porto Santo at 8 am.

Sensing Captain Gomes' restiveness, Fenwick decided it was time to close matters. 'Right. Well, thank you for your time, captain.'

Gomes bid them farewell and, with a sly wink to Sofia, turned on his heel.

Alerted to his own forgetfulness, Fenwick shouted after him: 'The bar receipt!'

Gomes turned and dug deeply into his trouser pocket, retrieving a single length of crumpled printout, which he duly surrendered to Fenwick.

'*Ciao*,' said Gomes breezily to Sofia, ignoring Fenwick. Then he turned and headed to the bridge.

They had ten minutes to finalise their inspection and leave the ship, prior to its sailing. Fenwick seated on a bench on the deck, unfurled the blueprints of the vessel. With a sharpened pencil, he cross-hatched areas of the top elevation plan, which showed the extent of the passenger decks. His detailing was precise, with sharp angles. The lines were wrought with careful spacing, like those of a draftsman.

Sofia looked over his shoulder, admiringly but bewildered. 'What are you doing?'

'Marking the CCTV blind spots,' he replied, gesturing to the sole security camera that surveyed the deck.

He looked up and smiled at Sofia. 'Finished,' he said. 'Now let's take a nice photo of you.'

Sofia stood in exactly the place Fenwick indicated. She adopted a cover-girl pose, neither preening nor pouting, but enticing, warm and sexy.

He took the snap.

Whether port or starboard he might never know, but of one thing Fenwick was certain: Sofia now stood on the exact spot, on whichever deck, where Tyler had met his death.

TWELVE

ABC

Fenwick wallowed in the deepest and most luxurious bath of his life. He had even treated himself to several squeezed dollops of amber-coloured bubble bath courtesy of Reid's. He laughed joyously, realising what a buffoon he must look, with huge pillows of white foam and bubbly froth covering his everywhere, and not just his modesty. Two miniature whiskies with ice from the minibar eased his pains also. He had a conference call at 6 pm and would then spoil himself rotten with dinner for one, booked at Reid's affiliated restaurant *Villa Cipriani*.

In navy chinos and a white short-sleeved shirt, he now sat on his room's balcony, marshalling his thoughts. He dialled the Knightsbridge direct line using his mobile. It was time for Springer's first briefing and he wanted to keep it concise and based solidly on the facts.

Springer answered immediately; the echoing acoustics suggested that he was on speakerphone. Fenwick wondered if anyone else was on the call. If so, they were not introduced.

With the usual greetings concluded, Fenwick didn't mince his words:

'There's no indication Tyler was attacked or involved in a struggle. The toxicology indicates his blood alcohol level was three times the EU legal driving limit. Ostensibly, it's a suicide. The police are treating it as such… but the blood alcohol count is troubling.'

After a brief pause, Springer, clearly taken aback, replied, 'I agree, it's very odd indeed.'

Fenwick elaborated:

'He'd driven safely on to the ferry at around six in the evening. If the stated booze level is right, he must have hammered it all afternoon or gone a bit berserk in the ferry's bar, but the till receipt shows just a single glass of white wine. We should try to get his card statements for the day.'

Using his leverage and contacts, Springer could obtain Tyler's bank records, which Fenwick considered crucial: *where*, *when*, *how much*, *for what* and *to* and *from whom*?

'Three times!' Fenwick emphasised. 'I'm sceptical.'

There was a longer pause. Springer was evidently shocked — it was most unlike him to be lost for words. At last, he spoke: 'It's certainly not in character, not from when I knew him.'

At that moment, there was an interruption. Fenwick envisioned Montserrat within Springer's office, perhaps with some documents for his attention.

The intrusion was brief. Then Springer spoke, this time with urgency: 'We need to refute the blood alcohol result, or at least question it. Send me copies of Michael's documents and I'll get some enquiries underway at this end.'

Fenwick was more than happy to comply — anything that reduced his workload was most welcome, as there was a huge amount still to be completed on the island. 'I'll send them this evening,' he confirmed. 'But Tyler's alcohol level isn't our only problem. I inspected the ferry this morning. There's nothing hazardous about the safety rail. It'd be impossible just to tumble over it, even in a faint or blind drunk.'

There was another prolonged silence. Fenwick imagined Springer's cogs whirring in London, weighing up the possibilities. At last, Springer responded: 'So, either Michael took his own life, or someone killed him?'

'Precisely. Absent cogent proof otherwise, the coroner will rule suicide. There were also traces of a drug called Xanax in Tyler's blood. It's prescribed for anxiety, so he may have been fearful or stressed before he died.'

Springer looked out of his large office window. It was dark and rainy in London, but the immense geosynchronous animated wall-clock in his office still showed Madeira bathed in sunlight. 'You sound increasingly confident he didn't kill himself.'

'It's possible Tyler was murdered,' replied Fenwick. 'There are several CCTV blind spots on the ferry's decks. A killer, or killers, could have thrown Tyler overboard and remained undetected.'

'But surely the autopsy would reveal signs of a struggle?'

'Not if they took Tyler by surprise.'

'Tyler's death was a hit?' Springer sounded shocked that the misgivings he'd expressed about Tyler's death might actually be vindicated.

'It's a working hypothesis,' replied Fenwick. 'ABC: Assume nothing; Believe no-one; Check everything.'

'The motive?'

'Too early to say.'

Springer decided to hold Fenwick's feet to the fire, testing his theory to destruction. 'Surely throwing Tyler overboard wouldn't guarantee his death? He might have been rescued. Simply hurling a man into the sea would have left too much to chance.'

Fenwick knew he had to be on his mettle. Springer had a razor-sharp intellect, and any inconsistency or weakness in the proposition would be vigorously exposed and torn apart.

'I suspect it was planned and executed at short notice. It was opportunistic, a judgement call. Tyler was well past his prime and unlikely to survive the conditions. A hailstorm, a freezing swell and a dense low cloud-base to impede aerial observation or rescue. Better to dispose of him at sea than on dry land.'

Fenwick took a slug of his iced whisky and admired the view from his balcony, still rich in the sunset, shimmering and vibrant. He didn't want to alarm Springer, but the man needed to know.

'You should also know there's a clean-up operation underway: a man in police uniform using a fake ID lifted Tyler's laptop from the hotel a couple of days ago. So, whatever's going on, it's well-resourced and professional.'

A more prolonged silence now. The ramifications of this development, which all but confirmed foul play, would not be lost on Springer.

'That's affirmative, then,' said Springer. 'That laptop is key. So, what next?'

'I'll send you Tyler's documents — the chief of police here has given me a small data dump. It's not much, but helpful nevertheless. Tomorrow, I'll search the hire car Tyler was driving. The car keys are missing and there's an issue with his mobile phone.'

'Soonest, please,' said Springer, 'You're doing a fabulous job out there.'

The call ended.

In Cheltenham, Martyn Stowell finished his Curry King pot noodle and uploaded the telephone intercept — designated 'SCAVENGER FLASH PIR-3/-1' for immediate transmission over an encrypted link to MI6's specialist cell. Fenwick's mobile number had been designated a priority intelligence requirement (PIR) and had been monitored since before his flight to Madeira. In this respect, and with Fenwick entirely unaware of the fact, his name and number were now linked inextricably to Danusia Ziętek and the late Michael Tyler, in a tight-knit targeted 'cluster'.

But Stowell and the Scavenger team were not alone in their focus.

Unbeknown to them, Montserrat in Knightsbridge had also recorded Fenwick's and Springer's call, using a trip-switch pre-installed in Springer's office intercom. She, however, felt no immediate need to report what she'd heard. As far as she was concerned, this particular conversation — interesting but hardly revelatory — could wait.

The harsh overhead lighting hummed and glared — the mortuary's sterile white tiles glistened blindingly. On the steel gurney, a male body lay shrouded, the face concealed by a folded linen cloth. A sickly-sweet scent of formalin lingered in the air, acrid, cloying and heavy.

The mortician, an elderly and surly man, stood obstructively over the corpse, his back turned.

'Cause of death?' Fenwick asked, his voice hesitant and uneasy.

'Drowning,' the old man replied, his voice rasping, wheezy with nicotine. 'But he was clearly out of his depth,' he added, with evident disdain.

Fenwick moved closer, compelled to see for himself. 'Identity confirmed?' he asked, half knowing the answer.

The mortician's lips curled in a grotesque caricature, revealing hideous rotted teeth. Grasping the corpse's forearm, he turned the wrist slowly, savouring the moment as he revealed the printed identity label:

1-090124
FENWICK, Charles.
14/05/1981

Transfixed and breathless, Fenwick froze in horrified recognition of his own dead self.

His body hit the mattress with a sickening thud, as if he'd crashed to his death in freefall. Shaken awake by the sheer horror, Fenwick sat bolt upright in the darkness. His pulse raced as his torso poured with salty rivulets of sweat. Every synapse was electrified and sparking, his nerves racked by the energy.

He looked at the luminescent dial of his watch. It was 3 am — the witching hour. He was reeling, paralysed with fear, locked awkwardly in fight or flight mode, panting deeply and gasping for air.

The seconds ticked by, and the effects of the assault on his mind and body gradually eased.

Utterly drained, Fenwick curled up on the mattress in the foetal position, quivering like a wounded animal.

Unable to resume sleep, Fenwick went early to breakfast. He was greeted personally and shown to the table of his choice, outside on the terrace by the pool.

He chose a Spanish omelette, which had the freshest, most flavoursome eggs he could remember ever tasting.

Still recuperating from his nightmare, he at last recognised the mortuary assistant in the dream: it was the ghoulish old man from *The Grenadier*.

With a final cup of coffee, he exorcised the demon.

Fuck him, thought Fenwick. There was work to be done.

THIRTEEN
THE HOLY GRAIL

Sofia went with a police officer to the airport to oversee the X-ray inspection of Tyler's luggage and property. Fenwick had instructed her to watch the X-ray imagery and its operator like a hawk, and to keep a close watch on the property at all times, lest allegations of tampering, loss or damage might later arise. He'd prepared a property list and had given her a crash course in maintaining the chain of evidence.

Fenwick assigned himself a separate task — one that he knew would be somewhat more arduous and time-consuming.

The Hertz rental office was a short walk from the hotel. Fenwick made a very specific request to the agent: he wanted to hire a charcoal grey Fiat Punto, registration FE-37-BD, for a single day and to return it the following morning.

With the formalities completed, Fenwick approached the car. As was his habit, before signing for the vehicle he inspected the exterior, noting any scrapes or dents — he didn't want to be accused of damaging the vehicle upon its return. The Fiat was in near-pristine condition, except for the external locks of both the driver's door and the passenger door, which showed several thin striations on the paint work — scrapes consistent with rudimentary lock-picking. He photographed the damage and showed it to the Hertz agent, making sure she logged it in the company's records.

Hertz had spare keys and had used them to collect the Fiat when it had been abandoned on the ferry's car deck. Fenwick concluded that whoever had tried to break into the car was not a Hertz employee. He suspected that the CCTV coverage of the car deck from the day of Tyler's death would reveal the attempted break-in. The ferry's CCTV imagery was now crucial — he'd discuss it with Teixeira later.

With the striations duly noted, Fenwick took off, heading out of Funchal, east, past the airport and towards Machico, then veering off to Caniçal. He drove carefully, mostly in the slow lane, keeping a watchful eye on the procession of yellow taxis passing him as they hurtled along the highway. He had nowhere specific in mind; he sought merely a quiet side-road, not overlooked.

A rutted, bumpy dust track at last presented itself, which challenged the Fiat's suspension and led to a small grove encircled by pine trees, densely spaced and tall enough to conceal the car. Fenwick did not want an audience.

Was there any sign of sabotage? Were there any indications the brake linings had been cut, or the disk brakes interfered with? Had the seatbelts been damaged, perhaps jammed from deployment? Might even a car bomb have been wired to the ignition, or a mercury tilt-switch affixed? Even a slow-deflating cut in a tyre could cause havoc at high speed, as could over-inflation. Fenwick thought it all extremely unlikely, but he would check nonetheless.

More realistically, and with signs of a clumsy break-in now evident, he needed to answer a different question: what had been in the car, or perhaps remained there undetected?

'If you don't look, you don't find.' Fenwick recalled the maxim of a police inspector with whom he'd worked in the distant past.

He unfurled a black leather tool-case on the front passenger seat and took out a pen torch, a dental mirror, a larger circular shaving mirror, a wallet of small screwdrivers and a pair of needle-nose pliers, which he placed in a pouch secured to his belt. Then he donned bright purple rubber gloves — not so much to preserve fingerprints or forensic traces, but to prevent electrocution.

Lifting the bonnet, he photographed the engine compartment with his iPhone. The electrics were housed securely and the cabling and contacts were intact, pushed home and seated. Under the car, using the shaving mirror and the torch, he could see nothing unusual. The wheels and wheel hubs were also fine. He inspected the boot, using the mirror and torch again to search crevices and inner linings, but there was nothing. Lifting the mat in the boot, he searched the spare wheel and its housing, also to no avail.

The sun was high in the sky, and the trees were selfish with their shade. Fenwick, by now stripped to the waist, was sweating profusely. He'd had the forethought to bring a bottle of spring water purloined at breakfast, which he now swilled and swigged. The water in the plastic bottle was unpleasantly warm and left a sour chemical aftertaste.

The interior was next. Fenwick started with the glove compartment, the door panniers and behind the sun blinds. A red plastic service manual in the driver's pannier revealed nothing — Fenwick flicked its pages at speed, doubting that in its entire existence the manual had ever been consulted.

The rear seats without doors were easy to check; the mats lifted easily as well. Searching under the front seats, however, required almost gymnastic contortion. Now thinking of fiendish concealment, Fenwick unscrewed various internal fittings: coat hangers, grab handles and air vents. He even unscrewed the rear-view mirror. Some of the fittings were moulded or modular, offering no opportunity for removal or concealment.

After two hours, Fenwick had nothing to show for his efforts. It had all been a tedious waste of time.

Thoroughly dispirited, he slumped against the front wheel-well, stealing what little shade the Fiat had to offer. He thought momentarily of stripping the car with machine tools, tearing it to pieces in the way that a full drug-bust inspection might entail.

No, complete overkill, he thought.

Rising to his feet, he wiped himself down with a packet of wet wipes, cleansing oil and grease from his hands, and purging the sweat from his torso, armpits and face. The breeze felt pleasantly cool on his cleansed skin. He put his shirt back on and prepared to depart.

In the driver's seat, with the windows closed and the air conditioning on full blast, he waited for the ferocious temperature to subside. He'd have another look at the car's maintenance manual — might it disclose some hidden 'priest hole', perhaps installed by the manufacturer?

He again withdrew the red plastic wallet from the door pannier; its rear cover, this time, feeling oddly rigid. Pressing with his thumb, he detected something solid — metallic — wedged deep within. Heart racing, he scrambled for his toolkit. Grasping his needle-nosed pliers, he gingerly pried the object free.

Stumbling from the Fiat, wide-eyed and barely daring to believe, he marvelled at the sight, which glinted in the setting sun.

Before him shone the treasure he sought; a USB flash drive; silver, razor slim. It bore a small red circular sticker, marked in biro: MT.

The Holy Grail!

Fenwick, weak with the effort but utterly elated, slumped by the Fiat's front wheel.

The sun was low on its arc and the shadows extended.

FOURTEEN
RACHEL

A t her desk in Knightsbridge, Montserrat read the email that had appeared in her inbox:

```
M,
SFS requested the attached:
Tyler's info and some other bits.
Thanks,
Fenwick
```

The attachments were key: Tyler's passport, his telephone numbers — mobile and home landline — from the hotel registration and car rental deal, and his residential address, which was also shown on his driving licence. Springer — 'SFS' — had asked for these documents to be printed immediately and left in a folder on his desk.

Unbeknown to Springer or Fenwick, this information was also of critical interest to Montserrat's handler. Closing the door, she retrieved a lip-balm stick from her tote bag. It was a functioning lip-balm, but with a simple counter-clockwise twist, its cap detached to reveal a twenty-four-gigabyte thumb drive. To Montserrat's amazement, the USB ports had never been locked down at Winchcombe HQ. She now copied Tyler's information quickly and efficiently to the thumb drive. With the lip-balm reassembled, she placed the device in her tote bag.

Montserrat then prepared the printed file for Springer as requested, and left it on his desk, marked 'SFS - Tyler'.

Fenwick returned the Fiat to the Hertz office at 5.30 pm. He was done with the car. Hot and sweaty, he just wanted to soak in the big bath in his hotel room.

Refreshed and sporting his fluffy white bathrobe, he sat in the evening sun at the table on his balcony. There remained perhaps another ten minutes of sunset to enjoy — the sky still burned, with striking orange and purple hues.

Fenwick set Tyler's silver-plated memory stick before him. He knew he really shouldn't. All the rules shouted: 'NO! Do not, under any circumstances, examine the damned thing — wait for an expert!'

Oh, what the hell? He had to know. He inserted the drive into the USB port of his laptop and examined the file listing:

Name	Date Modified		
README.DOCX	27/12/2023	16;41	Microsoft...312 KB
NEPHILIM_TRUST_1.XLSX	15/03/2023	12:45	Microsoft...483 KB
NEPHILIM_TRUST_2.XLSX	15/03/2023	13;27	Microsoft... 562 KB
NEPHILIM_TRUST_3.XLSX	15/03/2023	14:12	Microsoft...508 KB
TRIAL A-BSL4.ZIP	17/10/2023	00:12	Compressed...912 KB
TRIAL B-BSL4.ZIP	17/10/2023	01:15	Compressed...987 KB
TRIAL C-BSL4.ZIP	17/10/2023	02:36	Compressed...902 KB
ROLLOUT.XLSX	23/11/2023	22:34	Microsoft...540 K

He knew better than to proceed. And yet, after a few brief moments of self-restraint he clicked to access the files. To his great surprise, the README document opened gracefully. But its content was unremarkable, just a listing of the files and a single instruction: 'Use password.'

The other files were completely intractable, in each case he was presented with a password prompt which glared at him contemptuously. Every file was encrypted.

Nephilim? He checked it on Google. There were references to ancient giants and fallen angels. A strange name for a trust company — a dark sense of humour was at work, he thought.

He checked the files' properties, but the key fields — author and affiliation — were all blank.

Fenwick could make no more progress. This was a job for a professional — and only one person fitted the bill.

Fenwick reached for his mobile phone and dialled her number.

Rachel Chen, twenty-nine, was the daughter of a Chinese Malay father and an Austrian mother. Having studied internationally, she'd settled in the UK, contracting in forensic support. Specifically, she'd chosen digital forensic investigation as her adopted career, the discipline representing to her the perfect amalgamation of scientific process, technical innovation and logical inquiry.

Fenwick had been privileged to meet and work with many brilliant people, but he considered Rachel as at the top of the tree — quite simply one of the finest minds he'd ever encountered.

He'd once asked her in how many languages she was proficient. Rachel had paused to calculate, and had then answered — fifteen: French, Spanish, German, Italian, C, C++, Python, Pascal, BASIC, COBOL, Fortran, Assembly, Lisp, Java and SQL. Sixteen, in fact, if you included English, and she was learning Russian! Fenwick marvelled at the achievement and had chortled at the answer.

'No-one likes a smartarse!' he'd retorted.

'I know,' she'd said sweetly, the very picture of guileless innocence.

Rachel was — to use the vernacular — 'kick-arse', and effortlessly stylish too, whether in Doc Martens or stilettos. She rode a Norton Commando motorbike and had attained black belts in both karate and taekwondo. Rachel was larger than life and more than merited her own Marvel Comics incarnation. Needless to say, she had many admirers, of whom she was either charmingly unaware or effortlessly dismissive.

The telephone rang as Rachel was inspecting a RAID storage array. The display on her mobile phone read simply: 'Mr F'. She put down a Philips magnetic screwdriver and answered.

'Mr Fenwick! How nice to hear from you. How are things?'

'I need your help, urgently. I need you to decrypt some files. They're my best chance for motive and suspects.'

He sounded stressed, she thought.

'You know the deal, Mr Fenwick,' she said. 'Decryption can take weeks, months, even years — we could all be dead before a breakthrough. There's no guarantee.'

Fenwick appreciated Rachel's honesty. She'd always explained to him the limits of her capabilities. But this was not the time to agonise over semantics.

'I know,' he said, 'but you succeed more often than not.'

'I get lucky,' she replied with calculated modesty.

'You do, *more often than not.*'

Rachel made her luck, thought Fenwick — one percent inspiration, ninety-nine percent perspiration: she had built one of the fastest and most powerful commercially available processing facilities in Europe — at twenty quadrillion floating-point operations per second it even required bespoke water cooling.

There was a pause while Rachel calculated the relative chances of success and the resources she required to commence processing.

'Send the files by secure mail,' she said at last. 'I'll see what I can do.'

The call had been intercepted at 18:29 GMT. Martyn Stowell in Cheltenham had forwarded the download directly to the Scavenger team in London over the secure line.

The intelligence assessment cell now reviewed the content.

Rachel Chen and her company — Quantum Dynamics LLC, which operated from an industrial park in Guildford — were known to them. She was talented, for sure. Quite a pioneer, in truth.

But ultimately, an enthusiastic amateur.

Fenwick sat at the writing desk in his hotel room. With care, he transferred the encrypted files from Tyler's memory stick to a secure mail account and sent them on their way. Rachel, he knew, would commence processing upon receipt — in just a few minutes.

He contemplated the security of his own computer and of the memory stick itself. The safe in his room was large enough to accommodate his laptop, a Lenovo L390 ThinkPad, which was protected by fingerprint-activated biometric access control and had BitLocker disk encryption. In addition, Tyler's files also were themselves encrypted, seemingly to a high standard.

Despite these safeguards, Fenwick's sixth sense implored him to keep the computer equipment within his sight and reach at all times. Hotel safes, with their four-digit codes, always had an override — a backdoor. Tyler's passport, he recalled, had been retrieved exactly this way.

He popped the memory stick into the laptop's travel case. He would take both it and his computer with him.

FIFTEEN
CIDADE VELHA

S ofia had invited Fenwick to dinner in the Old Town. It was a gracious and welcoming gesture which he'd readily and appreciatively accepted.

It was a warm, inviting evening and they sat outside on the terrace of *Cidade Velha*, a restaurant nestled protectively beneath the city's seventeenth century sea fortress of São Tiago, with its high walls and abutments painted a rich and striking yellow. The setting sun radiated, flooding the scene, with the azure Atlantic in the distance, as placid as a millpond.

Fenwick and Sofia shared a starter of *lapas*: grilled limpets seasoned with garlic, lemon juice and butter, and served with local bread. Sofia wore jeans with sandals, a white blouse with sharp pleats and a brown leather bomber jacket. Her long dark hair was tied in a ponytail and her makeup was subtly applied to good effect. Fenwick felt guilty for stealing Sofia's time on this glorious evening. He pictured her, happy and content, at her home, rightly beside her husband and son.

Sofia, curious and still perplexed, scrutinised her mysterious dinner companion. Fenwick, in a short-sleeved shirt and jeans, had a navy-blue jumper tied carelessly around his waist — not casually draped over the shoulders in the European style. She was amused he'd brought his laptop computer with him — was he planning to take a deposition?

Fenwick, clearly on guard, was the proverbial 'coiled spring'. She quite liked the man's intensity and occasional flashes of humour; the tea at Reid's had been lovely, too. What more surprises had he in store?

Shocked and slightly bruised by the details of the case, Sofia only had herself to blame. The man was just doing his job, and she should rise to the challenge. This evening was an opportunity to test him, and to tease out the truth.

She opened rather too apologetically. The X-ray scan of Tyler's luggage and of his possessions had revealed nothing. The drugs swab was also negative. A fruitless exercise then, but as Fenwick explained, a necessary one and he thanked Sofia for overseeing it.

On route to the restaurant, Fenwick had happened upon the city's *Cathedral of Our Lady of the Assumption*. He had stepped inside, even lighting a candle in remembrance.

'Beautiful cathedral,' he ventured.

'Yes, it is, in its modest way. It's also my church. I go every Sunday. I try to be devout, but I lapse often. Are you religious?'

'Not in a formal or practising sense. I like candles and the smell of incense,' he replied breezily.

'Do you believe in good and evil?' asked Sofia earnestly.

'Evil, most definitely.' Fenwick surprised even himself with such a quick and affirmative answer. Sensing that Sofia was pursuing a dark path, he sought to lighten the tone. 'The Devil? I don't revere him, but I admire his talents,' he jested.

Sofia chuckled. It was a nice quote, but alas not his own and paraphrased also.

She leaned in inquisitively. 'Mr Tyler was a victim of evil?'

'I think it possible. I have less faith in Occam's razor than your chief of police.'

Sofia recalled William of Ockham from her university days in Lisbon; a Franciscan friar of the fourteenth century. *When seeking a solution, introduce as few assumptions or variables as possible.*

'Occam's razor?' she enquired, feigning ignorance.

'The presumption that simple explanations are preferable to complex ones. So, if a drunken man falls from a ferry, it's a suicide or a death by misadventure. It's a neat and tidy approach.'

'But you think it's wrong?

Fenwick paused to refill their glasses — *Caldas Douro*, rich and red.

'Not necessarily,' he replied, 'but it's flawed: it takes no account of ingenuity, guile, deceit or ruthlessness.' Context, he explained, was also key. A penniless man drowning was quite different from a millionaire drowning. Tyler had subscribed to a substantial life insurance policy and he also had a small fortune to bequeath. He had high-level and influential contacts also, with his nine fingers in many pies. Occam's razor, wielded without such context, was a crude and blunt instrument. 'Favoured by the lazy, by the stupid, and officialdom,' he concluded.

Sofia resented Fenwick's mansplaining. 'So, which is our chief of police?' she snapped. 'Lazy or stupid?'

Sensing a trap, Fenwick chose his words carefully. 'Neither. He's extremely shrewd… and provocative also. But he is an official. What was it he said? "It would be best for all concerned to close this file quickly." What he meant was it would be best for him. It definitely wouldn't be best for Tyler or his grieving widow.'

At that moment, the waitress appeared with the main courses. Fenwick had ordered *espetada* — skewered beef — while Sofia had black scabbardfish. They fell silent while the waitress completed the service with rice and vegetables.

With her departure, their conversation resumed.

'It's an intriguing case,' said Sofia, looking out to the sea, '…but sad. You've considered I suppose the possible involvement of Mr Tyler's wife in his death. She will inherit a lot of money, as you've explained. That is surely a motive for murder.'

Fenwick nodded. 'I'll see Tyler's wife when I'm back in London. I'm reserving judgement on her… for the time being.'

They fell silent.

Reanimated now, Sofia turned and smiled. 'So, Mr Fenwick… Charles, tell me: are you married? Do you have children? Family?'

The enquiry was inevitable. Fenwick, with nothing to hide, opted for brevity. 'Divorced. No children, parents long gone. A brother, also departed.'

'I'm sorry for your loss,' said Sofia with genuine sympathy.

Fenwick, seeing an opportunity to lighten the mood, grinned and eyed Sofia artfully. 'Believe me, my ex-wife was no loss!'

Sofia laughed, a little ashamedly. She couldn't picture a wife — Fenwick seemed so perfectly complete and resolutely independent.

'But your brother — an illness?'

'No,' he answered bluntly. 'Murdered. Knifed.'

Sofia gasped and instinctively covered her mouth with her hand. 'Oh my God!' she exclaimed, in shock. 'The killer?'

Fenwick was instantly transported eight years back to the bloody pavement in Canary Wharf, the pale blue forensic tent erected in the street, and the SOCO in white overalls, scouring the surrounds.

'A boy, fifteen,' he replied. 'Pled guilty to manslaughter. Since released.'

'You're not bitter?' asked Sofia, clearly alarmed.

It had been a squalid, unprovoked, juvenile assault: Wayne Masden was his name, a gormless, soulless, moronic and ultimately pitiful product of broken Britain. James hadn't even spoken to the boy, who was high on amphetamines at the time. A mere look — a facial expression — had sent Masden into a frenzy. Five savage wounds from a lock-knife were inflicted, one of which had pierced James' aorta, causing a lethal haemorrhage.

'Retribution is pointless,' Fenwick declared vaguely. He flashed Sofia a diffident smile. 'Life is fragile,' he said simply. 'And precious, too.'

She stared at him dolefully. 'Hence your commitment to this case?'

Fenwick had never thought of his motivation. For him, it was just another assignment, albeit quite an unusual one. Thinking of it now, perhaps there was a nobler calling.

'Maybe,' he conceded with a shrug of his shoulders, imagining Tyler's corpse on some cold slab in Lisbon. 'When the dead are silenced, we can perhaps be their voice.'

The conversation lapsed, momentarily. Fenwick emptied the wine into their glasses in equal measures. An alley cat — in black and white tuxedo — eyed their table longingly, relishing the prospect of some scraps of scabbard fish.

Eventually, Sofia leaned in, almost intimately. 'Tell me. If *you* fell into the icy sea, would anyone miss you or come looking?'

Fenwick laughed at the prospect. 'My guardian angel maybe? Well, I hope someone might, but there'd be no national "day of mourning" or twenty-one-gun salute.'

Sofia liked his answer. The man knew his limitations, but not his worth?

'You underestimate yourself,' she said reassuringly, with a modicum of affection.

It was dark now, and colder. Fenwick paid the bill, folding the receipt as an expense.

As they prepared to leave, Sofia turned to him. 'There's

something I forgot to mention, relating to the file. It may be nothing, but…'

'Go on,' he said.

'This morning, I noticed an attachment, a fiche, stapled to the pathology report with an address in Poland. It was stamped "URGENT". I thought it strange.'

'Where in Poland?' Fenwick pressed, with sufficient restraint not to alarm her.

Sofia shook her head. 'No, sorry,' she said, frustrated. Teixeira had forbidden copying and she hadn't made a note of it. It was similar to a postcode, like a French CEDEX or an American Zip, but she didn't recall a street or city.

But it was definitely in Poland.

Telephone and electronic mail intercepts from targeted ELINT had picked up the prospective meeting between Fenwick and Sofia at *Cidade Velha*.

The subjects were to be watched at the restaurant, and the man was then to be followed and, if necessary, incapacitated — but not killed. A simple theft with no violence at all was preferable. The woman was not to be harmed in any way, nor should she be an eyewitness to any theft or assault. All electronic and data storage devices on the man were to be secured for immediate return and inspection. His hotel room at Reid's should also be searched covertly.

Nathan and Xavier tracked the target, maintaining their distance — one waiting in advance, the other following several paces behind. The old boys who habitually played chess at the tables in the park had long since departed, leaving just a few teenagers still petting, smooching and fumbling in the darker recesses. Some young diehards still rolled and clattered distantly in the skateboard park, near the cable car terminus.

Nathan identified an adequate ambush site: concealed, far from street lighting, in the shadows of the night and with no casual onlookers.

As the target approached a low flight of stone steps, Nathan steeled himself.

A single judicious punch to the man's face should suffice.

SIXTEEN

LEFT HOOK

Fenwick regained consciousness lying flat on an examination couch in the semi-darkness of a quiet room. The door was slightly ajar and he could hear muted discussions outside, considered and serious — professionals conferring in Portuguese. Electronic systems beeped rhythmically and steadily in the corridor. A drip perfused saline solution venously into his arm, and a pulse oximeter gently squeezed his middle finger.

He turned and retched violently, sufficiently aware to avail himself of a papier-mâché vomit bowl, leaving no spillage. The sick was pale and watery with no solids — he'd long since parted with his dinner of the previous evening.

He dimly remembered the evening with Sofia, and then walking through the park on his way back to the hotel. The blow had come from nowhere, a left hook, and a haymaker. All else was a blank.

Unbeknown to Fenwick, his slumped body had been found by teenagers returning home from the skateboard park shortly before midnight. With the alarm raised, an ambulance had rushed him to the *Hospital Particular da Madeira*.

Several plasters were now stuck to his chest, peeling off, their adhesion weakened by a wet film of sweat. Metal studs from an electrocardiogram remained taped in place. Lines and drips had been inserted in his hand and arm also, the infusion sites secured with gauze dressings.

With dawning consciousness, Fenwick was suddenly thunderstruck by an alarming reality. Heart racing and instantly energised, he staggered from the examination couch, stumbling and fumbling towards the door and out to the bright ward outside.

The nurses were shocked at his sudden appearance, his face wan with a gaudy headwound and his torso bared and slick with perspiration. As he staggered towards them, he looked like a filmset zombie.

'My laptop!' he exclaimed. 'Where's my laptop?'

The ward sister intervened, moving quickly to hold him firmly and insistently by his shoulders. 'You need to rest. There is no laptop.'

A nurse scuttled forward with a transparent possessions bag. Fenwick grabbed it, scrutinising its contents: his passport, wristwatch and wallet were there, with payment cards all present and correct.

But the laptop was gone, and with it, Tyler's memory stick.

There was no sign of Fenwick's mobile phone, either, nor of his electronic keycard to room 509 at Reid's. Instinctively, he knew his hotel room had by now been broken into and ransacked.

Anxious and trembling, he was accompanied attentively by the nurses back to the side room. At their insistence, he lay back down on the couch. Dejectedly, he pulled a blanket over himself in protection against the harsh air conditioning.

Injured, robbed and violated. For Fenwick, it was a new low.

Doctor Guimares, consultant neurologist, studied the patient notes, while Fenwick sat on the edge of the examination couch, still naked to the waist, clutching his soiled shirt and shivering in the cold.

Guimares looked up from his notes at Fenwick. 'It's a severe contusion but the scan shows no sign of subarachnoid haemorrhage or CVT.'

'Which means what?' asked Fenwick impatiently.

'There's no significant bleeding or clotting. But, should either present and you're not in hospital, you could die before the ambulance even reaches you. You've suffered a serious injury.' He handed Fenwick a mirror. 'See for yourself.'

Fenwick was shocked at the extent of the bruising. His left eyelids and cheek swelled shiny purple and black, like an aubergine. His lip was cut and there were three stitches, neatly applied.

'Hmm. All right,' he conceded. 'I'll come in tomorrow for a checkup.'

Guimares, used to such obstinacy, was forceful now. 'You should remain under observation. I don't have the authority to restrain you but it'd be utter madness for you to leave this hospital.'

'But I am allowed to leave?' asked Fenwick, earnestly.

Guimares, resigned to the inevitable, shrugged his shoulders. 'Yes.'

'I'll be off, then,' said Fenwick quietly, gathering his remaining possessions.

SEVENTEEN
SIMPLICITY ITSELF!

S tripped of his mobile phone and laptop, Fenwick felt naked and lost. He re-camped immediately and now marshalled a fresh battle plan.

A taxi — yet another bright yellow Mercedes — arrived quickly at the hospital forecourt, and Fenwick was soon ensconced again within the protective cocoon of Reid's. The receptionist gasped, barely concealing her shock at Fenwick's injured face. Presented with his passport, she solicitously generated a fresh key card for room 509.

On entering his room, Fenwick envisioned the intruders rifling through his suitcase and clothes, tearing, pecking and scavenging like vultures. He tried his four-digit PIN for the room's safe; it no longer worked. Had they opened it using a default and then reset it?

Paradoxically and inexplicably, his assailants had left him functional and solvent, with his passport and payment cards intact — as though they wished him God's speed, never to return. The attack in the park, albeit nasty and violent, had been just a warning.

Fenwick used the internet in the hotel's business centre to obtain Rachel's landline number from her Quantum Dynamics LLC website. Several streets away, downtown, he dialled from a public phone booth in a shopping precinct. The line rang and rang. Fenwick cursed himself for not keeping a printout of Rachel's mobile number.

Then, to his huge relief, she answered.

His call had been auto-forwarded to her mobile phone.

She answered at a height of about forty feet, inverted as she now was, clasped to the negative incline of a climbing wall at a sports centre in Surrey Quays. With her 'three points of contact' securely established, and hearing Fenwick through wireless earpods, Rachel listened attentively.

'You need a secure phone, urgently,' he blurted. 'My mobile is compromised. I was attacked last night. They stole the memory stick with the files I sent you. You alone know about the stick. Someone was listening in.'

Rachel, defying gravity and clinging perilously, re-chalked her hands. She swung out and secured a fresh anchorage, from which she pivoted athletically to a further staging point. She resented the club's mandated safety harness and much preferred free-climbing, as she had in the Dolomites, Patagonia and Yosemite.

'Someone attacked you? Are you okay?' she asked breathlessly, straining to reach her next purchase.

'Yes, I'm fine. Just a few bruises.'

'Where did you make the call?'

'The balcony of my hotel room,' he answered.

'Have you swept it for bugs?'

'No. I don't have the time, skill or resources.'

Rachel wondered how Fenwick even survived. He was a dinosaur.

'I'm calling from a payphone,' he said.

'I forget payphones still exist,' said Rachel in wonderment, pinned now to the climbing wall with no obvious pathway to ascend.

'Thank God they do,' said Fenwick. 'I'll make no more calls from my hotel, only from a burner phone. Contact me on that number only. It's probable your lines are also compromised. You'll need a burner, too.'

Her lines compromised? Rachel doubted it. And a burner? Fenwick was being paranoid, surely? A nasty and random mugging she suspected, but she would fall in with his narrative, just to ease the way.

'I'll activate a SIM this afternoon,' she replied cheerfully. 'I'll send you the number by secure mail.'

She considered the final stage of the climb which demanded some extreme contortions, both physical and mental. Reaching the summit and impressed with her own kinesthetics, she then descended balletically, spiralling downwards with acrobatic prowess along the nylon support cable, to loud whoops of applause from a coterie of appreciative fellow climbers.

Landing on the ground with a studied pirouette, she signed off: 'The decrypt is underway. There's nothing to report yet.'

Fenwick entered a phone shop in the basement floor of a shopping precinct. He paid in cash for a cheap mobile phone, with an additional sum of €200 prepaid for text and voice services, with full European coverage. No contract, no name or address required, nor any awkward questions asked. He could top up the SIM as and when required, also in cash.

At an internet café, he wrote down the number for Rachel's burner phone, which she had transmitted to his secure mail account. He replied in kind, with his own newly assigned number.

He now sat at a table overlooking the sheltered marina, with a tightly grouped armada of yachts, sailboats, catamarans and dinghies that bobbed placidly. The day was a little overcast, with a slight drizzle. Fenwick remained dry beneath the table's parasol. He sipped from a black caffè americano, appreciating the strong hit of caffeine. Gulls soared and screeched overhead, alert to the rich pickings to be had, whether discarded, or inadequately safeguarded by the waterfront clientele.

Rachel was inspecting the files from Tyler's memory stick when the mobile rang. Her newly activated burner displayed an unfamiliar number.

'Anything?' Fenwick urged, without introduction or pleasantries.

'Alas, no,' she replied, somewhat taken aback. 'Nothing from the decrypt.'

She was running the target files as seven subsets in parallel across nine processors, but she knew better than to say this to Fenwick, knowing it would be meaningless to him.

Besides, she had a pleasant surprise to convey.

'There's metadata in the README file,' she said, masking her excitement. 'I've extracted the file properties.'

Fenwick blinked, momentarily lost.

'But I checked the file properties myself,' he responded. 'There was nothing there! All the fields were empty!'

'The files have been anonymised, stripped of identifiers.' Rachel paused, letting the import of her words sink in. 'But I've found classification data recorded by a content management system. Whoever created the file didn't realise this information was logged.'

Fenwick frowned, trying to piece it together: a background process? An invisible exchange between the corporate server and the file?

Rachel clarified. 'The network's CMS has remotely embedded the software registrant and username.'

Fenwick's heart raced. This was the breakthrough he had been hoping for. 'Jesus!' he exclaimed. 'That's a massive lead!'

He fished his notebook from his jacket pocket and pulled a pencil from its spine. Pressing the speakerphone to his ear, he switched to hands-free.

'Spell the names, please,' he said, his voice calm, his mind racing.

Rachel didn't hesitate. 'Danusia — D-A-N-U-S-I-A — Ziętek — Z-I-E-T-E-K.' She spelled it out, each letter crisp and clear. 'There's an accent on the first 'e', called an "ogonek", by the way.'

Fenwick wrote the name in bold and precise capitals, wary of the slightest mistake.

'And Saurian Group,' Rachel continued. 'S-A-U-R-I-A-N.'

Fenwick exhaled. He looked down at the notebook, his mind spinning as he scanned the names he had just written.

'Rachel, you've surpassed yourself,' he said, his voice low, profound in admiration.

'It was really nothing. Simplicity itself!' she replied sweetly. And with that, she hung up.

Springer was in the third-floor drawing room of his magnificent London townhouse in Addison Road, Holland Park, when the call came in. He didn't recognise the incoming number, prefixed +351, but instantly knew the familiar voice of the caller.

Fenwick was open about the attack, the theft and the hospitalisation.

'A head injury?' said Springer. 'That's appalling. Go straight back to the hospital and get a full assessment.'

'No need,' replied Fenwick. 'I'm fine. No headache or neurological issues. I'm just sorry I've lost my only piece of promising evidence so far.'

'In that case, I accept no liability. You understand?'

'Yes.' Fenwick understood the rules. The injury was an occupational hazard and came with the territory.

Springer now broached the real issue. 'Apropos the memory stick, you saved its data before it was stolen?'

'Yes, thank God. The files are currently being decrypted by...'

'Stop!' interjected Springer forcefully. 'Don't say another word.'

He was right — Fenwick had momentarily let his

guard down. Springer's line was potentially exposed, as were many others.

'Return home now,' commanded Springer.

'But Sir Frederick…'

'But nothing. I have a duty of care towards you, as well as Tyler's widow. Leave Funchal immediately.'

It was an order, not a request.

The line went dead.

EIGHTEEN
'FRENEMY'

Fenwick visited the police HQ alone. He didn't want Sofia to see his injuries, intent as he was on wishing her farewell by telephone only, mentioning nothing of the assault or the theft. Composing his report without a laptop had proven arduous, and he now thanked Teixeira's receptionist for her efficient transcription.

His priority was to secure the CCTV footage from the ferry and from Reid's, for which he'd raised a formal request. He was certain Tyler's assailants had been caught in the frame, and that his hotel room had also been entered surreptitiously and searched.

Fenwick had issued a further request: immigration data for one Danusia Ziętek. Had she been in Madeira or Porto Santo? He hadn't explained Ziętek's relevance or his reasoning: the less Teixeira knew, the better.

The wily police chief looked relaxed now, seated behind his desk. The meeting was a formality. This man, Fenwick, had brought nothing but trouble, and the police chief wanted him off the island forthwith.

He casually flicked through Fenwick's report, a concise document of three pages, which focused primarily on the maintenance and safety of the island's ferry.

'Thank you for granting the *Lobo Marinho* a clean bill of health,' he said. 'Your assessment has no regulatory status, but your efforts are appreciated nonetheless. I shall notify the captain this afternoon.'

Fenwick thought of Captain Gomes in his pristine white uniform, flirting so outrageously with Sofia. 'Yes, the ferry seems fine and in good working order.'

Teixeria studied Fenwick. The black eye was a real shiner. He noted the precise stiches on the man's upper lip also.

'But you appear not to be,' he said with a sneer.

Fenwick had spent the night with an ice compress, but despite his best efforts, the swelling and bloody discoloration had only worsened.

'It's nothing,' he shrugged. 'A fall in the Old Town.'

Teixeira's relaxed demeanour changed abruptly. He leaned forward and snarled with cold fury, 'Don't lie to me, Mr Fenwick, or dare to insult my intelligence.'

For the first time in the police chief's presence, Fenwick felt a frisson of fear, sensing the volatility and pure menace of the man.

'I heard about your visit to the hospital,' Teixeira said. 'Nothing escapes my attention on this island. Furthermore, I can state categorically: whoever did that to your face was not from this island. I know the people here.'

Teixeira was right. The people of the island were lovely — gentle, welcoming and playful. The violence visited on Fenwick was from an altogether darker place.

'What did your attackers steal?'

Fenwick noted Teixeira's use of the plural. Fenwick, too, sensed that a team was at large, not a 'lone wolf'.

'Nothing irreplaceable,' he replied. 'My laptop... and phone.'

It was a lie by omission. Fenwick had no intention of telling Teixeira about Tyler's hidden memory stick. Nor would he mention the Polish address on the autopsy report that Sofia had seen. Teixeira had quite possibly lied about the necessity for the corpse to be transported to Lisbon. Doctor Guimares at the hospital, responding to an offhand enquiry, had assured Fenwick the island had a fully functioning and well-resourced pathology lab, with two expert pathologists and a pharmacology unit also.

'Another stolen laptop!' Teixeira scoffed, slyly eyeing Fenwick's report, clearly typed in the distinctive style of his own secretary. After a short pause, he added: 'You clearly don't think Tyler killed himself.'

Fenwick gestured to the file in Teixeira's hands.

'As I stated in my report...'

Teixera interrupted him, quoting from memory:

'"*Although the evidence that Mr Tyler was murdered is circumstantial at best, it is nevertheless sufficient to cast reasonable doubt on the supposition that he took his own life.*"'

Fenwick was taken aback at Teixeira's astonishing recall. 'Verbatim,' he murmured, grudgingly impressed.

'I pay as close attention to my work, as you do to yours. For what it's worth, I'm inclined to agree with you about the safety railing. It's indicative that Tyler's death was no accident.'

'But...?' There had to be a 'but' thought Fenwick.

'But... there is absolutely no actionable evidence of foul play. And to persuade a coroner to reject a verdict of suicide, you'll need more compelling evidence than some CCTV blind spots, the theft of some laptops, or your assault. Besides, if you're right, the culprits arrived on the island undetected and most likely have departed likewise.'

Fenwick, aggrieved at the brush-off, shot back: 'Which means they're professionals.'

'Skilled and ruthless professionals,' admitted Teixeira, 'who are now targeting you.'

'In that case, we should review the CCTV footage immediately,' declared Fenwick, pointing to his printed access request.

Teixeira looked witheringly at the typed page. 'Your request for disclosure is with the department's lawyers. There are data protection and privacy issues to be considered.'

Data protection — that old chestnut. Fenwick thought of the countless times when CCTV imagery had been withheld by the authorities to protect 'privacy' and 'human rights' — and when crucial cameras had conveniently failed to record during critical moments. He was certain the CCTV recordings from the ferry, and possibly the hotel — if not already destroyed or irretrievably 'lost' in the bureaucratic morass — would never again see the light of day. 'ACCESS DENIED', the official stamp would declare.

'Don't misunderstand me, Mr Fenwick,' said Teixeira with emollient dispassion. 'I wish you no ill, but I don't have the resources to guarantee your safety. I suggest... *I strongly advise...* that you leave the island.'

Whether Teixeira was corrupt, coerced, lazy or just disinterested, Fenwick didn't know, but it was clearly time to leave — from this shuttered office and Madeira also.

'I'll notify you should anything arise,' said Teixeira as Fenwick rose and approached the door.

'I won't hold my breath,' Fenwick seethed, exiting.

Fenwick brushed swiftly past the reception desk towards the exit, when a woman's voice called after him: 'Senhor Fenwick, Mr Fenwick!'

He turned abruptly to see Teixeira's receptionist fast approaching him.

'The superintendent left this for you,' she said, urging a sealed document upon him. 'He insists you must have it,' She promptly turned on her heel.

Fenwick opened the envelope and was astonished to see an immigration record for Danusia Ziętek from Porto Santo airport. He'd presumed the police chief would sit on his request for entry and exit data with the same casual disregard with which he'd treated his other leads.

Yet, lo and behold, here was the answer.

Yes, Ziętek had been in Porto Santo. She'd even departed the island for Lisbon on the very afternoon on which Tyler had drowned!

The immigration form showed her temporary residency

on the island with a suite at Excelsior Apartments, along with details of her flights and points of embarkation.

Fenwick was amazed. For all of Teixeira's sneering and obstruction, now this! A crucial lead, willingly tendered. So, was the wily police chief a friend or foe?

He was neither, Fenwick concluded, observing the receptionist now behind her desk, who smiled back at him benevolently.

Teixeira was following his own arrow.

He was, at best, a 'frenemy'.

NINETEEN

EXCELSIOR

F enwick wasted no time. With no commercial flights available, he was now the final passenger of six strapped luxuriously into the passenger seat of a chartered Beech BE90 King Air twin turboprop that taxied for take-off from Madeira to Porto Santo. The seat had cost a king's ransom, for a flight that would perhaps take thirty minutes at most. It was by far the greatest extravagance of Fenwick's entire life.

His fellow passengers comprised the core personnel of a fashion shoot; a stunning auburn-haired female model worthy of *Vogue* or *Cosmopolitan* but sweetly demure and refreshingly modest, an extremely camp artistic director who was very much older, a bearded and muscular male photographer, a butch female dresser tattooed and encrusted in metal studs, and a somewhat browbeaten young girl, apprenticed as a hair and make-up artist. All were bound for the deep blue sea and blinding white sands of the diminutive island. The road not travelled, thought Fenwick, lost in wild imaginings, envisioning the high life that such an exotic entourage must lead.

The short flight was uneventful through cloudless, serene skies. Fenwick, feigning disinterest, earwigged attentively, astonished at the unguarded gossip and truly shocking fashion industry revelations of his fellow passengers.

It was an hour after landing, and from a small café opposite, he now surveyed Ziętek's registered address — Excelsior Apartments, a tenement of serviced suites on the outskirts of Vila Beleira.

'Walk-ins' were notoriously tricky, dependent entirely on the self-confidence and charisma of the actor. In the performance, there was no room whatsoever for hesitation or self-doubt. Every expression, facial tic and movement had to ooze sincerity, imbuing an unquestionable authority and authenticity. The story, however ridiculous or contrived, needed to hold water. It was a very fine tightrope to walk. Fenwick, with little experience of such visceral subterfuge, nor any acumen or appetite for it, was daunted by the prospect.

With no opportunity for rehearsal, he now steeled himself. A fundamental rule when gathering information from such raw intimate human interaction was to live completely in the moment, mentally absorbing every single detail — however small — for subsequent retrieval and analysis. As best he could, Fenwick now summoned his super-senses, with his visual and auditory cortexes on full alert and his memory engaged in overdrive.

With an admittedly weak and hastily assembled cover story, Fenwick crossed the road.

'Hi,' he breezed. 'I'm having lunch with Miss Ziętek, Apartment twelve.'

The young woman looked at him, clearly befuddled.

'Ziętek?' She recalled the name. The woman had left two weeks ago, she said, shaking her head.

'There must be a mistake. We have a booking at *Vila Alencastre*, at two.'

The receptionist checked her computer. No, she confirmed, Miss Ziętek had left.

'That's odd,' he said, looking perplexed. 'She left no note for me?'

There might be an email, perhaps? Or some explanation?

Checking the hotel's inbox, the receptionist's face lit up. An e-mail had arrived that morning.

'There's a parcel,' she said brightly… 'to be forwarded. Let me check.'

She disappeared to the mailboxes in the administrative office behind.

Fenwick knew he could simply lunge across the receptionist's desk to catch a glimpse of Ziętek's forwarding address, or even take a snapshot with his phone of the screen, but he desisted. Increasingly in control of the situation, he calmly awaited the young woman's return.

She now placed two letters, one sellotaped to a small parcel, on the desk. Fenwick now scan read, upside down, concentrating most intently on postmarks and the points of origination. The letter, a cream vellum envelope handwritten in beautiful copper-plate black ink, was most definitely a personal communication. Its emblem, large and distinctive, showed crossed gold and silver keys bound with a red cord and surmounted by a silver tiara. Fenwick recognised it as the Papal coat of arms, Vatican City. The parcel attached was the size of a thick paperback book. A New Testament possibly?

The second envelope, with printed address label, was formal and business-like, clearly containing several folded pages and looked contractual. *'Casa di Cura Sant' Antonio da Padova,'* it read, imprinted in blue ink.

The young receptionist viewed her computer records. There was a problem. Miss Ziętek had left no payment card — the parcel, she explained, would be costly.

'I can take them,' Fenwick said, helpfully.

No, it was against the rules.

'I'll pay then,' he said, reaching for his wallet, cash in hand.

The young woman smiled — his offer was most welcome, curtailing no end of administrative hassle.

She placed adhesive label stationery in the print tray and clicked the mouse to print two address labels. She then took the letter and the parcel into the office behind, to be weighed and franked.

Fenwick watched the printer like a hawk, the camera on his burner phone active and ready to take the shot.

The Fujitsu whirred efficiently, and the labels loomed into view, each with the all-important address:

    Danusia Ziętek
    Apartment 8,
    Distal 62, Old Town,
    31-036 Kraków, Poland

Fenwick, as focused as a marksman, pressed the button of his camera phone.

SNAP!

Fenwick took a charter flight back to Madeira — this time, on a Cessna 340 with three other passengers. He'd considered taking the *Lobo Marinho*, but the crossing took almost three hours, and Fenwick had no time to spare. As he reclined in his seat, sipping chilled champagne, he felt a pang of guilt. It was grubby of him to have tricked the Excelsior's receptionist; deceiving the young girl now made him despondent and downcast. He was saddened also by what he'd inferred from Ziętek's mail.

Letters from Rome. A priest or cardinal ministering the last rites, perhaps? And a document from a hospice. Experts in palliative care, according to their website.

He instinctively knew Ziętek's days were numbered.

The clock was against him, too.

TWENTY

HENDERSON

F enwick, trapped on a red double-decker bus, waited impatiently for the driver to open the rear exit door. He greatly missed the old Routemasters, with their open platforms, from which you could simply hop on and off at will. With a high-pitched siren squawking, the bus's door grudgingly shuddered open, and Fenwick at last stepped out.

It was yet another overcast grey London day, damp with freezing drizzle. Fenwick, head bowed and with umbrella aloft, headed swiftly to the offices of Henderson Galbraith & Partners in Bedford Row, Holborn.

Geoffrey Henderson, sixty-seven, had been the family solicitor for as long as Fenwick could remember, deftly handling matters of tax, property, inheritance and probate. Fenwick liked Geoffrey. The man had a fine-tuned, irreverent sense of humour, supported by an inexhaustible supply of the tallest stories, which were invariably outrageous and scurrilous. He liked to insinuate that he had an informant in every bordello, fetish club and bondage dungeon of note. He would frequently regale Fenwick with the alleged peccadillos and exotic practices of society's great and good, all recounted in vivid and lurid detail with a knowing twinkle in his eye. For a lawyer, Geoffrey was surprisingly nonchalant about the threats of libel suits and litigation.

For all his jocularity and abject silliness — and part of the fun was that Geoffrey knew many of his stories were utter nonsense — Fenwick respected the man immensely. In addition to a long and distinguished legal career, Geoffrey had shown great commitment to several causes — most notably the horribly debilitating condition spina bifida, which had afflicted his daughter Charlotte.

Fenwick, not himself an academic achiever of any note, revered Geoffrey's erudition. A graduate of history at Balliol, Oxford, Geoffrey had written many monographs, with his scholarly essays published in respected journals, and was an authority on the Plantagenet kings, and Richard II in particular.

Geoffrey was 'on the square' — a Freemason. For a member of a secret society, he was remarkably indiscreet, captivating allcomers with his gaudy descriptions of the various initiation ceremonies and elaborate paraphernalia. He took delight in the absurdity of it all, gathering tittle tattle from the various lodges as a bee collects pollen. Geoffrey had once enquired whether Fenwick might like to handle his 'Masonic trowel'. Fenwick had roared with laughter at the innuendo, marvelling that such an instrument might even exist.

Fenwick now sat with Geoffrey, partaking of an obligatory glass of dry Amontillado sherry. A portly figure, Geoffrey enjoyed his food and drink a little too much, as he himself readily admitted. The broken red veins on his flushed cheeks and nose — as spindly and fine as cobwebs — spoke to a life well lived.

Through his thick spectacles, Geoffrey observed Fenwick's bruised and swollen eye, which still flared grossly and unmissably. 'You've been in the wars, Charles.'

'I would claim it as a rugby injury, but no,' replied Fenwick, hoping to deflect.

Geoffrey smiled. 'I'm a cricket man myself. Fielding — usually in a deckchair. That said, I'm soon destined for the stairlift to Saint Peter.'

This was news to Fenwick. 'You're ill?'

'High blood pressure, cholesterol off the scale, type-two diabetes and a wife with a platinum Harrods store card. Still, at least I don't have the big "C".'

Fenwick recalled from the distant past Geoffrey's description of Mrs H. 'She spends what I earn,' he'd said plaintively at the time.

Geoffrey now produced Fenwick's last will and testament, printed with various 'track changes' visible, in reds, blues and yellows. There was also a lasting power of attorney, which Fenwick had assigned to Lucia.

Fenwick noticed that Geoffrey's hand shook violently and uncontrollably as he placed the printouts before him.

'Parkinson's,' said Geoffrey. 'Degenerating rapidly. Keep that to yourself, Charles.'

Fenwick nodded. His discretion was assured.

'I've drawn up a lasting power of attorney and your two codicils to the will. Check it all carefully before signing.'

At that moment, the telephone on Henderson's desk rang.

'Excuse me, Charles,' he said, lifting the receiver. 'Henderson Galbraith. A provincial service at London prices.'

Fenwick smiled. The caller was evidently a good friend. Geoffrey winked at Fenwick, sharing the jest.

With Geoffrey chatting away inconsequentially, Fenwick scrutinised the documents prepared for him now splayed on the desk. He'd composed two codicils, simply worded but each bearing concise instructions, to be followed to the letter.

Ending his call, Geoffrey peered at Fenwick, the fingers of his clasped hands steepled. 'As ever with wills, the Devil's in the details.'

'Yes,' replied Fenwick. 'He very well may be.'

TWENTY-ONE

BARTS

Fenwick arrived early at Saint Bartholomew's Hospital, and he was now seated with his briefcase on a low cushioned podium in the foyer of the Department of Clinical Pharmacology. While he waited for his appointment, he checked his messages but was disappointed to see just a routine update of no consequence from Rachel: the decrypt was churning, but still without result.

A female clinician in a white lab coat appeared and greeted Fenwick, who then accompanied her down a spiral staircase and into the subterranean bowels of the department.

The nameplate on the door read: 'Professor Jairaj Anand — Senior Clinical Pharmacologist'. Anand, a forty-nine-year-old British-Indian man in a smart, double-breasted suit, was seated at his desk in a windowless office. Fenwick was surprised by how cramped it was. Bookshelves groaned with weighty tomes and clinical journals, and the desk was piled high with analytical printout. The office was a haven of organised chaos in which only the professor could navigate.

Anand now studied a printed email which Fenwick had sent him, appended with an anonymised summation of Tyler's autopsy findings.

Fenwick had contacted Anand in the hope he might volunteer his time and expertise. Experts in any field were often keen to talk on their given subject, it being an opportunity to showcase their knowledge and prowess. The professor was at the pinnacle of his chosen discipline, an authority on the clinical effects and toxicity of drugs, whether trialled, prescribed or illegal. Anand had provided crucial testimony in several high-profile cases where drugs or other substances had caused disability or death.

The professor at last raised his head and peered over the rim of his spectacles. 'You seek to contest a toxicology report?'

'Yes. I have a suspicion someone falsified a blood alcohol count. Is that possible?'

There was a brief silence as Anand considered the question. 'Near effortlessly,' he replied at last. 'If so minded, they could just add ethanol to the sample.'

Fenwick was shocked. Was it really that simple?

Anand explained: 'They'd need to keep the blood alcohol level within realistic parameters, but any toxicologist would know how to do that. As for errors, I believe there are broadly three possible causes. First, ambient heat tends to raise the blood alcohol count, so refrigeration is essential.

'Second, contamination could occur where the

stomach is ruptured and undigested alcohol leaks, perhaps into the chest cavity or elsewhere. If blood were sampled from a site contaminated in this way, the count would be elevated.'

'Understood,' said Fenwick. 'What about the third possibility?'

Anand shrugged. 'They could simply have taken the sample from the wrong body.'

Fenwick was stunned. 'The wrong body?'

Anand nodded.

'Surely they have safeguards to prevent such a profound mistake?'

'Yes, but they're not foolproof,' replied Anand. 'Continuity of evidence is crucial to prevent such mix-ups. The gold standard is to authenticate the samples using DNA, but that rarely happens. For all practical purposes, meticulous record keeping is obligatory.'

Fenwick thought immediately of the ID labels on Tyler's ankle and wrist, both showing '1-090124'.

'And the Xanax? Could that be a false reading?' he asked.

'I doubt it. The diagnostic printout is machine-generated, and the hardware and software would be difficult, if not impossible, to manipulate. There is a marginal risk of miscalibration, either by the manufacturer or in the laboratory. I'm not sure if a therapeutic quantity of raw Xanax could simply be added to the blood sample — I haven't studied the precise metabolism of the drug — but I think it unlikely.'

'If someone drank alcohol while on Xanax,' asked Fenwick, 'what effect might it have?'

Anand consulted a database. Reading from the monitor, he replied: 'Drowsiness, dizziness, imbalance, impaired reflexes, and lack of coordination.' Fenwick thought of the non-slip decking and the height of the ferry's safety rail. Even if Tyler suffered these effects, his fall overboard couldn't be explained by them.

'There are many variables,' added Anand. 'Xanax is a benzodiazepine. Alcohol is contraindicated; driving on the mixture would be utter recklessness.'

Recklessness — it didn't bode well.

Fenwick pondered, and then struck up. 'So, to appeal the findings?'

Anand replied: 'You'll need to obtain the DNA of the deceased to establish whether the sample tested came from the same body. Your best hope is that it didn't. But if the DNA matches... well, it'd be almost impossible to prove that anyone tampered with the sample, let alone the test apparatus. Unless the culprit confesses, of course.'

'Which they won't. So how do I...'

Anand interrupted Fenwick mid-sentence and rummaged through his desk drawer, retrieving a pamphlet entitled 'DNA: COLLATION AND PRESERVATION', which he passed across the desk.

'Check for hair roots from a comb, dried saliva or blood debris from a toothbrush, discarded skin flakes, bodily fluid from bed linen...'

Fenwick, envisioning the unsavoury direction of travel, held his hand aloft and smiled.

Anand fell silent with a knowing grin.

'To confirm,' asked Fenwick at last, 'a 175-millilitre

glass of wine would not, of itself, account for the stated level of intoxication?'

'A single glass? Almost certainly not. Given the subject's sex, weight and reported stomach content of a meal in digestion, I think it unlikely.'

Fenwick put the pamphlet in his briefcase and stood up, and the two men shook hands.

On reaching the door, Fenwick looked round at the professor. 'Just one more question. If a UK national dies overseas, is there any reason for the host jurisdiction to send an autopsy report to an unconnected third country? Under an EU protocol, perhaps?'

Anand peered at him, evidently thinking it a strange scenario and an even odder question. 'I'm a pharmacologist, not a pathologist… but no, I'm not aware of any such arrangement.'

It was the answer Fenwick had expected.

'Professor, thank you,' he said mutedly. 'You've been most helpful.'

TWENTY-TWO
UNIT 07

It was twilight on the M3 southbound. Desperate for a pee and a long-overdue pitstop, the driver signalled, left the motorway and eased his tanker along the designated lane to a hardstand in the HGV and lorry park at Fleet Services, Hampshire. Withdrawing the key and electronic fob from the ignition slots, he climbed from the cab and hastened to the service's hub, brightly lit and welcoming in the burgeoning dusk, a few hundred metres away.

Unhindered by the enveloping darkness, Xavier watched the driver's every move, viewing events with powerful illumination through the eyepiece of a Pulsar Lexion XQ38 infrared nightscope. In his rush, the driver had left the cab unlocked; this was strictly against the rules. Xavier presumed there was nothing of value inside. The HAZCHEM notices on the fuel bowser, in orange and flame red stencilling, showed: '*3YE 1203 — petroleum spirit — Highly flammable liquid and vapour, no smoking or naked light, switch off engine, mobile phone & radio.*'

The tanker was ideal: a six-wheeler of medium

dimensions and weight, with nine thousand litres of fuel — a shade under two thousand gallons.

The tanker driver, with his bladder relieved, now paid at the till.

A tenner? For a sandwich, a packet of Walker's crisps, a Coke and a Mars bar? Diabolical, he thought with a grimace.

He'd snatch a short break and then finish the run, a delivery of premium unleaded to two forecourts in Maidstone, Kent.

Ten minutes later, feeling suitably refreshed, the tanker driver inserted the ignition fob and the key, turning it. The engine rumbled and growled to life healthily, as if eager to depart. There was the customary hiss of the airbrakes as he released the handbrake and engaged the gears.

And then, from nowhere — BANG!

Nathan struck with the speed, accuracy and concentrated viciousness of a rattlesnake. In a split-second, he smashed a thick, translucent polythene bag over the driver's head, compressing it around the neck. As the driver flailed, Nathan tightened his grip, constricting the windpipe in a vicelike hold. With the man suffocating, Nathan hauled him bodily from the front seat, dragging him backwards and into the cab's rear sleeping quarters, where he and Xavier had lain in wait.

The driver's arms struck out, thrashing out violently, desperate to land a blow but striking aimlessly and hitting only thin air. In the rear compartment and fighting for his life, the driver felt Nathan's grip tighten around his neck, crushing his airway with thumbs pushed forcefully into his carotid arteries. Meanwhile, Xavier forced his full bodyweight on to the tanker driver's chest, pressing down mercilessly with both knees, compressing the sternum to breaking point.

Squeezed as if by anacondas, the driver's breath, rapid at first, now shallowed, and then ceased altogether. The heavy-duty polythene bag over his head, which had sucked in and out so noisily, quietened as his desperate gasps subsided. The bag, now opaque with carbon dioxide, was grey, moist and misty with the exhaled gas. The driver's body juddered in its death throes, its extremities twitching autonomically to a close.

Xavier checked his stopwatch: forty-seven seconds. He was pleased. It had been a quick and clean kill, with no blood or mess.

Xavier and Nathan climbed into the front seats and strapped themselves in. Xavier, with a claw hammer produced as if by routine, smashed the cab's tachometer and GPS tracking system to pieces, ensuring the chips within were severed from possible transmission.

Driving free — below the radar and undetectable — Xavier and Nathan headed for the A322, towards Guildford.

John Smith — an alias so ridiculous as to be incontestable — had leased Unit 06 on the Guildford industrial estate with a downpayment of four thousand pounds in cash. Smith had applied three selection criteria: the unit should be available for immediate occupation; it should have a large internal bay accessible from the road, sufficient for a six-wheel HGV; and crucially, it should be adjacent to, or nearby Unit 07.

Smith had then worked tirelessly in Unit 06 for three days, taking delivery of various supplies and equipment, soldering, welding, and testing his design to perfection.

He now waited in the darkness of the small administrative office, monitoring the unit's CCTV surveillance cameras. He was expecting a large consignment.

Rachel Chen, next door in Unit 07, had stayed very late. Fenwick's decrypt — which involved nine processing rigs and had been running for sixty-seven hours — was churning satisfactorily. The ZIP compressed files were scrambled with the powerful AES-256 encryption standard — the most secure algorithm publicly available while the Excel spreadsheets were protected by Microsoft's proprietary algorithm. Rachel thought the Excel files were the most likely to unravel. If a single file cracked, the remainder might follow suit using the same password — or so she hoped.

This evening, however, she'd focused her attention on an unrelated matter: cryptocurrency mining on behalf of an investment client, a hedge fund in Zurich. She'd allocated ten percent of the platform's processing resources to the exercise. She configured the cryptocurrency-specific processes shortly before midnight and executed them; the run commenced, reporting no errors.

Satisfied with her work, Rachel then checked on the platform itself, as was her habit before closing the office. The rigs, mounted in racks in bespoke housings at the rear of the unit, hummed loudly, like miniature jet engines. Rachel wore ear-defenders when in close proximity to the rigs for any length of time. The machines were cooled by high-powered fans and water-lined pipes and radiators, which absorbed and distributed the immense heat generated by the core processors. The risk of fire was always a concern. Each processor was mounted on cinder blocks, and the processing compound was fitted with smoke and carbon monoxide detectors and halon fire suppression. Rachel had set strict safety parameters, with the operating systems configured to send an SMS text alarm to her phone if her predefined performance restrictions — her 'speed limits' — were interrupted, or if temperatures rose unexpectedly.

She'd once tried to explain to Fenwick the architecture involved, but his eyes had glazed over. The only detail he'd understood was that graphic processing units accelerated the performance of each of her rigs to up to four hundred times that of a typical high-end PC. Or, as he'd put it: 'So, what you're telling me, Rachel, is that it all moves like shit off a hot shovel.'

Viewing the counters on the various monitors, Rachel calculated that the total number of hashes and password attempts now exceeded 627 billion on each processor, with a throughput for each file targeted of about 2.6 million attempts per second.

It was past midnight. Rachel, in her leathers, set the alarm, donned her gloves and helmet, and exited the building, striding towards her beloved Norton Commando motorbike.

As she left the compound via the retractable steel entrance gates, which remained open even at this late hour, Rachel couldn't help noticing the petrol tanker now turning into the industrial estate.

She thought its arrival on the scene, so late at night, quite odd.

With a shrug, she rode away.

Xavier contacted Smith on a walkie-talkie: he should bring the tanker in — the bay would be open.

With the press of a button, the unit's steel shutter awakened with a mechanical shudder and rose smoothly. Xavier aligned the tanker and, with Smith's guidance, drove it straight into the bay, careful to avoid a battered Hyundai parked outside the internal admin office. The air brakes hissed as the tanker shuddered to a halt.

Smith had been tasked with the demolition. He needed to ensure the unit's destruction, and his team's safe escape before it exploded.

He'd devised a simple method, using cylinders of propane gas, auto-ignition acetylene torches and three reliable twenty-four-hour mechanical segment timers — available at £14.99 for a pack of three from Argos. Pairing the timers with the auto-ignition mechanisms had proved problematic, but with ingenuity, and after some improvisation and adept soldering, he'd cracked the nut. The timers offered delays in fifteen-minute segments, and Smith had determined that forty-five minutes would be ample time for the team to flee the scene.

Xavier and Nathan now jammed the propane cylinders

tightly against the petrol tanker's outer skin. They aligned the acetylene torches four inches or so from the gas cylinders, secured in place by crude welded cradles that Smith had manufactured for the purpose.

Three gas cylinders with timed initiators — improvised time bombs — now nestled tightly under the belly of the tanker. Mains extension cords snaked across the bay from the timers to the mains power supply — to be plugged into the sockets, with the timers set and the power switched on only at the last minute.

Timers set, the team now cleared the scene, leaving no traces of Smith's occupancy of Unit 06 and, most importantly, purging the CCTV system of its recordings. Smith moved the Hyundai out to the forecourt.

At 5.20 am, the stage was set. Smith checked the three timers, each set to forty-five minutes. Satisfied, he signalled to Xavier and Nathan, who inserted the plugs into the mains sockets and flicked the switches on. The timer clocks instantly commenced their countdown.

Smith activated the roller shutter's mechanism, which started to close. He rolled adroitly beneath the ever-narrowing gap of the descending shutter out on to the forecourt. Strapped in, with kit stowed, they sped off into the night.

Next door in Unit 07, in the semi-luminescence of the processing compound, the rigs continued the decryption effort. The heat and noise of so many processors churning in parallel was immense.

The third processing rig of the nine had been set

to break one of the encrypted Excel files using a 'brute force' attack: all combinations of all available characters, in sequences of all lengths. The brute force attack was a blunt instrument most suitable when nothing about the password was known or presumed.

The output monitor of this rig — #3 — suddenly froze, and instantly flashed an alert on-screen:

```
SUCCESS! FILE DECRYPTED —
PASSWORD
— 'BSL4-KHARKIV~TRIAL_10-T9'
```

The explosion that now hit Units 06 and 07 was so powerful that the blast and its subsequent fireball could be seen and heard forty miles away; it even registered on national seismic monitoring. Pilots approaching Heathrow, 10,000 feet above, reported what they believed to be a missile strike or even an atomic bomb detonating.

The propane sub-ignitions obliterated the walls of Units 06 and 07 instantly, but it was the compressed fuel in the petrol tanker — exploding at 6,000 feet per second — which levelled the entire complex. The supersonic shockwave fractured and warped the building's supporting 'I' beams, causing the roof and upper floors to buckle and collapse; they now showered downwards in a murderous cascade of toxic debris.

Bricks, breeze blocks and concrete were pulverised, and cladding was shredded, the fragmented shards becoming lethal projectiles that tore through the air. Furniture, storage racks, cabinets, computers and equipment within the complex were all instantly dismembered, the pieces blasted outward concussively.

Several hundred metres from the epicentre, smaller components rained down in a deadly hailstorm. Two vehicles in the car park overturned. Others were pummelled, their steel bodywork battered and bruised, with windscreens and glass instantly shattering, rubber tyres igniting and aluminium hubcaps melting. Petrol tanks in some vehicles exploded, and descending embers soon ignited distant roofs and set trees and foliage on fire.

For miles around, a cacophony of car alarms screeched discordantly. The 999 public emergency system, inundated by hundreds of alarmed callers, was soon overwhelmed and paralysed. The local electricity substation failed also, causing a power outage that plunged entire streets and communities into darkness.

It was a scene of utter devastation. The entire complex had disintegrated, laid completely to waste.

Smith, Xavier and Nathan had surpassed even their own expectations.

Rachel, many miles away in the sanctuary of her bed, had sensed the deep bass rumble of the explosion even in her sleep.

Awake now and fretful, she was lucky to be alive.

TWENTY-THREE

ESTHER

The doorbell rang as Esther was on the phone to her mother. The babysitter had phoned in sick, or hungover more probably — could granny stand in?

'Mum, I'll have to go,' said Esther wearily. 'There's someone at the door.'

It was before eight in the morning. No-one was expected. Esther thought it must be some special delivery or package to be signed for. Wearing the uniform of many tired and busy young mums, she opened the door in a scruffy T-shirt and tracksuit bottoms. Her shoulder-length blonde hair was unwashed, knotted and tousled, and her daughter Caitlin, quiet with a dummy, nestled in the crook of her arm.

Fenwick, in suit and tie, stood on Esther's doorstep, holding his battered black briefcase and clutching a white plastic shopping bag with what looked like a small box within.

Esther was annoyed by this unannounced appearance. Why the hell hadn't he called in advance? And at this ungodly hour, too.

'Look, Caitlin,' she said resignedly, 'the Gruffalo!' Her nickname for Fenwick, apposite she thought, had stuck.

Witnessing mother and baby, Fenwick was momentarily taken aback. He was still adjusting to the new Esther, who was a far remove from the single, carefree, dynamic girl about town of old. Her new home, a semi-detached new build in a suburb of Bromley, was equally incongruous — the kind of place the Esther of yore would have considered intolerably dreary and restrictive, but was now obligatory for a newly married couple with a small child.

He'd first met Esther when she was working as an intelligence analyst with Kroll Associates, the elite corporate investigations and security consultancy. An expert practitioner in open-source intelligence (OSINT), she'd since gone freelance, still assisting Kroll but also working for other clients.

It is reckoned that OSINT accounts for up to ninety percent of the information used by law enforcement and intelligence agencies. Publicly available information, universally accessible from printed archives — books, newspapers, journals and such — had since been supplemented by electronic data. The internet had revolutionised the process, and more recently, social media had extended the knowledge base near exponentially, forming a whole new intelligence sub-discipline known as social media intelligence, or SOCMINT. The analytical tools to reap and assess all this data were advancing rapidly also, with Artificial Intelligence representing a quantum leap in capability.

The skill was not only in finding the right information

— the proverbial needle in the haystack — but also in assessing its veracity, setting it in context, joining the dots to see the commonalities and connectivity between entities and events. Using the right tools was key — Google, for instance, indexed less than five percent of the internet. Consequently, there were vast undiscovered seams of information to be explored and extracted, but only with the right knowhow.

Fenwick knew that if the answer he sought was in cyberspace, Esther would surely find it.

'Well, don't just stand there, you buffoon,' she scoffed. 'Come in!'

Closing the front door behind him, he noted several packing cases in the hallway. The house was chaotic — Esther, Caitlin and Mike her husband had only recently moved in. Fenwick now felt abashed at his sudden intrusion.

Esther had worked with Fenwick on several complex matters over the years and was very fond of him, teasing him at every opportunity, as women often do when they like a man. An Essex girl and proud of it, she had a ribald and earthy sense of humour, which Fenwick much appreciated.

She couldn't help but notice his black eye, yellow and healing at long last, as was the stitched upper lip.

'Whose wife is it this time?' she enquired jokingly, for Esther knew that Fenwick was a most unlikely candidate for an affair.

She yawned deeply, clearly exhausted. 'Sorry. Bloody car alarms throughout the night. Some of them went on for hours.'

'Sorry to hear that,' said Fenwick. 'I was attacked.'

Esther gasped. 'Who? Why?'

'That's what you're going to find out.'

'Christ! That's heavy. They won't bash down my door, will they?'

Fenwick gave Esther a stern look. 'We all need to be very careful. I'm deadly serious.' He produced a scrap of paper from his jacket pocket and handed it to her. 'My best and only leads.'

Esther skim-read the scant information, hastily scrawled with pencil in Fenwick's spidery hand. 'Nephilim Trust... Danusia Ziętek... Saurian Group,' she read aloud. 'Well, it's a start, I suppose,' she remarked wearily.

'Pull up the floorboards, Esther,' said Fenwick. 'The Saurian Group is located in Kraków; there's a ton of stuff on Google. I think Ziętek is Polish, too. I have an address but you'll need to confirm she's there. I suspect she's very ill, so she may be in a hospice possibly in Rome, I have the details.' Esther should exploit any and every resource, all the relevant databases, social media, Polish commercial archives, property and rental data. Funds were readily available, said Fenwick: for database subscriptions, software tools, subcontractors or other resources as indicated.

'I'll need a chart of the Saurian Group, its management and associates. Also, find out everything you can about a forensic accountant called Michael Tyler, recently deceased. There are some newspaper reports.'

He produced an A4 envelope from his briefcase. 'A copy of his passport, driving licence and some financials.'

'That's all,' said Esther, clearly unimpressed.

'Not quite,' replied Fenwick. 'I also need you to dig up everything you can about Tyler's relationship with a Sir Frederick Springer, chairman and CEO of the Winchcombe Group. It's unlikely you'll find anything — their dealings were discreet — but give it a go.'

Esther was happy to comply — she would enjoy the challenge and appreciated the fees, which would help immensely with the mortgage.

But there was a payback to be had.

'I need a favour in return,' she said archly. 'Look after Caitlin this morning. I have a dental appointment in town and my babysitter has called in sick.'

Fenwick groaned inwardly. There was much to be done, and a morning of babysitting did not appeal at all.

'I must be gone by one,' he said tersely.

Esther promised to be back very much sooner — by eleven, she promised.

As she skipped up the stairs to shower and dress, Fenwick intervened. He looked up the banister sternly. 'Before you go, an instruction,' he said. 'For your safety, you must adhere to it without exception. My phone was monitored round the clock and then stolen. I've tried repeatedly to deactivate it but all my attempts have failed, which means the number is being forcefully held active and continually intercepted.'

He dug into the plastic shopping bag and pulled out a smartly packaged box, hastily torn open. From within, he took a mobile phone.

'This is a factory-fresh burner,' he explained, holding the handset aloft. 'Exclusively for this issue and nothing else. I have one, too. I've programmed both with our numbers. Never, ever, contact me except on this mobile.'

Esther looked down at Fenwick in the hallway below. She perceived in him a trepidation and uncertainty she'd never previously witnessed. A frisson of fear now seized her, too.

'Understood,' she said solemnly, the warning heeded.

Esther reappeared in the kitchen, dressed in jeans, Reeboks, a blouse and puffer jacket. Her shoulder-length blonde hair was brushed and she had applied a subtle smattering of makeup also.

She turned to Caitlin, seated in a high chair.

'Mummy's going out, so you're going to spend the morning with the Gruffalo! Won't that be fun?'

Fenwick could help himself to anything in the fridge or freezer, and there were various tubs of baby-food also — a feed at about ten, she indicated. With a smile, she turned on her heel and left.

He fried two eggs with two rashers of bacon, washed down with orange juice and coffee. He now set to, with Caitlin's brunch — choosing a pot of carrot and coriander goo, which looked quite disgusting.

Caitlin sat in her high chair, facing a wall-mounted TV with volume muted. Fenwick tried to feed Caitlin but she resisted, determinedly turning from the teaspoon with mouth clamped shut.

'I know, Caitlin — it's yuk,' he said. 'I have the same problem, but with avocado.'

At least there was no tantrum. Just resolute non-compliance.

Looking Caitlin in the eye, he commenced a line of enquiry:

'You think the decrypt will fail,' he said contemplatively to the toddler, who gurgled incoherently. 'A randomised alphanumeric sequence via a password generator, you suspect.'

He tried more goo, but Caitlin was having none of it. Fearing a crying fit, Fenwick desisted, placing the pot to one side. Wiping snot and dribble from the little girl's nose, mouth and chin with a sheet of kitchen roll, he pressed on:

'And you also think my mobile was monitored by an intelligence agency... remotely and globally, in real-time, but not through a compromise of my handset. Direct cell-tower or satellite signals interception, you suspect. Hence, they knew my every move.'

GCHQ or NSA, thought Fenwick. But why?

Dispirited by his lacklustre efforts at feeding the tot, he resolved to ask her a final favour.

'Now, Caitlin, summon your Delphic powers,' he said quietly. 'What do you foresee?'

Suddenly, there was a bright fluorescent flash which lit the darker recesses of the kitchen. Caitlin squealed; her eyes now fixed on the television screen behind Fenwick. He turned to check the television also. It was a Sky News report, showing captured CCTV images of a huge night-time explosion — an industrial complex outside Guildford, according to the rolling yellow ticker tape at the bottom of the screen.

With the remote control, Fenwick adjusted the volume. A male news reporter, some distance from the industrial estate, was reporting from a road cordoned off with blue and white tape. His commentary was interspersed with helicopter footage showing the epicentre of the explosion and a circumference of destruction extending several hundred metres outward.

'The entire complex has been pulverised, everything reduced to charred rubble. It's a scene of utter devastation — as if a small nuclear bomb had gone off. A fire brigade investigation is ongoing into the cause of the blast, but Sky News understands that police suspect a fuel heist that went disastrously wrong. Tragically, the driver of the tanker is understood to have died in the explosion, but no other casualties are reported.'

Fenwick's blood froze. He knew the location — he'd visited Rachel at the industrial park on several occasions. He reached for his burner phone.

After an eternity, Rachel answered. Her safety was Fenwick's overriding concern and it was a huge relief to hear her voice. She'd clearly been crying and was now extremely angry. Fenwick knew better than to raise the issue of insurance. The financial loss was nothing compared to the investment in blood, sweat and tears — Rachel had dedicated thousands of hours of her life to designing, building and optimising the processors. The hardware and software costs were irrelevant — it was the knowhow, ingenuity and adaptive engineering that were priceless. Moreover, however sound were her backups and disaster recovery plan, she must have lost important client records and unique evidential exhibits, irretrievably.

Fenwick couldn't be sure it was sabotage, but if it was,

Rachel was now a prime target. He had some difficulty persuading her, but eventually she agreed to vacate her residential address temporarily, even if only for a few weeks. She promised to find a hotel and he guaranteed emergency funds, to be sent straight away.

'Forget the decrypt,' he said. 'Just get out of town now and disappear. I'll cover your relocation and all expenses. Do so immediately, I implore you. You've been a great help.'

By now, Rachel's anger had dissipated somewhat. 'What are you going to do?' she asked.

It was a good question.

Fenwick couldn't quit now. He was in their crosshairs and they wouldn't stop, so neither could he.

TWENTY-FOUR
CAT AND MOUSE

I t was time to return home. Like a submarine, Fenwick was about to submerge; but before doing so, he needed to gather some clothes, other essential bits and pieces and complete some unavoidable administrative tasks.

Acutely aware of the risk of physical pursuit while returning to his house, he'd scrupulously adhered to the rules of counter-surveillance: sudden changes in transportation and direction to avoid being followed. Jumping into and out of tube trains and buses and backtracking down pavements and alleyways. It had felt most unnatural, but he'd sustained the regime diligently since his return to London. Looking in every reflected window, and squatting abruptly as if to tie his shoelace, he'd detected no tail.

He lived in a three-storey Georgian town house on Chiswick Mall, a waterfront street on the north bank of the Thames. The house, purchased in the mid-noughties, was now worth a small fortune. Fenwick had paid for it with his contingency fee for financial and asset recoveries from a securities investment fraud originating on the Mumbai Stock Exchange. By means mostly fair but occasionally foul, Fenwick had broken the fraudsters' fiendish Hawala operation — a remittance channel outside the control or monitoring of traditional banking systems — which they had used to launder the stolen funds. After much legal kerfuffle, injunctions had been served and assets had been frozen in several jurisdictions, amounting to over \$438 million. Of these recoveries, Fenwick had negotiated a cool three percent.

For Fenwick, the domestic arrangements at Chiswick Mall were ideal. The lower ground was a 'grace and favour' occupancy, which Fenwick let at a seed-corn pittance to his housekeeper Evelyn Braybrook and her husband Duncan. Fenwick occupied the two upper stories. 'Mrs B' took charge of the cooking, cleaning and almost everything else, while Duncan dealt with maintenance and security, which encompassed a sophisticated CCTV system and a safe. It was a happy setup, secure when Fenwick was away, and companionable, with celebrations, festive meals and special occasions often joyfully shared.

Fenwick's ownership of the property was concealed by design. Chiswick Mall had been purchased using a front company, and he was at pains to keep his name out of public records. Utility bills and council tax were settled by a limited management company, and he was ex-directory and off the voter's roll. He knew he'd never be entirely untraceable, but he'd done his best to remain invisible. As a fundamental rule, observed at all times, Fenwick never cheated the tax authorities — there was no need to do so, nor any point in it. His front company filed yearly, on time and accurately, to the penny. Fenwick's concern was anonymity and nothing else.

On entering the study on the second floor, he now encountered Neville, who stretched out on his desk, languorously and evidently without a care in the world. The sun's heat was magnified significantly by the study's large window panes, and Neville was clearly in his element, luxuriating blissfully in the amplified warmth. Fenwick smiled, amused at Neville's impertinence; possession was nine tenths of the law, after all, and it would be most impolite to ask his friend to move.

With a hastily purchased replacement laptop attached to a docking station, Fenwick composed and printed a note for the Braybrooks: contact numbers for he and Lucia, Geoffrey's direct line at Henderson Galbraith, a bank account with access codes for the upkeep of Chiswick Mall, and some other instructions and directions. He would be gone, the note stated, for the foreseeable future.

In case management, Fenwick habitually devised a 'knowledge base': a matrix showing the incidents that had occurred, the people potentially involved, their access or knowledge, and a method to show linkage or any commonality between events and players. The murderers, and those who instructed them, remained in the shadows, but patterns and associations were now forming and clearly discernible. He tabulated a spreadsheet, to be updated as events unfolded, completing the entries known to date.

Neville remained unperturbed by the noise of the

clattering keyboard or of the printer as it whirred into action. He dozed throughout, oblivious, with just the occasional twitch.

Probably dreaming, thought Fenwick.

Eventually, the cat stretched with claws unsheathed, and yawned with sharp incisors bared, shaking his head from side to side vigorously, startling himself awake. He licked a paw and started to clean behind his left ear, circling it again and again with his spittle transferred from his rough pink tongue. The triangular ear, compressed with each insistent pass, repeatedly sprang back to form.

A short-haired tabby with large white paws and impressively long whiskers, Neville belonged to Evelyn and had the run of the house, appointed in the role of Chief Mouser, at which he was supremely proficient. Fenwick had often watched Neville in action, hugging the ground and stalking his prey, creeping incrementally ever closer, until the strike — so fast that the unwitting mouse, sparrow or chaffinch stood no chance. A natural born killer, then. Cunning and ruthless. Neville, admirably instinctive, was a handsome devil, too.

Tactics and strategy — subtle movements, silent, unpredictable and unseen. Like a game of chess — it always paid to be three or more moves ahead of the opposition.

At that moment, there was a discreet knock at the door; it was Evelyn.

'Neville!' she exclaimed, on seeing him now, repositioned and sprawled obstructively across the keyboard. 'Come on out of there this instant! You know you're not to disturb Mr Fenwick!'

'Leave him be, Mrs Braybrook,' said Fenwick without censure.

Neville, in his inimitable way, had been extremely helpful.

Stepping out on to Chiswick Mall, with his battered briefcase and tightly packed flight bag, Fenwick was a fugitive on the run, but he looked more like an itinerant salesman. He was going to ground. Weeks, or even months, of dismal hotel rooms and sofa beds beckoned uninvitingly. He had no idea when he would return to the house.

He was inextricably caught in the deadliest game of cat and mouse — and right now, he was the mouse.

TWENTY-FIVE
THE WINE LIBRARY

E sther exited at Tower Hill tube station and walked briskly, passing on her way the imposing battlements and revetments of the Tower of London to her left. She'd worked on Fenwick's project solidly for five days and now bore the fruits of her research, with a concise report in her shoulder bag and, most conspicuously, a grey cardboard tube, ungainly at three feet in length.

She didn't know the wine bar but found it quickly enough. Monday mornings were usually quiet, Fenwick had assured her, but if it was busy, they'd decamp elsewhere.

The Wine Library on Trinity Square had a discreet entrance down a flight of steps from street level. Fenwick had enjoyed several long lunches there, with fine wines recommended by the proprietor, variously accompanied by cheeses, charcuterie and pâté.

For Fenwick's purposes, the venue offered two other advantages. As a brick-built, subterranean cellar, it offered no street-view; and, just as importantly, the solid walls were resistant to drilling, concealment or any covert electronic installation. It was a convenient hidey-hole but timing was everything — the place would start to fill with customers from midday. Eleven on the dot, he'd told Esther.

They now found themselves alone, deep in the cellar's inner sanctum with a bottle of Côtes du Rhône, as recommended by Tom, the owner, who had then promptly departed on cue. Esther enjoyed a drink and held it well. Fenwick applied the same rule to drinking in cellars as he did to boozing on aeroplanes: any time was appropriate.

They had only an hour and there was no time for small talk, so Esther got straight to the point: 'Nephilim Trust. It's a "brass plate" administered in Grand Cayman, beneficiary unknown. The notary is a local attorney, an American expat called Hector Mendoza.' Esther suggested a pretext using a retired Customs Drugs Liaison Officer who knew the Caribbean like the back of his hand. The former DLO now lived in Barbados and had made a name for himself for elaborate sting operations against various trusts fronting for drug running cartels. There was another chap also — Oscar — based in Switzerland, who had infiltrated offshore financing and tax havens administered in Liechtenstein and Luxembourg. Might he be able to help?

Fenwick weighed the options. Elaborate pretexts and stings were prone to failure, depending as they did on people's greed or gullibility. Mendoza would not be gullible — he was the gate guardian and probably employed an entire army of security officers to screen every approach, whether electronically or in person. Nor would there be any hapless secretary or guileless novice employee to court and cajole into an act of treachery, or even a minor indiscretion. Nephilim would be secured against such 'social engineering' by a ring of steel — of that much, Fenwick was certain.

Mindful of 'Nephilim', and the non-existent opportunities it proffered, Esther and Fenwick drank a sardonic toast to the 'fallen angels'.

Esther opened her report at an appendix. It was the delegate list for a conference in London the previous November — the proceedings had cost £170 she informed him, slightly abashed. Ziętek had attended as a compliance officer of Saurian Group. Tyler had been there also, presenting on fraud investigation. The thumbnail photo of him in the proceedings was too small for identification purposes, thought Fenwick, abstractly.

Normally, this "nexus" — the association — would have been a stellar finding, but Fenwick was distinctly underwhelmed. Ungrateful bastard, thought Esther — he really could be an old curmudgeon at times.

Resolutely, she ploughed on. 'No evidence of any links between Tyler and Springer,' she said. 'Nothing. Zilch!'

Fenwick smiled. 'Never mind,' he said, resignedly. 'Keep digging. Anything on the Saurian Group?'

Esther, with thinly veiled pride, withdrew several tightly rolled sheets of pristine white paper from the cardboard tube. Before she could open the content, Fenwick gently but firmly clasped the roll shut, alert to security cameras in the cellar. Detecting none, he gestured for Esther to commence.

Unfurled, the sheets were enormous, nearly three feet

by four — the rarely encountered 'A0' beloved by architects and graphic designers.

The first chart, which Fenwick now held close to his chest, was one of four instalments which, when combined, displayed the totality of the Saurian Group. Spread before him was a vast and complex web of companies, subsidiaries, trusts and associated enterprises, all shown with their directors and company secretaries where publicly disclosed.

Esther had clearly burned the midnight oil. Fenwick marvelled at her representation of Saurian, its global reach now so explicitly and exquisitely depicted. Hundreds of tiny icons crowded each page, revealing the expanse of the structure, its people, its known assets and the links between them.

Esther was a master at visualisation. Fenwick thought her striking and beautiful charts akin to works of art, to be framed and displayed — perhaps at the Tate Modern — in an exhibition dedicated to modern villainy.

But for all their aesthetic appeal, the charts quantified a seeming imponderable, veering perilously close to information overload. Sucked into such a morass, for all of its delineation and codifying, where to start? Other than the Saurian Group headquarters, which squatted inescapably at the centre of the spider's web, there was no other obvious focal point.

Sensing Fenwick's unease and studying his expression, suggestive of his unwrapping a pair of gaudy socks at Christmas, Esther interjected:

'I picked ten of the larger companies at random; the

submitted filings show them heavily resourced but all other published data shows them unviable. A back-of-a-fag-packet analysis, admittedly, and my professors at the LSE would be horrified, but these companies should have gone tits up several years ago. We're dealing here with some alternate channel of funding.'

Esther twirled the stem of her wine glass, deep in thought. 'In addition, the group isn't listed on any global index; it's beyond stock market regulation or investor scrutiny.'

Fenwick listened attentively and nodded, gratefully. Fraud? Or money laundering, he wondered.

At that moment, three punters — young men in dark suits with brown shoes and no ties — could be heard clattering down the street steps into the atrium, loud and exuberant on closing a deal, or jubilant at some sporting victory.

Fenwick rolled the charts tightly. Esther rotated them deftly into the confines of the tube.

The joking and laughing continued good-naturedly as the young men occupied seats near the exit, at a distance but within earshot. Esther and Fenwick eyed each other furtively, recognising this restriction now imposed on them. The place would soon be packed.

Esther still held an ace up her sleeve. As she refilled their glasses, she decided it was now time for a major revelation.

Casually, almost as if it were an afterthought, she said, 'There's a Saurian company that's not on my charts.'

Fenwick recognised Esther's 'tell', for she looked as

pleased with herself as Neville did when depositing a dead mouse at his feet.

'Do tell,' he said, leaning in, enthused and a little flirtatious.

With a theatrical flourish, Esther brandished a page from her report and held it directly in front of Fenwick's face. One entry, to which Esther now pointed with an immaculately manicured cherry red fingernail, had been underlined and highlighted in dayglo yellow.

It was a Polish company: *Polmilitask Sp z.o.o.*

'It's a shadow operation,' she explained breathlessly, 'beneath the organisational umbrella, with administrative HQ in Kraków. It's a shell company and there's been a concerted attempt to erase it from the records.' They had failed to scrub it from the 'Wayback machine', Esther exclaimed triumphantly.

Launched in 2001, the *Wayback Machine* enabled users to travel backwards in time to discover website content from the past, including defunct web pages and long-removed entries. By 2024, 860 billion web pages had been archived so. It was an investigative tool of incalculable value, and had featured also in several notable legal cases.

'You're a genius!' declared Fenwick, but his delight quickly gave way to doubt. 'How do you know Polmilitask is still active?'

'A woman's intuition!' Esther smirked. Then, earnestly: 'Polmilitask doesn't appear in the National Court Register, but the Wayback records prove it was incorporated and active. I doubt that it ever traded — at least, not in the commercial sense. Somebody has been weeding the archives. That takes time and effort… and access and influence.'

Fenwick and Esther drained the bottle of wine equitably between them.

'Was there any SIC?' he asked — a Standard Industry Classification.

'No,' she replied, 'the purpose, operation and activities of the company are a complete mystery. For all intents and purposes, Polmilitask is a "ghost ship".

'It's the first place I would look,' she said, raising her glass in celebration, and looking Fenwick sternly in the eye.

Martyn Stowell's shift in Cheltenham had almost ended. With three days' leave in store, he looked forward to an interactive multiplayer bonanza of *Call of Duty*, with deliveries of Domino's pizzas and unlimited Peroni on tap.

The target cluster — the pool of intercepted numbers and email addresses — had expanded considerably through the Scavenger cell's iterative analysis. In the past week, a residential landline telephone number in the affluent village of Forest Row, Sussex, had been added.

Stowell loaded the latest intercepts as 'SCAVENGER FLASH PIR-4/-9' and merrily released the package for onward transmission to the MI6 analysts in London.

He headed to the exit and the prospect of a long weekend.

Let battle commence!

TWENTY-SIX
GREEN LIGHT

A few years earlier, Fenwick had witnessed Springer berate a hapless junior employee, a young man who had entered his office distinctly dishevelled and unshaven. 'Smarten up, Davis!' Springer had barked. 'You look like you've dismounted an elephant having tried to shag it on the way down!'

SFS placed great store on personal presentation — particularly for male staff. Pressed shirts for all and no beards, bum-fluff or designer stubble. Nor Windsor knots, which he considered vulgar. Bow ties, rings, piercings, earrings, jewellery and tattoos were also forbidden for men, and even cufflinks were frowned upon — Springer thinking them effeminate.

Fenwick, on the run and living out of a suitcase, had scrubbed up as best he could for this meeting. He was 'suited and booted', with black single-breasted jacket and matching trousers, and a factory-fresh white shirt from M&S.

Montserrat knocked on Springer's door and peered in. 'Mr Fenwick is here, sir,' she said, coolly.

Beautiful but charmless, thought Fenwick, as

Montserrat cold-shouldered him on the way out, closing the door behind her.

Fenwick fleetingly observed the bright geosynchronous clock mounted on the wall; Madeira, London and Kraków were bathed in light, with the Far East and the Americas now shrouded in darkness. He'd always admired this striking and ingenious feature within Springer's spartan office; for the umpteenth time, he promised himself he'd equip his own study likewise.

The office was expansive but soulless in flat white, furnished with a few sizeable illustrated books on the great artists — Cezanne, Mondrian, Picasso — and some other coffee-table 'eye-candy', randomly selected.

Springer now pinned Fenwick across the desk with his inquisitive blue eyes. 'Your injuries are healing?'

'Yes,' replied Fenwick, whose eye and lip had almost fully recovered.

'Your computer man had a narrow escape,'

Fenwick just nodded in agreement without correcting Springer. Rachel had gone to ground, and her status and location remained strictly on a 'need to know' basis.

'No fuel heist, then?' Springer had evidently followed the television news reports, which parroted the official Surrey Police inquiry into the cause of the explosion.

'Absolutely not,' declared Fenwick. 'The tanker blast was targeted sabotage with murderous intent.'

Springer remained silent. Fenwick could sense that the cogs of his formidable mind were whirring.

After lengthy deliberation, Springer said curtly, 'We should take it all to the police. It's too dangerous to continue.'

'No, not now,' insisted Fenwick. 'It's all entirely circumstantial. We have no case yet: no suspects, no motive, no proof.'

Fenwick felt despondent as he realised how true this was. Despite all his efforts, and the input and the sacrifices of others, the investigation had made hardly any progress at all.

Springer gestured to a coffee pot and cups at the end of the desk. He reclined in his grand office chair, presumptuously awaiting service. Fenwick, unfazed by such entitlement, responded to the cue and poured the coffee into two cups of fine white porcelain.

Montserrat had activated the intercom 'trip switch' twenty minutes prior to the meeting. She now recorded the men's conversation, listening in simultaneously through earphones.

This meeting between SFS and Fenwick, scheduled by Montserrat herself, had been prioritised for coverage, with the afternoon's 'product' — the recording — to be submitted for immediate assessment at the earliest possible opportunity.

She listened to the disembodied voices in the office next door.

Springer now: '*The eavesdropping is very worrisome. I've ordered a groupwide sweep.*'

'*That's wise,*' said Fenwick flatly.

Montserrat made a mental note: to avoid detection, she'd have to deactivate the intercom 'trip', or even deinstall it altogether, however temporarily.

Springer eased forward and scrutinised Fenwick closely. 'So, Michael was murdered!'

Fenwick took a sip of his coffee. 'All I can say is that the man who fell from the ferry didn't tumble into the sea by accident. I'm still having some problems with identification.'

Springer cocked his head quizzically. 'I thought you'd confirmed Tyler's identity from the passport.'

'I did. But the passport photocopy was very poor, and I haven't been able to secure a passable likeness of the man from any other source.'

After a few moments, Fenwick continued: 'Sir Frederick, you knew Michael Tyler well and had extensive dealings with him. Can you remember any distinguishing physical features, either on the face or the body? Moles, scars, birthmarks, tattoos? Or some accidental or congenital deformity, perhaps?'

Springer looked nonplussed. His lip curled in distaste. No, he said. There was nothing odd or distinctive at all about the man. Nothing whatsoever.

Fenwick, silent now, nodded affably. He sensed Springer's unease and was keen to respect the natural ebb and flow of the conversation. There was an etiquette to observe in these discussions.

'As regards Tyler,' Springer struck up, at last, 'do we stand any chance of contesting the drink driving? Quite apart from the insurance payout, it's a terrible stigma for his widow to bear.'

Fenwick replied, 'Yes, there are several grounds to question the result. But if someone simply added ethanol to Tyler's sample, we've no way to prove it.'

'Then what can we do?'

'I can obtain Tyler's DNA. If it doesn't match the DNA in the sample tested, then the assay must have been taken from the wrong body.'

'Well, that will solve your identification issue most definitively, I should think,' said Springer, looking rather pleased with himself. 'Where will you get Tyler's DNA?'

'From his home. I need to speak to his widow in any case. I have her address from Tyler's driving licence and a landline from the hotel registration. She's ex-directory and off the electoral roll. Tyler valued his privacy, for good reason.'

'You've found her?'

'Yes, Montserrat has the details,' said Fenwick. 'The wife may be sitting on relevant documents, and I can hunt for DNA and Xanax at the house also.'

Springer stood and stretched his long, thin, wiry body. He'd forgotten about the Xanax.

Fenwick, observing the man silhouetted in profile, was quietly amused. He'd noticed that posh older men wore braces — never belts — and rolled their sleeves above their elbows with the crisp, bed-linen sharp folds of the ward matrons of old. Perhaps it was a nanny thing.

Springer looked desolately out of the large office suite windows down to the busy Knightsbridge high street below. 'I don't know. This whole DNA malarkey sounds like a long shot. Then again, if it's our only hope, we should give it a try.'

Fenwick, aware that Montserrat had imposed a timeframe of just one hour, now accelerated the pace. To further the investigation, he needed Springer's express permission to proceed.

'I also need to go to Poland,' he said, 'but only after I've seen Mrs Tyler.'

Springer raised an eyebrow. 'Poland?' This was news to him, evidently.

Montserrat now listened intently. Poland was the cue — this segment would be critical. The sound remained crystal clear in her earphones, with no ambient noise or interference. She made a note of the recording point:

Fenwick commenced at 41:07.

'*We pulled a woman's name and a company from the memory stick: Danusia Ziętek and Saurian Group. They're both based in Kraków. It's not much, but it's all I have. Well, apart from a Cayman outfit called Nephilim Trust, but we'll get nowhere with that. It's impenetrable.*'

Fenwick was taken aback now by Springer's indifference — the man seemed disinterested in this Polish angle, almost as if he had not registered it at all. Perhaps he was distracted by some other pressing matter, thought Fenwick.

Springer just shrugged his shoulders.

'Go wherever the evidence takes you,' he said, casually. 'Draw funds as you see fit. You can pretext as an executive at the Winchcombe Group. Send Montserrat your photo with an alias. I'll expedite the passport and Winchcombe ID.'

This was the all-important green light. Fenwick couldn't

proceed without a credible alias and documentation. SFS had the connections to pull such strings; the passport in particular would have been impossible without his say-so.

'Thank you,' he said quietly.

Montserrat's schedule for this meeting read '1400 / AOB / close'. She and Springer were punctilious. It was ten to two, and Fenwick had said as much as necessary. It was time to leave.

'Any other business?' asked Springer, reading the same schedule.

Fenwick shook his head and eased himself to his feet.

As Fenwick reached the door, Springer raised his voice. 'Oh, and Fenwick?'

He turned.

'Don't be pushy or insensitive when you approach Mrs Tyler. The poor woman must be going through hell. Your best bedside manner, please.'

TWENTY-SEVEN

THE WIDOW

I t was a heaving Saturday and parking spaces were limited. Susan Tyler eased her black Audi RS4 into an awkward and tight lot of the Sainsbury's superstore at East Grinstead and walked to the cafeteria terrace. Her close friend Celia remained secreted in the passenger seat as a remote observer, quietly thrilled and most intrigued to have been co-opted on such a mission.

The call had come out of the blue. A man, middle-aged by the sound of him, had requested this meeting, calling the Tyler home's only landline. Something about an insurance policy connected to her late husband. It initially had the feel of a nasty prank or a tabloid sting, but as the story unravelled, with the details laid bare, Susan surmised that the caller was both well informed and sincere.

Today, she would hear the full story, assessing the man eye to eye, with Celia under instruction to alert the staff in the superstore — and, if necessary, the police — should anything untoward happen. The women had their mobiles to hand, and a panic phrase they'd agreed in advance.

Fenwick and Mrs Tyler now sat at a bench table with

large cartons of coffee. She had chosen the venue sensibly, thought Fenwick, their conversation veiled by the din of children at play, teenagers and young families. There were plenty of people for her to run to, should things turn nasty.

A sensible, precautious woman then, and an attractive one, too, with tousled auburn hair, lightly bronzed skin and warm expressive and inquisitive brown eyes. Fenwick knew from Google that Susan was an acclaimed fashion buyer, born and raised in New York. Her tasselled chamois jacket, jeans and moccasins spoke to a Native American influence. Michael Tyler and she were strange bedfellows, thought Fenwick, who had never fathomed the mysteries of human attraction.

'Murdered?' exclaimed Susan in horror, causing a few heads to turn sharply.

Fenwick cringed at his clumsiness and awkwardly signalled to her, urging hush and restraint. 'I think it possible,' he murmured. 'In truth, I think it probable.'

Susan didn't know which was worse: her husband killing himself, or his being killed by someone else. She knew nothing at all about the life insurance policy of which the man now spoke.

What was his involvement anyway? Flaring now, she demanded proof of identity.

Fenwick proffered his driving licence. Susan glanced at it, more as a formal observance than as a genuine check.

'Michael was a trusted colleague of a client,' explained Fenwick. He could not disclose the identity, but an insurance settlement in her favour was his client's priority, as was a thorough investigation of her husband's death.

Susan remained unconvinced. 'Why aren't the police on the case?'

Absent any obvious indication of foul play, he explained, it was quick and convenient for the Portuguese police to close the file and move on.

Fenwick knew he now needed to venture onto sensitive ground. 'Forgive me, but did your husband have any health problems?'

Susan considered the question superfluous; the man surely knew all of this already. 'It's all in the post mortem report,' she said tersely. 'He had cardiac ischemia. A heart attack was not inconsistent.'

'Again, not wishing to pry, but his state of mind?'

Susan let out an impatient sigh. 'As I've told the coroner's office several times, Michael showed no signs of depression, anxiety or any mental health issue.'

'So, as far as you know, he wasn't taking Xanax? It's also called Alprazolam. It's for anxiety.'

'I know what Xanax is, Mr Fenwick,' she shot back. 'Michael never took any tranquilisers. Why do you ask?'

'According to a toxicology report, Xanax was present in Michael's blood. Might you search for evidence of it? Prescriptions, packaging, blister packs?'

Susan retrieved an Apple iPad tablet from her leather shoulder bag and started to make notes. Fenwick watched appreciatively — it was a good sign.

'This may sound silly,' he said bashfully, 'but it is quite important. Michael's missing index finger — do you remember the incident?'

Susan looked at Fenwick aghast. What possible

relevance could this have? Lost for words, she chuckled now, and her expression relaxed somewhat. Her natural charm and beauty now radiated.

'Jesus!' she exclaimed. 'The finger! Well, no, I wasn't there at the time,' she laughed. 'Michael never levelled with me on that one. The story changed on a daily basis. One day, it was a tiger shark, The next day it was a motorbike chain or a helicopter blade. Once, he even said he'd lost his finger in a wager. It was a running joke.'

'But it happened recently?' asked Fenwick solemnly.

'God, no! I married him fingerless, over thirteen years ago. As long as his other equipment was present and correct, it didn't bother me.'

Fenwick was warming to Mrs Tyler. He wished he'd met her in different circumstances. 'Michael's luggage has been returned?'

'Mostly… other than his laptop.'

'Did he own a wristwatch?'

'Several,' replied Susan, 'including this one.' On her left wrist, she wore the stylish Rolex GMT-Master. 'It was returned undamaged from Funchal. I also have Michael's wallet, with his cards and banknotes inside. All ruined, but still there.'

No theft or mugging, evidently, thought Fenwick.

'Did your husband have associates or business dealings in Poland?'

'Poland? No,' she replied. 'But he was working on something to do with Ukraine.'

'Ukraine?' Fenwick, covertly recording the conversation, was now on full alert — this was a significant new line of enquiry. 'Did he tell you anything about it?'

'No, nothing. There's a folder marked "Ukraine" but I didn't open it. Michael's files were strictly off limits. I never read them. Frankly, why would I?'

The folder was instantly a priority. Fenwick was relieved to see Susan make a note of it too. She looked up from the iPad, levelling with him. 'So, what do you need from me?' she asked, business-like.

'Anything that might yield Michael's DNA: a toothbrush, a comb with hairs, unwashed clothing. I've compiled a list with some guidance.'

Susan watched as Fenwick rummaged in his briefcase, a battered old warhorse by the look of it. She found the obvious wear and tear and its modest lines reassuring — reliable, old fashioned and devoid of ostentation.

Fenwick retrieved a typed crib-sheet and set it before her.

'DNA?' she asked, on seeing the document's heading.

'It's technical and complex, but essential. I needn't trouble you with the detailed forensics of it.'

Susan bridled; she found Fenwick's answer dismissive and patronising. She would test him now.

'When you called me yesterday, I thought you were another of Michael's cranks. They called him all the time, asking him to investigate their crackpot theories.'

Fenwick smiled wanly, a little taken aback. 'I'm certainly not one of them,' he said, slightly aggrieved.

'Actually, the jury's out,' she said coolly. 'I'm certain you're not telling me the whole truth.'

It was the insurance story that puzzled her most. Michael would certainly have advised her had such a policy existed. As for murder, the notion was preposterous. This man Fenwick was lying to her, but why?

With the facts exhausted, and the little evidence he could divulge less than persuasive, Fenwick was despondent.

He needed now some desperate appeal to the woman's core, but was at a loss. The harsh facts, which presaged only further carnage and mortal danger, would only drive her further away.

Telepathy, alone, might save the day.

'Will you help me?' he now urged, simply.

Surveying this man before her, Susan screened his very being. For all his undeniable guile and evasion, Susan sensed in him only benevolence and good will.

'I'm trusting entirely in my own intuition,' she answered at last, guardedly. 'But yes, I will help you. Meet me here on Tuesday, at the same time. I'll bring you what I can find, including Michael's Ukraine folder.'

Fenwick inwardly sighed with relief. If Ziętek was a key to the safe, then Susan had the code to its combination lock. Without her, he feared, the mystery would never unfold.

'Thank you, Mrs Tyler,' he said, humbly, with head bowed. 'This is extremely important — for you, but for others also.'

Scrutinising the man before her — rapt, stripped emotionally and baring his soul — Susan nodded.

'Yes,' she said, in muted recognition. 'I suspect it probably is.'

In London, intercept 'SCAVENGER FLASH PIR-7/-6' had caused a commotion. Fenwick, confirmed as the caller by voice recognition, had dialled Susan Tyler's landline from a BT-registered phone box at 20:43 GMT the previous evening. He'd telephoned to confirm her mobile number and the meeting scheduled for the following week. Inadvertently, Susan Tyler had mentioned 'Ukraine' during their conversation, which had tripped a 'CARNIVORE' key word monitoring module.

The Scavenger Team now convened in an urgent and secure online conference.

TWENTY-EIGHT
THE TUNNEL

Turning sharply from her driveway onto the road, Susan Tyler paid no heed to the fibreoptic cable installation team that had swarmed the area the previous Friday. They'd swiftly ripped up the tarmac in the road and then set to work with an eerie efficiency. The cable team now watched intently as Susan sped past. Oblivious to the foreman making a call in her rearview mirror, she signalled right at the junction and disappeared from view.

On the passenger seat beside her was a laundry bag containing Michael's unwashed clothing which had been returned from Funchal: pants and shirts mostly, as well as a toothbrush, a comb and some other bits and pieces. Nestled beside them was his sea-drenched wallet and the pale blue 'Ukraine' file from Michael's office, along with a thin stack of papers. Among them were some notes and grid references in her husband's hand that had caught Susan's eye, the strange scripts intriguing and mysterious. These jottings, which Susan had photographed, clearly related to the bible, incongruous and gaudy in red, that she had instantly spotted on her husband's office desk. Yellow Post-it notes were stuck to its pages at intervals, with letters and numbers within the body text circled in pencil and biro. A key, written in a neat and unfamiliar hand, was inscribed on the flyleaf of the bible. Michael, a godless and opinionated atheist, had clearly indulged in some scriptural puzzle play — Susan would do the same, time permitting. She had left the bible where she had found it, but would advise this man Fenwick of its discovery and obvious relevance.

Susan adored her Audi RS4, a thoroughbred that responded to her every command. She floored the accelerator, pushing the speedometer a good twenty miles per hour over the limit, easing off only for the speed cameras she knew too well. Her satnav chirped out precise alerts, guiding her through the familiar terrain.

A quick glance in the rearview mirror revealed a motorbike — a powerful-looking machine with two riders, their faces hidden by dark visors — trailing her by about fifty metres. Ahead, three hundred metres down the dual carriageway, a small, dark saloon car was weaving erratically between lanes.

The driver must be drunk, thought Susan, her mind already devising a strategy to bypass the wayward vehicle.

Suddenly, the motorbike surged forward. Susan's heart pounded as the bike materialised alongside her, its engine's guttural roar loud and menacing. Its rider moved with unsettling precision, the machine throttling aggressively, as if intent on collision. Susan's knuckles whitened on the wheel, her movements sharp and jerky as she struggled to maintain control. The motorbike backed off, then lunged again, closer and more insistently, like a predator toying with its prey. Panic surged through Susan as she swerved desperately, determined to avoid an impending crash, her breath quickening with every chaotic manoeuvre.

Both the Audi and the motorbike were now hurtling along at ninety miles per hour, rapidly closing on the gaping concrete maw of a railway tunnel. Susan's heart raced as she saw that she was on a collision course with the weaving saloon car ahead, which was now straddling the midline and blocking her path. Panic set in as the Audi was forced leftward, perilously in the direction of the concrete abutment of the tunnel entrance, which now loomed like a giant's mouth, ready to swallow her whole.

The motorbike accelerated again, tearing ahead of the Audi. The pillion rider suddenly turned rearward, balancing adeptly, and with both hands he levelled a military issue 'dazzler' at the Audi's windscreen and fired.

FLASH!

A blinding beam of white light, like sheet lightning, obliterated Susan's vision. Nathan had used the LED stun device on several missions. At 200,000 lumens — a sensory denial weapon as bright as the sun — it was a proven method to blind and disorientate a target.

The Audi fishtailed violently. Susan, responding, stamped hard on the brake pedal, the ABS juddering hard to slow the car. Overcompensating, she reflexively oversteered, clipping the unruly saloon at the tunnel's entrance with a loud bang. Glass shards and shattered

Perspex fragments tumbled and clattered far along the road. The two cars had connected for only a fraction of a second — a tangential blow, but of sufficient impact to force the Audi further off its track and initiate a chaotic zigzagging.

With her optic nerves overwhelmed and her retinas whited out, Susan didn't stand a chance. From the motorbike, Nathan targeted the Audi a second time, illuminating the windscreen once more.

FLASH!

Two hard taps on Xavier's shoulder from Nathan signalled 'mission accomplished'. With the Audi now irretrievably beyond control, Xavier gunned the motorbike and rocketed through the tunnel at maximum acceleration, fleeing the scene.

The Audi hit the abutment at a devastating sixty miles per hour, striking the concrete edge slightly off its midline, which caused the car to bounce and turn, spinning full circle before coming to rest facing the wrong way into the oncoming traffic lane of the eastbound carriageway. The Audi had decelerated from its closing speed to a shuddering standstill in less than three seconds.

The small, dark saloon car braked to avoid a secondary collision, then swerved past the wreckage and exited the tunnel, disappearing from sight.

The horn blared incessantly, like a banshee's wail. A thick pall of acrid smoke from scorched tyre rubber filled the air, and an oil slick from the smashed engine compartment spread slowly across the road. The Audi's crumple zone had disintegrated, having failed to dissipate the energy of the head-on collision, which concentrated the force of the impact at a single point at the front of the vehicle, unleashing a devastating shockwave throughout the chassis.

The airbag had activated and deflated — which, along with the seatbelt she still wore, had spared Susan from instant death. No external wounds were apparent, but she'd suffered an internal venous tear typical of such sudden deceleration. Hospitalisation would be critical; disoriented, temporarily blinded and utterly terrified, Susan required surgery. Time was of the essence.

From nowhere, a yellow-and-green chequered motorbike with emergency panniers and blue flashing lights now drew up alongside the wreck. With a sterile gloved hand, the paramedic reached in and expertly cut the electrical leads to the blaring horn, silencing it instantly.

Susan twitched and grimaced, hyperventilating, in fear and shock, blinded and in pain.

'Paramedic. The ambulance is on its way,' said the man reassuringly. 'I need to assess your injuries.'

'They tried to kill me… they nearly killed me!' she screamed.

'Stay calm,' he implored. 'Breathe deeply and slowly. Where does it hurt?'

'Ribs, chest…'

The man produced a catheter and a preloaded syringe, deftly locating a vein in Susan's forearm before injecting the contents. With the mix infused, he checked Susan's pulse and watched as her breathing slowed. It was a lethal concoction. The fentanyl would ease the pain, while the midazolam — at a dosage grossly exceeding therapeutic levels — would depress her breathing and ultimately stop it. Within the limits of detection, the drugs, he knew, would evade discovery by standard autopsy.

Shrouded by his helmet, with a bike bought at government auction and disguised with a false registration plate and call-sign, Smith watched the dual carriageway attentively. Seeing the motorbike's flashing blue lights, a few cars passed, slowing briefly to 'rubberneck', but soon accelerated away, their curiosity sated.

'Soon be comfy,' he intoned gently, waiting for Susan's pulse to stop.

Smith now rummaged through Susan's leather shoulder bag, retrieving a set of house keys and her mobile phone. The overriding priority was the blue folder and its contents, several pages of which had cascaded into the passenger footwell amid other scattered documents. Along with a wallet and a laundry bag, he gathered the material and locked it in the pannier of his bike.

Rechecking for a pulse, finding none, he removed the catheter.

Susan Tyler looked serene, as if sleeping.

Nice and clean, he thought, unclipping her seatbelt and letting it hang.

The bike's engine sparked and turned over with a high-pitched whirr and then roared throatily.

Smith rode off through the tunnel, disappearing as if never there.

TWENTY-NINE
DEEP CLEAN

Fenwick was no stranger to opulence — he'd worked for many wealthy clients over the years — but even he was awed by the Tyler residence, which struck him as one of the more grandiose homes he'd visited.

Perched on the outskirts of the affluent village of Forest Row, it was sprawled across two acres, boasting a large pond — practically a lake — beside the driveway. The mansion had a sixty-metre façade and gabled roofs with tall, narrow chimneys of variably coloured bricks, arranged decoratively in the mock-Tudor style. In an adjacent large garage, with doors open, Fenwick noted a red Jaguar E-Type and an Aston Martin.

Those cars fitted Tyler's self-projection as an action man, thought Fenwick, having parked his own hire car — a modest Avis Budget rental — several hundred metres away, out of sight.

With his trusty briefcase, Fenwick now rang the doorbell.

After a delay, longer than was excusable or explainable,

the door opened to reveal an astonishingly beautiful woman in her mid-thirties, svelte with model-like features, expressive brown eyes and a professionally styled and subtly tinted shoulder-length bob.

French, Fenwick surmised instantly.

'The Tyler residence?' he enquired.

'That's right. I'm Mrs Tyler's social secretary.'

Odd. Susan had never mentioned her.

'My name is Charles,' he said. 'I was supposed to meet Mrs Tyler this morning but she didn't show up. Is she in?'

'No, there's been an emergency.'

'Is she okay?' asked Fenwick, concerned. 'She didn't answer my calls or texts, so I came straight here.' Fenwick had called Susan repeatedly and had sent her several text messages — not with his burner phone, but using the replacement iPhone that he was running in parallel.

Yes, the woman assured him — a relative had taken ill.

'You are to examine Mr Tyler's belongings,' she said flatly, 'and some documents.'

Fenwick nodded, masking his thoughts. This woman had clearly read his text messages; Susan's phone had to be nearby.

'Please follow me,' she said, leading him across an expansive, marble-floored hallway. She opened pine double doors into a lavish living-room with a patio overlooking a vast, well-tended garden dotted with outbuildings, including what appeared to be a restored hostelry or a small tavern at the far end.

The woman then led him to a less grand door leading

to a small annexe. 'Mr Tyler's office. Copy what you need, but please leave the original documents where you find them.'

'Thank you,' replied Fenwick. 'One request: might I use the bathroom?'

'The bathroom?' A little thrown, she pointed to a magnificent winding flight of stairs, in the shadowy eaves of which Fenwick now noticed Tyler's Samsonite and his attaché case, both freshly adorned with adhesive customs declarations.

The bathroom cabinet was empty — no toiletries, not even a packet of sticking plasters or a bottle of cough mixture. The shower, bath, bidet, floor and surrounds were spotless, as if scrubbed and meticulously scoured. Fenwick flushed the unused lavatory, pleased that the noise resonated.

Returning downstairs, in Tyler's office he commenced his search.

A single steel filing cabinet had been crudely prised open, the dividers bare, their contents ransacked. The wooden desk drawer had likewise been forced, its flimsy brass lock smashed, with nothing within. An ancient and dilapidated desktop computer sat dormant, its antiquated SATA hard disk removed, with the connectors and wires hanging loose. Observing the skirting board, Fenwick noted that the phone cable socket for the WIFI network router had also been ripped violently from its housing.

Everything had been systematically sanitised and cleansed.

Fenwick realised he had stumbled into a deadly trap.

His heart pounded as he heard the woman speaking softly but urgently on a phone somewhere distant. Straining to listen, he caught a few words: *'He's here. I'll stall him. Bring silencers.'*

As stealthily as possible, he slid the sash window open, dropped his briefcase outside and contorted his body painfully, dropping awkwardly on to the patio. He moved swiftly across the ornate garden, heading for the tavern at its edge, hoping to hide there and plan his next move. He knew he had only minutes — the hit team would arrive any second now.

Approaching the building, Fenwick noticed a thick, viscous, repulsive cloud of flies — bluebottles, in a frenzied mist of feasting and egg laying. Looking closer, he saw an Irish red setter — a young dog, he thought — riddled with bullet holes, which appeared to be small calibre, fired at the animal's head and upper body. He recoiled in horror, fearing that his own fate would be far worse, with torture also.

With seconds to spare, Fenwick refined his plan. Behind the restored building was a tall wall, about ten feet high. Instinctively, he hurled his briefcase up and forward, and it descended in freefall, hitting the ground on the other side with an audible thud. Summoning all of his youthful cadet-force training, he charged at the wall, kicking it hard with his left foot, propelling himself upwards and hurling himself to its summit. With adrenaline and determination, he heaved himself over, falling without injury but most unceremoniously, straight into a compost heap that nestled in the neighbouring garden.

To the front of the mansion, the motorbike screeched to a halt. The helmeted and visored men dismounted immediately and commenced their manhunt. Giselle ushered Xavier through the hallway, while Nathan proceeded at pace to the rear garden via a side entrance. Both men wielded silenced handguns with laser sights at the ready, intent on hunting and killing their quarry.

Reeking of fear, sweat and now also rotting compost, Fenwick sprinted across the neighbouring lawn, a grand and formidable expanse that culminated with yet another high wall. Summoning all his energy, he threw his briefcase over it, scaled it and dropped heavily, winding himself and impacting a rib in the process.

Cowering behind a viburnum bush and wary now of unchained guard dogs, he shivered with fear. He needed to reach his car — time was running out.

Exhausted and dishevelled, Fenwick approached the hire car cautiously. He'd parked on a tree-lined avenue flanked by grand homes with expansive lawns stretching far back from the pavement. His heart raced as he scanned for his assailants, fearing pursuit and a possible pincer attack launched from each end of the street. Seeing the coast was clear, he slipped into the driver's seat.

At that moment, a klaxon blared and blue lights flashed. A paramedic, clad in a dayglo yellow hi-vis jacket, roared past on a green-and-yellow checkered motorbike, speeding towards the Tyler residence.

There but for the grace of God, thought Fenwick, as he shifted into gear and pulled sharply from the kerb.

Peter Hennessey, a former sergeant and seasoned combat veteran with 264 (SAS) Signal Squadron, knew better than to ask questions. The unexpected call was brief and direct. His mission was clear: go to Kraków, rent a modest apartment on a six-month lease, wire the place for covert audio and video with heat and movement sensors, test the installation for remote transmission, and then hasten home.

Peter didn't hesitate. He'd worked with Mr Fenwick several times — the man was discreet, knew the rules and paid on time, and his money was as good as anyone's. It was nice to be on the clock, too, and a generous advance payment of five thousand pounds had already been banked.

With the necessary equipment to hand, Peter loaded his SUV. There was no direct car ferry to Poland, but that didn't matter. He would set off in the early hours. With luck and a fair wind, he should be in Calais by mid-morning, driving into Kraków overnight.

THIRTY
THE BRIDGE

S
pringer was having lunch at the Guards Polo Club in Windsor Great Park, seated in the veranda of the clubhouse that overlooked the field of play. He was enjoying watching his son-in-law play the fifth chukka of eight, riding a gelding from his Tennessee stud: a muscular and feisty chestnut thoroughbred at fifteen hands, with a white blaze and fetlocks, named Heracles.

Just about to tuck in to a tartlet of duck liver, damson and pear, the call could not have been more inconvenient or less welcome. From a bloody landline as well... some salesman, perhaps?

Fenwick, dispensed with the pleasantries.

'Susan Tyler is dead,' he snarled. 'The local newswire has some detail of it this morning. A traffic accident, yesterday, at about midday. We were to meet but she didn't show. I went to her house but had to flee.'

Springer was shocked. He did not care for Fenwick's tone at all. He excused himself from his luncheon partners and headed to the exit.

Amidst horse boxes and Range Rovers, Springer paced, the gravity of the situation sinking in. 'This is neither the time nor the place for this discussion,' he snapped. 'Be at the bridge tomorrow,' he barked.

'At ten sharp.'

The blue bridge in St James's Park, termed 'the bridge of spies' amongst those in the know, had been Springer's venue of choice on previous occasions. With distant views of Buckingham Palace and Horse Guards Parade, the location, favoured by screenwriters and film directors, was convenient for parliament, government offices and Springer's beloved clubs. On a day such as this, overcast and cold, it was an ideal setting for a private conversation. Even at the peak of summer, crowded with tourists and passers-by, the chance of being overheard amidst the hubbub was slim.

Fenwick thought the rendezvous melodramatic; Springer revelled in such cloak-and-dagger theatrics. Both men now stood warily by the railing.

'God Almighty!' snarled Springer, agitated and fearful. 'It's a hornets' nest and we need to stop kicking it. They'll be after me next! We must call it off and leave it to the big boys: Scotland Yard and Six.'

The self-preservation society, thought Fenwick, ruefully.

'With respect, Sir...'

'Stop there!' interrupted Springer. 'Statements prefaced "with respect" are invariably insolent!'

'With the greatest respect...'

'That's worse. Go on, man, spit it out. What's on your mind?'

Fenwick was riled now, angered by Springer's insensitivity and evident lack of moral fibre. In a calm, measured tone that masked his rage, he replied: 'When you assigned me, you said you had a duty of care towards Tyler's widow.'

'I did, but there's not much I can do for her now she's dead.'

'Yes, there is,' snapped Fenwick. 'We can find out who killed her and her husband, and nail the bastards.'

Springer felt nothing but disdain for Fenwick's indignation. The man lacked detachment and bordered on insubordination. 'I dislike moral crusades. You've done your best, and in any event the insurance issue is now moot.'

Fenwick knew better than to push back — Springer would not stand for any unauthorised action and could cut him off at the knees with a single telephone call.

At an impasse, they stood momentarily in silence.

Springer, reflexively disliked confrontation and now sought rapport. 'I appreciate that you and others are suffering,' he said, quietly, now sympathetic. 'I also understand the need for closure.' He calculated a way forward. There could be no free-wheeling, however; he would need to keep Fenwick on a tight leash. Should Fenwick pursue the matter, strict conditions would apply. He was not to interfere with any ongoing police investigations, or stymie any covert efforts. Springer had already briefed Vauxhall.

Fenwick knew of Springer's MI6 connections and had assiduously avoided any entanglement with such people, distrustful of their integrity, and doubtful of their competence and methods. He resented their being informed of events, let alone any active involvement by them.

'Are my ID and passport ready?' Fenwick now asked, mutedly.

'You mean, are Charles Richardson's ID and passport ready? Yes, they are.' From his mohair overcoat, Springer produced a tightly packed envelope, which contained the passport, a Winchcombe Group platinum credit card, a block of Group business cards in the guise 'Charles Richardson, Global Strategy', and some other assorted 'confetti' to support Fenwick's cover story.

'Poland, then?' Springer asked, contemplating the next stage of the investigation.

Fenwick nodded.

'You've found this Ziętek woman?'

'I think so… I need to confirm the address.'

'Hmmm,' Springer snorted, somewhat dismissively. 'I'll arrange a meeting for "Mr Richardson" with the Saurian Group.'

A man called Jakub Schwartz was the CEO, he said. Springer had never met him.

Departing towards Queen Anne's Gate, Springer turned. 'I should like your assessment of Saurian,' he said. 'Schwartz interests me, as does his operation.'

The man — greying, bearded, of indeterminate nationality — sat in the windowless room. It was a SCIF — a secure compartmentalised information facility stripped of independently operated communications capability, in a bunker buried deep beneath Menwith Hill, North Yorkshire. Before him was Montserrat's distinctive lip-balm memory stick, one of several with which she'd been issued, now attached to a laptop computer.

'Poland,' said the bearded man over an ultra-secure line, reading from Montserrat's submitted content on screen. 'He's using an assumed name: Charles Richardson. I'll forward the passport details.'

There was a pause as his correspondent asked questions.

'Yes,' replied the man. 'Danusia Ziętek. She's somewhere in Kraków.'

Springer's PA had confirmed the fact. Springer evidently didn't suspect Montserrat, but Fenwick almost certainly did, having notably withheld Ziętek's address in his emails to her.

'We'll need to shadow him,' advised the man.

THIRTY-ONE
TEETHING PAIN

The early hours had been horrendous. Caitlin woke at around four, screaming from her cot with teething pain — a persistent, high-pitched squeal that Esther feared would awaken the neighbours. She'd given her daughter a dose of Calpol the previous evening, but now a fresh milk tooth was searing through the gumline. As with animals, there was no way to explain the root cause or transitory nature of pain to a baby or toddler.

Esther considered an overdose — but for Caitlin or herself?

Needless to say, her husband Mike was away, at some godforsaken installation up north, nowhere to be seen. Exhausted from yet another sleepless night, feeling soiled and squalid in a dirty onesie, and desperate for even a few hours' sleep, Esther had rarely felt so deserted or alone.

A warm drink might comfort and distract Caitlin, but against the background of the child's shrieking, the milk on the hob was now boiling beyond control. Esther snatched the pan away, but she was out of time. The boiling milk cascaded over the hob and spilled messily on to the kitchen floor.

'Caitlin, for God's sake, give me a break, will you?' she shouted, near breaking point.

There was a loud 'ping' from her laptop; it was an incoming email she'd been expecting, which she now read quickly. Realising its urgency, she instinctively reached for her mobile, pressing the speed dial for Fenwick's number, which went straight to voicemail.

Tired and stressed, she spoke hurriedly: 'Ziętek's address is confirmed. She's there, spotted at the apartment this afternoon.'

Dismayed by the messy floor, Esther exhaled and ruffled her matted hair distractedly.

Regaining her composure, she looked at her phone and checked the last number she'd called; she realised straight away she'd transmitted her voicemail to Fenwick's previous number. Her eyes shot immediately across the kitchen to the secure burner phone she'd been instructed to use, which was still in its box.

'Shit!' she groaned mutedly, resigned to the silly mistake.

Should she confess this minor mishap to Fenwick? He would never hear her absent-minded voicemail, and need never even know of it.

She would resend the update securely, as instructed, but only after clearing up the mess once Caitlin was finally asleep.

THIRTY-TWO
KRAKÓW

Fenwick, wrapped in a red woollen rug provided by the café in winter, sat with a cafetière of freshly brewed coffee. He snuggled close to an outdoor heater. It was a sharp, frosty morning, and the sun had yet to make any impact.

Kraków's fourteenth-century market square, the second largest of its kind in Europe, showcased the magnificent Cloth Hall at its centre. Even at this early hour, the square bustled with vibrant movement and colour; there were florists' stalls, gift shops, beer gardens and horse-drawn carriages, which carried sightseers eager to explore the Old Town and the majestic Wawel Royal Castle, Poland's medieval and Renaissance seat of power.

The clock of Saint Mary's Basilica chimed ten. Right on time, a trumpet sounded mournfully from the taller tower of the church. Known as the '*Hejnał mariacki*', the plaintive tune abruptly cut off mid-stream, commemorating a trumpeter fatally shot through the throat while sounding the alarm of a Mongol attack on Kraków in 1241 AD. A sudden death, remembered on the hour, every hour.

The thought made Fenwick grimace; his own unwitting complicity in Susan Tyler's death nagged at him now.

He pondered Springer's latest directive, which insisted on timely written reports and updates, 'to itemise all intended actions and outcomes.' It was a bloody nuisance — time-consuming and frankly dangerous. The weakest ink outlived the strongest memory, and written records in the hands of third parties dangled like the sword of Damocles. However, Fenwick was in no position to disobey, so before flying to Poland, he'd delivered by hand his first such report to Springer. For Sir Frederick's eyes only, the single page was heavily self-censored and tactically seeded. Two can play at that game, thought Fenwick with a sardonic smile.

Pouring himself a third cup of coffee, he familiarised himself again with the controls on his replacement iPhone, deftly activating the ringtone and smiling briefly as its asinine tune played.

A loud and jovial wedding party was now assembling in the square, the women colourful in satins — red, yellow, gold, and blue — and the men in suits or tails with bright, fresh buttonholes. A gleaming white carriage appeared, drawn by two white ponies, quiescent in blinkers, with red-feathered plumes and nosebags. There was no sign yet of the bride or groom.

Another couple to the slaughter...

'Mr Fenwick?' said a young woman, startling him from his introspection.

It was Magdalena. She had come highly recommended by Esther. Described as a formidably bright graduate of the Sorbonne, Magdalena had somehow slithered into a niche between government service and the shady world of corporate intelligence. Esther had assured Fenwick that Magdalena was not only reliable — she was almost psychic.

Fenwick doubted it. On seeing her now, he thought she looked disconcertingly like Tank Girl, an anarchic cartoon character of old that he vaguely remembered.

Now seated, Magdalena asked: 'I'm to visit your informant alone?'

Fenwick smiled, amused at the thought of working with this punky elf. 'Yes. Miss Ziętek is more likely to be open with you than with a strange foreign man.'

Magdalena smiled faintly, scrutinising him. 'You don't seem strange to me, Mr Fenwick.' Observing the busy square, she continued: 'I'll tell you what is strange: that address you showed me for the company Polmilitask.'

Fenwick leaned in. 'Why? What's strange about it?'

'It's in a residential area — the elderly and retired gravitate there, and it's a bit run-down.'

Fenwick hadn't checked the location. He wondered whether Esther had supplied the right address. 'Hmm... That is weird. We'll check it out later, after you've spoken to Miss Ziętek.'

Magdalena stepped out of the lift on to the fifth floor of the tenement block, walking the corridor in search of apartment eight. She had prepared for various outcomes and was wearing a wire, in hope of a lengthy interview. Standing before the door, doing her utmost to appear sympathetic, approachable and relaxed, she rang the bell.

Danusia Ziętek was on the phone with a taxi company. She had a flight to Rome via Katowice that evening and wanted to ensure she reached the airport at least two hours before the flight. She instructed the company to send a people-carrier for her numerous suitcases and the wheelchair.

The doorbell buzzed a second time, more persistently. Confident her instructions were at last understood, Danusia ended the call. Irritated and alarmed by the unexpected visitor, she struggled to the door, exhausted by the effort of manoeuvring her heavy, unresponsive wheelchair. The osteoporosis was pushing her to the brink, her frame crumbling daily beneath her.

Danusia approached the door hesitantly. She'd lived in constant fear for months, dreading such a visit. She applied the brake and activated the hallway VDU, viewing the visitor on the screen at an angle, staying out of sight.

'Who are you? What do you want?' she rasped.

The voice was wheezy and gravelly, sounding much older to Magdalena than Danusia's forty-eight years.

'Miss Ziętek,' she said brightly, 'my name is Magdalena. I'm assisting with an insurance claim. Might we have a brief chat?'

'About what? I have nothing to say to you.'

'I understand you were in Madeira recently? Porto Santo?'

'I repeat, I have nothing to say.'

'Does the name Michael Tyler mean anything to you?'

Danusia shivered even at the mention of his name. This woman knew too much; she had to be an insider. There'd be accomplices, men with guns.

'Leave me alone,' she said, her voice haunted and tremulous. 'I'll call the police.'

Magdalena, losing hope, pleaded, 'Please, Miss Ziętek...'

Danusia was furious, both at this upstart intruder and at herself for now being trapped in this wretched rented apartment. 'Go away! Now!' she spat venomously.

The VDU monitor went blank.

THIRTY-THREE
RECCE

The taxi driver, unfamiliar with the neighbourhood, followed the satnav, dropping Fenwick and Magdalena at the end of a quiet street. They were far from the city, beyond its ring-road, with its busy traffic sounding as a distant, droning hum. The buildings were squat, prefabricated blocks — unremarkable dwellings designed solely for utility, typical of postwar communist brutalism.

Fenwick checked the address again. It was so incongruous, yet Esther was adamant: this was the right location.

As the taxi disappeared from view, Fenwick enquired: 'So, Ziętek?'

'I failed spectacularly,' replied Magdalena. 'She threatened to call the police. She was terrified when I mentioned Michael Tyler's name.'

Fenwick smiled. 'Good. That affirms their association. And if she won't talk to you, she most definitely won't speak to me.'

Magdalena's phone pinged — an inbound text message from her colleague Agnieszka, who had reserved a table at the *Cyrano de Bergerac*, an acclaimed basement bistro in Sławkowska Street. Through Springer's auspices, Fenwick, under the guise of Charles Richardson, had been invited to lunch with Jakub Schwartz and Saurian Group's senior executives. Agnieszka and her colleague Stephan would shadow the meeting from a table nearby, using directional microphones. Fenwick was impressed — Magdalena's people were clearly accustomed to the clandestine world and demonstrated initiative too.

'So, Polmilitask?' Fenwick queried, frowning. Was this really the right location?

Magdalena shrugged. 'Yes,' she replied, equally astonished, surveying the shabby surrounds and envisioning the net curtains twitching. 'It's the last place I'd expect to find a prestigious company headquarters.'

Magdalena had volunteered to walk by — if confronted, it had to be a Polish speaker. A young woman with a 'Gen Z' streetwear aesthetic, she was perfect for the job. She had even brought her skateboard and pads. Beneath her baggy dungarees was the full rig — concealed bodycams — wide-angle and directional, zeroed in at twenty metres and activated by switches in her oversized pockets.

'Okay,' said Fenwick. 'Find the exact address; there will be cameras, possibly hidden. Stay focused and remember every detail.'

None of it needed saying. Magdalena was a natural.

She glided down the street, hopping on and off her

skateboard, noting each house number as she passed. With surveillance, silence and stealth were not always the best approach. In this instance, noise and carefree bravado applied — clattering along on her skateboard, she deliberately caused it to fly ahead as an unguided missile, steering it in her every intended direction.

Polmilitask was listed unusually as a double plot. Magdalena approached the building with the same carefree spirit that marked her noisy progress along the rest of the street. It was a strikingly large bungalow, set far back from the street, in poorly maintained and wildly overgrown grounds of perhaps a fifth of a hectare. Even from a distance, she could see CCTV cameras and alarm boxes.

As she approached the bungalow, Magdalena appeared on one of several CCTV monitors, but the security guard within was too engrossed watching television to notice her.

She spotted a side alley leading far to the rear of the building. She deliberately misfired the skateboard, which shot off down the alley, freewheeling with a loud, satisfying clatter. She trotted after it, acutely aware of the wire mesh fencing and the dense foliage blocking her view.

Magdalena knew she'd have to draw blood. Pretending to trip, she fell to the ground, grazing her elbow. She staggered to her feet, concentrating on the slick of fresh blood oozing from the self-inflicted wound and carefully aligning her torso with the target. There were sufficient gaps in the wire and foliage to film the infrastructure concealed within. She flicked the switches in her pocket and the bodycams started firing rapidly, each at twelve frames per second.

Fenwick stood at a bus stop. He was starting to worry about Magdalena, who'd been gone for too long. He scanned the locality, longing for her reappearance.

A tap on his shoulder caused him to spin around, startled. 'Oh, it's you. Thank God. You're okay?' he asked, anxiously.

'Of course! Why wouldn't I be?' replied Magdalena cheerily.

'Hmm, nothing,' he mumbled. He noticed her grazed elbow, but she seemed fine. Flesh wounds always appeared worse than they were.

'So, tell me, what did you see?' he asked.

'I'll tell you what I *didn't* see,' replied Magdalena. 'There's no signage for Polmilitask — nothing at all to indicate the company's presence. Just a large, shabby bungalow at the front, covered in surveillance cameras and heavily alarmed. The grounds are wildly overgrown and out of control.' Deliberately, as camouflage she thought.

As Fenwick took mental notes, Magdalena continued: 'The backyard is really weird, there's a concrete slab bunker. I'm guessing it runs deep underground. It's festooned with satellite dishes and aerials. It's serious hardware, far beyond a radio ham or a hobbyist setup. It looks bespoke, professionally installed, capable of international transmission.' A critical communications hub, most likely military she assessed, all concealed by wire fencing and dense foliage.

'I have it all on film,' Magdalena declared, licking blood from her forearm and winking at Fenwick mischievously.

THIRTY-FOUR
CYRANO DE BERGERAC

The *Cyrano de Bergerac* bistro, a hidden gem, was tucked away in a back street of the Old Town. The dining area, located underground, was set in a seventeenth-century brick-built cellar with high, vaulted ceilings. Tapestries adorned the walls depicting scenes from the baroque and renaissance past — of hunts, jousts, coronations, balls and madrigals. The restaurant had a cosy, intimate grotto-like atmosphere, with candlelight adding a romantic touch. The cuisine had been described as the best French fare outside of France — classically prepared and served without undue fuss or fanfare.

That said, it was a strange venue for a business lunch, thought Fenwick.

He paid no attention to a couple seated nearby: two lovers rapt in intimacy, engrossed in each other. They were in place and on time, he noted. The proximity was about right also — their recording equipment should pick up a significant proportion of the meeting.

Jakub Schwartz, the head of the Saurian Group, greeted 'Mr Richardson' with warmth, cordially gesturing for his guest to sit and make himself comfortable.

A lean, bald, tanned man in his early sixties, Schwartz appeared deceptively youthful, affable and exuberant. He radiated confidence and power. Behind an academic countenance, accentuated by stylish steel framed spectacles, lay a boyish charm most evident when he talked of his passions, which encompassed all things at the extremes of technological innovation. His entourage — two men and a young woman, hung on his every word and gesture, the woman in particular was seized in almost hypnotic veneration. Fenwick recognised Schwartz's sharp intellect — the man held a Doctorate in biochemical engineering from the Max Planck Institute in Berlin — but detected in him also a latent fanaticism, which he was certain would soon surface.

Shwartz, with punctilious yet strongly accented English, introduced his team. Jozef Bako, the Chief of Staff, bespectacled and nerdy, was dressed casually in the manner of some 'tech' innovator, with a purple turtleneck and a pink cashmere sweater. Stanislaw Kamiński, 'without portfolio' and in his late thirties, was an altogether tougher proposition. Severe, in a tightly fitting suit and tie, he looked like an enforcer, ready to strong-arm the doubtful, and silence dissenters. The young woman, Jolanta, unnerved Fenwick the most. Her intense scrutiny, laser-like, felt as though she was dissecting his every tic and foible.

Kamiński, without deference or consultation, ordered the wine — a fine Riesling from Alsace.

Schwartz raised his glass in a toast, entreating a long and harmonious partnership. 'To our combined endeavours!'

'Welcome indeed, Mr Richardson!' he enthused. 'Sir Frederick has a reputation for opening doors,' he declared. 'We're delighted he has knocked on ours. We foresee many synergies with the Winchcombe Group.'

Schwartz gestured to Bako, who on cue produced a sleek brochure.

'The Saurian Group:' Bako indicated. 'Finance, pharmaceuticals, freight, transport, energy, aviation, manufacturing, software, and distribution.'

Fenwick reviewed the content, finding it a gross oversimplification compared to Esther's immaculate charts in London, which revealed an altogether more complex and obfuscated structure.

'Is that all?' he said, with gentle sarcasm.

Shwartz, evidently offended by such flippancy, looked him sternly in the eye. 'In addition to such conventional pursuits, Saurian and its subsidiaries are pioneers in the fields of nanotechnology, crypto-currency, sentient artificial intelligence, robotics, quantum mechanics, cyber-kinetics, bioengineering, gene editing and trans-humanism.'

'With a view,' Schwartz now added zealously, 'to attaining global autonomic singularity.'

Christ! thought Fenwick. What the hell did that mean?

'That's a very packed Christmas stocking,' he quipped, imagining such a smorgasbord. '"Global autonomic singularity" — good heavens!'

Shwartz, impassioned and in full flow, continued.

'The Singularity: the point in time at which machines become more intelligent than humans — superhuman — outperforming us, out-thinking us, and capable of self-replication and evolution.'

This was clearly a hobby horse, thought Fenwick, thinking the man more robotic, fanatical and ridiculous with his every pronouncement.

'A distinct life form, in reality.' Schwartz declared, buttering a sesame-seed roll fastidiously. 'The most important problems and decisions will be made by computers, not mankind.'

Schwartz was now in full flourish. 'Men and machines will merge. The best life forms will not co-exist. Instead, they will coalesce, combining in hybrid form. The Man Machine Interface, currently a boundary, will disappear.'

'But the rest of us?' Fenwick enquired.

'You Mr Richardson will adapt perfectly,' Schwartz laughed, his eyes twinkling. 'As for the rest of mankind, huge questions remain… which is a discussion for another day.'

Schwartz now caught the waiter's eye. A different wine this time, a Pouilly-Fumé to accompany the main course.

Fenwick braced himself for the next round.

'We're at the vanguard of the Fourth Industrial Revolution,' Schwartz continued, grandiosely. 'A well-oiled and immensely powerful machine. Of course, we have to fulfil our social, ethical and environmental responsibilities. But we also have regional influence; political clout, so to speak.'

'Clout', thought Fenwick, glancing at Kamiński, muscle-bound in his ill-fitting suit.

'So, if you need new laws or regulations to be introduced, you can make it happen?' Fenwick asked, leading, with studied indifference.

Bako took over, 'Not directly, no,' he answered in a whiny mid-Atlantic adenoidal twang, 'but we do use gentle persuasion to make sure our lawmakers see sense. Repeals and amendments are thus facilitated. Conversely, if we need old laws or rules to be abolished, we can massage them out of the system.'

Kamiński, surly and silent, interjected now, determined to impress his own message.

'We do the same thing to people... when necessary,' he said, flashing a smile, that was no smile at all.

Fenwick imagined Kamiński's 'massage' techniques, which were to be avoided at all costs, he was sure.

Such 'massaging' didn't subvert parliamentary democracy? Fenwick asked, with wide-eyed innocence.

'What a quaint notion, Mr Richardson!' Schwartz snorted, derisively. 'Democracy — *as we know* — goes to the highest bidder.'

An awkward silence followed. Fenwick focused on his wild boar tenderloin, savouring the dish and appreciating his choice. It was time to think and prepare. He checked the mobile phone in his pocket, sensing with his index finger the preset ringtone button, indicated by a rough sticker.

'Sir Frederick informed me that you have an interest in our JIT system. You understand Just-In-Time management,

Mr Richardson?' Schwartz looked at Fenwick, discerningly, with genuine enquiry.

'Not really,' Fenwick answered buoyantly. 'It's management, I suspect — *just in time.*'

Laughter now, from Schwartz and Bako, while Jolanta and Kamiński glowered. Fenwick knew better than to blather. He had acquainted himself with the process, but his knowledge was wafer thin.

'We will arrange some site visits for you, or more appropriately for one of your process engineers. Saurian has several plants — manufacturing, packaging and bottling — most of which are fully automated.'

With his free hand, Fenwick picked up Bako's brochure and studied it afresh.

'Reading this, there is something remiss,' he announced.

Schwartz, his mouth full of turbot, looked up, sharply. 'Remiss? I think not. It's all fully explained in the brochure.'

'No,' Fenwick assured him. Having studied the group chart in London, he noticed that an important company was missing.

'Missing?' Schwartz looked aghast, as if the cutlery of the table setting was out of alignment. Asperger's, thought Fenwick.

'Yes. Polmilitask,' he announced, casually.

With that bombshell, Fenwick now pressed the button. The ringtone sounded at full volume. Retrieving the phone from his pocket, he checked the display.

'Excuse me,' he said, 'I must take this.' He stood and headed towards the solid stone stairway to the street above.

There was a momentary silence, with furtive looks exchanged. With Fenwick absent, Schwartz discreetly consulted his team. The conversation, huddled and subdued, was entirely in Polish.

Adjacent, Agnieszka and Stephan stared longingly into each other's eyes, silent in their mutual adoration. In addition to the advanced rigs hidden in their bags, Agnieszka had now placed both a pen and a car key recorder discreetly on the table.

Schwartz turned to Jolanta.

'How the hell does he know about that?' he hissed.

'I've no idea. I totally erased it,' she murmured, clearly vexed.

Kamiński interjected. 'Well, you evidently didn't. What shall we say?'

Bako answered, 'The same thing we told the tax authorities… it was a feasibility study for the Polish military.'

'Assure me, please,' said Schwartz gravely, 'that the project, and T-9 in particular, are not compromised.'

Kamiński and Jolanta both nodded, affirmatively.

With calculated timing, Fenwick reappeared, commencing his descent down into the restaurant. Nodding politely, he retook his seat, burying his nose in the dessert menu.

Bako spoke at last. 'Polmilitask was a NATO financed study,' he stated, 'to support the Polish military with logistical support and infrastructure. Rapid deployment and so on. Nothing came of it and the project was closed.'

'It was so long ago, I'd completely forgotten about it,'

Schwartz declared. 'Frankly, I'm amazed you stumbled across it,' he said, forcing a smile.

Fenwick shrugged, diffidently. 'Winchcombe Group has an excellent research department,' he said, simply, thinking briefly of Esther and Caitlin.

Jolanta, aggrieved with this meddlesome interloper whom she had studied like a hawk, struck up now.

'We conducted some research on you also, Mr Richardson,' she said, with a heady mix of flirtation and menace. 'You have a surprisingly low profile within the Winchcombe Group; we found nothing about you online.'

Fenwick had prepared for this moment. There was minimal information to support the Richardson 'legend' — just the passport, and some business and payment cards, but no real depth to the cover.

'Good,' he answered, simply. 'Eminence Grise. The low profile is deliberate. As with the Saurian Group, Winchcombe has power and influence... but it is best preserved by avoiding unwelcome attention or exposure.'

Fenwick thought the answer rather good, but Jolanta, scenting blood, leaned in.

'We were surprised at such a low — *non-existent* — profile,' she purred. 'It's as if you were a ghost... or a "spook" perhaps?'

The silence now was deafening. Would she reel him into the catch net, or release him to swim away?

It was Schwartz who broke the silence — as though embarrassed at his employee's discourtesy.

'Forgive Jolanta's impudence, Mr Richardson!' he

insisted, with a light-hearted chuckle. 'You don't look at all like a spy!'

Fenwick also sought to lighten the mood.

'Well, as a good spy, it pays not to look like one!' he punned, summoning his quicksilver wit. 'In any case, what does a spy look like?'

Jolanta leaned in, as alluring and deadly as a siren.

'Oh, suave, dark, handsome,' she quipped, staring at him knowingly.

'Charmed, I'm sure!' he countered, self-effacingly, amused but fearful.

They all laughed, the simmering tension somewhat abated, each realising that this was neither the time nor the place for an inquisition, let alone an execution.

Fenwick, with Schwartz and his team, now stood awkwardly on the pavement outside the restaurant. The sky was overcast and a few raindrops fell, with distant black clouds threatening a downpour.

Apart from Jolanta's probing and Kamiński's glowering the lunch had been convivial, even jovial, but underpinned throughout by mutual suspicion and distrust. Talk of cooperation and joint ventures continued even now, but everyone involved sensed the inherent hollowness of the promises exchanged.

'Can we order you a taxi, Mr Richardson?' Schwartz asked.

'Thank you, no.' replied Fenwick. 'I'm enjoying my tram rides.'

He knew to avoid any cab, whether hailed or

summoned, as its driver would almost certainly disclose the location of his hotel.

'Very well,' said Schwartz, his ploy thwarted. 'Have a safe trip, Mr. Richardson,' he added, inwardly wishing him the very opposite. 'I look forward to our further discussions.'

Fenwick smiled, shook hands with each in turn and then walked towards the tram stop, turning at the junction.

Schwartz and his colleagues watched as the imposter disappeared out of earshot.

Schwartz turned to Kamiński. 'Ziętek?' he demanded.

Kamiński read a text message on his phone. 'Done!' he replied.

THIRTY-FIVE
BLUNT FORCE

F enwick rode the tram to the Novotel West, determined to retrieve his luggage and head straight for the airport. The tram was crowded but comforting in a gentle, antiquated way. Reassuringly mundane, too, filled with commuters going about their daily business.

Usually mindful of surveillance, Fenwick now drifted somewhat, lost in his thoughts, marvelling at the audacity and extent of Schwartz's vision, whilst also amused and aghast at its absurdity.

The blare of screeching sirens jolted him to reality. Emergency vehicles with flashing blue lights shattered the calm, speeding past in a convoy, with their sirens shrieking painfully in his ear. The tram shuddered to a halt, its driver braking abruptly. An ambulance, escorted by two police cars, raced across the tram tracks ahead, disappearing at an intersection.

At that moment, the burner phone in Fenwick's jacket pocket rang, inaudible amidst the clamour. On its thirteenth ring, alerted by the phone's vibration, Fenwick at last answered.

On viewing the transmitted footage, Peter Hennessey had dialled Fenwick immediately.

'Your rat trap has sprung,' said Peter, referring to the booby-trapped apartment on the outskirts of Kraków that Fenwick had instructed Peter to wire.

An old hand at this game, Peter had guessed straight away the purpose of the exercise — the apartment was a deliberate lure, designed to smoke out a leak or to unmask a double agent. He'd even installed the weakest lock he could find on the apartment's front door, readily pickable, to ease the way.

As ghostly shimmering apparitions, the intruders glowed brightly, their infrared signatures glaring within the room's darkened confines. Two men had broken into the apartment, their faces concealed by COVID masks and peaked caps. They were armed — handguns with long-barrelled suppressors.

Alerted so, Fenwick stepped from the tram. In an alleyway, he studied Peter's chilling footage on his burner phone. The 'rats' in his trap, he could tell, were professionals... and Danusia Ziętek, unequivocally, was their target.

Only three people had known the false address: he, Peter, and one other.

With heart pounding, Fenwick knew he had only minutes to spare. He ran towards a distant taxi rank; on reaching it, he jumped breathlessly into the rear passenger seat of the lead taxi.

Mehmet, his driver, considered Fenwick's urgent instruction to be a 'follow that car!' moment — quite the most invigorating instruction of the day's shift, and probably of his entire driving career. He powered his Skoda through the backstreets and rat-runs of Kraków, breaking countless laws, hustling through traffic lights and defying one-way streets.

Screeching to a halt with a satisfied grin, in the rear-view mirror Mehmet now looked his passenger in the eye. Fenwick, awash with cash, shoved several notes through to the driver's compartment. 'Shalom' and 'Inshallah' they exchanged, as Fenwick hastened out.

Running fast, Fenwick was immediately aware that an upper floor of the immense high-rise building before him was Ziętek's apartment. On closing, he encountered a police cordon, taped off with two tall, surly officers. The young sergeant shrugged and gestured to a fifth-floor balcony, with police and detectives high above, already in attendance. 'A woman fell; that's all we know,' he said.

The paramedics and ambulance crews — whom Fenwick could see in the distance at the foot of the building — had fought like lions, desperate to resuscitate the victim, their kit strewn widely and chaotically. Having administered CPR determinedly and unrelentingly for more than thirty minutes, and with their stocks of noradrenaline completely exhausted, the young doctor in charge called a halt. There were no vital signs. The woman was dead.

Fenwick watched with contrition as the teams retrieved their equipment and walked forlornly to the ambulances.

The hapless body, sprawled lifeless on the ground, caused Fenwick to retch — not through revulsion, but from guilt; for he, most assuredly, was responsible for Danusia Ziętek's death.

The face in the washroom mirror was unrecognisable — gaunt, weary, pale and etched with stress lines. Fenwick now realised just how much weight he'd lost in the past weeks, possibly a stone or more. Events were taking a severe toll. His hands were trembling with fear. With horror, he realised he was in physical shock.

They — whoever 'they' were — had followed Magdalena to Ziętek's apartment. Both he and Magdalena had been under surveillance the entire time, and Ziętek's fate had been sealed the moment Magdalena had left the café in the square. Fenwick, with blood on his hands, felt sick to the core.

Preparing to go through the airport's security gate, he removed the wiring taped to his clammy chest, along with the miniature microphone and covert recording rig. Agnieszka had also transmitted four MP3 audio files to his phone. A section was in Polish, unintelligible to Fenwick, and of varying clarity. He briefly checked the integrity of her recordings through an earpiece.

He made the call from a payment-card landline within a discreet, partitioned bureau of the business lounge.

'The informant Danusia Ziętek is dead,' he said. 'A fall. Blunt force trauma. Whether pushed or jumped, I don't know. It's too dangerous for me to stay in Kraków. I'll return, but only when prepared. I'll need backup and your continued support.'

Springer hardly responded. He seemed stunned and in shock.

THIRTY-SIX
THE FARM

The morning was bitterly cold, with a relentless wind from the North Sea sweeping across the flatlands, causing the distant tall grass to ripple in shimmering grey waves. Large, menacing crows cawed murderously from the stripped branches of the trees that demarcated the fields.

Fenwick parked beside a tall hayloft, then stepped carefully between cowpats to avoid soiling his leather shoes, cursing himself for not packing his wellies. The farmyard was chaotic, filled with all manner of farm machinery.

A large Massey Ferguson tractor pulled up, and Peter climbed down from the towering cab. With a welcoming grin, he approached Fenwick and gave him a bone-crushing bear hug. 'Mr Fenwick! You made it! Bloody good to see you, sir! Takes me back. Happy days.'

Peter Hennessey, forty-nine, had shared several adventures with Fenwick, as well as a few narrow escapes. Many pints had been downed between them over the years in hostelries worldwide.

The two men now sat in the farmhouse at a large, sturdy kitchen table strewn with bits of tech and other kit, drinking builders' tea from outsized mugs.

A former special forces soldier and signals specialist, Peter could transmit anything to anyone, anywhere, with just a coat hanger and a clothes peg. By any metric, Peter was the right man to have on side.

He dwelled in the 'Twilight Zone' — a hybrid specialist occasionally summoned from retirement for necessary but deniable tasks. Fenwick never asked about these 'grey ops', thinking it prudent not to know, but he always listened with interest to any titbits Peter volunteered. Peter's current assignments he described as sporadic and mostly for private clients — counter-surveillance for the usual suspects — dodgy MPs with their rent boys, shag-around footballers, and druggy Z-listers from reality TV. There were some offensive operations as well, which Fenwick presumed had targeted Putin's Russia, but which were actually aimed at European diplomats and embassies in Paris, Strasbourg and Brussels, which made sense, post-Brexit.

Fenwick approved of the farm — it was quite a departure. Did it earn its keep? Barely, said Peter, but it was an excellent cover. 'Farmer Pete, horny-handed son of the soil,' he chortled. After a shady career of digging, planting, sowing, plotting and burying, the transition to agriculture had been apposite.

Peter produced a bottle of Captain Morgan and a couple of battered tin cups. Fenwick hesitated — he was driving — but then conceded. A toast was permissible.

'So, what's the target?' asked Peter.

'As with this farm, it's hidden in plain sight. A large bungalow with a drab and inconspicuous façade on a residential street in Poland. But there's something very nasty in the woodshed. It's heavily alarmed with cameras everywhere.'

Peter took a few moments, envisioning the scene. 'In that case, I won't be able to get you in or out.'

'Understood. What I need are clear photos — preferably videos — of arrivals and departures, and some capacity to follow them.'

Peter nodded. 'Surveillance ought to be feasible. Any chance of an OP?'

'None at all. All the overlooking buildings are occupied, and there's nowhere in the street to rent or squat.'

'In that case, our best option is a rigged vehicle on the road,' said Peter. 'A car, not a van. With Polish plates.'

Fenwick made a note. Then he said, 'There's an antennae farm in the backyard. It's a slab bunker with aerials and dishes. Any chance of an intercept?'

The transmissions would almost certainly be encrypted and unreadable, with the data streams compressed. Peter would undertake range and traffic analysis to determine the strength, likely coverage — or 'footprint' as he described it, and the frequency, duration and structure of the signals. 'It might provide a clue to the extent and purpose of the installation,' he said.

'Any difficulties with customs?' asked Fenwick, thinking of the exotic equipment necessary, and how best to transport it to Kraków without hindrance.

'The kit's not contraband. I always blag my way through,' said Peter with a grin. Fenwick didn't doubt it — Peter had more front than Selfridges.

'My client has muscle,' said Fenwick. 'We may be able to use the diplomatic bag.' On second thoughts, maybe not — the fewer government actors or civil servants involved, the better.

One thing was for sure: come what may, they should prepare for any and every eventuality.

'Best bring the kitchen sink,' said Fenwick, only half-joking.

Peter's pride and joy was a wartime Willys jeep in olive drab, adorned with white stars and US Army insignia. He kept it in pristine condition and now powered it down a rutted, muddy track, with Fenwick riding shotgun. With its four-wheel drive engaged, the jeep bounced athletically and powerfully as Peter ably manoeuvred past hazards and obstacles, heedless of floodwater, ditches and cattle grids. The jeep was open to the elements, and the coastal wind whipped harshly against the two men's skin.

Peter pulled up directly beside a ramshackle outhouse. It extruded shoddily from a reinforced concrete gun emplacement which had once guarded Sheerness, the Isle of Sheppey and the Thames Estuary from wartime invasion.

They now stood outside the outhouse's dilapidated door, its black paint peeling and sloughing off. The crumbling brickwork urgently needed re-pointing, and the structure was overgrown with lichen, weeds and wild brambles. Random graffiti added to the sense of abandonment and dereliction.

Fenwick watched, intrigued, as Peter pressed a key fob. To his utter astonishment, the entire shoddy façade disappeared from view, smoothly descending underground as a single unified module, powered by pneumatics or electric motors. Upon a second click of the fob, an armoured shutter slid open gracefully with a satisfying hiss. Fenwick was amazed by the ingenuity of the installation's concealment, marvelling at its finesse and engineering.

An alarm bleeped insistently, which Peter disarmed by entering a PIN.

'Welcome to Mission Control,' he said, summoning Fenwick inside. They crossed a gantry and stood on a small steel platform with a waist-high handrail, which began a controlled descent into the complex. The subterranean chamber was sizeable and brightly lit, immaculately presented and lined with state-of-the-art surveillance monitors, communications hardware and analytical processors. The complex featured a network of auxiliary chambers and heavily reinforced ammunition caissons, converted to workshops and offices.

'This must have cost an absolute fortune,' gasped Fenwick.

'A small business grant,' said Peter with a wink.

This was critical national infrastructure, government funded, and they both knew it. Fenwick thought the vault was almost certainly reinforced against a nuclear strike or an EMP attack.

Peter sat at a Linux workstation. 'The address?' he asked.

Fenwick handed him a slip of paper, which Peter converted rapidly to GPS coordinates.

'Right. Let's have a look,' he said, firing up the internet.

'All this wizardry, and you're using Google Maps?' exclaimed Fenwick.

'Hey, if it works, don't knock it,' Peter shot back. He trusted his virtual private network and was using an anonymised web browser — an 'onion ring' that weaved between global relays and IP addresses as traceless as Scotch mist. There'd be no record of the search.

'Take a look at this,' he said at last, zooming in on the aerial view of the bungalow in Kraków.

Fenwick peered at the large high-definition screen. The pixelation, which Peter now expanded, was most evident. The bungalow was in focus, but the slab bunker behind it had vanished, with no sign of the extensive array of dishes and aerials.

'I've read about this,' said Peter. 'There's been online chatter — conspiracy theories — about digital camouflage and "invisibility cloaks" to hide secret locations: Area 51, ghost operations, rendition "black sites." I've never seen any proof of it, but there's clearly interference here.'

Peter toggled to 'Street View'. 'Yes, it's the same at ground elevation. See the fuzzy edges?'

The bungalow was clearly shown in oblique elevation, but the infrastructure to its rear was obscured, imperceptible in a haze of pixelation.

Peter turned to Fenwick. 'If we weren't looking for it, we'd never have seen it. As you said, Mr Fenwick, they're hiding in plain sight.'

THIRTY-SEVEN
THE LAMB

The man in the shadows watched attentively as Fenwick turned from the pavement and walked into the darkened confines of *The Lamb*, a small Victorian pub in Bloomsbury. The man noted that Fenwick appeared slighter and more world-weary than when they'd first met at a reception at the Latvian embassy some six years previously. He would follow Fenwick inside presently, but only after a precautionary pause, to ensure no surveillance or undue attention.

The Lamb, with its period decor, antique furnishings and brass beer taps, enforced a no-music policy. On weekday afternoons the pub was a subdued, discreet and congenial backwater. Fenwick settled into a booth with a double Scotch and his battered briefcase. It was 3 pm and the pub was empty, except for a bored barmaid in her early twenties, engrossed in her smartphone and concealed from view by the bar's etched glass 'snob screens'.

The MP3 files which Agnieszka had forwarded to Fenwick were surprisingly clear, and Peter's audio specialist had further sharpened and clarified the definition, rendering more than ninety percent of the material interpretable. Fenwick had used an Olympus DS-9000 mini-recorder with headphones to review the output; it was now in his briefcase.

The saloon door creaked open with a high-pitched, unoiled squeak, closing behind the newcomer with a jarring bang. Alerted, Fenwick looked up, reacquainting himself with the man's features, which had faded from his memory. He'd forgotten how strikingly handsome Aleksy was, with chiselled features, sharp grey eyes and tousled shoulder-length hair. Of indeterminate age, but older than he appeared, Aleksy looked like a catalogue fashion model, dressed today in a classical leather jacket and black polo neck jumper.

According to his card, Aleksy was based in Portland Square, not the Polish Embassy but nearby, and he was a 'Counsellor', which was diplomatic speak for an undeclared intelligence officer.

Fenwick was indebted to Aleksy. A potentially very nasty situation in Bahrain a few years earlier had nearly ended in Fenwick's indefinite detention. Investigating a private banking collapse, he'd stepped on influential toes. Stuck in Manama, his passport confiscated, abandoned by the Foreign Office and facing imminent arrest, Fenwick had turned in desperation to Aleksy, who had facilitated his escape from the country, taking considerable risks and showing great tenacity and ingenuity in the process.

It was a debt Fenwick could never truly repay.

After a lengthy delay as a pint of Guinness was

poured, Aleksy now sat opposite Fenwick and raised his glass in greeting. He cut an imposing figure, shrewd and dispassionate. Fenwick discerned a ruthlessness in him also. Confiding in the man was a judgment call, the outcome uncertain.

'How's the plumbing?' asked Fenwick, referencing a long-running joke between them.

'I told you, I'm a cabinet maker,' replied Aleksy. 'Solid stuff, well connected,' he added, with a faint smile. 'So, why have you bought me this pint?'

Fenwick placed the mini-recorder on the table. 'I'd like you to translate and interpret something. I had assistance in Poland, but I left before we could review it.'

Aleksy eyed the mini-recorder. 'Yes, you had to leave in a hurry.'

'Perceptive of you,' replied Fenwick coolly, slightly perturbed by the remark.

He prepped the Olympus and handed it and the headphones to Aleksy. 'There's background noise,' he explained, 'but the conversation is audible. It was the only time during our meeting when my hosts spoke in Polish.'

Aleksy donned the headphones and pressed the 'play' button, while Fenwick took out his notebook. They sat in silence as Aleksy listened intently, his eyes closed in concentration.

'Hmm… the first man, senior — and aggressive — wonders "how the hell" a man knew about something. Two men, his subordinates, advise him. The unnamed man is *you*, presumably.'

Fenwick nodded as he wrote.

Aleksy rewound the recording and played it again, immersed.

'Yes, it's evident now,' he said at last. 'The older man doesn't know what to say, and the younger men advise him. The tax authorities… a feasibility study for the Polish military. The young woman — tonally she sounds in her late twenties — says they had "totally erased it". They admonish her.'

Alesky looked at Fenwick with a sardonic smile. 'Clearly she hadn't!'

He translated the next segment, speaking slowly for Fenwick to annotate precisely in his notebook.

'"*Assure — me, — please, — that — the — project, — and — T-9 — in — particular, — are — not — compromised.*"'

Agnieszka had already alerted Fenwick to 'T-9', which — whatever it denoted — was a crucial new hook, another inflection point. Lodging this snippet with Aleksy might just cleave the case open, fracturing its fault lines. Fenwick was playing the long game. 'T-9' was a useful lead for Aleksy, but inactionable at this stage. It was a calculated risk. With 'T-9' now etched indelibly in Aleksy's mental index, Fenwick was entirely dependent on the man's discretion, lest the matter might escalate beyond his control.

With the marker set, Fenwick picked up a beer mat from the table and tore it diagonally in two. He handed one half to Aleksy, placing the other in his briefcase.

'A keepsake for you,' Fenwick said, without explanation.

Aleksy grinned at this archaic fieldcraft.

'You're a very skilled cabinet maker,' Fenwick mused.

'I'm just a humble carpenter,' said Aleksy with a shrug of his shoulders.

As was Jesus, thought Fenwick, rising now and heading to the door.

THIRTY-EIGHT
THE BUNGALOW

The grey Nissan Micra was as good as invisible. It was a 1998 model, soon destined for the scrapheap. Peter had spotted the car on *otomolo.pl*, Poland's top used car website. Magdalena had negotiated a cash purchase, charming the seller, an elderly widower from Sułoszowa, north-west of Kraków. She assured him sweetly that she'd register the car immediately upon exchange.

Peter was an old hand with Q-cars: beaten-up bangers subtly modified with surveillance equipment and sometimes fitted with high-performance engines and powerful brakes for hot pursuits. Q-cars should be humdrum and unnoticeable but never derelict eyesores, which might attract neighbourhood complaints or be towed away as scrap by the authorities.

Peter had rented a workshop and toiled night and day to rig the cameras inside the Micra's headlamps and the engine compartment. He installed a wide-angle lens for general review, an adjustable telescopic zoom lens for panned coverage and close-ups, and an infrared night-sight, all capable of remote transmission. For good measure, he replicated the setup at the back, concealed in the car's boot and rear lights, which extended the options for stationing.

Magdalena and Agnieszka took turns, parking the Micra each day before dawn, ensuring unobstructed coverage of the Polmilitask headquarters. To avoid unwanted attention or detection, they never left the vehicle overnight, driving it away each evening after dusk.

Five blocks away, in the shaded corner of an abandoned industrial unit, Peter and Fenwick were stationed in a rented SUV with impenetrable tinted windows. They wore the nondescript uniform of urban surveillance: hooded tracksuits in dull greys and greens, and trainers. As instructed, Peter had packed the proverbial 'kitchen sink' — equipment for pursuit and surveillance in any and every situation.

Fenwick was online, speaking with Rachel Chen. Following the explosion, her insurers were quibbling and she was close to tears, not in self-pity but with anger and frustration. Fenwick, racked with guilt, owed Rachel. He also needed her back on the case, urgently.

Peter, in the driver's seat, kept a casual lookout on his laptop. The streamed footage from the street was uneventful, with just the occasional dog walker or passer-by. He opened a second tube of Polo mints. Having skipped breakfast, he thought longingly of succulent beefburgers and crisp French fries.

Frustrated at the lack of progress, he vented: 'Day four... and nothing!'

Fenwick looked up, taken aback. 'I disagree,' he said calmly. 'You've established the bandwidth and captured several burst transmissions. That's a result.'

Peter had intercepted a series of densely compressed messages, broadcast in split-second packages on an unusually low wavelength. The bungalow was communicating, but with whom, or about what, they had no idea.

It was late morning. Fenwick drowsed, half-asleep, when he was shaken abruptly by the shoulder.

'Stand by — we have a bite,' said Peter, bristling with anticipation.

The laptop showed a military truck — a Russian built GAZ Sadko, according to Peter — pulling up to the kerb.

Fenwick and Peter watched as two men — unkempt and casually dressed, probably in their thirties — got out of the truck and headed towards the bungalow, out of shot, loitering at its entrance.

'We're recording this?' asked Fenwick anxiously.

'Yes...' replied Peter, his eyes fixed on the laptop screen. 'Come on, you bastards,' he growled, awaiting the men's reappearance in the frame.

Within the headlamp of the Nissan Micra, the adjustable camera whirred mechanically, tracking and closing on the scene now unfolding.

Fenwick and Peter watched as the two men emerged from the bungalow and reappeared in view. Notably stooped, they carried a wooden crate, of medium size but evidently heavy, which they placed in the truck's cargo compartment. They repeated the process several times, taking more crates from the bungalow to the truck.

'Zoom in,' instructed Fenwick.

Peter adjusted the camera. 'Twelve-point-seven millimetre,' he murmured, viewing the stencilling on the crates. 'That's not flatpack from IKEA.'

12.7mm was 0.5-inch calibre ammunition for heavy machine guns. Peter recognised the packing and stencilling instantly. There was a lot of it, too. He backed up a few frames, viewing other crates, which indicated 7.62mm armour-piercing rounds to penetrate ballistic armour — suitable for Kalashnikovs and other assault rifles.

Ten crates were loaded — enough to start a small war, noted Fenwick, calculating five thousand rounds in total.

He turned to Peter. 'Are we good for fuel?'

'A full tank, and plenty of spare. We need to place a tracker, which won't be easy. If they see us in a wing mirror, we're done for.'

Peter searched hurriedly through a utility bag and retrieved a GPS tracking device. Fenwick watched silently as Peter, after some testing and configuration, activated the device on his laptop.

With the tracker functioning, he handed it to Fenwick. 'Shove it under the bumper or in the wheel arch. It's magnetic so keep your watch away from it.'

Fenwick unclasped his Swiss Army watch and placed it gingerly in the glovebox. He looked at the tracking device; it was the size of a matchbox and weighed less than three ounces. He marvelled that something so miniscule could track the lorry over thousands of miles. For all its wizardry and stated capability, he didn't fancy placing the tracker at all, fearing the most ferocious beating, even death, if rumbled in the process.

Suddenly, Peter froze — unsure of what he'd just witnessed. It had been a mere glimpse — almost subliminal — that could easily have failed to register. Fenwick looked equally bewildered as he and Peter exchanged glances. Peter rewound the footage.

The dash to the truck had been fleeting, deliberately rushed so as to escape notice. But here, caught on video, were two girls — very young — being ushered into the cabin.

'Christ! What the hell is this?' gasped Peter.

The girls were almost certainly minors, aged fifteen at most. Both slouched, they staggered as they were herded by the men towards the truck, shown less respect than farm animals. The girls seemed to be drugged, as if stupefied by a chemical cosh.

The ammunition was alarming enough, but the criminality Fenwick and Peter now witnessed was of a different magnitude.

'That's horrific,' said Peter. 'The younger one can't be more than thirteen.'

Fenwick had not suspected human trafficking, let alone the exploitation of teenagers and children. He wondered how many others might be beneath the bungalow; he suspected that it hid an extensive underground complex.

With the truck's tail ramp locked, the driver climbed into the cab and fired the ignition. With a dense cloud of black exhaust smoke, the truck set off.

THIRTY-NINE
THE CHASE

'Hang tight,' said Peter. 'Tricky, but I should be up to it.'
Fenwick had attempted vehicular surveillance only twice, losing his targets on both occasions within minutes. Tracking the lorry would normally have required a sizeable team in several vehicles, so Peter needed to summon his finest reflexes.

Travelling through the streets of Kraków, Peter hung back at a distance, three to four vehicles behind. He worked the SUV's gears and the brake and accelerator pedals with all his skill, jumping two lights in the process and aggressively nudging several cars out of their lane.

Seeing an intersection ahead, Peter spoke quickly: 'I'll place you in their blind spot. When I say "go", walk straight to the target. Place the tracker firmly. Walk calmly to the kerb and down a side street. Meet me at the same exit point once they've moved on.'

Fenwick's heart raced. As long as he kept out of view of the offside wing mirror, all should be fine. The magnetic tracker was slippery with perspiration. He mustn't drop it. Countdown: four... three... two... one...

At that moment the lights changed and the truck set off again.

'Fuck!' growled Peter, accelerating after the quarry at full throttle.

The elaborate dance between the vehicles continued for several more miles, through urban sprawl and out into the suburbs. Peter thought about the GPS tracker — it should last at least forty-eight hours on constant transmission, but a battery failure would kill the entire operation. To optimise power, he would change the setting to intermittent signalling at the next available opportunity, but right now he needed to concentrate on keeping the distant truck within view.

To Peter's relief, the target turned on to a motorway and headed towards the city of Tarnów. On the expressway, Peter weaved tactically between lanes and behind other road users for a distance of twenty or so miles, at which point, on the approach to a service station, the GAZ suddenly and unexpectedly signalled and took the right exit.

'Thank you, God!' exclaimed Peter. 'Bloody hell, this is perfect! I'm following him in. I'll park up out of sight.'

Peter parked away from the truck, nestling the SUV amongst dozens of other cars. They watched as the driver of the GAZ dismounted and started to fill the truck's low-slung fuel bowsers with diesel.

Peter snatched the tracker from Fenwick and grabbed a Michelin continental road map from the glovebox, which he slammed shut. 'Stay there,' he barked, jumping from the driver's seat and heading to the filling station.

Approaching the GAZ, Peter instinctively knew there was no opportunity to affix the tracker without being seen.

If not by stealth, then by guile.

Summoning his inner actor, he boldly walked to the cab and knocked loudly on the side window. The man in the passenger seat turned curiously, while the two girls beside him took no notice, staring blankly into the distance. When the passenger window opened, Peter thrust the road map under the man's nose and pointed assertively to a small town on the Michelin guide. 'Tarnowska?' he asked urgently. 'Tarnowska?'

The man shrugged, annoyed at this aggressive intrusion. He took the atlas grudgingly from Peter and studied it. The bloody idiot — some British jackass — couldn't even read a simple road map. The man pointed emphatically to the town, clearly marked on route 73, thirty kilometres north of Tarnów.

The exchange lasted less than thirty seconds, during which time Peter, with his left hand hidden, affixed the tracker firmly under the truck's offside mudguard, near the inner wheel-hub.

Fenwick watched from afar, amused and amazed at Peter's audacity, which reminded him of the magician and illusionist Derren Brown: '*Look into my eyes, look into my eyes...*'

Peter watched cautiously as the truck departed. Taking a long detour on foot, he returned to the SUV ten minutes later and climbed back into the driver's seat.

Confirming the GPS signal on his laptop, he turned to Fenwick.

'We may be in for a long haul,' he said, handing him an empty one-litre milk carton. 'We still have to piss into milk bottles. Be grateful — they're plastic and have screw-caps these days.'

The next thirty hours were amongst the most gruelling Fenwick had ever experienced. The military truck drove relentlessly along main roads and motorways, heading towards the Belarusian border — a distance of 800 kilometres. Fenwick wondered whether the truck would cross the border. With the war in Ukraine, strictures applied, and he checked his iPhone to see whether such a crossing was even permitted.

Fenwick and Peter took turns driving in three-hour shifts. The GPS tracker, broadcasting intermittently every three minutes, kept them close to the GAZ. Occasionally, the truck would stop in a layby, forcing them to park up after a forced exit at a junction. The hard shoulder of any motorway was not an option, with regular police patrols scouring, intent on interference and inspection. Boiled sweets and parmeńska ham bagels were their only sustenance, with no chance for deep or restful sleep.

Finally, around six o'clock the following morning, after a wearying overnight pursuit, the truck stopped. The GPS signal was stationary, some ten kilometres to the east. Peter turned the SUV off-road and bounced along a rutted track for about half a mile before coming to a dead end.

'Come on,' he said. It was time to dismount.

FORTY
THE FOREST

Fenwick shivered in the freezing morning air and peered into the great Białowieża Forest. Unsure why, he felt a sense of dread.

The backpack weighed as if filled with lead, as did the various pouches strapped to the webbing that bit cruelly into his chest. The two rigid, heavy-duty plastic cases he now lugged grew heavier with each step. Their contents were a mystery, but Peter had sternly warned him of the cargo's fragility.

'Handle like eggs,' he'd said solemnly.

The forest floor was a chaotic, treacherous landscape of fallen trees and boulders smothered by moss, lichen and thick, dense undergrowth. Peter, on point and burdened even more than Fenwick, hacked at the ferns, thorns, and brambles with a compact machete, carving a rudimentary path through the dense vegetation.

The Białowieża Forest was a sprawling, forsaken, prehistoric wilderness, untouched by man. Towering oak, hornbeam, ash, spruce, aspen and pine reached skyward, the dense canopy obliterating daylight, plunging the forest floor into a murky twilight, where only a few spectral shafts of sunlight dared to penetrate.

Every step through the forest felt like a battle for Fenwick, who had never encountered anything like this primeval woodland. It was timeless and eerie, the stuff of childhood fairytales — or nightmares. The forest's sounds were as sinister as its appearance. Unseen birds — as alien and fearsome as pterodactyls — high in the trees or wheeling above, let out bloodcurdling squawks and shrieks.

As they ventured deeper, Fenwick's senses prickled with unease. The feeling of being watched, a primitive instinct that had saved him before, gnawed insistently. He scanned the shadows intently for any hint of menace.

Flying ants and mosquitoes tormented them, biting exposed flesh, leaving itchy welts and painful bleeding protrusions.

They came to a river, shallow but fast flowing. To ford it, they would have to wade waist-deep — no easy task with such heavy equipment. Fenwick cursed as he lost his footing, nearly plunging fully into the water and drenching the precious equipment. He grabbed instantly for Peter's outstretched hand, whose firm grip saved him from a watery mishap.

'My fitness is not good,' said Fenwick, righting himself and gasping for breath.

'It's all in the mind,' replied Peter. 'Take a break. We're not far now.' He checked the GPS tracker. 'Two more miles. The truck's been stationary for several hours.'

'Two miles?' Fenwick chuntered. 'This stuff weighs a ton.'

'Welcome to my world, mate,' retorted Peter. 'Join the army — an entire career of hauling useless, back-breaking shit around the world like a bloody pack mule.' His tone was jocular but veiled an underlying irritation.

Peter had a point. It was a team effort and there was much to be done.

Fenwick forced a weak smile. 'Back-breaking, yes, but not useless, I hope. You should be in advertising Peter; you're a natural.'

Peter forged ahead. Fenwick, weary and aching, followed doggedly.

By early afternoon, Peter and Fenwick had trekked some ten kilometres through the forest. The GPS signal indicated that the truck was parked in a narrow lengthy clearing, stretching several hundred metres.

As the forest canopy thinned and the trees began to part, Peter instructed Fenwick to stay back while he moved forward to reconnoitre, checking fastidiously with each footfall for tripwires and ground sensors. He chose an observation point hidden by a dense cluster of beech saplings, further concealed in the shadows of taller spruce trees and pines. With a Praktica LRF-7 laser rangefinder, he observed not just the GAZ but several other trucks in the distance — mostly military, but also cranes, diggers and construction vehicles, along with jeeps and uniformed personnel. He activated the rangefinder's laser against the chassis of one of the vehicles, recording a distance of 312 metres — about a fifth of a mile, an ideal distance for mid-range surveillance.

Upon further scrutiny, Peter realised there was an aircraft landing strip, perhaps two thousand feet long — not a metalled or concrete slab surface, but one hastily installed with Marston mats, consisting of corrugated aluminium plates staked securely to the ground. There was also a sizeable bunker with no windows, with aerials and dishes, similar to the bungalow in Kraków.

None of this infrastructure appeared on the GPS tracker map.

FORTY-ONE
THE HIDE

enwick joined Peter in the 'hide', a shallow dugout behind the saplings and beneath the trees, further concealed by netting and foliage. On Peter's insistence, his face was streaked with greasy black-and-green warpaint. Spotter scopes, rangefinders and night sights, some stabilised by tripods, were wired into an array of minidiscs and data stores, ready to record at a moment's notice.

Through the HH35L multi-spectrum binoculars, Fenwick's view was crystal clear. Uniformed personnel assembled a series of crudely constructed human mannequins on wheeled dollies, which they configured in expanding circles from a central point, all based on a wide concrete apron away from the airstrip.

Fenwick observed as Peter pressed the 'record' buttons on various scopes and sights, causing miniature red lights to blink recurrently.

With the mannequins arranged in concentric circles, the personnel jogged away, disappearing behind a deeply embedded culvert.

'Any idea?' asked Fenwick.

'Not a clue... but now we've got them on candid camera.'

A solitary shrike dived steeply. In the distance, a buzzard hovered, searching for its prey. From the meadowland that encroached, pipits and skylarks sang a discordant symphony of high-pitched chirping and warbling.

The tranquillity was broken by the jittery motion of another mannequin, mounted on a chassis with caterpillar tracks, steered by remote control. It emerged unannounced from the culvert and moved erratically to the epicentre, eventually shuddering to a halt amidst the other dollies.

'Jesus wept!' growled Peter, as he focused his range finder. 'That thing's wearing a bomb vest!'

The explosive belt was unmistakable — twenty or thirty pounds of densely packed RDX. Fenwick pressed the camera button on the binoculars, taking several photographs, and then began video recording.

'They're going to detonate it,' said Peter. 'Stand by... any minute now.'

They crouched expectantly. Fenwick had never witnessed an explosion. He clasped his palms firmly over his ears, unsure whether to watch or to shield his eyes.

Suddenly, there was a blue electric flash, a sharp crack, and instantaneously, a supersonic white shockwave that vapourised everything in its path. A deep, reverberating boom followed milliseconds later, causing thousands of birds to flee the treeline, screeching skyward in total panic.

Fenwick, reeling but responsive, refocused the

binoculars. The test mannequins in the inner reaches had been blown to smithereens, eviscerated by the blast, torn to shreds by thousands of nails, nuts and bolts that had been packed tightly around the explosive core. Those on the outer perimeter were hideously twisted, deformed and in flames, charred and smouldering with acrid black smoke.

'God almighty!' gasped Fenwick.

The drone flew at twenty feet above the forest track, skirting the perimeter of the clearing with eerie precision. A quadcopter, the size of a large eagle, it weaved deftly between the trees.

Peter, ever vigilant, caught a fleeting glimpse of the drone hovering menacingly near the edge of the airfield. Its faint buzzing grew shriller by the second.

'Listen... do you hear?' he whispered.

Fenwick nodded, with eyes strained, peering into the distance.

'Fuck,' growled Peter. 'It's coming this way!'

With no time to waste, Peter rifled through his backpack. He hauled out two camouflaged thermal blankets, tossing one to Fenwick, frantically enshrouding himself in the other.

'Infrared sensors... heat seeking!' he barked. 'Cover yourself completely: hands, feet, head!'

The drone's approach was relentless. Hovering intermittently, it inched ever closer to the hideout.

Controlled by a handheld console with a touchscreen interface, its multi-spectral high-definition cameras and radiometric imaging now captured Fenwick and Peter beneath their feeble foil blankets — two distinct heat signatures, stark and unambiguous. The GPS coordinates were logged and relayed instantly, indicating a remote spot, north-west of the command post.

Now the drone hovered directly above the dugout, its four propellers whirring ominously. Stationed on point like an alerted bloodhound, it broadcast a stream of live video and telemetry, designating the illuminated targets as hostile.

Peter and Fenwick lay prostrate and petrified, their faces pressed desperately to the ground, the veins in their necks flushed and pumping, their pulses racing. Peter feared the drone might be armed with freefall grenades, which had been used to devastating effect in Ukraine, or with an explosive warhead, capable of inflicting instant decapitation.

At the airstrip's command post, the remote console lay in its cradle, the drone's urgent warnings unseen and unheeded. Its operator had more important matters on his mind. With the Polish football league on its winter break, he was watching Real Madrid play in Spain's La Liga, rapt with attention and hungry for goals.

The drone's onboard AI module performed rapid calculations, dictating its next move. The threat presented was clearly hostile, and the drone flexed responsively, preparing a lethal mission package. The whirr of the propellers grew louder as the drone edged closer still, until it hovered directly over Peter and Fenwick.

It presided commandingly, stable and focused, like a kestrel monitoring its prey. Neither man dared to look up, or break cover. If they bolted, they would be hunted down — by a swarm of these devilish things and by men also, on the ground with quad bikes, guns and dogs.

Any second now, Peter feared, his heart pounding.

Fenwick, too, sensing the end, thought of his last will and testament, and his final instructions, all rushed too chaotically.

Suddenly, the buzzing changed pitch as the propeller blades shifted in unison, each cutting the air with a distinctive whine. With no countermanding instruction issued, the drone disengaged and reverted to the default mission plan. It banked sharply, speeding away to resume its patrol along the perimeter.

It was another ten minutes before Peter dared to emerge from his heat shield. Overwrought and exhausted, he anxiously scanned the sky and the surrounds.

The drone had gone.

He peered at Fenwick, huddled and fearful beneath his thermal blanket. Shaken, they both exhaled with relief — it had been the closest call.

'A near death experience!' Peter gulped, re-calculating the odds.

The sun hung low in the winter sky, casting long, weakly defined shadows along the treeline and the far reaches of the airstrip. With the hide compromised, it was time to vacate, swiftly and without delay. As they were packing, the distant roar of engines and men shouting caused them to halt and witness this renewed activity. They lay prone against the cold, hard earth, their scopes at the ready.

'Christ!' Peter muttered, his voice barely above a whisper but brimming with urgency. 'They're putting out more dummies, three truckloads of them... I count forty.'

Peter adjusted the rangefinder for sharper focus, watching the now-familiar ritual, as a pattern of concentric mannequins was assembled before him on the concrete apron. The formation completed, the men climbed into several jeeps, which sped from view behind the culvert.

Other than birdsong, the airstrip was quiet. It was the sudden movement across the ground that alerted them — shadows, cast from above, moving at speed towards the dummies. Looking up, they were astonished by the sight of dozens of quadcopter drones, flying in perfect, coordinated formations from all directions. They moved at speed, weaving left and right, high and low, their paths crisscrossing with aerobatic precision. Fenwick thought of a murmuration of starlings; frantic, rapid and erratic, yet hive-minded in formation.

The drones converged, most on the periphery, others centrally, hovering above the assembled mannequins. Fenwick, enthralled, watched through his binoculars. The machines were clearly controlled from a single console — the coordination was balletic, the execution mesmerising.

Five drones now ascended vertically in unison to an immense altitude of about six hundred feet. Fenwick struggled to keep the formation in focus, instinctively pressing the record button on his binoculars, sensing an imminent display.

Right on cue, the drones unleashed their payloads, the canisters freefalling for fifty feet or so, before exploding like a chain of firecrackers. The released capsules, now exposed to oxygen, ignited instantly in an exothermic reaction fierce enough to melt metal. Explosive trails of white phosphorus rained down, cascading to the ground in deadly, shimmering trails, like long spectral fingers. The mannequins were engulfed instantly, the phosphorus showering them with an incandescent sticky wax that seared ferociously. Most turned to ash in seconds, while others, further out, burned and smouldered forlornly.

Fenwick imagined the scene, but with real flesh-and-blood victims. Even amidst the barbarity of warfare, white phosphorus stood out as particularly iniquitous — being pyrophoric, igniting by contact with oxygen and difficult to extinguish, even when embedded in organs or seared into tissue, and liable to reignite instantly upon re-exposure to air.

Smoke and the acrid stench of burning filled the air. As the phosphorus finally combusted, the scene of devastation emerged — a hellscape of smouldering remains and sporadic fires.

The exercise completed, the drones soared away at high speed, disappearing as swiftly as they'd appeared. Silence fell over the scene, broken only by the distant crackle of dying fires. Fenwick and Peter remained still, their minds grappling with the sheer scale of the obliteration they had witnessed.

'That's one hell of a party they're planning,' muttered Peter, more to himself than to Fenwick.

Firefighters were already on the scene, battling the flames that still licked at the airstrip's edges. After thirty minutes, with the remaining embers doused, the fire crews and their vehicles departed.

A truck — an old DAF 7.5 tonne flatbed — rumbled across the airstrip and halted on a hard stand, its driver dismounting and walking to the safety of the culvert several hundred metres distant.

Peter knew instinctively. 'Cover your ears tight, don't look, and when I say, exhale completely and hold your breath. Stay as flat as possible.'

He started to count down, guessing as best he could the moment of ignition. Five, four, three, two, one...

The truck's cargo bay, packed tightly with Semtex erupted in a cataclysmic explosion that tore apart everything in its path. The lorry simply disintegrated, shards of glass and twisted metal became deadly projectiles, as random sections of the cab and chassis fragmented and powered skywards, falling chaotically as twisted confetti.

The shockwave sucked the air in a vacuum and, despite clasping his ears, Fenwick was deafened. He feared permanent hearing loss — a frightening sensation far worse than flight decompression, to which he was accustomed. He gulped and swallowed repeatedly to relieve the pressure, but to no avail.

He looked across the airstrip, focusing the binoculars on the lorry, which had been squashed flat like a beetle underfoot. The cab, cargo compartment and wheels had vanished, as if atomised. The force of the explosion had fractured and cratered the concrete apron, and what remained of the vehicle's chassis — which looked like a crushed and mangled bedstead — had fallen into the chasm.

Peter, his ears ringing from the vacuum, surveyed the chaos. 'That would take out an entire city block.'

Fenwick, lip-reading, nodded. 'Or an embassy compound,' he shouted unwittingly, over-compensating.

'Uh oh...' said Peter, '...here comes the cavalry.'

A convoy of military trucks, eight-wheeled BTR-80 armoured personnel carriers and jeeps stormed into the compound, accompanied by tracked BMP-1 infantry fighting vehicles, squat and menacing, belching thick black exhaust fumes. The armoured vehicles bristled with 30 mm automatic cannons and wire-guided anti-tank missiles. As the vehicles came to a halt, hundreds of paramilitaries, clad in military fatigues, poured out to parade, assembling in squads with precision and discipline.

Fenwick recognised the weaponry — Russian-built, or manufactured under licence.

Peter's voice, tight with anxiety, cut through the tension. 'Those are Russian divisional markings on the trucks and APCs.'

Fenwick's hearing was recovering. 'You're certain?'

'Yep, Russian uniforms, weapons and kit, too.'

Fenwick's mind raced. 'A training exercise?'

Peter hesitated, cautious with his answer. 'Possibly. It could be a NATO "OPFOR" — a simulated opposition force for wargaming.'

'Do NATO forces test suicide vests and truck-bombs?'

Peter frowned. 'Not sure — maybe to devise protective measures? I doubt they'd test white phosphorus against personnel. It's banned from use against civilians and urban targets.'

'What the hell are they doing now?' asked Fenwick, as the assembled paramilitaries fanned out, with automatic rifles and machine guns shouldered and zeroed-in. 'Stay down!' urged Peter, sensing an onslaught.

Suddenly, the militia burst into frenzied activity, with a cacophony of shouting and a deafening firestorm of automatic gunfire that peppered and shredded all before them.

They fired indiscriminately, serially reloading, wantonly spraying at anything and everything in their path.

Petrified as stray bullets now rocketed just inches overhead, Fenwick hugged the ground. With the enshrouding trees shattered and splintered by the fusillade, Peter squinted in horror, recognising these brutal manoeuvres as a terrorist massacre in rehearsal.

The de Havilland Canada DHC-4 Caribou, renowned for its ruggedness and unparalleled ability to land and take off from impossibly short runways, was pushed to its limits tonight. The pilot, a seasoned veteran of narcotics runs across South America and mercenary operations in Africa and Asia, knew every nuance of this aircraft. Yet even he acknowledged that landing on the makeshift Polish airstrip hidden deep in the remote wilderness was a formidable challenge.

As the Caribou's beacons flashed rhythmically, stark white and red against the darkening backdrop, the plane swooped low over the treetops, far below radar detection. The pilot banked sharply, commencing a brutally steep descent towards the narrow strip. With ailerons and airbrakes extended, the plane touched the runway and bounced a few times in harsh deceleration. Throttling down forcefully, the pilot fought the plane to a shuddering standstill. The aircraft taxied, rotating deftly on a dime, its engines roaring, propellers gradually winding down to a stop.

Peter watched the scene through an image intensifier. He saw no civil aviation code or registration on the fuselage or tail. The plane, in drab camouflage, was ex-Canadian military, he surmised. Checking various aviation flight trackers, there was no sign of its existence or flightpath — it had evidently flown in with its transponder deactivated.

The cargo ramp at the rear lowered. Fenwick, with a night-vision scope, watched intensely. He counted now, as a huddle of twenty adolescent girls, some barely in their teens, were herded onto the airstrip by stern paramilitaries. A couple of the girls looked happy and excited as if unaware of their fate, while others were clearly miserable and sullen. A few were crying and fearful. Some appeared drugged, their movements sluggish with eyes vacant.

The girls were shepherded in groups on board two trucks. Upon reaching the command bunker, they were forced to stand in lines, where they were brutally strip-searched. The guards jeered, mocking and leering at their charges, before forcing them inside.

Fenwick recoiled, sickened by the depravity, dreading to think of the appalling fate that surely awaited the poor wretches assembled. Peter filmed everything, his stomach churning as he scrambled to devise a rescue plan.

Darkness enveloped the airstrip as the runway lights dimmed. In the distance, a convoy of vehicles approached, headlights piercing the night. SUVs, all-terrain vehicles and sleek limousines pulled up beside the command bunker. Paramilitaries and burly minders jumped out, swiftly opening the doors of the luxury cars. Men in suits emerged, their faces obscured by shadows. Not a single woman accompanied them.

In the shadows, Fenwick watched through the night-sight. From the deferential treatment they received from the paramilitaries and minders, he inferred that the men in suits were VIPs — senior politicians, judges, police commissioners, high-ranking civil servants or similar.

Suddenly, his spotting eye widened in recognition.

'Schwartz!' he exclaimed, on seeing the man's bullet head. Bako, nerdy in a pastel cashmere jumper and ludicrously tight skinny jeans, trailed slightly behind. Kamiński, in his ill-fitting suit with arms folded commandingly, oversaw the security arrangements.

As the dignitaries and VIPs approached the command bunker, its large door swung open, revealing bursts of flashing multicoloured lights. Loud, hypnotic trance music, greatly amplified by the solid concrete of the structure, boomed out incongruously into the nighttime wilderness.

'Sick bastards,' growled Peter.

At that moment, there was a flash of fork lightning in the night sky and a distant rumble of thunder. It was as though the heavens agreed.

FORTY-TWO
DEMON SPIN

The steel elevator doors slid open and a fleeting blast of blaring trance music resounded from the floors above. As Schwartz, Kamiński and Bako stepped out, the doors closed behind them with a muted hiss, silencing the music instantly. They emerged into a vast chamber, deep underground.

Large monitor screens lined the walls, displaying live black-and-white feeds from several scientific complexes. Workers, diminutive from afar and as precise and industrious as ants, dismantled equipment, packed boxes and loaded vehicles. In some locations, bonfires blazed, consuming mountains of printout and documentation.

A larger screen activated suddenly with a broadcast of Ellen Wilson, a poised and elegant senior State Department official in a cream trouser suit, speaking from a secure conference facility in Washington DC.

Immaculately coiffured with a professionally tinted blonde bob, Wilson's features, gentle and feminine in youth, were hard and unforgiving now, annealed by decades of criminality and corruption. Her rise through the ranks had been fuelled by a relentless greed and a cunning that knew no bounds. On a salary of nearly a million dollars annually, Ellen was the highest-paid civil servant in the United States, but that was chicken feed compared to the kickbacks and bribes she banked offshore from arms manufacturers, pharmaceutical companies, narco-terrorists and other shadowy interests. Much of Ellen's wealth had been accrued through sanctions busting, misappropriating US military and civil resources to facilitate black market oil and gas shipments from embargoed states such as Venezuela and Iran, and more recently Russia. Her criminality was legendary, aided and abetted by others in power, who benefited themselves by turning a blind eye to her villainy.

Ellen, now seventy, was a doyenne of the Deep State. She'd spent over thirty years orchestrating the clandestine operations that kept the wheels of global power turning in favour of the few who pulled the strings. She was a master of deception, a woman who had lied to Congress, the Senate, successive Presidents and the American people without flinching. Her loyalty was not to the President, the people or the Constitution she ostensibly served, but to the Cabal — the shadowy, unelected council that truly governs world affairs.

The United States had officially renounced the development of offensive biological weapons back in 1969, a stance reaffirmed by every administration since. But the reality was far more sinister. Bioweaponry research had merely gone underground, outsourced and offshored to over three hundred facilities in compliant nations, far from the prying eyes of regulators. The research was disguised as defensive, a means of developing therapeutics and countermeasures, but the truth was undeniable: these programmes were designed to kill.

Ellen, with her connections and her unyielding ambition, was perfectly positioned to further the Cabal's goals. Ever since her teenage years, she'd been an advocate of eugenics, believing in the superiority of the few who stood at the summit of the global hierarchy, and the perfectibility of the human race. Now, with the advent of 'The Singularity' — the point at which machines would take over all societal tasks — the Cabal's agenda had shifted to depopulation. In this new world order, ninety-seven percent of the populace would be redundant, 'useless eaters' consuming resources that the elite believed were theirs alone. The Cabal's solution was as ruthless as it was efficient: reduce the global population from 7.9 billion to just 250 million, with further reductions as deemed necessary.

Ellen fretted now, flustered by the latest directive from the Cabal. The timeline they had scheduled was unrealistic, and the methods they'd proposed — aerosol toxins, respiratory viruses — had proven ineffective and uncontrollable. The only viable solution was to convince the populace to kill themselves, to submit voluntarily to injected toxins disguised as therapeutic vaccines. It was a grand deception, one that would require a coordinated global effort and the complicity or unwitting assistance of the world's governments, health authorities, the pharmaceuticals industry and the media.

Jozef Bako, a coldly brilliant scientist in his early thirties, had devised the most chilling solution yet. His intramuscular injectable delivered lethal payloads via lipid nanoparticles, variably triggered by specific radio frequencies. This method offered a precision that was as insidious as it was effective, allowing for the targeted extermination of selected groups, in incremental and scalable volumes, stealthily evading public health monitoring or surveillance. Using gene editing, Bako had further augmented his 'kill switch' with payloads that could trigger aggressive cancers, rapid neuro-degeneration, miscarriages, and targeted infertility, potentially sterilising entire communities with a single injection.

But even as Bako pushed the boundaries of his dark arts, new threats loomed. The US National Counter-Proliferation and Biosecurity Center had commenced a rigorous inspection of all laboratories and research facilities under US control, as well as those affiliated globally. The incoming US administration was determined to enforce compliance. If the illicit depopulation studies were discovered, it would spell the end not just for Ellen, but for the entire Cabal.

To complicate matters further, several prominent laboratories were based in Ukraine, where the ongoing war with Russia posed a significant risk. If the facilities were captured by Russian forces, Putin would exploit the issue unremittingly for his own propaganda purposes, and might even cite the discovery of such deadly bioweapons as sufficient grounds for a nuclear strike. Equally problematic, should the lethal technology fall into Putin's hands, it would comprise a quantum leap in his offensive biological warfare capability, to be exploited by his forces on the battlefield and beyond.

Ellen's voice, calm yet commanding, resonated through the chamber:

'The Russian offensive in Ukraine has lost traction, which affords us more time. So, we're in the business of damage limitation. What is the current status?'

A map appeared on the screen highlighting the status of various biolabs: active, decommissioned or sterilised. Schwartz stepped forward, addressing the camera:

'The evacuation effort is progressing. The biolabs within reach of the Russians have been purged, with all evidence removed. The core feasibility studies have been relocated.'

Ellen's expression remained steely. 'And the whistleblowers?'

'We have eliminated seven deemed security risks,' reported Kamiński in a flat tone. 'A further three have fled Ukraine, but we've located them, with hit squads assigned. The test subjects have also been eradicated — the corpses incinerated beyond identification.'

Ellen's gaze sharpened. 'You need to move faster. All dissidents and defectors must be eliminated. The latest directive demands the configurable targeting of any ethnicity, genetic subgroup or demographic. Do your experts think this achievable, given the disruption in Ukraine?'

Schwartz nodded. 'We remain confident. We will meet the deadlines for both the pathogens and the vaccine payloads.'

'Very well,' said Ellen in an icy tone. 'And the neurotoxin tests?'

Kamiński remotely loaded a video clip on the large screen. It showed a corner shot, an elevated view of an Asian man in a white T-shirt and shorts, seated at a table, eating from a bowl of rice with a spoon. The room was clean but sparse, with no windows. Only a cup of water and a mobile phone rested on the tabletop.

'This clip shows the effects of lipid nanoparticle payload infusion through the blood-brain barrier,' explained Bako. 'The test subject, pre-injected with Thanatacyn-9, is seen here following a microwave burst at a preset trigger frequency. Notice the telephone on the table: it activates, its screen flashes, and the subject reacts.'

On screen, the mobile phone's display flashed. A timer commenced, ascending in milliseconds. The man looked stunned. His head then turned upwards and to the right, his face contorting with an expression of utter terror — as though confronted by Satan himself. With his left arm outstretched in a spasm, he stood awkwardly, knocking over the chair. His body started to rotate clockwise, frenzied in a series of ever-faster and more chaotic circles, spiralling out of control, until he lost his footing and crashed violently to the floor. The man's entire body convulsed with tremors. With extremities rigid and the victim in violent shaking seizure, his death throes continued until the timer clock stopped at 00:00:19:17.

With the remote, Bako froze the footage.

'Thanatacyn-9 is invariably lethal,' he said. 'Death occurs rapidly, in under twenty seconds. The clockwise turn and the abject terror observed are not design features. These symptoms are possibly caused by a stimulus of the sensory cortex interacting with the hippocampus.'

With a faint smile, Schwartz interjected, 'We call the phenomenon a "Devil's turn", or a "demon spin".'

Ellen's eyes narrowed, dismissive of such whimsy. 'You say "invariably lethal" — how many test subjects?'

'Sixteen, all dead, all in under twenty seconds,' replied Schwartz.

'Through microwave initiation,' added Bako.

'Good. I will report that the lethality trials are progressing,' said Ellen. 'Thank you, gentlemen,'

Her image faded from the screen.

FORTY-THREE
HEART OF DARKNESS

The rain fell incessantly throughout the night, the downpour a relentless beating percussion on the dense forest canopy. Amidst the freezing morning mist, Fenwick shivered. The cold gnawed at his bones, a deep chill that no amount of protective gear could repel. He and Peter had taken turns on watch, sharing the four-hour shifts with a resigned weariness. They'd been vigilant, eyes scanning the skies for night-flying quadcopters, and all their senses on high alert for approaching patrols.

Peter was now lost in the blessed deep sleep that followed exhaustion. His earlier anger had dissipated, replaced by a weary calm, and the adrenaline that had fuelled him was long spent. He lay motionless, his breathing deep and steady, oblivious to the world around him.

A metallic squeal pierced the air, setting Fenwick's teeth on edge. The large steel door of the command bunker shuddered open. Fenwick watched, counting as precisely as he could, as the girls from the night before stumbled out. They looked dishevelled and raggedly re-clothed, and their departure was disorganised and uncoordinated. Paramilitary escorts lined their path, funnelling them towards the embarkation apron a few hundred metres away.

'Wake up, Peter,' said Fenwick, nudging Peter's shoulder. 'The party's over. Literally.'

Peter stirred, blinking in the dim light. He sat up, rubbing his eyes, as the distant roar of its twin turboprops heralded the approach of the Caribou. The aircraft had parked overnight out of view, somewhere to the east of the airstrip. Now it swung into sight, taxiing, its nose wheel and forward fuselage bouncing gently before lurching to a halt. Fenwick and Peter watched as the girls were ushered hurriedly up the cargo ramp, the plane's propellers spinning at full revolution, while the pilot undertook his preflight checks. After a short delay, the Caribou surged forward on full throttle, executing a stunningly precarious take-off, roaring skyward at a precipitous angle before stabilising and swooping low, skimming the treetops and then powering from view.

Next, the VIPs emerged. Some looked shamefaced; others looked frightened, cowered or wary. A few looked callous and cocksure, indentured and without remorse. The men were escorted to their waiting limousines and SUVs by their minders.

Peter filmed every second, determined to capture the facial features of each attendee, his camera set to maximum magnification and the highest resolution. He'd witnessed sexual brutalisation in Bosnia, Kosovo, East Timor and other places, and the implications of what he'd just seen infuriated him.

An officer, conspicuous in a braided peaked cap, emerged from the bunker, barking orders at the paramilitary escort, scattering them like cockroaches. With the ranks disbanded, the officer turned to the bunker's exit, expectant, and eager for his prey.

Suddenly, a girl, perhaps fifteen, burst out — running frantically, naked and screaming in abject terror, like a trapped animal fleeing captivity.

Peter and Fenwick watched in horrified disbelief as the officer calmly levelled his pistol and fired a single shot. The girl crumpled to the ground. He sauntered over to her motionless body, oozing casual disdain, and fired again, pitilessly; the fatal bullet to the back of her head resounding across the clearing as a murderous full-stop.

With a contemptuous boot, the officer rolled the girl on to her back. Seeing the exit wound in her forehead, he barked instructions into a walkie-talkie before returning to the bunker.

Peter, incandescent with rage, stood up. 'I'm going in!' he growled, preparing to charge.

Fenwick instantly tackled him, hurling Peter's muscular frame down, astonishing himself by the speed and strength he'd summoned. They crashed to the ground, landing heavily.

'You and whose army? Don't be absurd!' exclaimed Fenwick, struggling to restrain the far stronger and fitter man. 'They'll kill us both. Besides, we're a quarter of a mile away, and we have no weapons.'

Peter, felled so unexpectedly, regained his composure. It had been a moment of madness and he knew it.

Abashed, he crouched back down, his face ashen with shock, his hands trembling. He watched and recorded as two paramilitaries, with practiced efficiency, used steel rods with hooks to lift a concrete breeze block, revealing a large manhole. The men tipped the dead girl into the abyss, dispatching her with less reverence than if they were taking out the trash. Her small frame struck the storm drain below with a hideous muffled thud.

Minutes later, the men brought forth yet another body, carried on a makeshift stretcher. Freshly slain, this victim bore the marks of her violent end. She too was tossed into the manhole with the same callous disregard.

As the paramilitaries restored the block, Fenwick watched frozen in revulsion and fear, horrified by the barbarity and carnage he and Peter had witnessed. This was systematic, methodical slaughter. Fenwick's instincts screamed that this was but one of many such places, hidden from view, where the lost and missing were disposed of without a second thought.

'Who are these monsters?' he murmured, stupefied and sickened.

FORTY-FOUR
APOTHEOSIS

The *Apotheosis* was anchored serenely off Bridgetown, Barbados, its sleek lines and understated elegance a testament to Springer's refined taste and purposeful sense of design. Sedate and anchored in untroubled waters, the 120-foot yacht whispered a quiet but emphatic message: true wealth needed no proclamation.

Springer reclined on a sun lounger, a sharp lime daiquiri in hand. Montserrat, demure in a classic white swimsuit, languished nearby, resolutely detached and inscrutable behind large-framed sunglasses, her nose buried in the latest *Tatler*.

Springer had been tickled by the Prime Minister's call, but it also irritated him — for the Cabinet Office to disturb him while he was wintering abroad was a diabolical liberty. The PM was understandably rattled: Murdoch, with an eye to the next incumbent at Number Ten, was swinging to the Labour Party and increasingly hostile. Might Winchcombe Group buy Murdoch out?

Springer, attuned to the political winds, scoffed at the absurdity of this suggestion.

Jonty, the yacht's bartender, emerged from behind his lavishly stocked bar, quaintly bearing Springer's mobile phone on a silver platter.

'Some honky for you, bwana,' he said with a derisive laugh. Only Jonty could address Springer in this way — a Cayman Islander renowned for his wit and irreverence, he and Springer had formed an unlikely bond, based largely on mutually playful disrespect.

'Get back to the plantation,' replied Springer with a wry smile and a dismissive wave. He wondered if Jonty's 'honky' might perhaps be the PM on re-dial. He viewed the incoming number and placed the phone to his ear.

'There's been a murder at a Polish airbase this morning.' The voice, urgent and breathless, was instantly recognisable, though the number was not. Fenwick was clearly in a motor vehicle, and travelling very fast by the sound of it. He continued: 'A young girl shot in the head, and another girl, also murdered. It's all recorded. I'm taking it to the police.'

Springer was stunned. This was all completely out of the blue. 'God Almighty!' he spluttered. 'What the hell were you doing at a Polish airbase?'

'I'll explain when we meet,' said Fenwick, as Peter thundered along the fast lane of the S8 motorway towards Warsaw.

'It's connected to Tyler and the Saurian Group?' asked Springer.

'Yes.'

Montserrat, out of Springer's view, eavesdropped

intently. She studied her magazine, feigning interest in Meghan and Harry's latest tawdry escapade, but noting Springer's every word.

'Listen to me,' commanded Springer. 'Do not under any circumstances approach the Polish police. They're notoriously untrustworthy — communist recidivists steeped in corruption. You'd face instant arrest on spurious charges. When did this murder take place?'

'In the small hours of this morning.'

Springer, anticipating events, was already formulating a strategy. 'Who pulled the trigger?'

'A paramilitary officer billeted at the airstrip. You can see his face clearly on film, but we'll need official help to identify him.'

Springer knew that the video was a guaranteed death sentence should Fenwick be intercepted by the wrong people. Conversely, if apprehended by legitimate law enforcement, he and Fenwick risked losing control.

'Let's keep this in the family,' urged Springer. 'Then work out our strategy.'

Fenwick was unconvinced, wary of MI6 adventurism, foreign office mendacity and civil service meddling. 'Sir Frederick, we urgently need to inform the Polish police. It's not only the murders; there were weapons tests, suicide vests, a truck bomb, even white phosphorus — I have it all recorded. These people are armed to the teeth — a private army — and extremely dangerous.'

Springer was having none of it. 'Think, man! If there's a major criminal enterprise operating on the local police's patch, at least some of them must be complicit.'

'I take your point, but…'

'But nothing! Let's deal with this in London. I'll brief the Yard, Five and Six straight away. Fly home today. Put together a presentation with your findings, and I'll organise an intra-agency summit. Send Montserrat the videos and whatever else you have.'

Fenwick's reluctance was palpable. 'All right. I'll head back. I'll "Dropbox" the footage, encrypted.'

'I'll be in touch about the summit,' said Springer. 'It'll be a mixed bag of about four or five. You'll need to show your evidence and explain it. Steel yourself — you can expect a forensic inquisition.'

Springer ended the call.

Montserrat, sphinx-like behind her Ray-Bans, was calculating now. The situation was escalating rapidly, and she had much to do.

FORTY-FIVE
ATHENS

The Porsche 911 eased to a halt. An alley cat, roused from slumber, darted away, vanishing into the shadows. The facility, codenamed 'Athens', was an insalubrious workshop and lockup garage embedded within Hounslow's grimmest outreaches. Montserrat had never ventured to Isleworth before — entering the unfamiliar postcode into the satnav was as alien to her as programming a mission to Mars.

She now keyed the PIN, and the solid iron door unlocked with a loud clunk. The scent of Oud and Bergamot cologne wafted ahead, presaging her arrival. The technicians on site — tech-savvy beta males — had never encountered anything quite like Montserrat. In her sea-grey Céline midi-dress and her Bulgari earrings and accessories, she appeared in their midst like a goddess, striding forth with the grace of a supermodel on a catwalk.

The facility, which reeked of stale armpits and discarded fast food, was larger than it appeared from the outside, like the Tardis. Montserrat, determinedly exhaling, strode past several Ford Mondeos from the car pool, oblivious to the furtive ogling of the support team and unaware that she'd boosted the testosterone level in the building to stratospheric levels.

In stark contrast to the nudging, winking and muted catcalls outside, the atmosphere within the supervisor's office was deadly serious. The instructor, a nondescript man in his forties, placed the device on the table before them and looked Montserrat directly in the eye. 'If you don't understand anything I say in the next twenty minutes, please say so immediately,' he said, his tone stripped of politeness or humour.

Montserrat nodded and gave a winsome smile, tolerant of the gulf between their respective IQs. Her gaze fell upon the device: a sleek black box, slightly larger than a twenty-pack carton of cigarettes.

'This is a 5G GEM-CELL LTE audio and video transmitter,' said the man. 'The device is a "store and forward" — it records and transmits simultaneously.'

Montserrat really didn't need the lecture but nodded nonetheless.

The man continued:

'On a full-mains charge, the battery sustains six hours of live streaming over a 5G network. Audio and video are transmitted globally by satellite, receivable on any suitably configured and authorised cell-phone. Recording is voice activated. We'll listen and record in real time. With GPS we can also track the transmitter to within ten metres anywhere in the world.'

The tracking facility would be pivotal — Montserrat

needed to guide the team within striking distance. This device, as described, sounded about right — a powerful transmitter and a beacon.

'You indicate there's no opportunity to preinstall, and you tell us the subject is surveillance aware,' droned the man. 'That being the case, you'll have to work out how best to infiltrate the device. We can help with packaging and disguise.'

He wasn't wrong. The number of sweeps for bugs and surveillance devices had risen alarmingly in the last few days, with the TCM teams on occasion stripping furnishings and all else before them.

In any event, this imbecile had overlooked the blindingly obvious. Wearisome of the man's ineptitude, Montserrat interjected: 'You've overlooked a critical factor,' she said scornfully. 'The target building is in the middle of nowhere and there is no 5G coverage.'

The man looked at her with wearied disdain. She clearly thought him an idiot. 'As of six o'clock this morning, there *is* coverage,' he said. 'At our request, Ericsson erected a 5G tower overnight.'

Montserrat was dumbstruck. She yielded now — scolded, a little resentful, and slightly in wonderment.

FORTY-SIX
THE RANGE

Peter's team had spent three hours on the range, familiarising themselves with the Browning Hi-Power automatic pistol. Two boxes with ten handguns had been delivered to the farm — factory-fresh ex-government stock with the serial numbers milled clean off. Into the bargain, each weapon was supplied with a sanitised and untraceable 9mm suppressor from Advanced Armament Corporation with threaded barrel adapters. Three thousand rounds of ammunition had also been shipped for range practice and close-quarter battle training.

It had all been delivered by the Royal Mail — or at least the chap who had dropped the kit off, named Pat, was dressed like a postman and he drove a red van. If they needed more ammo, or anything else, Peter should just text 'Pat' using simple, preassigned codes — useful, as the team was burning up rounds at a phenomenal rate.

The farm was ideal for combat training, being miles from anywhere. Some abandoned outhouses — former labourers' cottages — served well for room clearance and urban warfare practice.

The team had finished at the range and Peter's three colleagues were seated, their clothes heavily impregnated with cordite, having descended into the bowels of Mission Control.

There'd been no time to build a model, let alone a dummy practice building, but they had studied the architect's plans carefully and had been advised of the key rooms and locations. The apps on the phones had been installed and tested, the earpieces and microphones integrated into headbands were working, and Peter was assured of local coverage — they would test the signal and communications integration live, prior to execution.

They had just two days left before deployment.

Peter addressed his team:

'The mission is protective overwatch. That said, it may be necessary to engage, even in close-quarter battle. The use of lethal force has been authorised — let's hope it isn't necessary.'

He pointed to a whiteboard, on which he'd written:

DURESS CODES: - OPULENCE

                              - KISMET

                              - HUBRIS

'If things escalate, the following phrases apply: "Opulence" is "action stations", "Kismet" is "standby", "Hubris" is "execute." Sear these codewords into your brains, and don't mix them up.'

The room was silent, each man appreciating the grave implications should any of these words be uttered operationally.

'Questions?' said Peter.

Soldier A, who had bushy sideburns and a grand old Western-style moustache, responded: 'Gaining access to the premises… you say we're not breaking and entering, but it's not a building assault or a lockpicking job. Explain.'

Peter was not at liberty to disclose too much. He chose his words carefully. 'We will have guaranteed entry to the building and "access all areas". I'm still working on contingencies. If the situation on the ground changes, we will adapt.'

Soldier C, a short, wiry Scot, piped up: 'What's the escape plan?'

'Exfiltration will be after dark by helicopter. The RV is shown in your briefing packs.'

The men disbanded, trustful in the leadership, their training and the plan.

Peter, apprehensive and fearing incipient revolt, recalled the time-worn maxim: 'No plan survives first contact with the enemy.'

FORTY-SEVEN
SAGE ADVICE

Fenwick stepped off the train on to the well-tended platform at Thetford railway station, nestled in the heart of Norfolk. The small, rural town lay beside the largest lowland pine forest in Britain, a place steeped in natural beauty and quiet mystery. Today, however, Fenwick had no time to appreciate the scenery. He was here for the inter-agency summit at Seaton Hall, a sprawling Elizabethan mansion and the ancestral seat of the Springer family.

As he waited outside the station for a taxi, his mind churned as he tried to order his thoughts. Montserrat had all the material for the presentation, but the knowledge matrix — his intricate Excel spreadsheet tracking who knew *what*, *when*, *where*, *how*, and *why* — occupied his thoughts. From the data, the conclusion was clear: only one person fit all the criteria. The other suspects had all been eliminated, one by one.

Fenwick had visited Seaton Hall once before, for a grilling testimony in the Tank, a 'secure speech environment' within Springer's grand conference chamber. Shielded by a Faraday cage to block electromagnetic fields and insulated against electronic eavesdropping, the 'TEMPEST' facility was a steel freight container elevated within the room by non-conductive support stanchions. Accessible by a steel gantry and stringent security controls, it was reserved for discussing the most classified matters.

Fenwick thought back to the previous occasion he'd been there — a briefing, intense and testy, which had uncovered a catastrophic security breach that threatened the integrity of the UK's Trident submarines and their missile launch codes.

A taxi — a London black cab, unusual for this provincial market town — arrived with a rumble. As they drove along a secluded road flanked by towering pines, the driver was startled by a young roe deer leaping across his path, causing him to slow.

'I'm running late. Is it far?' asked Fenwick, glancing at his watch.

'Another ten minutes,' replied the driver, a personable middle-aged man with a thick beard and a Millwall T-shirt. 'It's off the beaten track. Haven't done this run for a while.'

Fenwick, keen to avoid football guff at all costs, was intrigued. 'You know it? How so?'

'Yep, about five years ago. I was ferrying loads of journalists to the place — BBC, Sky, GMTV, loads of them. A young couple — backpackers — found dead on the estate, in the woods. Skeletons, been there all winter, torn apart by foxes.'

Fenwick imagined the gruesome scene. 'It made the

news?' he asked, vaguely recalling the story. 'Thanks, I'll check it out.'

The taxi emerged into a clearing and turned through imposing wrought-iron gates, proceeding down an oak-lined avenue to Seaton Hall. The mansion stood majestic amid extensive, beautifully manicured grounds. Fenwick observed the dark limousines and Range Rover backup cars parked under the trees, alongside marked police cars and motorbikes. Heavily armed officers in flak jackets and full counterterrorist gear patrolled the grounds.

'Blimey! This is heavy!' exclaimed the cabbie, eyes wide. 'What's going on?'

Fenwick, equally taken aback, muttered, 'I could tell you...'

The driver interrupted: '...but then you'd have to kill me. Haha, very good!'

As Fenwick climbed out and handed over a twenty and a ten, the driver leaned out and handed him a card.

'For the return journey,' he said with a wink. 'Have fun — just don't go into the woods!'

Fenwick watched as the taxi executed a tight turn and drove off towards the surrounding forest, the late morning winter sun already low in the sky. A pristinely uniformed police commander approached, beckoning him forward.

'Follow me, sir,' he instructed, leading Fenwick across a lengthy gravel forecourt towards the grand stairway, the ceremonial entrance to Seaton Hall. They passed meticulously trimmed evergreens, sharply rendered with topiary, and a giant ornamental hedge maze that decadently encapsulated the estate's sprawling magnificence.

As he stood alone in the grand hallway, Fenwick's eyes roamed over the portraiture of Springer's illustrious ancestors. Some paintings were familiar in style — perhaps the work of Frans Hals or Jan van Eyck?

'Charles!' A deep, resonant voice boomed, shattering the silence.

Fenwick turned abruptly to see Springer directly behind him, his sudden appearance as surprising as his casual familiarity.

'You found us!' exclaimed Springer.

'Just about. The driver had the "knowledge".' Fenwick thought fleetingly of the two young backpackers, lifeless in the woods.

'Yes, it is remote and isolated, but blissfully peaceful.' Springer gave a warm, inviting smile.

'The grounds are magnificent,' murmured Fenwick uneasily.

'Oh, I do my best with it all. It's a pity you're here in the winter; it's spectacular in the summer.'

It looked perfect even in February, thought Fenwick, imagining the army of gardeners and groundsmen required to maintain such grandeur.

'So,' asked Fenwick, 'is everyone here?'

'Ready and waiting,' replied Springer affably.

Montserrat appeared, clutching a stack of printed and stapled documents.

'Ah, right on time,' said Springer.

Montserrat eyed Fenwick with cool detachment. 'Mr Fenwick, this way, please,' she said, gesturing ahead.

'Turn right at the Rembrandt,' Springer called out after them, helpfully.

FORTY-EIGHT

THE SOUND OF SILENCE

The sign was emphatic: 'RESTRICTED AREA: NO MOBILE PHONES OR ELECTRONIC DEVICES BEYOND THIS POINT.' Fenwick knew the protocol: nothing was to enter the anechoic chamber that might record or transmit the discussion within.

Springer and Fenwick turned out their pockets, placing the contents into plastic trays. They stepped through an airport detection loop, overseen by two burly security guards. Once through the arch, the guards additionally swept them bodily with metal detectors.

Springer casually observed the meagre contents of Fenwick's tray: a leather belt, a cheap wristwatch, a biro pen and a wallet.

'No phone?' he enquired.

Fenwick nodded towards the sign. 'I'm travelling light.'

The guards whisked the trays away. Each man was ushered up the gantry. Fenwick's eyes narrowed as the guard entered a four-digit PIN. There was a loud, mechanical clunk as the lock released. With a grunt, the guard heaved open the armoured door.

'Welcome to the Tank,' said Springer, gesturing for Fenwick to step inside.

The interior of the chamber was lined with thousands of wedge-shaped Styrofoam cones, like inverted egg-boxes, arranged in precise geometric rows to absorb sound. It was unnervingly silent, a disconcerting sonic vacuum that accentuated each breath and heartbeat inordinately.

'This is where it all happens,' said Springer, his voice sounding oddly flat in the soundproofed room. 'No leaks, no interruptions. Just pure, unfiltered, candid discussion.'

The zonal analogue clocks, an engaging feature of the Tank that displayed the local hour in twelve capital cities, were conspicuous by their absence. Removed deliberately, thought Fenwick. With no wristwatch to consult, he'd lost all sense of time.

The interrogation was relentless, with every detail dissected exhaustively. Vulnerable, isolated and exposed, Fenwick sat on an unforgiving, hard plastic office chair — a torture stool, really — and was denied even a glass of water.

Squinting into harshly focused spotlights, he struggled to discern his inquisitors' identities, shielded as they were in near-impenetrable darkness. Fenwick knew all about staging — the layout and props were configured here to control, intimidate and disorientate. Near blinded, he was more a criminal suspect than a helpful volunteer or compliant witness.

Through the fierce beams of light, he could just discern a few details amidst the silhouettes: a male army officer in crisp fatigues, a senior policeman in uniform, two middle-aged men in suits, and a woman, smartly dressed. The spooks in suits were obvious, the woman with them completely unfathomable. No-one had been introduced by name or affiliation. Springer sat, consciously apart, his chair at a curious angle in self-imposed dissociation.

The video evidence recorded at the airstrip played, muted, in a loop on a screen to the side — the graphic mayhem and violence clear for all to see.

The disparity of power was blatant. Fenwick sat before these officials, stripped and laid bare. Springer hadn't exaggerated when he'd warned of an inquisition. Torquemada had nothing on these people.

Two hours must have passed. The deliberations, tense and fractious, simmered, bordering on outright aggression and even physicality.

The junior intelligence officer spoke now, 'You say your clips show terrorist training. Remind me, how did you reach that conclusion?'

Fenwick, weary of this obduracy, could restrain himself no longer. Catching a moment of eye-watering violence on the video screen, he flinched. 'Well, they weren't rehearsing for *Mamma Mia*,' he snapped.

The senior spook erupted: 'Don't be so damned facetious and answer the bloody question. How is this activity paramilitary?'

Not again! Fenwick groaned. 'Because — as I've already explained — no legitimate army uses car bombs, suicide vests, or white phosphorus against civilians. Nor would they carry out the hit-and-run assault training you've witnessed. Even special forces wouldn't do that.'

The army officer intervened, sneering. 'So now you're an expert on military training, Mr. Fenwick?'

Was not the video self-evident? thought Fenwick. 'I'm no expert,' he conceded, 'but I have testimony that the exercises filmed accord with terrorist attacks, such as those in Mumbai in 2008, in Tunisia in 2015, and at the Bataclan in Paris.'

The three savage attacks had been inflicted by gunmen rampaging with assault rifles on full-automatic. Fenwick's answer, observant and thoughtful, took the sting out of the question. The army officer, more receptive now, struck up again, quieter and less haranguing.

'The equipment filmed was Russian, and the personnel had Russian uniforms. What do you make of that?'

More prevarication, thought Fenwick, having already pronounced on this at least twice. 'Possibly a simulated opposition unit for NATO wargames and training exercises,' he repeated, yet again. 'More probably, a phantom unit to support some kind of "false flag" operation.'

'What evidence is there to support that theory?' snapped the junior spook.

Fenwick sighed, exhausted and in disbelief. 'The outfit is masquerading as a Russian army unit. If it launches a provocation in contested territory, it could drag NATO into war with Russia on false premises. As I've said, there's this Ukrainian dimension still to resolve: the missing folder, content unknown.'

Fenwick had faithfully recounted the circumstances

of Susan Tyler's death, but had deliberately said nothing about 'T-9' or Aleksy. The higher scoring cards remained close to his chest and off the table. Nor had he identified any of his other contacts, informants or operatives.

The senior spook, contemptuous from the start, was withering in his dismissal. 'Sir Frederick, I really must protest. Why have you dragged us up from London to listen to this pantomime of circumstantial evidence and paranoid claptrap?' He turned to Fenwick. 'You have provided no evidence of any criminal syndicate, just the parochial deaths of the two girls, which is a matter purely for the Polish police.'

'Parochial.' The use of the word was disgraceful — an affront. Fenwick grimaced, shocked and repelled.

Springer, head bowed, feared an unseemly squabble.

'With the greatest respect,' said Fenwick, with such abject disdain it caused Springer to wince, 'the stakes are phenomenally high: a drone attack with white phosphorus! I cannot discount the possibility — no, the *likelihood* — that this was a rehearsal for an imminent terrorist assault against civilians in open assembly: a football match, a rock concert or a mass demonstration.'

'You may surmise whatever you like,' said the senior spook, 'but you have absolutely no evidence of the purpose of this operation, nor any insight into its intent.'

Fenwick counted to five, then spoke in the calmest, most considered tone he could muster: 'This is a heavily armed, highly resourced paramilitary force, operating independently of any legitimate command structure, acting with impunity within a NATO and EU member state. They have the proven capability to deploy weapons of mass destruction. If unleashed, these people will commit mayhem and could even provoke a nuclear exchange.'

There was a pause. It was a cogent argument. Perhaps, at long last, the gravity of the situation might dawn on his inquisitors.

Now the woman intervened, for the first time in the entire meeting. Her identity and role remained a complete mystery. She was conciliatory, imploring even: 'Mr. Fenwick, we understand your misgivings, but you must realise –'

Fenwick interrupted her: 'No, *you* must realise: all indications are that these people will commit mass murder imminently, with devastating effect. You are witnesses to events and cannot claim ignorance. You stand advised, all of you!'

The room fell silent, the quiet massively amplified by the uniquely engineered acoustics of the chamber.

Fenwick stood up, his backside and lumbar region sweaty and aching from the rigid and airless confines of the vile plastic chair. With cold fury, he declared, 'I have nothing more to say.'

There was a deathly silence. Drained and demoralised, yet energised by anger, Fenwick rose and turned on his heel towards the armoured exit door. Seeing the keypad, he stalled. Other than Springer, those assembled smirked.

Defiantly, Fenwick keyed in the PIN, which he had 'shoulder-surfed' prior to entry. The door released with a satisfying mechanical clunk. Fenwick, escaping this torment, strode out.

Fuming, Fenwick walked briskly along the black-and-white chequerboard marble floor. Montserrat's concise itinerary indicated an informal debriefing within Springer's secluded study. Fenwick had examined the layout and now followed the corridor to the hideaway.

Springer, in hot pursuit, was half-running, his leather soles resonating on the marble floor, both men's footsteps resounding with a discordant clickety-clack.

'Damn it, man, slow down!' cried Springer.

Fenwick eased his pace. Springer caught up with him, and the two men continued, Fenwick slightly ahead.

'So much resistance and pushback,' growled Fenwick. 'I did my best.'

'Which was excellent, as always,' said Springer cheerily.

'You are alone in that verdict.'

'Never mind them,' said Springer. 'You uncovered an impending cataclysm that they and their sumptuously funded departments completely missed. Besides, the dissenting voices are not the decision-makers. My "A team" will assemble the formal briefing.'

'For COBRA?' asked Fenwick, presuming Springer meant the Cabinet Office's Briefing Room A, the governmental emergency committee.

'God, no!' replied Springer, shocked at Fenwick's naivety. 'This is far too sensitive for COBRA.' Springer considered COBRA intellectually substandard and delinquent also, as it leaked like a sieve.

Springer halted outside his study. Fenwick had walked past the discreet doorway without noticing it, but now he stopped and turned.

At that very instant, Montserrat appeared as if from nowhere, carrying a beautifully gift-wrapped present. It was the size of a hefty paperback novel and was tied with a decorative bow. Fenwick recognised the distinctive turquoise wrapping to be that of Tiffany & Co.

'Your gift for the Reverend Foster,' she said, looking Springer in the eye.

'Ah, good,' replied Springer. 'Pop it in the study.'

'Also, we should leave no later than four,' she advised him. 'Dinner is at eight.'

Montserrat entered the study and placed the gift-wrapped present on a sideboard, at waist height, adjacent to Springer's elegant yet functional walnut desk.

Exiting the study, she nodded and bade Fenwick farewell, walking the corridor but within earshot.

Springer, upbeat and smiling, gestured inwards.

'I have a fine single malt for us to share. A Macallan. Help yourself, but leave some for me. And make yourself comfortable. I must wrap up the meeting. Ten minutes, max — I promise.'

Springer turned on his heel and walked swiftly away, back to the conference chamber.

FORTY-NINE
THE STUDY

Fenwick, unaccompanied, entered the study. He surveyed the room, which notably had no windows, being lit entirely by subdued electric lighting. Doused in ambers and mellow crimsons, it had the ambience of a warm and welcoming fireside snug.

At the drinks' cabinet, he found the Macallan but opted instead for a different whisky — a blended malt — and prepared a tumbler with ice. He wouldn't touch the drink, suspecting the Macallan was almost certainly spiked, as probably were the other decanters and bottles, and even the ice itself.

Fenwick had repeatedly read the legal brief, an exhaustive discourse on the rules governing self-incrimination and entrapment. Geoffrey Henderson's recommended KC had outlined it all in painstaking detail, argued in three densely packed pages. The admission — or, better still, the confession — had to be voluntary, obtained without deception or duress.

Fenwick knew he was about to play chess with a grandmaster.

He pondered dispiritedly on the ghost of Cedric, who had been beaten to death at *The Grenadier* for cheating at cards. For Fenwick's imminent chess match, he knew the stakes were even higher, with many lives at stake including his own.

He sat in an upright leather armchair, less grand and set marginally lower than Springer's substantial ergonomic chair, opposite the refined desk — a sleek, minimalist design with integrated drawers, a custom leather blotter and a luminous green glass banker's desk light. Framed photographs of Springer with many world leaders and dignitaries adorned the walls and the desk — Kissinger, Soros, the Clintons, Obama, Biden, three Popes, Merkel, Macron, Trudeau... all the great and good, it seemed.

Fenwick placed the tumbler of whisky, untouched, on a table stand, conveniently sited next to his chair. He looked at the gift-wrapped present placed by Montserrat, distinctive in its inimitable turquoise wrapping.

An antique wall-mounted clock with weights counted down the hour:

Tick-tock, tick-tock, tick-tock, tick-tock...

Springer lingered in the Tank with the intelligence officers, both seasoned veterans. The other attendees had departed, leaving the trio to scrutinise the filmed recording of Fenwick's interrogation. The footage flickered as they paused and rewound critical moments, each detail under rigorous review. They concentrated now as Fenwick spoke, his image on the screen grainy and ethereal:

'*As I've said, there's this Ukrainian dimension still to resolve: the missing folder, content unknown.*'

Springer's anxiety was palpable as he turned to the senior officer. 'Your assessment?' he asked, nervously.

The senior officer, a slim man in his forties with saturnine, sharp features, exuded a cold confidence. He leaned forward; his eyes fixed on the man's image frozen on the screen. 'Fenwick hasn't seen the Ukraine file. You got to it before him.'

Springer exhaled audibly, the tension easing from his shoulders.

The senior officer continued: 'And through Fenwick, you've resolved the Tyler problem — namely the wife — and the folder. Her car crash was impressive, by the way.' He gave a satisfied nod, while his younger colleague stifled a grin.

'I thought so, too,' said Springer. 'We adapted the technique from the Stasi.'

A contemplative silence settled over them.

'But plaudits to your people for the intercepts and Tyler's toxicology,' blurted Springer, his relief now manifest.

The senior officer nodded. 'Our hobbits thought Fenwick's burner phones quaint.' It was an idle boast — his cadre at GCHQ had cracked only a fragment of Fenwick's network, with many of his contacts still elusive. They urgently needed to get into Fenwick's laptop.

'Tyler's autopsy?' the officer continued, his rhetoric clinical and dispassionate. 'Drink, drugs, a freezing sea and no questions asked. Compliant pathologists — we have them everywhere.'

Money talked, and twenty-thousand euros, in five carefully timed deposits, had found their way into the pathologist's private bank account in Lisbon, all courtesy of the Nephilim Trust.

Fenwick sat in the armchair, his whisky untouched, its hue a rich amber in the warm, subdued light of the study. He imagined the conversation now taking place within the confines of the Tank. He and Peter had racked their brains thinking how a bug might be infiltrated into the facility, but the opportunity was negligible, and the option had been ruled out.

The entire operation hinged now on just one mission-critical device, with a claimed battery life of a meagre six hours.

Fenwick glanced upward at the antique wall-clock, its mechanical rhythm resonating in his ear:

Tick-tock, tick-tock, tick-tock, tick-tock…

Secure in the Tank, the junior intelligence officer broke the silence. 'Your man came good. The memory stick particularly. Our hobbits found the password on Tyler's phone. We underestimated Ziętek — she'd hacked the entire portfolio.'

Springer was momentarily confused, but then recalled that Tyler's mobile had been recovered from the ferry's deck and airlifted to Cheltenham for forensic analysis.

The senior officer picked up. 'The Nephilim Trust — a veritable Pandora's box, a writhing can of worms. Ziętek also had the Thanatacyn-9 formula and the production and rollout schedules.'

Springer had incorporated Nephilim in the Cayman Islands some fifteen years earlier, running it as sole beneficiary, picking up Jonty as his bar steward and batman along the way. Nephilim was a 'black budget' fund supporting clandestine operations worldwide. All had run swimmingly until Ziętek — a cussed fly in the ointment — had somehow infiltrated Nephilim and downloaded the entire account using a zone transfer from the Caribbean to Poland. Her incursion had instantly triggered countless alarms, recorded in numerous logs and audit trails. Counterintelligence efforts had commenced within hours. The investigation had been complex and time-consuming, impeded by Ziętek's use of VPNs and TOR, none of which meant anything to Springer.

He exhaled with relief. It had been a close call. 'All's well that ends well,' he declared with an ingratiating smile. 'I knew Fenwick would trace Ziętek. He's tenacious for sure, but an obtuse fool also.'

The saturnine senior officer stared at Springer with a look that might kill. 'Climb off your high horse,' he growled. 'None of this should have been necessary, had your team not lost Ziętek in the first place. But yes, you were right to assign Fenwick.'

The subordinate officer interjected, enthusiastically, 'We're very fond of Fenwick. Your plan was sound: wherever he went, we followed!'

His boss looked quizzically at the frozen image of Fenwick on the screen. 'A "useful idiot" he exclaimed after a short pause. 'A pity to dispense with him, really. But needs must when the Devil drives.'

Restless and agitated, Fenwick remained in the armchair, his drink untouched. The entire case played out before him, every twist and nuance. The rat trap in Kraków had sprung impressively, but it was insufficient to prosecute. More probative evidence was required, hard facts that would nail the case; affirmative proof, teased or coaxed from the horse's mouth. Fenwick knew he was now gambling entirely on the man's arrogance and intellectual conceit.

This, then, was the denouement — but was he up to the task?

Tick-tock, tick-tock, tick-tock, tick-tock...

The senior officer studied the manicured nails of his right hand 'There remain loose ends,' he declared insouciantly. 'The computer woman in particular. All of Fenwick's associates must be tracked down and eliminated.'

Springer had only recently been informed of Rachel Chen's existence and relevance. Traced initially by ELINT, the wretched woman had since gone to ground.

'We dealt with one such thorny issue earlier this morning,' said Springer, eager for the senior officer's approval, as he recalled the extreme violence and brutality meted out in the early hours. 'Rest assured, Miss Chen is also on our "to do" list.'

Fenwick checked the hands of the clock. Twenty-two minutes had passed. He imagined his interrogators poring over the covert recording, struggling to interpret his every utterance and expression.

Tick-tock, tick-tock, tick-tock, tick-tock...

'And so, to Fenwick,' said the senior man. 'We've squeezed him like a lemon, but I'm not confident he's told us the whole truth. We need to push him further.'

Springer sensed that the man meant torture — messy and ineffective in his experience. He wasn't averse to inflicting pain, but torture was a blunt instrument — as he himself had observed in the small hours. With Fenwick in particular, more refined methods would be needed.

The junior officer spoke again: 'Fenwick's computer, lifted in Funchal — we need to get into it urgently.' Tracing Fenwick's contacts and the distribution of his files was an absolute priority. 'We need his password and his thumbprint. There's a "live and well" biometric sensor on the laptop; simply chopping his hand off won't do — there needs to be blood-flow, temperature and a pulse. We need Fenwick conscious and compliant to get in.'

The junior officer produced Fenwick's Lenovo L390 ThinkPad from a black attaché case, opening its lid and gesturing to the thumb pad. 'We suggest scopolamine. As a truth drug it's of marginal efficacy, but it has the benefit of erasing the subject's memory beyond recovery.'

His boss smiled malevolently. 'Once Fenwick spills his guts and we're into his computer, you can consign him to the living dead. He'll be a zombie.'

Thirty-three minutes had passed — far too long for a

simple debrief without complications. Fenwick sensed the gathering storm. Rising from the armchair, he stood near the Tiffany gift-wrapped present. Suspecting hidden cameras and microphones, with a faint grin and feigning appreciation of his surroundings, he exclaimed to no-one but himself, 'Such opulence!'

The wall-clock continued inexorably:

Tick-tock, tick-tock, tick-tock, tick-tock...

In the Tank, Springer was adamant. 'Fenwick has served his purpose. I want him out of circulation. Squeeze him like a boa constrictor, but then let's dispose of him. We have an incinerator on site.'

The cremation furnace, secreted in the bowels of Seaton Hall's network of chambers, burned at 1,300 degrees Celsius and could reduce a human body to a pile of gossamer-like ash in fifteen minutes.

'Hmmm,' thought the senior spook, aware of the relative risks of such a disposal. 'Very well. But if you cremate him, be sure not to leave any teeth rattling in the griddle.'

Springer, flanked by Xavier and Nathan in a tight arrowhead, marched the length of the chequerboard corridor.

In the study's armchair, Fenwick was a bundle of nerves.

Any minute now, he thought.

Tick-tock, tick-tock, tick-tock, tick-tock...

FIFTY
HARD KNOCKS

Suddenly, there was a tumultuous bang as the door to the study flew open. Fenwick jumped to his feet, heart racing, eyes wide with shock. Springer sauntered in, breezily. He carried his leather document wallet and a bulky padded airmail envelope.

'Whoa!' he exclaimed, amused at Fenwick's alarm. 'I didn't mean to startle the horses! Sit, sit. Relax.'

He strode to the drinks' cabinet, selected a whisky other than the Macallan he'd recommended, and poured himself a shot, placing the cut-glass decanter on his desk. He settled into his grand chair across from Fenwick, who found his demeanour affable but unsettling.

'We're all agreed — you've done a splendid job,' said Springer. 'There are just a few loose ends to tie up.'

Fenwick sat down guardedly, pondering his next move.

Without warning, Springer pressed a button on his desk-phone. Instantly, the study's door flew open again and Xavier and Nathan stormed in, charging at Fenwick and seizing him with brute force. Fenwick, in their iron grip, struggled and writhed as steel handcuffs were snapped expertly on to his wrists and the chair's armrests. The odds were insurmountable. With resistance futile, Fenwick buckled.

In an instant, the dynamic had shifted beyond recognition. The intellectual battle of wits that Fenwick had so meticulously planned and rehearsed now seemed a disastrous, arrogant and irrelevant fantasy. He faced imminent torture and death, having fatally misjudged his opponent.

Springer, behind the sleek walnut desk, donned his reading glasses and unzipped the document wallet. He took out a transparent plastic zipper pouch marked in bold red: 'FOR DESTRUCTION.'

From the pouch, Springer retrieved the items and laid them on the desktop. Fenwick immediately recognised the razor-slim silver USB flash drive he'd discovered in Tyler's hire car. A pale blue folder with a treasury tag was unfamiliar, but its provenance and importance were immediately evident from the large handwritten title in black felt-tip pen: 'UKRAINE'.

Springer looked at Fenwick over the rim of his half-moon reading glasses. 'These,' he said, gesturing to the items, 'along with other embarrassments...' — he paused dramatically, savouring the moment — '... will be destroyed in short order.'

Manacled to the chair, Fenwick hurled himself at the desk with all his might, toppling the chair and himself in the process, before crashing haplessly to the floor. Springer's whisky decanter shattered, and framed photographs, ornaments and assorted desk items clattered discordantly to the ground. Springer staggered backwards in alarm, stunned at the sudden violence.

Xavier and Nathan reacted instantly, striking Fenwick hard from each flank, hauling him backwards and forcing him down in the righted chair.

Springer, dabbing some blood from a cut on his chin with a pristine white handkerchief, regained his composure. 'Hmmm, that was an uncharacteristic loss of equilibrium — most undignified,' he sneered.

He took the Lenovo L390 ThinkPad laptop from the large padded envelope, placing it on the desk. Fenwick's eyes widened in instant recognition.

Springer turned to Xavier and Nathan. 'Slap him a few times. Not too hard — I want him sentient.'

On cue, Nathan knocked Fenwick out with a single practiced blow.

The room spun and mutated like the worst teenage hangover. With vision blurred at first but gradually sharpening in its focus, Fenwick viewed the turquoise wrapped gift, knowing it to be relevant somehow but unsure as to quite why. He struggled desperately to retrieve the basic elements of the plan from deep within the recesses of his mind, but important details evaded him.

A woman, her features indistinct, gently wiped his face with a damp cloth. The cool balm was comforting, soothing his bruised eye and cheek. Fenwick grimaced at the beating he'd taken, a sharp pain throbbing in his neck and jaw. Gradually, the features of the woman's face clarified and sharpened — it was the French beauty from the Tyler residence, Susan Tyler's self-proclaimed 'social secretary'.

Fenwick tensed his arms in frustration, the handcuffs digging tightly into his wrists. 'Oh God. You!' he groaned.

Springer addressed the woman directly. 'Thank you, my dear. Leave now.'

Grudgingly, Giselle complied, slightly aggrieved at her dismissal from the burgeoning onslaught.

Springer, whisky refreshed, sat at his desk, now restored in orderly fashion. Fenwick strained to see Xavier and Nathan peripherally. His heart sank as he noticed a steel stretcher on wheels, with leather restraining straps.

'Welcome to the School of Hard Knocks,' said Springer scornfully.

'You killed Susan Tyler?' asked Fenwick, realising the futility of any coaxing or subtle questioning.

'No! Don't even bother!' snapped Springer. 'We're not here to engage in meaningless supposition.'

Fenwick, reeling yet incandescent with rage, was determined to itemise the enormity of Springer's crimes. 'Tyler, his wife, the tanker driver, Danusia Ziętek…'

'Save your breath,' interrupted Springer.

Fenwick thought now of the missing index finger. 'Tyler… he never worked for you, did he? You never even met him!'

Springer flashed an enigmatic smile, provoking Fenwick to even greater rage.

'You truly are reptilian scum,' spat Fenwick. 'The girls

at the airbase? For God's sake, man, you have a teenage granddaughter!'

Inside the grey Ford E-transit van, parked six miles from Seaton Hall deep within the forest track, the three-man team listened intently. Springer's voice was as clear as a bell:

'The girls? Slavic street trash. Untermenschen. Bait for underage sexual blackmail, maybe? A couple of grifting little sluts who outlived their usefulness, perhaps? But who knows?'

Fenwick glared at Springer. The monster was assiduously side-stepping self-incrimination, picking his words as carefully as a craftsman selecting his tools.

Springer smiled demonically. *"'Assume nothing. Believe no-one. Check everything,'"* he sneered.

'Your lies about Tyler were transparent,' said Fenwick desperately, knowing that Springer now held all the aces.

'Were they? You asked Esther to investigate our dealings. You told her of my MI6 connections, "tread carefully" you said.'

Fenwick bridled. How the hell did Springer know that?

'Esther?' he blurted; his voice fearful and tremulous.

'Yes. *Esther.*' The tone was impassive, as cold as ice.

Springer drained his whisky, put down his glass and stood up. He picked up the gift-wrapped present and walked to the door.

Nearing it, Fenwick shouted: 'Kismet, Springer!'

The two monitoring personnel in the transit van listened

intently, as the third man — the controller — spoke live to the assault team on the ground through their headsets.

The monitoring continued as the tense exchange in Springer's study unfolded. Fenwick's voice resounded loud and clear:

'*Hubris also. You'll outlive your usefulness, too. Just give it time.*'

Springer looked at Fenwick with amused contempt. 'I doubt it,' he scoffed.

The antique wall-clock showed a quarter-to-four. 'Speaking of time,' he continued, 'it is pressing — dinner at the Athenaeum with the Bishop of Malmesbury. The old rogue is after funds again for the abbey. But it is a good cause, and very tax efficient.'

Springer turned and stared, his ice blue eyes drilling into Fenwick's skull. 'I'll bid you farewell,'

He motioned to Xavier and Nathan, who lurked expectantly in the shadows.

'You can exercise my demons,' he said, exiting.

FIFTY-ONE
DEVIL'S BREATH

D r Jeroným Řezníček stood over his latest assignment. The study was dimly lit, suffused with the acrid smell of sweat and blood. Fenwick was slumped before him, handcuffed to the chair and bruised, his face a mottled tapestry of violence. The brutality Fenwick had endured at the hands of Xavier and Nathan was evident in the deep bruises and swollen features.

Řezníček, an expert in narco-interrogation, was dismayed. The beating had been ferocious, crossing the threshold from interrogation to needless savagery, and Řezníček grimaced at the psychopathology of the men and their disposition to such violence. The injuries to Fenwick's head were particularly concerning, raising the risk of neurological impairment which might greatly complicate Řezníček's task.

Scopolamine — the 'Devil's Breath' — has a dual nature. In the hands of healers, it is a benign medication, used to ease motion sickness and post-operative nausea. However, the drug — a nightshade derivative — conceals a dark secret. A potent deliriant, scopolamine is a powerful psychoactive drug that strips away inhibition, severing the neural pathways by which lies are formulated and truths suppressed. Scopolamine loosens the tongue, much as wine does — 'in vino veritas'.

Řezníček's objective was clear: extract the password to Fenwick's laptop, then coax from him the names and whereabouts of every accomplice. A computer technician, jowly and middle-aged with thick-lensed glasses, stood by, ready to access the laptop using the extracted password and Fenwick's livid thumbprint. Once inside, the technician would copy the machine's contents, preserving every tract of data, byte by byte.

With the computer copied and the accomplices identified, Řezníček was to administer a lethal dose, rapidly inducing hypoventilation and death. He was no stranger to this final, grim task. The confines of the study, cramped and dimly lit, were ill suited for what lay ahead. Řezníček instructed that Fenwick, now strapped to the wheeled stretcher, be taken below ground in the lift, to a place where the interrogation and the final act could unfold in clinical sterility.

The rickety brass gates closed imprecisely with a shuddering rattle and the antiquated lift began its descent. Dr Řezníček surveyed Fenwick's battered face, steeling himself for the task ahead. His thoughts were focused on the delicate balance required to extract the truth without pushing Fenwick beyond consciousness. The line between life and death was wafer-thin, and scopolamine was a blade that cut both ways.

Forcing the clattering lift doors apart, Řezníček and the computer technician pushed the stretcher bearing Fenwick along an extended subterranean passage. They passed through thick, translucent rubber curtains into a large mortuary with steel gurneys and bright white tiles. Steel hooks descended from the ceiling, to which there was attached a peripheral haulage rail. The floor of the basement was configured to be hosed down via a single drainage duct, a sizeable steel plughole. A trickle of dilute blood streamed into its depths.

Řezníček and the computer technician were greeted by Smith, dressed in blue scrubs and eager to assist, who now wheeled Fenwick to a steel gurney. The heavyset, bespectacled computer technician set up a vantage point, arranging Fenwick's laptop on a trolley with adapter cables and external disk drives.

Fenwick drifted in and out of consciousness, his mind a fog of chaos and confusion. He writhed, flexing and flailing against the stretcher's unforgiving leather straps that dug harshly into his flesh. His head thrashed from side to side, eyes wide in horror, as a nightmarish image sharpened into focus, piercing his sanity with its stark, brutal clarity.

It was Esther!

Her lifeless body, stripped and savagely beaten, was compressed into a transparent polythene body bag which hung from the haulage rail. The sight was a grotesque obscenity, Esther's once vibrant form now a bruised and bloodied shell. Her face, gashed and smeared with blood, was pressed hideously against the plastic sheeting, her features frozen in a final, contorted grimace of agony.

Fenwick's mind reeled, struggling and uncomprehending, clawing for some semblance of understanding. Was this a sick reality, or some hellish hallucination? He convulsed in turmoil and excruciating pain. Tears streamed down his face. A primal shriek left his soul, a screaming wail that transcended human suffering, a cry from the very depths of despair:

'Esther! No! NO!'

Springer checked his Patek Philippe rose gold wristwatch; they were running slightly overtime, and the sky was darkening as night approached. He descended Seaton Hall's grand steps to the gravel forecourt, accompanied by Montserrat, who carried the turquoise gift-wrapped box.

An attendant opened the passenger doors of an immaculately presented vintage sedan — a 1939 Talbot 4-litre Sports Saloon, one of only three in existence. Once boarded, the chauffeur set off at a gentle pace, shadowed by a Range Rover backup car with three heavyset bodyguards. The vehicles proceeded along the extensive tree-lined driveway and towards the forest.

A solitary brick chimney rose defiantly from a peculiar, angular structure behind the grand mansion complex, spewing a sinister stream of jet-black smoke that twisted into the sky. Montserrat affected not to notice; her gaze fixed forward. But Springer, couldn't resist a glance over his shoulder. He glimpsed the dense plume in the twilight, a furtive smile playing on his lips.

FIFTY-TWO
REGIME CHANGE

Montserrat, tanned and lithesome in her classic white one-piece swimsuit, sprang from the midship's diving board and arced gracefully and expertly into the sparkling azure-blue Mediterranean Sea.

She and Springer had flown by helicopter that morning from Nice, touching down on the flight deck of the M.V. Potemkin, a 260-foot superyacht owned by the enigmatic and secretive multi-billionaire oligarch Maxim Tarasov. The sleek and stylish vessel was anchored thirteen nautical miles south of Monaco, outside territorial waters, free from inspection or interference.

Montserrat had the run of the ship, with the exception of a single mezzanine deck, an external dining area that had been quarantined for the exclusive use of Springer and a small delegation of VIPs. Such rare 'privy councils' afforded Montserrat some cherished leisure time. Having commandeered the ship's helicopter earlier for an extravagant shopping foray to Monte Carlo, she now luxuriated in the warm sea, relishing the prospect of the ship's spa, massage parlour and beauty salon.

Springer now sat with Tarasov's Chief of Staff, a flamboyant homosexual in his forties called Dupont, or the 'aide de camp' as he was known in the higher echelons of the Winchcombe Group. Although he'd never admit it, Springer secretly liked Dupont, who had an acerbic wit, an eye for the absurd, and a bon mot for every occasion.

With them on this glorious afternoon was Jakub Schwartz of the Saurian Group, who had arrived energised and upbeat, also transported from Nice by Jet Ranger helicopter.

A buffet of fine cold cuts adorned the sideboard, and the assembled company quaffed chilled *Château d'Yquem*, a premier Cru Supérieur wine from Sauternes, waiting for the encrypted satellite link from Washington DC to activate.

The crisp image of Ellen Wilson of the US State Department soon filled the screen, her trademark trouser suit sharply tailored in regal purple. The usual stars-and-stripes backdrop typical of the State Department was nowhere to be seen.

Dupont opened with a flourish. 'You look gorgeous, my darling!' he enthused. 'Love the pantsuit; is it Prada, Coco Channel or Stella McCartney?'

Ellen laughed, while Springer's lip curled derisively.

Sensing his disapproval, Dupont shifted gear, getting straight to the point: 'Mr Tarasov seeks the removal of President Kuznetsov. Installed with our backing, he now bites the hand that feeds him.'

The Cabal controlled hundreds of puppet presidents, prime ministers, cabinet appointees and heads of state — Kuznetsov was just one of several in the former communist bloc. Grudgingly, he'd been cajoled into hosting the bioweapons laboratories uprooted from Ukraine, but now he'd gone rogue, appealing to populist nationalism and seeking to expel all foreign influence, especially that of the United States.

Dupont turned to Springer, his tone beseeching. 'You helped us to install him; we now need him removed.'

In a steely voice, Ellen elaborated: 'Kuznetsov is threatening to expose our rehoused bioweapons programme. He's blackmailing us, threatening to go public. We're playing ball with him for the moment — but we can't do so indefinitely.'

Dupont, leaning forward in his seat, looked at Springer imploringly. 'We'd be most grateful for your assistance.'

Springer swirled a mouthful of crisp, chilled wine as he contemplated his reply. 'It depends on the time-frame,' he said languidly. 'When do you want him out?'

'May, at the latest,' ventured Dupont.

Springer retrieved a leather-bound diary from his document wallet. 'A Spring revolution then. We're currently mopping up your bioweapons programme in Ukraine. Not easy, what with the Russians all over it. But, all things considered, late May is feasible.'

Springer's remark was directed at Ellen more than Dupont — Maxim Tarasov was the financier and facilitator, but Ellen ran the illicit weapons programme — it was her baby.

Schwartz leaned in. 'The proven playbook?' he enquired of Springer, envisioning the planning, resources and mobilisation that would be required.

Dupont's ears pricked up instantly. 'The proven playbook?' he asked, echoing Schwartz but evidently bewildered.

Springer glanced at the crypto-box connecting them to Washington. Despite his usual aversion to exposition, he knew that this deal with Tarasov warranted clarity.

'Killing civilians,' he said at last. 'Women, children, the elderly and infirm, and Kuznetsov's opponents, making sure he gets the blame.' Snipers and assault squads disguised as Kuznetsov's militia would commit the atrocities.

Dupont recoiled, but Springer knew that Tarasov himself would not baulk at the prospect, appreciating the material rewards and returns. '*Pour encourager les autres*,' added Springer nonchalantly.

A brief silence followed, as Dupont grappled with the brutal realities of the situation.

Springer spoke again: 'Ellen, you'll know this: who is the most prominent dissident?'

Ellen, harder than nails and contemptuous of Dupont's diffidence, answered: 'The one Kuznetsov fears most is Morozov. He's exiled in Budapest.'

Schwartz made a note. 'Morozov... I'll pencil him in for April. A car bomb.'

Springer turned to Dupont, who was stunned by the steely dispassion and brute callousness unfolding before him. In an avuncular tone, Springer explained, 'To make Kuznetsov more isolated and reviled — the people's enemy.'

Ellen was a veteran of instigating coups and government overthrows. Her attention now turned to the practicalities. 'Will you deploy armour?' she asked, knowing that the populace would need a lead from the military, whether real or illusionary.

'Possibly,' answered Schwartz. 'Our vehicles are currently prepped for Russian ops but we can respray them with Kuznetsov's insignia.'

Polmilitask could muster a few hundred T-72 tanks and BMP-1s, scavenged from sundry brush wars and tinpot third world skirmishes, which could be transported in theatre overnight by rail. It would entail greasing several palms to ease the way, but that was readily achievable.

Springer, ever pragmatic, interjected: 'We can't have Kuznetsov escaping by plane.'

Ellen recalled Erdoğan's escape in 2016: an F16 pilot had the Turkish President's private jet locked in his gunsights but had refrained from taking the shot — with disastrous consequences.

'Langley will help with that,' she said, referring to her team at the CIA. 'An electronic warfare package and fighter jets on standby, based in Romania. We'll prepare a cyber-offensive as well, and a media package.'

Springer reclined in his chair, surveying the deep blue sea and the cloudless sky. With the Polish difficulty resolved so elegantly, and with the imminent prospect of Winchcombe Group's expansion and his further personal enrichment, life was good. Reflecting on his luck, he felt a little giddy.

For the benefit of Dupont, he would sum up now. 'And so, with the crowds enraged, our paramilitaries enter the Duma. Your candidate appears, order is restored, the crowd hails him as saviour of the nation and hey presto! You have a compliant new president.'

Dupont was aghast at such audacious geopolitical powerplay; he was also far from confident it would work. 'How will Washington, NATO and the Kremlin react?'

Ellen, authoritative and commanding, answered:

'We only start wars when we mean to. Washington and NATO will express grave concerns and then do precisely nothing. After all, we're doing their bidding. Kuznetsov has lost interest in joining NATO, but his replacement will be desperate to align. Or at least he will be if he wants to stay in power.'

Springer marvelled at such coherent realpolitik; with an ally such as Ellen, the world really was at his feet.

Ellen continued: 'As for Russia, Putin is bogged down in Ukraine. His forces are overextended; they don't have the resources to intervene militarily.'

Dupont, knowing he'd have to explain and justify this rationale to his boss, remained unconvinced. 'Won't Putin be angry about yet more NATO expansion?'

Ellen laughed, a breathy witch's cackle. 'He'll be furious. But, so what?'

A contemplative silence fell, providing Springer with the opportunity to produce a handwritten note from his shirt pocket — a shopping list of sorts. Handing it to Dupont, unseen by Schwartz and out of view of the livestream monitor, he murmured, 'At your next briefing with Mr Tarasov, please mention prospecting rights. I seek licence to all mineral and natural resources.'

Graphite, lithium, titanium and nickel were at the top of Springer's list — critical elements to advance The Singularity.

As the meeting wound down, Springer addressed the final question. 'Now, do you want Kuznetsov eliminated or exiled?'

'We want him dead,' declared Ellen without hesitation. 'Even if banished to the other side of the world, he could still wreak havoc.'

Springer chuckled. 'Well, we can't allow that. Our sole purpose is to bring order from chaos.'

Raising his glass, he initiated a toast. '*Ordo ab Chao*!'

Springer, Schwartz and Dupont clinked their glasses as Ellen vanished from the screen.

FIFTY-THREE
BEDFORD ROW

Rain yet again, incessant and heavy, poured on to the city streets. Lucia battled her way to Bedford Row, her umbrella sucked inside out several times by powerful gusts. Splashed most inconsiderately by a speeding car, she felt the damp from the roadside puddle clinging uncomfortably, seeping into her shoes and tights.

Now seated across from Geoffrey Henderson, she found his solid, cheerful and familiar presence comforting in her world, which felt increasingly uncertain and unstable. She'd known Geoffrey since childhood, his reassuring presence consistent through good times and bad.

Geoffrey was no stranger to bereavement and grief. His daughter Charlotte, to whom he and his wife were devoted, had died just years before at the age of thirty-four, the victim of the vicious congenital affliction spina bifida. Geoffrey had adored his only child, and the wound of her departure would never heal. He carried his cross lightly, but the scars were permanent, etched into his soul.

Geoffrey had foregone the habitual offer of a glass of sherry, thinking it inappropriate. Coffee was the order of the day.

Lucia sat upright across the desk, dignified and composed, her grey eyes fixed on him, level and enquiring.

Henderson, a little unnerved by the intensity of her gaze, broke the silence. 'Did you ever get to the bottom of his trip to Poland?' This remained a complete mystery to Henderson, whose private detectives — his 'enquiry agents' — had lost Fenwick after Madeira.

'No, it's an enigma,' answered Lucia. 'Like Charles himself.'

'Well, you found his passport at Chiswick Mall, so I think it's safe to conclude that his departure, in whatever circumstances, was a British occurrence.'

Lucia hesitated, pondering. 'Not necessarily. I found a second passport. His photo, but a false name. Polish visas, successive dates in both.'

Henderson was shocked. He had assisted many dual nationals with passport issues, but the use of an alias suggested criminality or some subterfuge. 'Should I make enquiries?' he asked.

'No, I think not. But thank you.'

'Very well,' said Geoffrey, respecting his client's wish. He took an envelope from Fenwick's file and placed it on the desk before her. 'He also left you this letter.'

Henderson watched inquisitively as Lucia read a single side of Smythson. Through the backlighting, he could discern Fenwick's spidery hand.

'I'm in danger,' she declared. 'Life-threatening,

apparently. Typical Charles! No explanation! Nothing! It makes me bloody angry, if I'm honest.'

In his recent meetings with Fenwick, Henderson had sensed the man's deep-seated anxiety and fear. Dark actors were clearly in the wings, and this latest pronouncement came as no surprise. He paused, thinking how best to broach the pressing issue that now demanded Lucia's attention. As executor with power of attorney, she had to consent; he needed her express permission to proceed.

Restrained and respectful, Henderson broke the silence. 'I seek your permission to activate a codicil in Charles' will. The court's declaration on Charles' death will take time. However, this codicil is urgent and requires immediate attention. Do I have your permission to act upon it?'

Lucia, still reeling from Fenwick's letter, looked up distractedly. It took her several seconds to gather her thoughts.

'Yes, granted, absolutely, whatever you suggest,' she declared at last. 'It may also throw some light on his disappearance. And why the hell he thought I was at such risk!'

It was a ten-minute hop to King's Cross by black cab, and Henderson now tentatively surveyed the bank of steel security cabinets as indicated in Fenwick's codicil. Identifying the precise locker, he typed in a PIN and inserted a key with which he'd been entrusted. On seeing the contents, Henderson frowned — yet another letter and what he recognised to be a hard disk, sealed in silver anti-static wrapping within an evidence bag.

A self-proclaimed luddite, Henderson knew he'd need help with the technical processing. He opened the envelope; Fenwick's spidery handwriting instructed Geoffrey to contact someone named Rachel immediately, listing a mobile number.

Rachel Chen strode towards the reception desk at Henderson Gilbraith & Partners, clad in skin-tight black leathers, shaking her lustrous hair free from the confines of her crash helmet. Summoned to the foyer, Henderson was instantly enchanted, delighted at the prospect of sharing a few hours with someone so intelligent, glamorous and youthful.

The content of Fenwick's hard disk, whatever it held, was likely privileged and confidential. Rachel duly signed a concise non-disclosure agreement without question or hesitation. Geoffrey sensed that the material to be processed might be disturbing, but Rachel assured him they should share the burden — after all, she'd been traumatised by this case and sought answers herself.

Fenwick had supplied a detailed written report, which Rachel promptly decrypted with the given password and printed. But it was the video clips from Poland that silenced the room. Geoffrey and Rachel sat transfixed as the imagery escalated in the levels of mayhem, violence and savagery shown. The shooting of the young girl and the disposal of the bodies caused Geoffrey to cry, the tears quietly rolling down his cheeks, which he dabbed away with a large white handkerchief. Rachel, too, sat in respectful solemnity, horrified by what they had just witnessed.

It was Henderson who had specified the colour red — distinctive and suggestive of an emergency. Rachel, following Fenwick's instructions, set swiftly to the task of reproducing the data, encrypted with the given key, across three sets, on one-terabyte USB 3.2 hard drives — each unmissable with striking crimson vinyl jackets.

As the data copied speedily in parallel, Geoffrey interjected, 'You had a lucky escape!'

'A few hours earlier or later and I'd have been toast,' she answered. 'I went to ground. I'd advise you to do the same. They'll hunt you down too.'

'The Grim Reaper is already knocking on my door,' said Henderson ruefully. 'He'll find me before they do.' He knew he had only months left at most. This act of public duty would be his swansong.

He thought back to the motive behind the petrol tanker explosion. 'You were decoding some files?'

Rachel smiled sweetly. 'Decrypting,' she said, gently correcting him. 'Until my computers were atomised. I have backups, but I'm stuck at the moment — it will take time to build the high-end processors necessary to decrypt — I'm still sourcing components and need a place to station the rigs.'

Henderson opened his desk drawer. It had been a long time since he'd handled a cheque; he looked at the crisp bank draft with the curiosity and reverence of a museum curator. The payee was MISS RACHEL CHEN, drawn against Samuel Hoare & Co, client account 'C', for the sum of £150,000. Samuel Hoare was amongst the longest established private banks in London, its pedigree immaculate with a reputation beyond reproach. Geoffrey had astutely unscrambled the identity of 'C' — correctly deducing it to be the same benefactor who favoured one Charles Fenwick.

Smiling benevolently, he handed the cheque to Rachel. 'This may help.'

Rachel froze, absolutely stunned. 'I can't possibly bank this!' she exclaimed, fearful of money laundering regulations and spot checks.

Geoffrey chuckled. 'It'll clear in the blinking of an eye. You evidently have friends in high places.'

He watched somewhat furtively as Rachel squeezed the cheque inside her leathers, close to her bosom. 'You have backups,' he said. 'That's most auspicious. Let me ponder on that.'

He surveyed the three red hard drives, so efficiently processed by Rachel and now ready for dispatch. 'Speaking of encryption…' he said, 'the content is protected?'

Rachel handed Henderson a printout with a password.

'Thank you, Miss Chen,' he said. 'One for the safe, another by courier, and the third to be delivered by hand. I have a meeting at three.'

FIFTY-FOUR
THE YARD

S enior commanders at New Scotland Yard were not in the habit of granting audiences to private citizens, but today was an exception. The chief constable of Kent had phoned the Commissioner of the Metropolitan Police with a somewhat garbled tale involving a shadowy terrorist group and alleged acts of unspeakable murderous violence. Geoffrey Henderson, sharing the same masonic lodge as the chief constable, had pulled innumerable strings to secure this face-to-face interview. He had hoped to see the commissioner himself, but in the wake of another week of explosive knife crime in the Metropolis, culminating in three teenage deaths, the Mayor of London had convened an emergency summit. The commissioner sent his apologies.

Henderson now sat opposite the commissioner's representative, a senior commander immaculately turned out in his uniform, foreshadowed by a wood-veneered nameplate on his desk which read 'DAC NEIL PLOUGHMAN'. The deputy assistant commissioner, a graduate entrant fast-tracked up the ladder, was known as a safe pair of hands, a man who rarely rocked the boat and did as he was told. Bright enough to pass the senior staff exams, and a diligent if uninspired detective and police officer, the DAC tended to plough his own furrow, sometimes against the better instincts of his subordinates.

As commander of SO15, Counter Terrorism Command, Ploughman had a UK-wide remit and served as the Met's principal liaison officer with MI5 and MI6. Knowing this, Henderson kept his counsel. He was surprised by the formality of his reception. The dark blue-black uniform, bearing even the man's extensive array of service ribbons, was imposing, but it was the stilted way in which Ploughman spoke, replete with strangulated officialese and facile verbiage, that alerted Henderson to the possibility that their interchange might be scripted or choreographed.

Henderson opened his battered brown briefcase and retrieved one of the red hard drives prepared by Rachel, which he now placed on Ploughman's desk, along with the printed password to access its content, his hand shaking uncontrollably, his Parkinson's ever more debilitating.

Ploughman's eyebrows knitted reflexively. 'Two murders? In London?'

'No, in Poland,' answered Henderson. 'Near the Belarusian border.'

Ploughman looked nonplussed. 'That's not really our neck of the woods. Have you contacted the Polish embassy?'

Henderson looked befuddled.

Ploughman's eyes narrowed. 'This isn't some elaborate hoax?'

Henderson's face loomed large, his voice clear, recorded by the office's covert CCTV camera and relayed to a monitor in a secret viewing room next door. The interview was not only being recorded, but the live feed was being assessed in real time.

'Absolutely not,' responded Henderson. 'I wouldn't waste your time otherwise.'

The response was genuine, the hidden assessor knew — Henderson was clearly sincere and motivated by conscience. The black-and-white footage continued as Henderson rifled through his briefcase, submitting Fenwick's printed report, detailing the facts his client had documented of the case, prior to his mysterious disappearance.

'My client Charles Fenwick waived privilege, so you may have his report. My assessment is that he has exposed a major criminal and terrorist network.'

'Terrorism?' asked Ploughman, aware of the ramifications, as was his undeclared colleague next door, viewing the covert feed.

'Terrorist training,' said Henderson. 'At an advanced stage with sophisticated weaponry.'

Ploughman was intrigued. 'How was this filmed?'

'Mr Fenwick was investigating a suspicious death, a drowning at sea. The trail led to Poland, thence the videos.'

It was an imprecise answer, but Ploughman could see that the full story was fastidiously recorded in Fenwick's report, which he now perused.

'Mr Fenwick was a UK national?' he asked at last. 'That might justify a Met investigation.'

'Yes. As was Michael Tyler, the drowned man. Both British.'

A suspicious death at sea and a missing person — they couldn't ignore it, especially with the filmed evidence of the murdered girls from the airbase.

Ploughman studied Fenwick's report, slowly turning the pages. 'There's a lot here to digest. Your allegations are astonishing, but this report appears very detailed and substantial. I'll review the videos and hand the file to Homicide and Major Crime Command.'

Henderson nodded uncertainly. He had studied the command structure with academic scrutiny. Surely, with an impending terrorist threat, this was a job for SO15, not SCO1? Had Ploughman just misassigned the case? And if so, why?

Ploughman tapped some details into a keyboard recessed in his desktop, the screen also secreted from view.

'I've assigned a crime reference number,' he said with a courteous smile. 'Pick it up from reception on your way out.'

Robertson, Ploughman's 'babysitter', watched the black-and-white CCTV monitor predatorially, his eyes tracking Henderson's every movement as the lawyer left Scotland Yard's reception area. Robertson switched immediately to external coverage. The outdoor camera feeds flickered briefly before displaying Henderson's portly, dishevelled figure hailing a taxi on the concourse, his battered briefcase in hand.

Ploughman remained at his desk, immersed in Fenwick's report, the distinctive red hard drive before him. A connecting door, craftily concealed by subtle tessellated panelling, suddenly swung open and Robertson strode purposefully into the room. Nervously respectful of his superior officer, Ploughman put down Fenwick's report, and Robertson sat in the seat Henderson had vacated.

'What d'you make of him?' asked Robertson abruptly.

'Clearly in ill health. I'd say late-stage Parkinson's.'

'How long d'you give him?' Robertson's eyes bored into Ploughman.

'I'm no doctor, but six months, maybe. If he twigs we're burying the case, he'll do immense damage in six days, never mind six months.'

'I agree. He's a ticking time bomb. And if he's dying, he has nothing to lose. We need to defuse him.'

Ploughman shifted uncomfortably in his chair. 'What do you suggest? Obviously, I'll withhold the file from the murder squad.'

Robertson considered the options — both SCO1 and SO15 — knowing the matter would be withheld from both departments, buried forever in a bureaucratic labyrinth.

He instructed his subordinate: 'In the first instance, read the report, watch the footage and then brief me. No emails, texts or calls. Keep it all in my safe.'

Ploughman stammered, 'Okay, but I'll need to convince Henderson we're on the case.'

Robertson sneered inwardly. A seasoned master of

dissimulation, he sifted through his mental playbook, selecting the most appropriate tactic. 'Do what we always do when we have no intention of doing anything.'

'A "scoping exercise"?' Ploughman knew the manoeuvre well, it being a standard tactic for sidelining and shutting down any contentious issue.

'Precisely!' exclaimed Robertson, like a proud tutor praising an enlightened student. 'Tell Henderson you've put your best men on the case, working around the clock. Give him the usual spiel about "national security" and "official secrets".'

Still uncertain, Ploughman sought reassurance. 'What if Henderson doesn't buy it? Threatens to go public?'

Robertson smirked, confidently. 'Have him sectioned under the Mental Health Act as a fixated person.' His voice was as dispassionate as the solution he proposed. He had utilised the tactic several times over the years, incarcerating many dissenting voices with the assistance of compliant doctors and psychiatrists.

Robertson's instructions had been explicit: any interference with Polmilitask or attempted scrutiny of the Nephilim Trust needed to be suppressed ruthlessly. MI6 deemed both entities inviolable.

If push came to shove, Henderson, the ticking time bomb threatening these operations, should be defused — definitively.

FIFTY-FIVE
WARSAW

The package had arrived at Portland Street by motorcycle courier, meticulously documented with a signature and photographed to confirm delivery. Within hours of reviewing its contents, Aleksy was on a flight to Warsaw, arriving at a government-leased apartment in Marszałkowska Street late in the evening. There, he worked through the night, fuelled by caffeine and cigarettes, catching just a few brief hours of sleep as dawn broke.

The diagonally torn beer mat had confirmed the package's authenticity, matching perfectly with the 'keepsake' Fenwick had handed Aleksy during their previous encounter. The bright red hard disk, now connected to the laptop, displayed a low-resolution video. Aleksy now watched it again.

The man and the voice were unmistakable.

'*I am in limbo, possibly held captive, perhaps in an induced coma, or more probably dead.*' Fenwick, in shirt-sleeves, looked pale and gaunt, a washed-out ghost against the plain white wall behind him. His voice echoed from another realm, hollow and distant. '*Elements of your military have gone rogue, but law enforcement and Polish intelligence are most likely complicit, too.*'

Aleksy paused the video.

It was a stark, unambiguous warning. Fenwick wasn't bluffing; who then to trust? In the small hours, Aleksy had prepared an order of battle — the legal, military, police, diplomatic, intelligence and reconnaissance assets necessary to assess and counter the threat. Several specialist units would be needed. Personal contacts would be crucial, to identify those who could be relied upon, and others to avoid.

Aleksy clicked on 'play'.

Fenwick held an external disk drive aloft. '*Herein, recorded, is all of the evidence: names, IDs, contact details, locations and GPS coordinates. The video recordings are self-explanatory.*'

Fenwick had done well, bequeathing Aleksy the most thorough and intricate mission package. Aleksy wasted no time, compiling the target list — names and locations, within Poland and globally. A few key players remained elusive — one man in particular.

The video continued. '*I need your assistance with a missing piece of the jigsaw,*' said Fenwick, cueing the gruesome task of identification.

Aleksy steeled himself, summoning his nerve to watch the clip.

The girl filled the screen, captured on a powerful video field scope. She ran as fast as her legs could carry her, naked, screaming in terror, weaving desperately to escape. The officer entered the frame, striding purposefully, pistol drawn. A muffled bang, and she crumpled to the ground, twitching in her death throes. Then the second bullet, the coup de grace, fired into the back of her head with monstrous precision.

Aleksy's lip curled with revulsion; he was reminded of old war footage of the *Einsatzgruppen* — paramilitary death squads in Eastern Europe that executed women and children, the elderly and infirm, beside the massed graves which the victims themselves had been forced to dig.

Fenwick issued a blunt instruction, his recorded voice eerie in the large, sparse apartment: '*Trace the man.*'

A high-definition close-up of the murderer's face — digitally enhanced using top-of-the-range filters — loomed large on the screen. The man's features were distinct beneath the military peaked cap. Aleksy studied the face carefully, freeze framing and noting its lines from several angles. He activated the facial recognition system and watched as the scanning process commenced, a complex grid assessing every facet, measurement and parameter of the face, rolling through the entirety of the clip, expertly producing a 3-D photofit. There was a pause as the software interrogated the combined services' intelligence database with which it was integrated.

In less than a minute, a match! A passport photo entry appeared on the screen. Aleksy now had a name — Jadranko Cvetkovic — along with several known aliases and a date of birth. Cvetkovic, sixty-three, a war criminal convicted in absentia for his role in the

Srebrenica massacre of 1995, was on the run and had gone to ground.

Aleksy pressed the print button; the murderer's cruel features now appeared in full colour on a single sheet, laid flat on his desk.

With a steely expression, Fenwick spoke determinedly from the screen: '*Deal with him as you deem fit.*'

FIFTY-SIX
A CALL TO ARMS

Chief Cabinet Secretary Jaroslaw Bekas' fingers drummed rhythmically on the highly polished surface of the large oval conference table. Bekas, sixty-two, was the most senior government minister in Poland, with a direct line to the president. He had summoned Colonel Robert Jastrzebski, the head of the Internal Security Agency, to an emergency summit at his secluded winter retreat in Zakopane in southern Poland. The grand timber hunting lodge was nestled in the foothills of the Carpathian Tatra mountains, close to the Slovakian border. Jastrzebski had flown in by helicopter that morning from Warsaw, accompanied by Aleksy, the Federal Intelligence Agency's cabinet liaison officer and their key man in London.

On the table before Bekas lay a printed copy of Fenwick's report and Henderson's distinctive red vinyl hard drive.

Bekas spoke first, breaking the tension. 'So, the woman murdered in Kraków… Ziętek. She was our asset?'

Jastrzebski shifted awkwardly in his chair, clearing his throat before speaking softly. 'Effectively, yes. We were introduced to her. She was embedded in the Saurian Group for eighteen months. She sent us short but precise reports. She resigned when she thought she'd been identified as a source. She went to ground.'

'Short and precise reports. Of what?' demanded Bekas.

Jastrzebski squirmed. 'Arms shipments, terrorism, narcotics, sex trafficking, money laundering.'

'And no-one thought to tell me about any of this?' simmered Bekas, his anger barely contained. 'Hmm. So, why did Ziętek go rogue and contact this Englishman Tyler?'

'She wanted us to act prematurely. I told her it wouldn't be wise to move so quickly. It was too early to strike — we were still assessing severity and impact. I assume she thought Tyler could expose the situation without compromising her.' The explanation rang hollow, even to Jastrzebski himself.

'You didn't neutralise Ziętek or Tyler?'

The use of the word 'neutralise' was unnerving. Surely not? Thought Aleksy.

Jastrzebski, also taken aback, was thinking on his feet. 'No. We assessed them both as manageable irritants, not as threats to national security.' It had been a bad call, and he knew it.

Bekas watched as the man's neck and face reddened. 'And these two girls at the airbase? Were they undercover?'

Jastrzebski turned to Aleksy, seeking confirmation. 'No,' he answered. 'We're trying to identify them. We suspect the first girl was tortured, overdosed or died during a forced sex act. Her friend perhaps saw the killing and was silenced.'

Bekas raised his hands, his eyes rolling skywards. 'God help us!'

Aleksy spoke now, to Bekas as an aside. 'Or maybe they witnessed something *else* they shouldn't have.'

Bekas nodded, for he and Aleksy had already discussed an alternative scenario on a secure line.

Bekas gestured now to Fenwick's printed report and Henderson's red hard disk. 'Remind me, how we came by these?'

Aleksy responded. 'I received them from a contact in London. Or rather, from his lawyer. My contact has vanished.'

'Should we be worried about him?'

'I think not. I suspect he's dead.'

Bekas looked at Jastrzebski in cold fury. 'So, let me get this straight. Your informant exposed a vast web of corruption and an entire criminal enterprise, including a covert paramilitary training facility, even supported by its own airstrip... and you did nothing about it?'

Jastrzebski looked down, abashed. 'As I explained,' he murmured, 'we were still assessing severity and impact. It was too early to strike.'

Bekas struck the tabletop thunderously with the flat of his hand. 'That was not your assessment to make, Jastrzebski!' he shouted.

A prolonged silence fell. At last, Bekas spoke. 'In time, the agent Ziętek will be awarded the Cross of Merit, and a funeral with full civil honours.'

The order broke protocol, but Aleksy would see to it.

Bekas continued, 'Drastic action is called for. What are the options?' The question was directed at Aleksy, Colonel Jastrzebski now an irrelevance.

Aleksy had already consulted several constitutional lawyers. 'Under Article 229 we can declare a state of emergency for a limited duration,' he said. The president could invoke martial law, but only with the consent of the *Sejm*, the lower parliamentary house. Operational security — the need to know — overrode such considerations; they would deal with the legal fallout, as and when.

'How limited a duration?' asked Bekas.

'Ninety days. Maximum.' Aleksy was working on an infinitely more compressed schedule, aiming to complete the operation in weeks, not months.

He passed a slim folder to Bekas containing a vellum form, pre-stamped with the Presidential Seal, issued before dawn at the *Pałac Prezydencki*, Warsaw. Bekas countersigned the document with his fountain pen. 'All necessary resources of the state are now activated,' he declared.

He pressed a button on the conference intercom. Instantly, the double doors opened, and two military police officers, in uniform and with holstered sidearms, marched into the room. Bekas issued the order, 'Colonel Jastrzebski is detained until further notice. No communication at all beyond the duty guard.'

Jastrzebski looked stunned as the officers manhandled him, gripping each arm firmly, then searching him, seizing his mobile phone, wallet and attaché case.

Bekas handed the officers a sealed envelope. 'Search warrants and detention orders for the colonel and his team. With immediate effect.' Aleksy had instructed that the upper echelon of the Internal Security Agency be arrested, pending investigation, with simultaneous office raids and residential searches.

The military police escorted Jastrzebski from the conference room, respectfully closing the elaborate double doors behind them.

Bekas turned to Aleksy. 'Your mission plan is approved. Execute it within thirty-six hours.'

Aleksy turned on his heel.

He was airborne within twenty minutes, carried aloft by a light and nimble 'Tawny Owl' helicopter of the Polish Air Force. Within hours, hundreds of personnel in dozens of disparate units across the country, all on standby for immediate deployment but with no indication as to why, would be activated by means of the state's emergency broadcast system. Aleksy had hit the ground running; he just hoped and prayed he'd selected the task force wisely.

First, however, Aleksy had one further task to complete — one that Fenwick had assigned to him personally.

FIFTY-SEVEN
THE MONSTER

The file on Jadranko Cvetkovic — the murderer at the airbase — was a grim litany of unspeakable atrocities, each page more horrifying than the last. His legacy of brutality reached a nightmarish crescendo during the Bosnian War. Cvetkovic and his Scorpions, a paramilitary unit as ruthless as their name suggested, orchestrated the massacre of over 8,000 Bosnian Muslim men and boys in and around the town of Srebrenica. The Scorpions killed mercilessly, but unleashed also a frenzied and sadistic orgy of terror, rape and torture.

Cvetkovic revelled in the carnage, mowing down hundreds with a gleeful ruthlessness. He set others alight, watching impassively as they writhed and screamed in mosques, barns and warehouses. Bulldozers pushed corpses into mass graves, some victims buried alive. Parents were forced to watch their children slaughtered before their eyes. Women and girls were subjected to gang rapes, and then permanently silenced. The violence spared no-one: men, women, the elderly, the disabled, children, even infants. Torture and beheadings were macabre routines.

At the International Court of Justice in The Hague, witnesses described Cvetkovic as a demon in human form, recalling how he'd beaten a pregnant woman to death with his bare hands.

Aleksy had assigned two of his most skilled analysts to trace Cvetkovic. An alias, one of several adopted over the decades, led to a tax return connected to the small village of Star Masiewo, nestled on the edge of the great Białowieża Forest near the Belarusian border.

Now Aleksy stood cloaked in the shadows of a narrow, isolated lane, lined with towering trees, which provided a natural cover, their thick trunks protective like embracing arms. In the distance, amidst a forest glade, lay a rustic homestead, shuttered with blinds and curtains drawn tight — a testament to Cvetkovic's perpetual fear of identification and arrest. Aleksy knew the fugitive would have surveillance systems and perimeter defences in place.

He placed the holdall quietly on the ground, retrieving a Kevlar tactical vest with ceramic inserts, which he strapped on. He donned a CQCM full-face bullet-resistant mask, as much to conceal his face as to protect it. The mask, in jet black with just slits for his eyes, made Aleksy look like some devilish knight of old. In his shoulder holster was a Charter Arms Pitbull .45 ACP five-shot snub-nosed revolver for concealed carry — reliable and deadly.

Aleksy's primary weapon was his great-grandfather's 1935 'Radom' 9mm. An exquisitely engineered automatic pistol, the Vis 35 had been a mainstay of the Polish officer class and the resistance in the war. The gun had killed several Nazis, and would now do so again.

He strode purposefully to the homestead, quietly ascending the short flight of stairs to the wooden veranda. He stood aside from the front door, out of the line of fire. Cvetkovic's features were etched into Aleksy's memory; he'd studied the 3-D generated images of the man from every conceivable angle.

Extending his arm, he rapped on the door, loudly enough to be heard, but not so much as to signal alarm. After a brief pause, the door opened. Cvetkovic stood there, hesitant, his eyes blinking and squinting in the early morning light.

Aleksy pivoted skilfully, square on to the target with the Radom firmly grasped with both hands, and fired twice in rapid succession — straight and level shots to the head. Cvetkovic reeled backwards, an expression of total shock and bewilderment on his face. Yet he remained disconcertingly upright, unsteady but not knocked off his feet as he should have been. Puzzled by the monster's astonishing resilience, Aleksy fired again — two further rounds to the head, and two to the upper torso, dropping the brute at last.

Alerted by the gunfire, a woman appeared from a room at the back, scuttling and stooped, her face visibly marred with the bruises of a severe beating. She looked at Aleksy in his macabre black mask, her eyes wide with terror. Then she beheld Cvetkovic spreadeagled on the floor, riddled with bullet holes.

Aleksy held his firearm aloft and clearly visible. The woman, heeding his warning, cowered and crouched. Sensing no threat, Aleksy backed away, the world a better place. Cvetkovic could go to hell. If Satan rejected his soul, God would simply snuff it out, as dismissively as squatting a fly.

Departing calmly along the track back to his car, Aleksy swore he'd detected a smile on the woman's face.

One thing was for sure — the Radom didn't have the stopping power. He would use the Pitbull in future.

FIFTY-EIGHT
HARD STOP

At the bustling intersection, the black BMW M760 idled at a red light, its gear-shift in neutral. Kamiński, at the wheel, was absorbed in the satnav, navigating the heavy traffic and fine-tuning the route to the Endpoint Pharmaceuticals laboratory on the outskirts of Katowice. Beside him, Bako, pretty in pink, was engrossed in his Android. Unusually, the team travelled as a foursome, with Jolanta and Schwartz in the back, immersed in printouts of the latest Thanatacyn-9 trials data.

Kamiński paid no attention to the car that eased to a halt behind them, its three male occupants clad in black tactical vests. Nor did he notice the SUV that now idled on the left side of the intersection.

The red light lasted an eternity as vehicles in the intersecting lanes sped across in front of the static BMW. Kamiński, in no particular hurry, awaited the green signal patiently, ready for the off. Green at last. He engaged the drive shift and eased off the brake pedal, the large luxury sedan beginning to glide forward, poised for a swift acceleration.

Over the tactical radio network, the command came: 'Strike! Strike! Strike!'

BANG! The SUV's bull-bar smashed into the BMW's front end with brutal force, shattering its windows and spinning the car uncontrollably out of its lane and hard right.

Kamiński had no time to react. His head slammed towards the steering wheel, the airbag exploding in his face, sparing him serious injury. Jolanta in the back screamed hysterically as another cruiser appeared out of nowhere, screeching to a halt beside her, boxing the BMW in. The passenger airbag had deployed, pinning Bako in his seat. He screamed in panic and confusion, bloodied and evidently in pain.

Doors flew open from the three assault vehicles, and black-clad commandos poured out in balaclavas, automatic weapons drawn and voices barking commands for instant compliance. 'Armed police! Get out of the car! Get out of the car! Hands visible! NOW!'

The driver's door was torn open. Kamiński, stunned but conscious, instinctively reached for his holstered handgun.

'GUN! GUN! GUN!' shouted one of the commandos.

Instantly, Kamiński received a sharp blow from a telescopic baton to the top of his head. Dazed, he was yanked from the car by his collar and hauled brutally to the ground. The commando ripped the handgun free and tossed it along the road out of reach. Others swiftly pulled the remaining occupants out, their cries drowned by the chaos, bodies hitting the road hard and painfully, faces pressed firmly against the asphalt.

Dominating the scene, three of the commandos drew bright yellow Tasers, holstering their firearms. The unit had orders to take the four alive — lethal force only if absolutely necessary. The captives' wrists were now cinched tight with red plastic flexicuffs.

The commandos, veterans of Poland's BOA — the elite antiterrorist bureau — had just executed a textbook vehicular 'hard stop' ambush. Over the tactical radio network, the unit's commander issued the codeword signalling 'mission accomplished'.

The next phase of the operation was about to begin.

The helicopters' engines thundered, rotor blades slicing the air with a deep, bass, rhythmic thumping. Four Sikorsky Blackhawks, each carrying six of Poland's elite GROM assault commandos, flew fast and low, skimming the tree-tops. Locked on to the target, they vectored on a predefined course clear of pylons, telephone wires and ground clutter.

Flanking the formation, two gunships — also Blackhawks — had their door-mounted M134D miniguns primed for devastating suppressive fire at six thousand rounds per minute. Marksmen aboard, armed with Mauser and Accuracy International sniper rifles, scoped out their shots with measured breaths.

The raid was scheduled for daybreak at 0723 CET (0623 Zulu), with sufficient daylight to initiate the assault without night-vision goggles. They were also free of the burden of respirators, with gas masks stored in pouches, readily accessible if required.

Sweeping in tight formation over Kraków's eastern suburbs, the helicopters closed on the target at 260 kilometres per hour. Civilians below, stunned by the noise and fleeting shadows, craned their necks skyward, catching glimpses of the powerful machines surging forward in a tight diamond formation.

The assault teams, clad in fire-resistant overalls and body armour, weapons at the ready, listened intently over the tactical radio network through helmet-integrated headsets. Each man was armed with a Colt M4A1 Bushmaster assault rifle or a Heckler and Koch MP5 machine pistol, their pouches brimming with ammunition in high-capacity magazines. Sidearms, Berettas with laser sights, completed their arsenal.

Framed charges had been meticulously tested and prepared to breach the roof and windows of the bungalow. Shaped charges and blocks of C4 plastic explosive were designated for the communications bunker to the rear of the complex.

GROM, Military Unit 2305, known as 'The Surgeons', had been on standby for days. The mission plan was explicit, yet the target remained a closely guarded secret. High-resolution aerial videos and photographs, transmitted by an RQ-21 Blackjack high-altitude reconnaissance drone, had shown the complex in stunning detail. The soldiers had presumed an overseas operation; they were astonished now to find themselves fast approaching a residential area in Kraków's suburbs.

Intelligence indicated that hostages were held captive, greatly complicating the mission's intricate planning. Gaining entry to the building would be difficult. The pretext of a gas leak was ruled out — the heavy firepower necessary to overcome the occupants deemed too conspicuous. A perimeter security team would impose a lockdown, confining residents to their properties. Mains gas supplies were now taken offline, and cell-phone coverage revoked for the duration of the raid.

Sergeant Tadeusz Zawadka, in a postman's uniform, wheeled his bright red handcart undemonstratively along the street. He had a special delivery for the large bungalow ahead. The street was quiet, with no traffic. Birds chirped the dawn chorus; dogs barked in the distance.

The countdown crackled in Zawadka's earpiece — the helicopters would arrive within the minute. He checked the compact Škorpion vz.61 sub-machine gun, concealed in a brown paper-wrapped parcel. The weapon had been rigorously field-tested, capable of firing from within the box — crude but effective apertures fashioned with a craft knife for the muzzle and ejection mechanism. Tucked in the small of his back, nestled a diminutive yet man-stopping Hellcat 9mm automatic, high capacity, in a quick-draw holster. Zawadka, GROM's top marksman, had volunteered for the job — the most perilous task on an already exceptionally dangerous mission. He was about to knock on a door, with no idea what awaited on the other side.

The lead Blackhawk pilot's voice cut through the radio. 'On my mark,' he stated, his voice calm and assured.

'Twenty, nineteen, eighteen…' Zawadka, hearing the countdown in his earpiece, pressed the entrance intercom, standing in plain view. The guard, seeing the postman on the VDU, rose lazily, a revolver tucked in his waistband.

The heavy steel door of the bungalow opened, its weight shifting on well-worn hinges. Zawadka grinned at the guard amiably. 'I need a signature,' he said, raising the parcel and instantly firing the Škorpion on full-auto. Twenty bullets tore across the man's torso in just over a second, cutting him down instantly. Zawadka dived to the ground, aiming the Hellcat pistol with its red dot laser sight beyond the man's slumped body, and along the dark corridor behind.

Overhead, the Blackhawks arrived precisely on time, engines roaring, the downwash from the rotors whipping up a maelstrom of debris in a chaotically swirling vortex. Abseil lines dropped, unfurling like serpents, at a hovering height of about thirty feet. Skilled loadmasters spaced each commando's rapid descent in precise drops at three-second intervals, the soldiers disgorged from both sides of the fuselages. Most commandos descended fluidly, their deployment precise and controlled. But Corporal Tomasz's rope snagged awkwardly in his steel carabiner, leaving him dangling mid-air, jeopardising the helicopter and the mission. The loadmaster instantaneously pulled a lever, dropping the rope from its sponson, sending Tomasz into freefall. He crashed hard on to the bunker's unforgiving concrete roof, narrowly avoiding being impaled by the structure's array of aerials and satellite dishes.

Vehicles screeched into the street, synchronising the

ground assault with the aerial strike. Toyota Land Cruisers and black Ford trucks surged forward, replete with overhead steel gantries and running boards. Commandos dismounted, running, weapons concentrated on the building, eyes scouring for any movement or threat. Two much heavier armoured vehicles followed — 4x4 MRAPs, mine-resistant and ambush-protected, with remotely controlled weapons stations, bounced to a halt in the bedraggled, overgrown forecourt, providing covering fire and shelter.

With the breach teams deployed atop both target buildings in less than thirty seconds, explosive charges were placed and detonated. A series of ear-splitting booms rang out, blowing sizeable apertures in the roofs of both structures. Laser red dots danced and flickered in the smoky haze, seeking targets and potential hostages in the exposed spaces below. With deft teamwork, the commandos dropped into the confines of the upper floors, commencing a top-down room clearance.

Deafening explosions and blinding flashes followed as stun grenades detonated, disorienting anyone within range, igniting fires. One commando engulfed momentarily in flames dropped and rolled, a colleague quick to douse him with a compact hand-held fire extinguisher.

Radio communications were clipped, urgent Polish commands and reports punctuating the channel as teams relayed their progress through the buildings and the labyrinthine network of chambers and tunnels that they now encountered.

Inside the bungalow, chaos erupted. A skeleton

staff — lightly armed but stunned and overwhelmed — scrambled to respond. The commandos had secured the entrances, moving like a dark wave, sweeping through rooms and basements with lethal precision. Stun grenades were primed and hurled along corridors and through inner doorways, their blinding light and deafening noise disorienting the captors within. Gunfire, sharp and sporadic, echoed noisily from both the bungalow and the bunker as the assault squads closed in, room by room.

Armed occupants engaged as best they could, their weapons blazing. But the commandos were quicker, their own fire cutting down the enemy with ruthless efficiency. Gunfire echoed through both buildings — short, sharp reports punctuated by the deeper booms of grenades. The captors were disorganised, their resistance sporadic and poorly coordinated. The commandos, in contrast, moved as one, each step calculated, every shot deliberate.

'Five dead. Hostages located,' came the situation report, the first team to enter having breached the bungalow's basement. Eight girls were huddled in fear, most crying, some screaming hysterically.

All inside the building were treated as hostile until proven otherwise, as the hostages could be boobytrapped or complicit — the commandos were acutely attuned to the risk of Stockholm syndrome. Forming a disciplined line at precise two-metre intervals, the eight girls were hurled like ragdolls from one burly soldier to the next, up steep flights of concrete steps to the ground-level exits.

In the crosshairs of the GROM sniper teams, the girls emerged into the daylight, terrified and dazed. The commandos hurled them to the ground, hooded them and secured their hands behind their backs with flexicuffs, before marshalling them onwards. Safe and secured, then thrown brutally inwards, they were whisked from the scene in two vans with blacked-out windows which had a police escort and motorbike outriders, sirens wailing.

The mission had its stumbles — Tomasz's wayward descent, and a soldier momentarily on fire — but the objective had been achieved: the hostages were safe, the captors neutralised and the crime scene secured.

An EOD team stood by, awaiting the summons to inspect the entire complex for bombs, unexploded ordnance and boobytraps. Only when the buildings were pronounced structurally safe and free of hazards would the intelligence and SIGINT cadres be permitted entry; the strange signals transmitted from the bunker were their absolute priority.

Major Bartek Filipowski of the Polish Air Force initially thought there'd been a mistake. A ground attack with live weapons on Polish territory? But the GPS coordinates were unambiguous and the Air Tasking Order was clear: a precise area denial mission with suppressive fire.

Filipowski, an F16 pilot and senior weapons instructor with the 10th Squadron based at the 32nd Tactical Aviation Base at Łask in central Poland, had been summoned unexpectedly from his home just after midnight, informed that he'd be flying a live mission within hours.

The operational requirements were specific: the destruction of a runway, the suppression of ground personnel, and neutralising a localised armoured force. It was to be a 'shock and awe' display, designed to intimidate and cower the opposition before a broader ground and air assault on the facility. A single building — a large concrete bunker festooned with transmission aerials — was specifically excluded from bombardment but was to be subjected to a low flypast at extremely high speed, in preparation for a commando assault.

Filipowski studied the surveillance photographs of the target, set deep in the great Białowieża forest. The runway was tiny, little more than 600 metres in length. A few vehicles were visible, but the majority of the force was hidden under the treeline, as revealed by heat signatures that glowed brightly amidst the thermal imagery.

In the small hours, Filipowski prepared the mission. He assigned three F16C fighter jets, each configured with conformal fuel tanks that extended their range. Fellow pilot Rafal would take the lead, with his wingman Marek trailing. Filipowski would follow through, flying the 'intimidation' run. The selection of ordnance for this mission was obvious — only one weapon met the mission's requirements.

Rafal and Marek, on duty with the Quick Reaction Alert team, reported for a briefing within minutes of being summoned. Filipowski removed the data transfer cartridges from the Mission Support System, pocketing one and handing the others to his team. The cartridges would transfer the flight plan and strike coordinates to the jets' onboard computers and Target Management Systems. Air Traffic Control had cleared a corridor for the ingress —

a relatively sedate approach at twenty-five thousand feet, followed by a phenomenally sharp descent to just three hundred feet on the run-in to the computed weapons release point, timed at precisely 07:40 CET — 06:40 Zulu. Radars and surface-to-air missiles were not anticipated, but anti-aircraft fire and shoulder-launched missiles — MANPADS — were deemed a clear and present danger.

Shrouded in the morning mist and darkness, the three elite pilots walked to the apron. The load crews and armourers, bright in yellow and orange fluorescent vests, prepared the jets, their breath misty-blue in the freezing night air.

The airbase was peaceful, with an assortment of trucks, jeeps, armoured personnel carriers and infantry fighting vehicles parked, their steel husks glinting dully in the dappled sunlight that filtered through the thick canopy above. Peripheral wooden barracks stood silent, their occupants — paramilitaries — slumbering in the stillness of early dawn. Only a few sentries patrolled, heedless and bored.

Skimming the trees, the jets thundered in just below Mach 1, approaching the airstrip at a heart-stopping altitude of three hundred feet, the minimum release height for the Mk-20 Rockeye cluster munitions to activate. The air erupted with the deafening roar of jet engines, shattering the morning calm, the jets' huge air intakes gulping the air greedily with an alien high-pitched whooping. The F16s hurtled down the centreline of the runway, their sleek forms slicing the air, a shimmering white shockwave afore their leading edges, nose-cones and canopies, a garbled haze of exhaust left in their wake.

Ejector racks beneath the two F16s' wings had jettisoned the munitions exactly at the computed release points, in a straight line some three hundred feet before the runway approach. The sub-munitions, propelled unaided by kinetic energy, hurtled forward, gliding to the ground in graceful formations, 988 bomblets detonating in a rapid, percussive sequence of crippling explosions, each capable of penetrating seven inches of steel armour.

The airstrip erupted in a maelstrom, eviscerated beyond repair. A frenetic chain of peripheral ground-bursts blasted the parked vehicles to pieces, reducing them to smouldering, twisted metal casks, obliterating the BMP infantry fighting vehicles and BTR-80 armoured cars concealed beneath the forest's cloak.

With a final, thunderous roar, the F16s engaged their afterburners and surged skywards, piercing the low cloud base and vanishing into the heavens.

Filipowski, summoning his nerve and all of his skills, now approached, skimming the treetops, flying marginally below the speed of sound at a death-defying two hundred feet. As he rocketed across the target, the ground a blur below him, 'Bitchin' Betty', the onboard terrain avoidance warning system, screamed incessantly in his headphones: 'Pull up! Pull up! Pull up!'

Streaking along the airstrip, a screaming blur of metal and fire that tore through the air, he stormed over the heavily fortified control bunker, the thunderous, deafening roar paralysing its occupants in sheer terror.

Filipowski gripped the controls, his heart pounding. He pulled the aircraft into a sharp ascent, his body crushed into the ejector seat by immense G-forces. ZSU-23 'Shilka' anti-aircraft guns, now alerted, opened fire, hopelessly late to the party. Tracers — white and red hot — blazed past, hosed skywards in futile arcs.

The F16 powered into a near-vertical climb, soaring out of enemy range. Through the tactical network, Filipowski heard the confirmation: the ground assault had commenced. Apache helicopters were tearing through the armoured vehicles and barracks, their 30mm auto-cannons and missiles precise and deadly. GROM special forces had stormed the command bunker, progress unknown.

Amidst the chaos, the airstrip lay in ruins, a testament to the ferocity and precision of the strike.

FIFTY-NINE
BLACK SITE

In the dimly lit room, Aleksy's specialist intelligence cell had been glued to the clip, rerunning it again and again. The three elite analysts — two men and a woman, as absurdly bright as they were young — scrutinised every frame, every syllable, hoping to uncover a clue or some nuance that had escaped their attention. They paused the clip yet again, dissecting each word with surgical precision.

Fenwick stared at them, a ghost of a man in his shirtsleeves, yet every word he spoke bore a gravity that demanded attention:

'*And so, to a folder marked "Ukraine". This file has been causative to several murders. "Ukraine" is the crux of the matter, a Doomsday file. I believe it represents an existential threat — globally.*'

'Doomsday', they knew, was a term Fenwick would not employ lightly.

The clip resumed, strikingly luminescent in the darkness. '*Sift every location for data or information pertaining to Ukraine. Deep dive at a forensic level. Digital, multimedia, online, printout, trash, everything.'*

The young female analyst pressed 'pause', and heaved a sigh of frustration. They had pursued every conceivable lead, yet a breakthrough remained elusive.

She restarted the clip. *'BSL4: the ZIP files on Tyler's memory stick — biosecurity laboratory category four.'* Fenwick didn't elucidate. Aleksy had instantly deduced as much from the filenames. Level 4 was the highest level of containment, reserved for the deadliest toxins and pathogens.

The narrative continued, severe and unyielding. *'Be warned. Computers may be hot-keyed to erase or auto-encrypt. You will encounter many hazards along the way, some of them life-threatening.'* The threat of boobytraps — both digital and explosive — loomed large, though none had yet materialised. The team was acutely aware of the risks.

'Also, signals intelligence: monitor the airwaves around the clock. Deploy your best people.'

A combined services SIGINT unit had examined the burst transmissions from the bungalow supplied by Fenwick. Despite their efforts, the encryption and compression had confounded them, leaving the identity and location of the correspondents shrouded in mystery, as were the messages themselves.

The mission Fenwick outlined was clear yet daunting. The dismantling of Polmilitask — branded an enemy of the state — was proving intricate and hazardous. Saurian Group posed an even greater challenge on account of its vast size, ambiguous legal status and multijurisdictional footprint. Intelligence efforts were currently zeroed in on Kraków and Białowieża.

Fenwick's brow furrowed. *'There is a project, or a specification or even a location — I don't know which — designated "T-9". Schwartz and Bako are sitting on it.'*

'T-9' was a deceptively simple designation that had yielded an avalanche of 'false-positive' data, burying the analysts beneath a mountain of digital chaff. Every laptop, computer, server, backup tape, media store and cloud repository seized from the Saurian Group, Polmilitask and Endpoint Pharmaceuticals had been combed through. The meagre and brutally succinct reference 'T-9' had generated millions of hits, a haystack far too vast for even the sharpest of minds to sift through. With no suitable AI tool at hand to ease the burden, the analysts were at an impasse.

'T-9' was now Aleksy's paramount concern, overriding all other considerations, a Gordian knot to be untangled — or preferably severed.

'And sweat all detainees,' commanded Fenwick. *'Use your best interrogators. Sodium pentothal, if need be, or whatever you people use nowadays.'*

Jakub Schwartz and his team, incarcerated under constant surveillance, were held at a 'black site' within the Intelligence Agency Training Centre at Stare Kiejkuty in north-east Poland, an impenetrable fortress supervised by the ultra-secretive Unit 2669. A cocktail of psychoactive drugs was under evaluation — 3-quinuclidinyl benzilate, flunitrazepam, sodium thiopental and amobarbital — each one a potential key to unlocking the truth.

Fenwick's gaze bored into the camera, his expression intense and severe.

'*Finally, a posthumous request,*' he said, his voice softening. '*The girls at the airbase. Disinterred, identified, and afforded a dignified burial. Paid for by my estate.*'

Silence fell over the room, the solemnity settling like a shroud.

'*Powodzenia,*' Fenwick said finally, before signing off.

The screen went black, leaving the analysts with a mission as insurmountable as it was urgent.

SIXTY
CHAMBER OF HORRORS

lurries of snow whipped chaotically, the tail end of a blizzard that had engulfed the Russian steppes and had then drifted westward, encasing the forest's clearing and the airstrip in a crisp white blanket. Aleksy huddled in his leather trench-coat, the ice particles stinging the exposed skin of his face, his freezing breath misted.

Military engineers had entered the chamber clad in hazmat suits and respirators, to examine its structural integrity and the storm channel that ran through it. They meticulously searched for tripwires, grenades, explosives and boobytraps. It took over an hour before they gave the all-clear. Only then did the forensic pathologist, accompanied by a scene-of-crime specialist with cameras and toolkit, begin the grim task of cataloguing and securing the evidence.

Even in the frosty air, Aleksy recoiled at the stench of death — a foul cocktail of cadaverine, putrescine and gaseous sulphides — which assaulted his nostrils in fetid blasts carried by the wind. It would be hours before the cadavers could be retrieved, and Aleksy, unable to meaningfully assist, took refuge from the biting cold in the concrete command bunker at the end of the runway.

Sheltered by the casement, secure behind its reinforced concrete, he spent an hour sifting through the evidence that had been collated. He thought of the price paid in blood — a commando had died in the assault on the bunker; another had sustained life-changing injuries. He shuddered at the thought, aware of his culpability.

The entire complex, above and below ground, had been wired for sound and vision. Hundreds, possibly thousands, of video recordings had been retrieved of unspeakable rapes and tortures, perpetrated mostly against young girls, most of whom appeared to be teenagers and even younger children.

The operation was a blackmail factory, expressly designed to compromise and entrap persons of influence, nearly all of whom were male. Aleksy thought of Jeffrey Epstein and his island in the Caribbean; these 'kompromat' operations, he knew, operated worldwide. The number of those so ensnared was incalculable; the harm that those blackmailed did to the public good, immeasurable. In instigating these outrages, the perpetrators used a range of mind-bending psychotropic drugs — a large haul of which now sat on the bench before him.

Aleksy's walkie-talkie sounded, its harsh robotic utterance summoning him outside. The disinterment was complete, the pathologist said, with the remains of the girls recovered intact.

The sleet and howling wind lashed Aleksy as he trod through fresh layers of crisp snow. In the distance he could see a military chaplain, two coffins, and undertakers. The chaplain looked incongruous, in military fatigues but bedecked with the baubles, sashes and colourful trappings of ceremonial office. Aleksy watched as the coffins were loaded on to the Mi-8M, a muscle-bound, camouflaged military helicopter requisitioned for the grim task. He climbed aboard and buckled in alongside the coffins. Each modest casket — piteously small — was braced against displacement by tightly ratcheted canvas straps.

Ascending rapidly, Aleksy in ear-defenders to protect him from the thunder of the helicopter's twin turbines, looked at the snowscape below. Bulldozers, dump trucks, recovery vehicles and a small army of contractors in bright orange-and-yellow hi-vis jackets were systematically disassembling the airbase, leaving dirty, muddy tracks in their wake. A shameful episode was being erased from history, never to be revisited.

As the helicopter banked tightly on a south-westerly course towards Warsaw, the pathologist's words resounded in Aleksy's head: 'There are more bodies down there,' the man had said, gravely. 'Many more.'

SIXTY-ONE
'REGNUM DEFENDE'

The vast, conspicuous and modernist headquarters of MI6 towered imposingly on the south bank of the River Thames in the London borough of Vauxhall. The building's grandiose yet deceptively childish block-like design had earned it the affectionate moniker 'Legoland' among those who worked within its walls.

Forsyth and Langford, veterans of the service, knew better than to discuss sensitive matters anywhere within the confines of the building. Instead, they utilised a series of commercially serviced offices, rented by the hour at astonishingly short notice, to minimise any opportunity for eavesdropping or surveillance.

They now found themselves in one such office behind Southwark Cathedral. Both men, impeccably tailored in Savile Row suits, watched the early evening news on a large flatscreen television mounted on the wall.

A young woman spoke earnestly to camera: '*There are reports this evening that Polish fighter jets have bombed a terrorist installation within Poland itself.*'

A female anchor, glamorous and severe, cut in: '*A terrorist base inside Poland?*'

'*The Polish Ministries of Justice and Defence have refused to comment, and we have no independent verification of the claim, but...*'

Forsyth switched the television off, abruptly.

'What a monumental fucking omnishambles. How did this happen?' he snarled, swirling his whisky in a cut-glass tumbler.

Langford stared absently at the blank screen. 'Springer's Polish operation was blown. We're not sure how, or by whom,' he said vaguely. 'According to Christie and Goodall, a man called Fenwick.'

Forsyth frowned. 'Fenwick?' he spat. 'Who the fuck is Fenwick?'

'A spanner in the works. Springer brought him in to conduct a counterintelligence investigation. Springer had soiled himself badly and his bottom needed wiping.'

Forsyth grimaced; the analogy too gross.

'Fenwick's dead, but he's left a "shit file,"' said Langford, referring to a posthumous 'insurance policy' — the occupational hazard they now faced.

Springer had become an intolerable liability. Nephilim and Polmilitask had been instituted as proxy assets to finance and fight foreign wars and support clandestine operations globally. Springer had increasingly treated both operations as his personal fiefdoms, misusing the funds and the mercenaries to further his own commercial ventures, especially in Africa. Enforcing land appropriations for Springer's oil companies in Nigeria, Polmilitask's paramilitaries had gone rogue, massacring entire villages, with hundreds killed and thousands displaced. Forsyth and his officers spared no effort to suppress the scandal — resorting mainly to hush money and bribes, but applying also coercion, intimidation, blackmail, incarceration and even localised murder to prevent the atrocity from hitting the headlines.

'Has Springer been arrested yet?' asked Forsyth.

Langford topped up his whisky with a jet from a soda siphon. 'No, but it's only a matter of time.'

Forsyth fretted, the cogs in his mind whirring. 'If they offer him a clemency deal, we'll all end up standing on trapdoors.'

Parliament's Intelligence and Security Committee didn't worry Forsyth at all — it was toothless and easily blind-sided. But meddling journalists, human rights charities and lone-wolf back-bench MPs could stir things up. Overzealous cops also, and the police were closing in. There were many corpses — both metaphorical and real — buried and hidden, rotting but discoverable.

'We need a "deep clean",' Forsyth said determinedly, thinking through the options. '"Donkey Bollocks"?' he ventured, referring to a seasoned 'odd job' man.

Langford had considered the options, too. 'No, it's not Donkey Bollocks' style. He's a master with guns, explosives, even toxins. But this calls for something more esoteric,' he said, the inference clear.

'I agree. Are "Smashie" and "Nicey" still on our books?'

Langford smiled knowingly. 'Off our books, yes.'

'Good, activate them — this needs to be done quickly.'

Langford, heedful of the order, sprang to his feet and headed to the door.

'Oh, and Langford?'

Langford stopped and turned, attentively.

'Make it hot and spicy,' said Forsyth with a glint in his eye. 'Blanket coverage, all channels.'

SIXTY-TWO
THE REMOVAL MEN

I t had been raining daily in London for weeks, but on this particular March evening, the downpour was of biblical proportions. The gutters overflowed from the upper storeys, pouring sheets of water onto the street below, a cascade that drummed the pavement with relentless force.

Seated at his desk on the fifth floor of his townhouse in Holland Park, Sir Frederick Springer was penning a letter to his legal team, each sentence meticulously crafted to fortify his defence, with every conceivable argument that might sway a court in his favour. Montserrat's absence was a bloody nuisance — her sharp intellect was sorely missed at this crucial time, but she'd unexpectedly and most inconsiderately taken annual leave, leaving Springer to fend for himself.

A quiet, respectful knock on the door interrupted his train of thought.

'Come!' he bellowed.

The study door opened to reveal Joan, his venerable housekeeper. She stood deferentially in the doorway.

'I plan to finish for the day,' she said softly. 'If there's nothing further, sir?'

'No, nothing. Cut along Joan,' he snapped, dismissing the woman with a casual wave of his hand.

Across the street, two men watched intently as Joan left the townhouse with raised umbrella. Their white van, parked diagonally opposite, bore side panels which read 'DISPOSAL / REMOVALS, 24/7', reflecting just one of many uses to which the ageing vehicle had been applied over the years. The passenger window was down, offering an unimpeded view of Springer's residence. The windscreen was misted by the occupants' breath, and the wipers swept back and forth, squeaking with each shrill, rubbery pass.

Smashie, forty-one, in jeans and a bomber jacket, and Nicey, thirty-two, bespectacled in a suit and tie, watched Springer's house with unwavering attention. The two men had bonded as bouncers at 'Whispers' nightclub in Braintree, Essex. A succession of more rarefied and lucrative side jobs had soon materialised from out of the shadows, all on the nod — *omerta* strictly applied. Ten grand each was their rate for tonight, in used fifties.

Through the downpour, a single light in the top-floor window now shone brightly.

'No LED. The alarm's not set,' observed Smashie.

Nicey retrieved a translucent document wallet from his holdall. 'Right. I'll open the door once the takedown is complete,' he said, before exiting the van and running across the road, stooped with his head bowed against the battering rainstorm.

Inside, Springer picked up the telephone. It was Roland, senior partner and lead counsel at Braithwaite, his principal solicitors. The man had hardly started to speak before Springer cut him off. 'No! You listen to me!' he hissed. 'There will be no trial, no taking the stand. King's evidence is out of the question, as is protective witness status. You guarantee me safe haven, a new identity — untraceable — and the preservation of my wealth and assets. Only when those conditions are met...'

The ground-floor doorbell rang. Puzzled, Springer looked at the wall-clock; it had gone half-past-eight. He ended the call abruptly and pressed an intercom button.

'What is it?' he demanded, clearly irritated.

Nicey spoke into the intercom, adopting his finest received pronunciation: 'I have an urgent dispatch for Sir Frederick Springer.'

'Press button two,' snapped Springer. 'The security detail will deal with it.'

'I've tried that sir, but there's no response,' said Nicey, apologetically.

Springer pressed a direct dial to protective services, to no avail. He felt a pang of unease — there should always be three bodyguards on duty round the clock.

'It's from Vauxhall; it requires biometric authentication,' said Nicey. '"Action this day" and "for your eyes only".'

Springer felt a frisson of unease. 'Wait there,' he barked, before heading for the staircase.

Descending speedily to the hallway, Springer scrutinised the VDU, eyeing the respectable-looking young man on his doorstep, who brandished an official-looking document wallet. With an impatient sigh, Springer opened the front door.

'Sir, may I come in?' implored Nicey. 'It's raining cats and dogs out here.'

Springer saw that the young man was drenched. 'Yes, yes, come in,' he growled, peeved at the imposition.

Nicey entered the hallway, soaking wet, and Springer closed the door behind him. Nicey dried his spectacles with a handkerchief before handing Springer the transparent wallet.

'Pray tell,' snarled Springer. 'What is so urgent that they dispatch a courier at this hour?'

Nicey shrugged. 'That's above my pay grade and security clearance, sir,' he said meekly. 'But, if I had to guess...' he continued, dropping the upper-class accent, '... I'd say it was your P45.'

In an instant, Nicey headbutted Springer with explosive force, shattering the bridge of his nose. Blood sprayed in a sweeping arc, splattering on the wooden parquet as Springer reeled backwards, losing his footing on the polished floor. He crashed heavily to the ground, his ribs cracking audibly.

Nicey moved in swiftly, producing a ligature from his jacket pocket, a thin leather 'cheese-wire' with wooden toggles at both ends. He wound it tightly around Springer's neck, tensioning it with successive, brutal turns. Springer's face contorted in sheer agony, his jugular veins bulging as his eyes swelled to bursting point. He writhed in pain, a ghastly, liquid gurgle rattling in his throat. His body convulsed violently at first, then twitched, before finally going still.

Panting with exhaustion, Nicey surveyed his latest victim. Springer's death had been excruciating, the strangulation lasting more than a minute, necessitating a constant winding and compressing of the ligature. The deceased's face was crimson, the tongue grossly engorged with blood, his eyes protruding hideously from their sockets. The blood vessels in Springer's head had nearly exploded from the applied pressure.

After taking several minutes to recover from the sheer exertion, Nicey dragged the corpse to the rear of the hallway, unceremoniously hauling it by the scruff of the shirt collar. Once Springer's body was out of sight from the entrance, Nicey switched off the hall light, opened the front door and flashed the white van's windscreen with a Maglite pocket torch.

Smashie, alerted by the signal, quickly crossed the road and entered the porch, carrying a sizeable valise.

The staging was always the fun part, thought Nicey, as they carried Springer's corpse upstairs to the master bedroom.

It had taken six hours in total. All evidence — papers and documents mostly — had been bundled for removal and shredding. Digital devices and media had been bagged likewise. Springer's laptop, his phone and SIM cards would simply vanish. The CCTV recordings for the entire night were erased by a technician from Department Q. A chap called Alfred had arrived in the early hours, breaking into Springer's wall-safe in less than an hour, the contents removed, never to reappear. Every surface was wiped down with Jeyes fluid, removing the blood on the parquet floor and all traces of DNA.

Smashie and Nicey surveyed their handiwork with the discernment of master craftsmen. They'd stripped Springer naked and added a couple of accoutrements: a medium-sized dildo inserted hard into the man's rectum, a ball-gag in his throat, and a tight black leather gimp mask with zipper over his head. The body, suspended inside his wardrobe by means of a dressing gown cord, slumped awkwardly amidst laundered suits and shirts. Several magazines lay before it — extreme sado-masochistic pornography, barely legal, that ought never to have seen the light of day.

It was a staged crime scene and any competent pathologist or moderately skilled detective would quickly deduce this was a murder. Not that it mattered. A compliant senior investigating officer had already been assigned, as had a cooperative pathologist and an amenable coroner. To eliminate any doubt, Nicey had left his signature calling card — a joker — tucked inside Springer's dressing gown pocket, now casually draped across the bed. It was a 'get out of jail free' card, imbuing total immunity from prosecution.

'Hot and spicy enough?' asked Smashie, looking at Springer.

Nicey smirked. 'I think so. A vindaloo.'

Smashie shook his head. 'More of a phaal really. But will the police suspect phaal play?'

They sniggered with dark amusement: two demonic schoolboys revelling in the macabre absurdity of their creation.

SIXTY-THREE
REFLECTIONS

I t was a balmy night, the kind that clung to the skin, whispering secrets through the rustling of the net curtain, which danced gently in the breeze. Intermittent flashes of lightning shimmered on the fabric, casting brief, ghostly illuminations across the oceanside apartment. Thunder rumbled distantly, not threateningly but like a benevolent, growling guardian.

Montserrat lay in the dark, sensuously attuned to the warm body beside her, each gentle rise and fall of breath a soothing rhythm. The marriage proposal had come completely unexpectedly, a bolt from the blue which had left her breathless. Yet she'd accepted without a moment's hesitation. It had been an intimate service at a registry office, with just the closest friends and family, before the newlyweds had flown off on honeymoon. The shack on the beachside at Cape Verde was paradise, an idyll framed by blinding white sand and a rolling blue sea — the perfect stage upon which to embrace and explore each other, without boundaries and free of the world's constraints.

Reports in the papers and on TV had talked of a scandalous sex game gone wrong; the coroner had conveniently ruled death by misadventure, attributed to autoerotic asphyxiation. Montserrat smiled in the moon's silvery light, imagining the scene. Springer's only passions had been money and power — the man was diseased by greed.

As cicadas whistled their nightly chorus, her thoughts drifted to Seaton Hall. Trusted implicitly by all sides, she'd played her part impeccably; summoning the three men into the building without hindrance or inspection, each given key cards and codes that granted them access to every corner of the estate. She'd later glimpsed one of them lurking in the corridor near the study, a sinister black-clad figure merging with the shadows, recoiling into the darkness.

She smiled now, imagining the bishop opening the gift she'd chosen for him: an 1837 hip flask in sterling silver. The technical department had prepared two identical boxes, matching in weight and size, each meticulously wrapped in Tiffany's turquoise, complete with a bow. One for the study, the other for the bishop.

And Fenwick? Their secretive dealings had been tense, but purposeful. His fate remained a mystery, and she hadn't enquired. She was content to be free of it all, untraceable and beyond the reach of her past, with an assumed name and a new passport.

As the night deepened, she spooned with her beautiful young bride, snuggled in the warmth and security of this new beginning. It was the best outcome imaginable, a fresh start in a world where she was finally safe and beyond caring.

Peter dangled his legs over the edge of the pier, gazing out at the serene expanse of the lake. The midday sun bathed him in warmth, with reflected rays from the water's surface playing on his face. The past two days had been a frenetic whirlwind of activity. The small British delegation had swept in under conditions of the utmost secrecy, entirely incognito, their presence never to be admitted, their very existence not even acknowledged.

The instant the RAF Voyager had touched down at Lausanne airport, Peter's team had been on high alert. They'd imposed control immediately, ferrying the delegation in a convoy of three sleek BMW saloons and a Mercedes, flown in specially from Brize Norton. The Americans and the Russians were also in town, their presence adding a layer of complexity and intrigue to the mission. All parties were ensconced at the Château d'Ouchy, a medieval castle turned luxurious hotel on the shores of Lake Geneva.

Peace talks were the order of the day, conducted behind firmly closed doors. No-one outside the conference room was to know anything of what was discussed or agreed — not the French, not the press, and especially not the Ukrainians. Counter-surveillance was of paramount importance, with everyone on edge about potential bugs and wiretaps. Peter's unit was thorough, conducting meticulous countermeasure sweeps in all vehicles, living quarters and assigned conference rooms, and before each plenary session. The

Russians had initially been wary, protective of their own methods and technology, but cooperation had gradually smoothed the edges of their interactions.

The incoming US administration was keen to extricate itself from the quagmire of Ukraine, ready to strike a deal with the Russians. Why the British had been invited to the table, Peter had no idea, nor did he particularly care.

In the strong sunlight, Peter closed his eyes and craned his head sunward. His mind drifted back to the strange events earlier in the year.

The GEM-CELL had worked beautifully, relaying everything said in the study and guiding his team in precisely. From the shadows, Peter had watched the wheeled stretcher's descent in the lift and the momentary departure of the doctor.

Killing the man in the strange chamber beneath Seaton Hall was horrendous, involving the most gruelling, vicious hand-to-hand combat imaginable, before a clinical 'double tap' to the head from Soldier A's silenced Browning finally dropped the bastard. The furnace came in useful, cleanly incinerating the thug's body and expunging all evidence of the episode. They hogtied the fat guy with the glasses, his limbs immobilised tightly with rope, his wrists flexi-cuffed, and mouth taped shut with several winds of duct tape.

Leaving the dead girl in the body bag had been an incredibly tough call. Acting on 'information received', the police later failed to locate the young woman's remains. Peter frowned, frustrated and dismayed by the futility of his anonymous tip-off.

Fenwick, strapped to the stretcher, had been unresponsive but had a pulse with shallow breathing. Time had been critical, the man in steep decline. Peter had the wherewithal to grasp Fenwick's laptop and four glass vials of whatever muck they had pumped into him — scopolamine at 0.65 mg, the labels read.

The team had escaped unchallenged in the dark using one of the estate's many Land Rovers — the heavy security and police presence they'd encountered earlier, nowhere to be seen. They were extracted from a point just beyond Seaton Hall's Victorian folly — a tall brick tower reminiscent of Rapunzel, right on the edge of the estate. Peter was astonished — in addition to an air ambulance, they'd sent two Army Wildcat gunships, each with a full troop. The extraction had clearly been sanctioned at the highest level.

Clearance had been given for the air ambulance to land on the helipad at University College Hospital, London, a crash team notified and on standby. Flying at its maximum speed, the fast and nimble Airbus H145 helicopter touched down on the roof of the hospital within forty-three minutes of boarding the patient. UCH, amongst Europe's foremost specialist units in poisons and the management of overdoses, had been on the case from the first alert. The antidote to scopolamine was a drug called physostigmine, a remedial dosage preloaded and waiting even as the medevac helicopter touched down.

A first-class paramedic and a doctor on board the air ambulance had kept Fenwick alive during the flight, but as the crash team removed him from the helicopter, he suffered a cardiac arrest.

Peter, climbing out onto the hospital's helipad, watched as desperate CPR efforts were administered, the medics struggling frantically but ever more forlornly. He stood alone, his teammates long since whisked away in the two army gunships, their whereabouts a mystery. He felt vulnerable — incongruous in combat gear and with a gun, exposed to unwanted attention, arrest or even worse.

Two youngish men in sharp suits had approached him from the shadows, with heavily armed police officers loitering in attendance.

'This way, sir,' they had said.

SIXTY-FOUR
IN MEMORIAM

Whether it was the stonemason's chisel or the precise imprint of some laser-beam, Lucia couldn't discern. The lettering was precise, the typeface formal, the layout well-spaced and proportioned. The inscription on the plaque was simple:

Charles Fenwick
1981–2024
Nil sicut videtur

Lucia had chosen Welsh slate and the epitaph itself, unsure quite why.

She stood now, hand-in-hand with daughter Beatrice, before the memorial wall of Mortlake Crematorium in west London. Desiccated wreaths and withered flowers lined the wall, dried and dishevelled following an unusually hot summer with weeks of cloudless skies and relentless sunshine.

Lucia sensed that Charles would very much have

approved of her chosen bouquet of oriental lilies, their traditional white petals fresh and strikingly bright against the grey slate. A bell tolled mournfully, heralding the distant arrival of a hearse and funeral cortege, a straggle of smartly attired mourners making their way towards the chapel.

Beatrice slipped her hand away and wandered off, chatting to herself, happy in her own company as children often are. Lucia watched her daughter for a moment before turning her gaze back to the plaque. She'd known Charles her entire life, and yet she hardly knew him at all. She tried to calculate the total number of hours spent in his company; it couldn't have amounted to more than a couple of months or so in her forty-four years.

Childhood memories were more vivid than adult ones: shared ice creams, roller skates and skateboards with grazed elbows and knees, sandcastles and donkey rides on the beach at Weston-Super-Mare, and being scolded for trailing sand across the landlady's carpet. In their teenage years, there'd been the angst and shared heartache of first love and break-ups, Charles always an attentive listener.

In adulthood, mutual respect — Charles notably appreciative of her career, Lucia sympathetic towards his ill-fated marriage and the dreadful sadness of his brother's murder. As godfather to Beatrice, Charles had been dutiful. Lucia smiled, fondly remembering his abiding present for her daughter: a bear from Hamleys when Beatrice was two. His name was Humphrey and Beatrice still had him.

Of Charles' work, Lucia knew next to nothing. It remained a mystery.

The issue of probate was pressing. Lucia had been astonished at the speed with which Charles, a missing person, had been declared dead. Geoffrey's contacts, perhaps? The process had somehow been short-circuited, the statutory seven years of absence condensed obscenely to just six months, with all documentation and a death certificate issued without hindrance or question, all deemed 'by order of the Court'. It was as if some hidden force had willed her cousin dead.

Lucia regretted that her last hours with Charles had been on that fateful night in the pub. Her premonition of mortal danger that evening had proved correct. Geoffrey had talked her through the horrific events in Poland; she'd resisted watching the video clips, fearing them too distressing. The Met Police were investigating, Geoffrey assured her. She'd fretted over Fenwick's demise, fearing the circumstances. She just prayed that at the end there'd been no pain or suffering.

She glanced again at the plaque. Unfussy and stylish, without maudlin sentiment. Charles would have approved.

'Right, come on, Bea,' she beckoned. 'Grandma has made shortbread, your favourite.'

It was late October. The air held the chill promise of winter, and the clocks would soon steal an hour, surrendering the evenings to early darkness.

Lucia, cradled with her cello, and her accompanist André at the baby grand piano, were rehearsing in the garden room. Contracts had been exchanged only in August, and the sizeable detached house in Twickenham

— purchased at a steal — was in a shabby state with peeling wallpaper, a wobbly banister and even the odd cracked window. Yet the surveyor had assured Lucia that the structural essentials were sound, with only some rudimentary fixes needed. The workmen were due on Monday.

More pressing was the upcoming recital at Bridgewater Hall in Manchester. The *Cello Sonata in G Minor, Opus 65*, by Frédéric Chopin demanded their full attention. They laboured now over the first movement, *Allegro Moderato*, the haunting theme setting the tone for the entire piece. The sonata's four movements were distinct in their individual demands, and mastery as yet remained elusive.

The music echoed through the house, seeping into the quiet street outside. A car pulled to the kerb. Through the windscreen, obscured by garish reflections from the streetlights flickering alight at dusk, the indeterminate forms of the two occupants were barely distinguishable. The driver, vigilant and watchful, stepped out and surveyed the street, her demeanour sinister. Opening the passenger door, she nodded towards the house. 'Unfinished business,' she murmured, her gaze fixed intently on the front door.

The playing continued, growing louder with proximity. A man's hand unlatched the gate. The front door was adorned with a stained-glass window with brightly coloured panes, obscuring the view.

The man knocked — three loud, deliberate raps.

The music ceased abruptly.

Startled, Lucia froze, her heart racing. No-one was expected.

Beatrice was at home for half term. From her bedroom upstairs, she shouted down, 'Mum, are you going to get that?'

Lucia, apprehensive, set down her cello and stood, shouting irritably in response, 'Yes!'

Turning to André, her voice trembled with urgency. 'Take Bea into the back garden. There's an alleyway,' she urged, gesturing.

'Why? What's wrong?' asked André.

'Don't argue. Do as I say!' she snapped.

Beatrice appeared before them. She looked puzzled. André moved quickly to her side, taking her hand.

'Mum, what's going on?' asked Beatrice, her voice quavering.

'I don't know,' responded Lucia. 'Just go with André.'

Three more knocks, slower this time, but more insistent.

With trepidation, Lucia approached the door. Through the kaleidoscope of stained glass, she discerned the outline of a man, his features indistinct. For a moment, she considered joining André and Beatrice in their flight to safety. But something held her back.

Resolutely facing her destiny, she opened the door.

She now beheld the man.

'Oh my God...! My God!' gasped Lucia, as tears welled in her eyes.

THE END

ACKNOWLEDGEMENTS

Noel and Kate Bonczoszek are core members of the Fenwick team. Noel assisted with plot and character development, while Kate has been a thoughtful critic and enthusiastic supporter of the project from the outset. James Taylor edited the story with judgement and skill. Marion Gosling first suggested that Fenwick's story might be told. Patrick Madden, Jon Walklin and Peter Old assisted with technical excerpts. George McKillop and Gill Rock provided Fenwick refuge and sustenance in Edinburgh. Insights and suggestions, in no particular order, came variously from: Allan McDonagh, Robert McKillop, Neil McCorquodale, Jean Whitelock, Zoe Willenbrok, Lucy Wilding, Clare Wilding, Susy Firth, Stephanie Firth, Katharine Augarde, Jon Rosen, Samantha Blunden, James Wren, Delphine Brès, Michele Ferguson, Paul Hallett, and Tim Christian. A few others remain in the shadows. Apologies to my former colleague Montserrat Barraclough for my theft of her first name. Plaudits to Neville, who appears in cameo. Thanks also to the teams formerly at 26 Dover Street, Queen Anne's Gate and at DGI… bygone eras for sure, but astonishing times nevertheless. Opinions expressed, or outlandish concepts or assertions herein, are entirely those of the author, or of his characters.

TRADEMARKS

Reid's Palace, a Belmond hotel.

Xanax is a trademark of Upjohn LLC, a Pfizer company.

Pulsar Lexion XQ38, www.pulsar-vision.com

HH35L Thermal Binoculars, HikMicro Habrok.

Praktica LRF-7 laser rangefinder, Praktica Ltd, UK.

Rolex GMT Master II, Rolex SA.

Swiss Military, Hanowa Ltd / AG, Switzerland.

Patek Philippe SA, Geneva.

GEM-CELL LTE, Acustek Limited, Dublin.

Advanced Armament Corporation, Huntsville, Alabama.

Hellcat, Springfield Armory, Illinois.

CQCM bulletproof ballistic mask, Atomic Defense, Clovis, California.

Pitbull .45 ACP, Charter Arms, Shelton, Connecticut.

Kroll Associates, Kroll, New York.

Céline, CELINE, 16 rue Vivienne, Paris.

Bulgari, Bulgari S.p.A., Rome.

Samuel Hoare & Co., London.

Smythson of Bond Street, London.

THE AUTHOR

Edward Wilding brings over three decades of experience of investigating cases ranging from cybercrimes and corporate frauds to extortions, sabotage, and murders. An expert witness, he has contributed evidence in numerous investigations, including the Hutton Inquiry into the death of renowned weapons expert Dr David Kelly. Specialising in digital forensics and computer crime, Wilding has lectured worldwide and authored two acclaimed books on the techniques and methods involved. His debut thriller, *Fenwick*, draws on his knowledge and experience of complex investigations and forensic techniques. Wilding lives and works in London, where he continues to explore the ever-evolving intersection of technology and crime.